"IF YOU'RE INTERESTED IN THE[...]
CRIME FICTION, [PARKER'S] SOMEONE YOU SHOULD READ."

—*The Washington Post*

Praise for the Novels of Three-Time
Edgar Award Winner T. Jefferson Parker

The Jaguar

"A crime writer as good as any when it comes to action, adventure, and downright down-and-dirty deeds."　　　　　　　　—*Los Angeles Times*

"Parker's latest elevates mystery to literature. . . . [He] has a gift for challenging readers with sympathetic villains. . . . *The Jaguar* is a weighty and entertaining exploration of vice and virtue."　　　—*North County Times* (CA)

"T. Jefferson Parker has stated that when he sat down to write *The Jaguar*, he wanted, among other things, 'to write a cracking good thriller.' This he has done, and to the tenth power. It is one of those books that transcends the genre. . . . Over the course of eighteen novels, Parker has consistently set and then exceeded his own standards; *The Jaguar* raises the bar into nosebleed territory. . . . [Parker] at the top of his game." —Bookreporter.com

"As usual, Parker's direct style, action scenes, quirky characters, and smooth plotting meld into a compelling read."　　　—*The Sacramento Bee*

"Excellent. . . . Parker demonstrates remarkable command of his material, from the gruesome realities of the Mexican drug trade to a surprisingly human portrayal of the monstrous Armenta . . . a crime thriller notable for its fine, insightful prose."　　　　　—*Publishers Weekly* (starred review)

"Action-packed."　　　　　　　　　　—*The San Diego Union-Tribune*

"Parker convincingly portrays Mexico, torn apart by the wars between the cartels and the government, and between the cartels themselves."

—*Suspense Magazine*

The Border Lords

"A breakthrough for a novelist whose accomplishments already are many and notable . . . a superior work of fiction."　　　—*Los Angeles Times*

continued . . .

"IF YOU'RE SEEKING A THINKING MAN'S BESTSELLER, T. JEFFERSON PARKER IS THE WRITER FOR YOU."

—The Washington Post

"Frenetic action and creatively insane characters . . . madly entertaining."
—The New York Times Book Review

"Part Raymond Chandler, part Carlos Castaneda, and all gripping . . . flat-out brilliant . . . Parker's deepest and most daring novel."
—The San Diego Union-Tribune

"Parker again demonstrates his mastery of the genre."
—Entertainment Weekly

"Adrenaline-fueled . . . [a] white-hot series."　　　*—Publishers Weekly*

"This is a rich book, packed with action, violence, love, lust, flashes of wit, moments of poignancy, and the occasional sharp geopolitical insight . . . extraordinary."
—Kirkus Reviews

"Moves at a white-heat pace from start to finish. . . . Parker ratchets up both action and suspense."　　　*—Alfred Hitchcock Mystery Magazine*

Iron River

"This is gripping literary entertainment with a point." *—Los Angeles Times*

"A can't-put-it-down-snappy-as-all-get-out corker. [This] series . . . just got a serious kick in the pants."　　　*—Chicago Sun-Times*

"The suspense in *Iron River* is terrific."　　　*—The Washington Post*

"[A] top-notch thriller. . . . With crisp prose and chilling detail, Parker brings a brutal, bullet-riddled world to light."　　*—Booklist* (starred review)

"While Parker has a serious message to convey, he is also a popular novelist with a need to entertain. In *Iron River*, he succeeds brilliantly at both."
—The Associated Press

"The indomitable Charlie is, as always, irresistible."　　*—Kirkus Reviews*

"Parker once more delivers the goods . . . rich, satisfying."
—North County Times (CA)

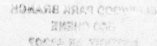

The Renegades

"Deft characterization and hard-boiled action played out against smartly detailed Southern California landscapes."   —*Los Angeles Times*

"Take[s] us in unexpected new directions. An interesting and inventive writer."   —*The Washington Post*

"In *The Renegades*, Parker surpasses himself in . . . a book that ranks among his most original."   —*The Toronto Star*

"A typically streamlined T. Jefferson Parker thriller. . . . Think of Parker's work as sunshine noir."   —*St. Petersburg Times*

"It's quite a showdown, done the Edgar Award–winning Parker way, in this engrossing tale of justice and redemption. Highly recommended."

—*Library Journal*

L.A. Outlaws

"Vivid writing, strong characters, clockwork plotting, agonizing suspense . . . *L.A. Outlaws* is popular entertainment at its most delicious."

—*The Washington Post*

"Totally compulsive reading."   —*The Seattle Times*

"Hard, fast, and etched with characters so sharp they'll leave you bleeding."   —Robert Crais

"*Out of Sight* meets *Gone in 60 Seconds*."   —*Entertainment Weekly*

"The best book of its kind since *No Country for Old Men*. . . . Simply stated, once again Parker has penned the best mystery of the year."

—*The Providence Journal-Bulletin*

"Both hard-boiled and heartbreaking, Ross Macdonald as sung by Marty Robbins."   —*Los Angeles Times*

"Suspenseful and original."   —*Chicago Sun-Times*

"Brilliant. . . . Parker takes a seat at the head of the class next to Michael Connelly."   —*The Sunday Oregonian*

T. JEFFERSON PARKER

A CHARLIE HOOD NOVEL

THE JAGUAR

NEW AMERICAN LIBRARY

New American Library
Published by the Penguin Group
Penguin Group (USA) Inc., 375 Hudson Street,
New York, New York 10014, USA

USA | Canada | UK | Ireland | Australia | New Zealand | India | South Africa | China

Penguin Books Ltd., Registered Offices: 80 Strand, London WC2R 0RL, England
For more information about the Penguin Group visit penguin.com.

Published by New American Library, a division of Penguin Group (USA) Inc.
Previously published in a Dutton edition.

First New American Library Printing, April 2013
10 9 8 7 6 5 4 3 2 1

NAL REGISTERED TRADEMARK—MARCA REGISTRADA

New American Library Trade Paperback ISBN: 978-0-451-23911-2

The Library of Congress has catalogued the hardcover edition of this title as follows:

Parker, T. Jefferson.
The jaguar: a Charlie Hood novel/T. Jefferson Parker.
p. cm.
ISBN: 978-0-525-95257-2
1. Hood, Charlie (Fictitious character)—Fiction. 2. Police—California, Southern—Fiction. I. Title.
PS3566.A6863J34 2012
813'.54—dc23   2011023376

Printed in the United States of America

For Those Who Make the Music

Every hundred feet the world changes.
—Roberto Bolaño, 2666

THE JAGUAR

1

THE BLACK VAN ROLLED ACROSS the barnyard in the rain and stopped beneath an enormous oak tree. It was a large vehicle but under the canopy it was poorly visible, a dark shape within greater darkness. From it the men spilled and advanced quietly to a stable where they paused, then to the flank of the barn, then in single file to the ranch house where they pooled in the overhang of the deck.

Upstairs a young man watched through a window as he buttoned on his jeans. He saw the dull glint of the van under the tree and men snaking through the night. He counted ten of them. He looked back across the bedroom at his security monitors but they told him that the gate had not been breached and none of the doors or windows of the outbuildings had been disturbed. No warning indicators, no audio alerts. Yet this. The dogs were kenneled for the storm. The rain belted the roof and he saw the silver lines of it slanting outside the windows and he understood that he might die here tonight but she did not have to. He was twenty-one years old.

He went to her and put a hand over her mouth and rocked her upward from sleep as he whispered. *Men are here.*

What men?

Men with guns. We only have seconds, Erin. Get up now. Please.

How can this happen?

They beat the security. Up. Hurry. We have our plan. .

She let out a small cry and held his hand tight and pulled herself up and out of bed. In the near darkness he put his arm around her and walked her across the suite and down a hallway and into another room lit by a faint night-light. Her shoulders were white and her hair was red. Outside the wind hit the walls and the rain raked down upon the world. He let go of her and slid open the door of a walk-in closet and threw a hidden switch. The interior pivoted away with a motorized hum and was replaced by an alcove with a leather recliner and a fire extinguisher and a small refrigerator and a rack of weapons along one wall.

He kissed her and pressed a hand against her middle and felt the slight warm bulge through her nightgown.

I love you, Erin.

I love you, Bradley. Is this a nightmare? Why us? I hear things downstairs.

I'll handle it. You wait here and I'll come to you by moonlight. Like in your song. This is a promise. Hurry.

He guided her by the hand into the alcove. She sat on the recliner and he kissed her and pushed the switch and they held hands and gazes until Erin glided away and was gone. Bradley pulled the silenced machine pistol from the upper shelf and slung it over his shoulder, then took another and pushed off the safety and trotted back out into the hallway.

He heard feet on the stairs. He backed away from the balustrade and when the first man came up and looked from under the brim of his helmet Bradley shot him and he arched back down into the stairwell. Another followed and Bradley shot him also but three more boiled up hydralike, shoulders hunched and faces down, and Bradley sprayed them but they surged toward him while he loosed his last few rounds and raised the second gun.

They knocked him over just before he could fire and pinned his arms to the floor. More men piled on. He expected their knives but he could barely move beneath their weight. He could smell their bodies and their breath and the gunpowder in the air and he could feel the hard ballistic armor that crushed down on him and none of his claw-ing or tearing or biting could damage that armor or the men inside it.

They grunted and cursed in Spanish and they kept their voices low and they had not fired a shot. He felt his lungs being squeezed empty and still the men were piling on, heavier and heavier upon him until the last spark of his breath flickered and he could not catch it. Bradley thrashed and grunted against them. He entered the darkness cursing them and he heard their voices above his own—profanities and ner-vous laughter.

He awoke and opened his eyes and saw nothing but black. He was on his back and tried to sit up but hit his head on something just a few inches from his face. He touched it with his hands: fabric over metal. There was a smell he knew. His knees were bent and he tried to straighten them but the space was too small. When he tried to raise them they too hit the low ceiling and Bradley felt the panic gathering in his body. He took a deep breath and let it out slowly. Breath, sweet breath. Calm. The panic sat and waited. Bradley had always suffered in close places—in sleeping bags and crowded elevators and below decks—as had his mother and their ancestors deep into history.

He reached out and felt the curve of his enclosure and the small-ness of the space. He heard one of the terriers yapping. I'm in the barn, he thought. His fingers found a plastic crate and when he got a hand into it he felt the familiar air compressor with its power cord wrapped snug around the bottom, and the spray can of tire treatment that smelled of cherry, and the rubber blade of the window wiper. The

Cyclone, he thought: I'm in the trunk of my old Cyclone, in the barn. Nineteen seventy, aftermarket trunk release. *Broken.*

The panic launched and Bradley shoved the crate away and braced both hands on the lid and pushed mightily but it did not give. He wriggled over onto his front side and got his knees under him and he drove his back up into the top. He felt the muscles of his thighs and groin flaring but the lid was unmoved. He turned over, breathing fast and hard, strangling on the closeness. Sweat ran off his face and neck and he felt it accumulating in the cleft below his larynx. He wondered how much oxygen was left. He heard voices from above him. He tried to calm his heart and listen to them but he could not.

The panic came again and he chopped at the ceiling with both elbows but the ceiling did not give. He flipped over again, and again drove his back against the lid but the trunk was Detroit-built and it gave not even the smallest sign of coming open. So he pushed up on his young strong arms, arms that could easily press his own weight and more, but they were no match for the steel.

Bradley flipped over onto his back again and screamed the scream of the living, and he knew that if he screamed loud enough the sound would rip a hole through the metal and he would be able to reach an arm through.

And the lid lifted. He sat up and looked into the faces of men and the barrels of their guns. Most wore helmets or bandanas or balaclavas. Beyond them he saw the lights and rafters of his barn. Some of the men poked at him with their barrels. Erin stood not ten feet away, one large armored man holding each of her arms, her nightgown torn and her feet bare and her eyes wild. Beyond her, along the far side, was the kennel and behind the chain link the twelve dogs paced or stood or sat and the terrier kept barking.

He gathered himself to climb out but a gun butt hit him square in the forehead and he dropped back into place in the trunk and looked dizzily at the man who had hit him.

"Excuse me, Deputy Jones. My name is Heriberto. You are now living because I have been asked to be merciful to you." He was tall and wide, his face below the eyes hidden by a bandana. His voice was soft and lilting. Bradley noted his new white athletic shoes, jeans, and the Mexican Army–issue armored vest and helmet.

Bradley nodded faintly and looked again at Erin. He didn't know how long he'd been unconscious and it was his belief that she had not been beaten or raped. He wondered how they had breached his security and discovered the hidden room so easily. He tried to climb out again but the gun butt corrected him as before. He saw the tears running down her face but he tried to stare at her in a way that imparted calm and strength. He felt the blood running from his scalp and down his lips and off his chin.

"You're going to be all right, Erin. I promise you that you will be all right."

"Deputy Jones, this is not a certainty," said Heriberto. "We are here to take your wife. You will see her again if you end your protection of Carlos Herredia and the North Baja Cartel in Los Angeles. And if you stop arresting the Gulf Cartel's Salvadoran friends. And if you offer one million dollars to Benjamin Armenta as an apology for the trouble you have caused and the money you have cost him. These are to be your labors, gringo Hercules. We give you ten days to complete them and your *esposa* will be released without harm. If you fail, Deputy Jones, then Saturnino will skin her alive. He is the enforcer *ultimo* and this is one of his methods. All of the lovely white skin. Off. *Sí, mis amigos?*"

The men remained silent and did not look directly at Erin. She tried to break away but the men yanked her back and her hair flashed red in the tube lights of the barn. Beyond them the big sliding door was open and Bradley could see the rain lightly falling outside. It was an unusual monsoonal storm from the southeast, brief and warm, but Bradley was trembling cold and bloodied. His ears rang badly. He wiped some blood off his face and looked at his wife.

"You have the wrong man, you sonsofbitches," she said. "He's a sheriff's deputy for the County of Los Angeles. He was second in his class at the academy. He's been awarded for bravery. Get off our property."

Heriberto looked at her. His expression was incomplete because of the bandana but his eyes crinkled with amusement. He opened both hands and gestured at the spacious barn with its Porsche Cayenne and the lovingly restored Cyclone and Erin's new Toureg hybrid turbo, and the tarped and trailered Boston Whaler and the gleaming quad runners and the John Deere and the profusion of tools and sporting gear. He nodded toward the big house and spread his hands in a gesture of inclusion, which included Erin. He laughed quietly and so did the men.

"All of this and a secret room with a motor? Why not a private jet? This is what the one-year policeman in *los Yuniates* earns? But the beginning pay is not forty-thousand dollars per year. All this? Where does all this come from, *roja*?"

"You've got the wrong guy, Heriberto," said Bradley. "I am not who you think I am."

Heriberto stared at him. "Tell your lies to the fools in your life. To your wife and your department."

"I do not lie to my wife."

Erin looked at Bradley with angry confusion. He saw the doubt on her face and, feeling judged by the one person he truly believed in, the doubt hit him harder than the gun butt. He gauged his chances of lunging out of the car and getting to her without being beaten or shot.

But then what? He saw the movement of the gunmen toward him and held still.

"Erin," he said. "I'll take care of this. I'll give them what they want. I'll give them twice of what they ask, whether it's in my power or not. You'll be free again. You'll see this home again and raise your children here and we'll walk that meadow in the spring and be in love."

She looked back at him through her tangle of hair but said nothing.

"If you fail us, Deputy Jones, we will send you her skin, rolled up in a small box," said Heriberto. "We will be in touch with you. Many details are to be coming. The Gulf Cartel will crush your master Carlos Herredia like a small dog. This is only the beginning. You tell him Benjamin Armenta says hello."

The two men pulled Erin toward the barn door just as four others stepped forward and pinned Bradley to the trunk bottom with their gun barrels. He looked up at their motley disguises and clothes and their vests with the military numbers stenciled in white. A moment later he heard a vehicle pull up outside the barn and one by one the gunmen backed away and disappeared.

He sat up and wiped blood from his face. Through the barn door he saw that the rain had ended and he heard Erin shout out to him: *"Come to me by moonlight, sugar!/Let the moon be your guide!"* These were words to a song she was writing and she'd been singing them in slightly varying melodies for the last week now. *"I love you, Bradley!"*

Love or loved? He sprang out of the trunk and ran to the door and saw the van heading down the dirt road toward the gate. He ran to the workbench, got the .357 Magnum revolver from a drawer, then to the all-terrain vehicles waiting side by side at the far end of the barn, gassed as always, keys in their ignitions. He chose the best one and jammed the gun into the holster strapped under the dash while turning the key.

He bounced through the barn and shot out the door, up on his hands and feet, head held low. Shirtless he shivered as he cut through the cool wind and found the road and gunned the quad runner through its gears. I will not fail you. He saw the taillights of the van as it cleared a rise, then he saw nothing but the pocked road.

Seconds later he was nearly upon the van. It was loaded heavily and the back tires slipped and spun in the fresh mud. The gate was not far away. He slid out the revolver and guided the whining quad with one hand and he raised the pistol and sighted down it. The van, big and easily hit, bounced along ahead of him but to fire was only folly and he knew they had beaten him this time. He backed off the accelerator and touched the brake and swung the ATV into a sideways slide that threw mud in a big rooster tail and finally brought it to a stop. He shivered with cold and his eyes filled with tears and blood as he watched the van leave his property not through the gate but through a large hole cut in the chain-link fence.

2

HE SHOWERED AND DRESSED AND bandaged the scalp wounds, then took the steps down into the bunker he'd built beneath the foundation of the barn. The vault was roomy and made of poured concrete with double rebar, heated and air conditioned, and the walls were painted white. The lights were recessed and low voltage and bright. There was a desk and three standing safes, file cabinets and a long table covered by colorful Mexican blankets.

He knelt and spun the dial on one of the safes. He swung open the heavy door and pulled out one million dollars, weighed and shrink-wrapped in one-pound bundles. There were twenty pounds of one-hundred dollar bills; four pounds of twenties and sixteen loose hundreds to complete the amount. He took out another ten pounds of twenties—ninety six thousand dollars to sustain himself and whomever else might help him get Erin back. This all fit into a piece of lightweight rolling luggage.

He sat at his desk for a short while, staring straight ahead at the blank white wall. Fury and fear. How could he not have known? How could Herredia's organization have no warning, no inside information? How could Armenta even *attempt* this? Erin, light of my life. Where are you and what are they doing to you? With the eyes of his mind he tried to picture her, but all he saw were the most terrifying pictures he had ever imagined. Ten days. Ten.

He forced away these images but now his thoughts came heavy with shame. He'd loved her to the point of obsession but what was that but a young man's foolishness, dwarfed in importance by his failure to protect her, his wife, sleeping, pregnant with their child, in their own home? *If you fail, Deputy Jones, we will skin her alive.* He knew this was not just a gruesome threat. Flayings had joined beheadings as statements of fact among the drug cartels.

Sitting in his vault, cold and hungry and assaulted by things he could not control, Bradley felt his former self step aside. She was gone; now he was gone. Into him flowed the rage and the shame, and they ran the miles from his heart to the narrow capillaries. He felt them turn into strength and will and he knew that only these could bring her back.

He went to the long wooden table that sat against one wall of the vault and carefully lifted the blankets that were spread upon it. Here were his mother's journals and many framed pictures of her and of his brothers, and of her family back into the time when photography had just been invented. He put his hand on the journals and looked down at the pictures, which he dusted every month. There was also a fine Western saddle and a tooled-leather scabbard and a pair of six-guns in a two-holster rig that he cleaned and oiled once a year. The steel and leather were dark and shiny and smelled of the past. Beside the saddle was a forged steel mesh vest that had been dented by bullets, some fired nearly a century and a half ago, but some quite recently.

In the middle of all this stood the glass jar containing the head of Bradley's ancestor, the great outlaw, *EL FAMOSO*, JOAQUIN MURRIETA, *1830–1853*. The blanched face was handsome as in legend but Joaquin's famed mane of black hair had fallen to the bottom of the alcohol and it rose slightly and lilted when Bradley picked up the jar in order to speak to his great-great-great-great-great-great-great-grandfather face-to-face.

"Give me your blessings," Bradley said quietly. "I need every last one of them that you can spare. Don't let them do to Erin what they did to Rosa. Or to me what they did to you."

The head bobbed gently as if in agreement. It looked forlorn. Bradley set the jar back on the table and wiped it clean with a cotton towel kept there for this purpose, then he snapped the colorful serapes before spreading them over the artifacts. Dust motes rose and swirled in the hard light.

Back up in the barn he stood at the open door. The wind was still blowing and the early sunlight sparkled through the wet trees to the east.

Bradley opened his cell phone and made his first call.

3

THE TWO DEAD MEN SAT fast in their restraints in the last row of seats, helmets low, bandanas over their faces, and heads lolling like they were asleep. Erin could smell their blood and the various odors of the living. She listened to the automotive sounds inside the van dampened by the sound-absorbing bodies of the men. The men did not wear their helmets or face coverings now and she saw that they were young to middle-aged but none were old.

At first they tried to ignore her but she caught them looking. Then they studied her more boldly and she looked down. She saw that some wore work boots and some cowboy boots and others athletic shoes and one a pair of huaraches with no socks.

She sat in the middle seat of the second row, still in the nightgown, a red-and-blue striped serape from the barn pulled over her shoulders. Her nerves were raw and her insides were clenched and in spite of the warm night she was cold. She listened to the engine and the tires on the asphalt and the arrhythmic breathing of the men and the defroster going on and off. She pictured Bradley sitting in the trunk of the Cyclone with his head bleeding, trying to tell her that everything would be all right. And she pictured the baby inside her, his heart tapping away and his cells dividing amid the jolts of fear that he must surely be receiving from her. Such terror and not yet born, thought Erin. This world will be his. His life, four months strong, such a blessing after her failures. She lowered her face to her hands and rubbed hard at her temples and willed the nightmare to end.

In the dark they drove Interstate Eight near the California/Mexico border, then got off at Jacumba and within seconds a boy on a motorbike was leading them from one dirt road to another and another. This road shrunk to a faint trail that allowed them to trundle slowly between hills of rocks. There was a narrow bridge and a short tunnel. Somewhere they crossed into Mexico and Heriberto said to one of his men that he was relieved to be home again where he could drink the water—no more Washington's revenge. Of course this must be funny to a gringa if she could understand it, he added. Erin's Spanish was good and she had always loved Mexican music and could play and sing norteño and marimba and fandango songs long before she knew what they were about. But she didn't laugh at Heriberto's joke.

Forty minutes later she was sitting in a small muscular jet shooting into the sunrise at four hundred miles an hour.

She dozed with her head against a window. Fear had always made her short of breath and groggy and she had always tried to let the grogginess work for her. It had helped her survive possible calamity for twenty-six years: the male tarantulas that emerged by the hundreds that spring evening in the campground outside of Tucson, the runaway horse on the ranch near Austin, the attempted assault in Las Vegas, the car accident in L.A. Panic kills, dad always said. A tough man, fabulous on the harmonica. He'd fought in Vietnam and read Hemingway. So she told herself to stay calm and deliberate and go to the cold place inside that her father had talked about. Steer yourself out of this nightmare.

She closed her eyes. She took a deep breath and tried to empty her mind but she did not sleep. The jet was full of sounds within the baffled roar of the engines. Her ears were trained for sound, and the waking world was a busy place for her. Now melodies and rhythms drifted into her as they often did, new melodies, strange and lovely, some carrying words. Gifts. In the long minutes of forced calm she let her rational mind speak: stay alive, girl, don't let them see your fear, or the shape of what's growing inside you. Bradley will save you. Bradley has always saved you. Bradley is good and truthful. Isn't he? Then why in hell is all this happening?

Several hours later, in sun-blasted day, she walked down a short stairway that deployed from inside the jet, four men ahead of her and four behind. Their guns were not drawn and they seemed tired. They had not searched her. Even with the blanket around her she made it a point to hold her tummy in. She could feel the first-aid tape and its hard cargo, strapped high and out of sight on her right calf. The air was heavy and hot and smelled strongly of the ocean. There was white sand and stands of coconut trees and flats with mangrove thickets stretching far back into a silver lagoon.

She was ushered into a white Suburban with blacked-out windows. The engine was already running and the air conditioner was on and the driver waiting. Heriberto took the front passenger seat but the other men did not board. As soon as they were moving she tried the door so she could throw herself out and run for it, but of course the child guard was on and she was trapped. Heriberto turned and looked back at her with no expression on his face.

"You are very happy?"

"Very."

"Maybe the worst is over."

"This is a terrible thing to do."

Heriberto pursed his lips and nodded. "There are many costs."

"Why do you do things like this to innocent people?"

"Your husband is a criminal and an enemy."

"You're wrong."

"And if I am not?"

"Then you should have taken *him*."

"But we have taken something much more valuable than him. We have taken what he loves. Anything we want from him is now ours."

"Who is Herredia? Who is Armenta?"

"They are men, Señora Jones."

"Are they criminals and enemies?"

Heriberto studied her. His face was wide and the planes of it were flat and hard. The stubble on his chin was gray but his hair was black. "They are honest men. They represent no authority except their own power to survive and prosper. Their cruelty is magnificent. But they do not deceive."

She considered his words and said nothing. Deceive? Could she say that much about her husband? What Heriberto had said back in the barn in Valley Center had rung true. If Bradley was a simple deputy then where had all of their treasure come from? From his mother's estate, he'd always said. The estate of a school teacher who died young?

First there was the white sand road, then a stretch of freshly paved asphalt. The road wound through the jungle away from the lagoon. She tried to reckon directions by the sun but it was straight overhead and defiantly still. There were few road signs and these were hand painted and announced small hotels or cabanas for rent, ecotours, fishing charters, ruins. The man drove fast and he gave no quarter to the other vehicles on the narrow road. Erin watched for a state or highway sign. Quintana Roo. Good. Good for what? She turned and saw that the silver Denali and the black Tahoe that had started the drive with them were still in place behind. Soon the signs vanished and there was nothing but the hunched shoulders of the jungle and the curve of road.

Heriberto turned and looked at her. "You will see that there is almost no wind now. This means a hurricane is coming. On the news they say in four days. There will be much rain."

"Good thing I packed the serape."

"Don't be afraid."

"Why would I be afraid? Because you invaded my home and beat my husband and want to skin me? Because of your guns and the smell of your dead men? No fears here, none at all."

"It is good that you fight fear with anger. Anger is like lifting a blanket from your eyes."

"What shit."

"Now you are beginning to see the real world."

They turned off the highway and onto a smaller asphalt road that brought them to a guard gate manned by soldiers in green camo. They were young and their weapons were strapped to their shoulders and two of them approached as Heriberto rolled to a stop and lowered his window. Erin saw a large stone-and-brass sign announcing the RESERVA DE LA BIOSFERA DE KOHUNLICH and the yellow-and-black striped barrier across the road. Heriberto and the young soldier talked for a moment, then the barrier lifted and they drove through. Erin turned and saw the vehicles behind them stopped at the gate, the arm lowered again.

Later they turned off onto a white-sand trail and when they came to a streambed the Suburban passed through it easily with the water swooshing up into the wheel wells. Just past the stream was a gate that Heriberto unlocked with a key and relocked after the Suburban and the two other vehicles had passed through. After that the road became wider and the land more hilly and they passed four more locked gates. Not a single vehicle came or passed them. Heriberto made a call on a satellite phone each time they went through a gate. Erin couldn't hear what he said. She saw an iguana napping on a log and a monkey striding upon the high branches of a tree and a small wild pig watching them from the jungle shade. She wiped away the tears running from her eyes but she did not make a sound.

They pulled up one last steep grade and at the top was another gate and three armed men standing outside a guardhouse. They wore the same varied clothing and body armor that her captors wore but no helmets or face coverings. The front windows went down and the three men took turns chattering away with Heriberto and poking their faces in to look back at her.

They rode up a long rise overhung with foliage to a level place and stopped. Through the windshield a structure rose, grand, immense, and disheveled. She stepped out of the SUV into the heat and looked up at it. It was a Mexican-Caribbean-Asian mongrel with curving red Chinese roof beams and turquoise Jamaican storm shutters and many balconies. The balconies had elaborate wrought-iron railings and they slouched, overladen with bright ceramic pots that sprouted flowers. Some of the walls were painted white and fingerprinted by vines long gone, although one entire level was festive yellow and another was lime green. The edifice was loosely V-shaped, with the two wings facing each other to form a colonnaded loggia and courtyard below. It seemed to have grown out of the steep green hills and it looked random and out of plumb, which made its stories hard to count: she saw four then five then four again. It seemed important to get that much right, but she could not. Thirty rooms, she wondered. Fifty? The plaster was ancient and spotty and portions of it were crumbling away. The roof was overgrown with trumpet vines and mandevilla and honeysuckle busy with birds that trilled and flitted anxiously.

Erin listened to the crazy notes of the songbirds and wished she was one of them and could fly away. She watched as two women came down a stairway from the third level and walked a path into the jungle. They wore long, loose white dresses and white rebozos that covered their shoulders and heads. One turned to Erin as they walked but her face was lost within the folds of the shawl.

Heriberto appeared beside her and together they looked up at the madly colored extravagance.

"Does it have a name?" she asked.

"El Castillo."

"The Castle."

"One of the homes of Benjamin Armenta."

4

THEY WALKED ACROSS THE COURTYARD and up the limestone steps to the porch and faced the massive copper entry doors. Heriberto stepped around her to mutter something into a speaker built into the wall. The doors swung slowly in with a low groan and the hiss of grinding sand.

Inside, the air was cool and smelled of stone, a lavender-scented cleanser and mildew. They stood in a tall atrium and Erin looked up through four or five stories of layered shadows at the distant ceiling. A black woman in a gray dress and a gray turban pushed a mop across the floor tiles, then stopped to watch her. Erin tried to look her in the eye but could not.

Heriberto barked something at the cleaning woman and Erin heard the backslap of his voice carom upward through the air from wall to wall. Heriberto's sneakers squeaked and Erin's bare heels clunked softly on the stone floor.

They climbed the stairs, past the parrots and macaws and toucans perched on the banisters, and the small monkeys clinging to the curtain rods high up, eyeing her widely and dropping seed shells, which floated down to the second-story landing. Here another black woman in gray swept the hulls into a long-handled dustpan and still another mopped up after the animals with the lavender concoction.

On the second-floor landing Erin froze when she saw the black jaguar napping on the shadowed tile. She had never seen a black jaguar and never known they got this big. The chain of its steel collar was staked to a ring in the stone wall but it seemed to her that the cat could pull it out.

"Everyone is afraid of him," said Heriberto.

"Why? Inside, I mean . . . why keep him inside?"

"It is a decoration. Benjamin loves all of nature. He gives the cats to friends. Some he sells for profit. This one was captured not too far from here. Sometimes it is useful."

"Useful for what?"

"Up. Climb, please. *Apurate!*"

But Erin stood still, pulling the serape tight around her, looking at the cat's black flanks moving in the rhythm of sleep. She saw a litter box the size of a small garden, made of gleaming hardwood and filled with beach sand, waiting back in the shadows. The cat suddenly lifted its big sleek head and looked at her with green eyes, then just as quickly dropped back into sleep.

"We can go," she said.

They climbed to the fourth floor.

"Why is there no landing for the third floor?"

"Because there is no reason to go there."

"Two women in white dresses came from the third floor outside."

"So it is."

He led her halfway down one of three broad hallways and opened a door with a plastic card as in a hotel. She stepped in and without a word he closed the door behind her and she heard the electric lock buzz and hum and clunk. When she yanked on the lever handle it did not move even a fraction of an inch.

She pounded on the door. "Hey, mister! Hey!" She listened and heard nothing but the clipped echo of her own voice. After a moment she took a deep breath and relaxed her stomach muscles and dropped the serape to the floor. Then she turned to face her new prison.

The room was spacious and richly furnished and Erin sensed it had been cleaned daily for decades if not centuries. It had a shiny dark hardwood floor and white plaster walls with many framed paintings. She looked up at a high copper ceiling with a dark brown patina, the copper sheets held fast by steel rivets that gave the appearance of a knight's armor. Trapped inside a suit of armor, she thought. She sang a short note and listened to its quick bounce and rapid absorption in the space.

The bed frame was dark hardwood, the bedding high and plump. A handsome leather armchair sat with its back to a window and a hardbound copy of García Marquez's *Of Love and Other Demons* propped up on its seat. It was the English translation. There were two hand-carved wardrobes and between them an oval full-length mirror in a swiveling frame. She pulled open one of the wardrobes and found it full of women's clothes, her size, new, with the tags on. She felt a ripple of invasion down her back and closed the door.

Along one wall were a long table and chairs and on the table was a basket of fruit and bread and bottles of wine and water and juices. She lifted the white envelope that was propped against a wine bottle. Her first name was written across the front of it in crude longhand. Inside was a card with the letters BJCA embossed near the top. More of the longhand: *Welcome to my home—Benjamin Juan Carlos Armenta.* Another unpleasant ripple went down her back and she dropped the card and envelope to the table.

In the far corner stood a desk and chair. There was a lamp and a DVD player on the desktop, and a yellow legal pad with what looked like an expensive pen lying across the top sheet. She thought of her mother, who had always laid out pads of paper and freshly sharpened pencils on her desk at home, to encourage her to write and draw. Between two gray onyx bookends carved as crocodile heads were a Spanish-English dictionary, *Rock 'n Roll in L.A.*, and three Harlequin bodice-rippers.

The bathroom was large, with a red marble tub and aged copper fixtures that had taken on the same deep patina as the ceiling. She looked at her face in the mirror and saw the exhaustion in it. Find strength. Create strength. *Come to me by moonlight, sugar!* You're going to have to do better than that, she thought. A whole lot better.

She sat down heavily on the edge of the tub and reached under her nightgown and slowly worked the derringer away from her upper calf. She felt the air hit the chafed skin and she rubbed the raw and painful indentation the weapon had left. It was one of the hideout options: take it if you need it. Bradley had shown her how to operate the gun but she wasn't too good. Two big bullets. Loud and lethal. Intended for pocket or purse.

But fifteen hours ago Erin had had neither pocket nor purse as she heard the men in the next room, their voices urgent. So she had used tape from the first-aid kit, and grabbed some fifties off the roll and folded them over twice and taped them along with the gun to her calf. She had barely gotten it all secure when the floor began to move and she grabbed the shotgun off the rack and plopped into the recliner as it swung out. When she looked at the eight armed men who had invaded her home she realized she was at least a captive and likely a corpse and her husband was almost certainly dead and her son would die unborn. She couldn't remember quite how the shotgun worked and they quickly got it away from her. She had hit at them and burst into tears and clung to the chair arms kicking as they dragged her away.

Now she stood and without counting the money she slipped it into the stack of fat white bath towels on a shelf. Then she lifted off the lid of the toilet flush box and set the gun underwater, down near the float assembly where it was difficult to see. Bubbles hurried up from the barrel. The water wouldn't damage the gun or the ammo, Bradley had said. He'd told her that a toilet tank was a good hide for a gun for a few days, even a week or two, if it ever came to that. Just remember to shake the water out of the barrel before you used it. Easy.

She stepped back into the room and went to the left wardrobe and set the tape carefully in the pocket of a light jacket. Through the glass and the vine-wound bars of one window she could see the balcony with its profusion of pots and flowers, and beyond the blossoms a swath of jungle, and a sliver of white-sand beach and pale-green water. Prisoner of flowers, she thought, prisoner of paradise.

Propped upright in the corner between two casement windows was a guitar case with its lid open. When she stepped closer Erin saw that it was a Gibson Hummingbird not unlike her own back home. She felt a powerful stab of sorrow and grief as she looked at this beautiful instrument and wondered if she would ever see her Hummingbird again, or her home or husband or even just one thing from her former life.

From behind her Erin heard the electric buzz, hum and clunk of the door lock opening and she turned to see a young man step into the room. He was tall and sandy-haired, solidly built, and wore a clean white Guayabera shirt and jeans and polished black cowboy boots. The door closed decisively behind him.

"I am Saturnino."

"Erin."

"You are in good condition?"

"Very good."

He smiled at her. He was handsome. "I am the boss of security here. I want to welcome you."

"I feel kidnapped, not welcomed."

"You are here. Everything here is my duty to protect. I am in command. Only my father is more powerful."

He walked close to her and she looked up into his eyes. They were tan, small-pupiled, catlike. She could smell the scent of his body and breath. "You are more beautiful than the many pictures of you I have seen."

She stepped around him and hooked the serape off the floor with her bare toe and caught it and wrapped it around her shoulders again.

"You are amusing," he said. "You cannot protect yourself. I will take you when I want you."

His smile is the devil's, thought Erin. "I'm Benjamin's guest."

"And there is nothing you can do. Or anyone can do."

"I'll be sure that Mr. Armenta knows that."

"He does not control everything, *pinche gringa*. You are far away from what was real to you. You are nothing in Mexico. Not even a person. You are entirely invisible and entirely alone. You are like the air. You need a strong friend."

Saturnino smiled again and came up close to her. When he leaned in to kiss her she slapped him hard across the face. In the silence that followed she watched his rage flash and hover, then slowly retreat.

There was a knock at the door. Saturnino unleashed a rapid-fire string of Spanish curses, of which Erin understood most.

"Edgar Ciel," said the voice behind the door. "*In nomine patri et—*"

"Go to hell you filthy goat!" yelled Saturnino. He looked at Erin then swiped his card key and pushed open the door.

In stepped a tall slender priest and two young novitiates—a boy and a girl. The priest was very pale, with a sharp nose and ears and thinning light-brown hair. Behind his wire-rimmed glasses his eyes were blue and luminous. He looked sixty. The boy and girl looked to be twelve or thirteen and they stood behind him, hands folded before them, looking at the floor. The priest looked at Erin, then turned his gaze to Saturnino. "What are you doing here, my vile child?"

Saturnino made the sign of a cross with his fingers and held it up to the priest as he circled around him and toward the door. When Saturnino went by he stomped the boy's foot with his boot and backed out of the room with a nod to Erin. Edgar Ciel pushed the door closed on him. The boy hopped wordlessly on his good foot four times then put the hurt foot back down tentatively.

"I am Father Edgar Ciel."

"I am Erin McKenna."

"Did he harm you?"

"He would have."

"Never be alone with him."

"He has a key to my room."

"I will speak to Benjamin."

"Can he control his son?"

Ciel studied her with his blue eyes. They had a light in them that was cold and possibly wise. Father O'Hora had had that light. "Of course."

"Can you do it right now? Talk to Benjamin?"

Ciel held her gaze and swung open his jacket and pulled a cell phone off his belt at one hip. Erin saw the walnut-handled revolver holstered at the other. She smelled vanilla. He raised the phone to his ear and walked to the window that framed the balcony and the jungle and beach. He turned his back to her and spoke softly in Spanish, then he waited for a while and spoke again.

"What's your name?" Erin asked the boy.

"Henry. Enrique."

"And yours?"

"Constanza."

"How do you like the Castle?"

They shrugged with their hands still folded before them and looked down at the floor. Enrique gingerly lifted his stomped foot, then set it back down.

"We come here because Benjamin Armenta donated four million dollars to the Legion of Christ last year," said Ciel. He walked toward her, fastening the phone to his belt again. "He has been donating such amounts for a decade. He convinces his friends to donate too. It's the largest Catholic league in all of Mexico. Last year we built two more schools in Chiapas State and were able to endow a chair to head the department of cinema in our university in Mexico City."

"Does that buy him a place in heaven too?" asked Erin. She saw the pain pass across the face of the priest. In that moment he reminded her again of Father O'Hora back in Austin, the way his emotions were always so ready and readable. A good and decent man, she thought. He had married two of her brothers and sat with her father for hours at the hospital and finally buried him. "Forgive me. It's been a long day."

He smiled. "Saturnino is not permitted to have a key. It will be taken from him."

"Can you make Benjamin let me go?"

"I will speak to him. I do not control him. But I can watch over you while you're here. And pray for your safe return."

"Why thank you so much, Father. When my husband gives Benjamin the million bucks he wants, maybe Benjamin can give it to you."

"Keep your heart pure and your thoughts clean."

"I was never a very good Catholic."

"Neither was I until the Lord opened my heart."

"I can't believe you and your Lord let these people get away with this."

"The world is complicated."

"So that makes kidnapping okay?"

"Benjamin will be here in a moment."

Ciel removed the card key from his pocket with a guilty smile. He swiped it through the lock, then ushered out his two charges and let the door swing shut behind him. Erin listened to the buzz and the clunk of the dead bolt thrown home.

She already hated those sounds.

He was not what Erin was expecting. Into the room pushed a large and disheveled man with a head of wild gray-black hair and a hangdog expression on his face. He wore a Cerveza Pacifico T-shirt and shorts and he was barefoot. He had a beer belly and stooped slightly, as if it were pulling him over. His complexion was pale for a Mexican and he had at least a two-day growth of whiskers. His eyes were black and shiny. She guessed him to be fifty years old.

He stopped and stared directly at her face. "Do you have everything that you need?"

"Everything but safety and freedom."

"That is up to your husband. He has ten days."

"Saturnino has a key to my room."

Armenta pulled two card keys from a pocket in his shorts, fanned them for her like playing cards in his thick fingers. "No more."

"How could you threaten to skin me alive?"

Armenta looked at her matter-of-factly and said nothing for a moment. "They tell me you are Erin of Erin and the Inmates. I believe I heard you on the radio."

"It'll just be the Inmates if you do what you've threatened to do."

Armenta raised a hand and waved it gently, as if shooing away a slow fly. "I love music of all kinds. We have performances here. I record music also. Many important people come here to listen and dance. Do you know the Jaguars of Veracruz?"

"Everyone knows the Jaguars of Veracruz."

"Do you like them?"

"I saw them in Los Angeles. Fantastic show. They played so long the fire department made them quit."

"They will be here this week. To perform."

"And do you skin them alive if they don't bring you millions of dollars?"

He smiled at her bleakly. "I grew up with them. I have been cruel in my life but I have never lacked compassion. I am strongly loyal."

"Your son threatened me."

"I will discipline him. Sometimes he has large ideas that are bad ideas. You don't worry."

"When I looked in his eyes I saw that he could do bad things and enjoy them."

Armenta nodded slightly. "This is his way. He will not hurt you while you are here."

"You seem like a good man. Let me go. Fly me home. I'll *mail* you the million cash if you really need it all that badly."

He studied her again and she studied him back. His hair stood out from his head, an unbrushed nest. His face was morose and his eyes looked exhausted and suspicious and piggish. She wondered if his paleness was from prison or illness or just from being inside all the time.

"Your husband has taken hundreds of thousands of my dollars in the last year. He has taken many pounds of my best products. He has cost me thirty men to be deported or prosecuted. He has allowed the murders of another nine of my men to go without any authentic investigation. Nine! He himself killed two more last night."

"You have taken the wrong man's wife. Bradley is a sheriff's deputy and you invaded our home."

"He has been paid large money for doing some things and not doing other things."

"His salary is not large."

"But he is also employed by the North Baja Cartel of Carlos Herredia. You maybe do not know this. Maybe you spend your time making music. As you should. But there are many secrets in a marriage, some small and some not small. Maybe you are not welcome to this type of information. Maybe he does not want you to know where your fortune comes from."

"I don't believe you."

"What you believe does not change the measure of things. Your husband is more than a thorn in my paw. He must surrender L.A. to me. Surrender it absolutely. Business is the thing we all do. Statements are to be made and answered. This is my example. A man must attend to the small things so that the larger things will occur properly."

"Fly me home and you'll get what you want from my husband. All of it. I promise."

Armenta beheld her and Erin looked back. His sad hound eyes appeared clear and calm, resigned to things she did not know, and apologetic for things she did not want to know. "I will fly you home when I get what I want from you."

5

Los Angeles sheriff's deputy Charlie Hood watched Bradley's Cayenne bounce up the dirt road toward his house. He's early, thought Hood, not surprised. Bradley had sounded intensely worried on the phone, though vague. He had never asked Hood for help in anything until now.

It was evening here in Buenavista but still 102 degrees, according to the thermometer in the shade of Hood's patio. Buenavista straddled the border and was often the hottest place in the nation. Hood was attached to an ATF task force working the Iron River—the gun trade—between the United States and Mexico, and he had moved here from L.A. to be near the action. Hood liked action and the idea that he was needed and that what he did mattered. He was thirty-three, tall and lanky, with a forthright face and strong eyes.

His rented home sat in the steep hills outside of town and from the eastern patio where he now stood he could see the little city huddled below, with its odd amalgamation of old and new: the ornate dome and cross of St. Cecilia's, the zocalo, the narrow cobblestoned streets of the old town. And around them, like the growth rings in a tree trunk: the Rite Aid and the Blockbuster and the Ralph's and fast food places on the U.S. side and the Sam's Club and Wal-Mart and the stretch of maquiladoras and new apartments on the Mexican side. Hood could also see the new twenty-foot steel border wall. This had recently replaced the old chain-link fence, a porous formality along which Mexicans and Americans used to meet friends and family, trade news, exchange minor goods. Beyond the new wall were sharp mountains to the south and west.

They sat inside with the air conditioner blasting. Bradley declined a beer. He had two butterfly bandages across gashes in his forehead. His eyes were rimmed in red and their hollows were dark and he had not shaved. He paced back and forth in front of the cavernous black fireplace, Hood watching him from an old sofa. Hood's dog, Daisy, lay on the paver tiles at his feet, her snout on the cool tile, her dark brown eyes tracking their visitor. She was black and slender with a white blaze on her chest, and had the high-standing, flap-topped ears common to the border dogs from which she had come.

Bradley told Hood the story of Erin's kidnapping. Hood's heart fell but he listened without interrupting. Erin had long been one of his favorite people and Hood had long believed that she would suffer someday at the hands of her husband.

When Bradley was finished he came to the couch and sat and buried his head in his hands.

"Can you get the money?"

"I've got the money."

"A million cash?"

"Mom left us plenty. I invested it in gold before the crash."

"A million cash?"

Bradley looked at Hood as if at an annoying child but said nothing.

"You're not going to talk to our people, or the FBI?"

Again that look from Bradley. "They can't help officially. You have to know that, Charlie. All they can do is get her killed. The more noise we make the faster she'll die."

"They're some of the best law-enforcement people in the world."

"Gringo law enforcement means nothing in Mexico. The government doesn't want us, and the cartels hate us. We're ants. You should know that better than anyone, after what happened to you with the Zetas."

That last word sent a breeze of nerves across Hood's scalp. The Zetas were military defectors, special forces men who had thrown in with the cartels and then become their own cartel. Hood had seen their violence, their beheadings, and their torture in Mexico and in the United States. "Calderón's government helped us get Jimmy back."

"Yeah, after he was tortured and broken. Jimmy was federal. Erin's a singer. How much help are they going to give her, Charlie?"

"So you're going to run that million dollars to the Jai Alai Palace in Tijuana tomorrow afternoon at three, and wait for a call from a guy named Gonzalvo?"

"Those are the orders."

"Then what?"

Bradley looked over at Hood. "When I show the money I get to hear her on the phone. Proof of life. Then I wait for the next order."

"When do you deliver the cash?"

"Ten days. I told you."

"After they run you all over Mexico."

"Probably."

"I hate your chances," said Hood. "But you don't seem to. Why?"

"I have a plan."

"Explain it."

"I've been working narcotics for almost a year now, right? Jack Cleary is my boss and he's smart and tough and he's taught me a lot. We've got friends in Mexico. Counterparts. They're smart and tough too. They'll help, but not through official channels. And I'm going to use my ten days and these guys to find her because you know what?

There's a good chance that the minute Armenta gets the money he'll kill her anyway."

Hood knew that this was more than possible. It was happening more and more in the narco kidnappings—murder left less witnesses and ignited even more terror in the living, more submission and compliance.

"How are you going to find her while you lug forty pounds of cash from California to God knows where?"

Bradley looked at Hood and offered a small smile. "I love your optimism, Charlie. I love your can-do attitude."

"That's not an answer."

Bradley marched out and a car door opened then slammed and a moment later he was back, pulling a piece of wheeled luggage across the pavers behind him. Daisy's head was up and she was watching. Bradley stopped in front of Hood and pushed down the handle and flipped the luggage over at Hood's feet. He squatted and unzipped the flap and threw it back.

"The answer is teamwork," said Bradley. "You and me. You deliver this while my friends and I are coming in the back door. If I can find the back door, that is. When Heriberto's men contacted me late this morning, I told them I have the money but I don't have the stomach for delivering it. This produced great laughter and witty insults. I am now a fag without balls with a kidnapped wife who desires real men. And many other things almost as bad. But I can dispatch a brave friend to deliver. Because money is money, after all. So, what do you say, Charlie? What do you say?"

Hood thought. He knew Bradley was brash, fearless and lucky. Knew that he was strong and bright and tainted. Hood suspected him of murder and lesser crimes but could prove none of them. Bradley's highest allegiance seemed to be to himself. He studied the young man's face. In it he saw Bradley's mother, Suzanne. He and Bradley had been trading blame and suspicion for the three years since her death, and now Hood wondered if he should just forgive and help him through the harrowing future.

"Why me?"

"Because you love my wife. In a chaste and honorable, Charles Hood kind of way. I know you wouldn't do it for me. But I think you'll do it for her. Will you?"

Hood looked down at the suitcase. Daisy sat beside it looking at him. He pictured himself waiting for a call in the parking lot of the Jai Alai Palace in Tijuana, three p.m. the next day. He thought of Gustavo Armenta, Benjamin's innocent, college-bound son, killed by an errant ATF bullet during an undercover buy that went bad. He thought of Armenta's vengeance upon ATF agent Jimmy Holdstock, of his own bloody journey across the border to Mulege, of the carnage enacted by the Zetas, of Sergeant Raydel Luna, his counterpart, slaughtered by his own countryman to prove that honesty and bravery and integrity were weaknesses in their world. And of course he thought of Erin.

"There's fifty grand extra in there," said Bradley. "Yours for trying. And another fifty for expenses. Fifty more waiting here if we actually get her back alive."

"I don't want your money."

"Donate it to Save the Dinosaurs or something. Her passport is in there, too. I'm bullish. It's all I can afford to be."

"This is all wrong, Bradley. How did Benjamin Armenta know where you live? And that you and Erin would be home? How did he know about the hidden room? How did he know to pick a night when the dogs were kenneled and you didn't have guests? How did he know that your gate was wired for security but the fence wasn't? How did he know the security code for your house? Or that you had a million in cash just kind of handy? Why did he take such huge risks and lose two men for a million dollars? He makes that in an average week. So why the pyrotechnics? What did you do to him to deserve all the special attention?"

Bradley gazed down at the money and toed the suitcase with his boot. "Maybe we'll find out. But I'm not going to beg. If you don't want to help, don't."

"Where were your homies last night—Stone the car thief and Clayton the forger?"

Bradley looked at him sharply. "Stone is a car *salesman,* Hood. There is a small difference. And Clayton is an artist. You know that."

Hood stared at him.

"Anyway, Erin encouraged them to find other lodging after we got married." Bradley walked to a window and looked out at an orange sunset. When he turned back Hood could see his silhouette framed in the falling light. "Hood, if I don't make it back but Erin does, I want you to take care of her. She'll be a mother by February and she'll need help. Take good care of her and of my boy. The ultrasound showed him healthy. There's plenty of money in the bank. She's the most wonderful person you will ever know."

"You can't pass her like a football."

"But I couldn't protect her, either, could I? It was my number-one thing to do in this life and I didn't. I'll do anything to get her back. I'll die down there to make it happen."

"You know I'm in."

Bradley pulled a cell phone from his belt and tossed it to Hood. Daisy watched its flight. "Their phone. Pre-paid Mexico minutes, non-traceable by Mexican law enforcement. Just answer it when good old Gonzalvo calls and do what he says."

Hood pictured himself alone in Mexico with a million dollars and maybe a handgun, lined up against the Gulf Cartel. He felt the dread leaking into his brainpan like rainwater through an old roof.

"And here's a phone just for you and me." Bradley unclipped the satellite phone and handed it to Hood. "Best satellite job money can buy. I've signed us up for unlimited Mexico calling for the next two weeks. My number's already programmed in. They promised reception in all thirty-one Mexican states, plus the federal district."

Hood considered the two phones, the million in cash at his feet, and bright, lovely Erin McKenna in the hands of killers. "We'll make it work."

"It has to work. By the way, I thought the name Charlie Hood might get Armenta buzzing after what ATF did to his son last year. So I told them your name was Charlie Bravo. Charlie the Brave. That okay?"

"It feels like an unfair advantage."

Hood watched Bradley's smile go from wicked to haunted. "Deliver her, Charlie. And if I don't come back, well, you three figure it out."

They stood outside on the stone porch while the bugs slapped against the light and the mantids walked their elongated shadows on the adobe.

"Any luck with Mike Finnegan, Charlie?"

"No luck with him."

"He'll turn up. He always seems to. Crafty little guy."

"Tell me if you see him."

"You bet. That's a promise, Charlie."

Bradley walked down the gravel path toward his Cayenne, then stopped and turned. "Thanks for doing this, man. I knew you would. I'll pray to God in heaven for you. And to anyone else who might help."

6

Later Hood took half of the extra fifty grand and distributed the cash among his wallet, his shave kit and his Expedition.

Out on his patio in the dark he felt the temperature finally drop. He called Frank Soriana, his managing ATF superior in San Diego, and cleared the next eleven days for personal time. He also talked Soriana into issuing him a diplomatic pouch to carry his gun into Mexico.

"Personal, huh?" asked Soriana. "Sounds like you should be on ATF time."

Hood laughed quietly. He pictured Erin in the hands of cutthroats. He wondered if the million dollars was all Armenta really wanted from Bradley Jones. "See you tomorrow early, sir."

Next Hood called his mother in Bakersfield. She was a talker. The Buick was making a funny sound and the strawberries at the market were plenty big but almost tasteless. His father was doing okay in assisted living but he had tackled an orderly that morning. He was an Alzheimer's sufferer and his mind was nearly gone but his body was fit and strong. His mother was trying to forget the man he was now, but to remember the man he used to be, trying to steel her heart, but Hood knew that this was breaking it instead. He invented a story about going back to D.C. for ATF meetings.

"Then I'll see you in a week?" she asked.

"A little over."

"Less than two, though?"

"Less than two, Mom."

He called Beth and left a message on her home phone. He rarely called her at work because she was a night-shift emergency-room doctor at Imperial Mercy in Buenavista and she was almost always busy. In the last year Hood had been working more and more assignments for the ATF Blowdown task force so it wasn't unusual for him to be out of touch. He told her he would call just as soon as he could. Although Beth had never said so, Hood knew that absences like this were taking their toll on them. She wanted more closeness not more distance, but he could only give her what he had. Thus he felt bad. The cool fog of disappointment had begun to settle down upon them. And Hood had started wondering if he worked long and sometimes dangerous hours so he could remain a distance from the demands of love and family and friends.

He told Beth's answering machine that he'd be gone ten days and asked her to come get Daisy if she could. He promised her he would call and write. As he rang off he pictured her face and his breath caught achingly and he doubted that he knew even one thing about love. He set a box of stationery and an elegant pen she had given him in his duffel, beside his gun and holster and three plastic wrist restraints, and the CD slipcase for the most recent release from Erin and the Inmates.

When he was done packing he sat on a bench in his home office—a picnic table in his dining room. He checked his Web site, Facebook page and Twitter, hoping for a tip that might lead him to a man he had been trying hard to find for the last year. The man had introduced

himself as Mike Finnegan, a bathroom-products wholesaler based in
L.A. But as Hood came to learn, Mike had also gone by other names
and claimed other occupations. It was very possible that he was insane, as someone close to him had said. And it was likely that he had
done some very bad things to some good people—good friends of his,
in fact. Then Mike had vanished.

Because of his dual citizenship with the Los Angeles sheriffs and
the ATF, Hood had many contacts in law enforcement. Once a week
he would blast:

Dear Paul (John, Barbara, Philip, Donna, Friends . . .),

Charlie Hood checking in. Anything on Mike Finnegan?
Here again are the six known photographs of him.
Please continue to distribute. I hope this note finds you
well and I truly thank you for all the help you've given.

Sincerely,

Charlie Hood, Los Angeles Sheriff's Department;
Alcohol, Tobacco & Firearms Blowdown Task Force,
Buenavista Field Office

But no e-mails back today. And no messages on the Web site. There
were several useless postings to his Facebook page, where he trolled
the general public, and some more irrelevant tweets.

A year ago, his opening inquisitions had led to some promising
"tips" about Mike. But these had trailed off quickly and Hood had
been forced to face a numbing truth: not one of his hundreds of contacts had anything at all on the Mike Finnegan he had met in L.A. He
was in no database. Not the IRS, not the DMV, not the Social Security
System. No one in law enforcement, intelligence or security had any-

thing. No fingerprints, no dental records, no DNA. And apparently, the world outside of law enforcement knew even less about him.

Hood sat straight-backed on the hard picnic bench and looked at his wall, where he had tacked copies of the eight photographs he had of Finnegan. Three were extracted from security video, and showed a small, thick, middle-aged man and an attractive younger woman. Possibly his daughter, as Hood knew, but likely not. The video was taken a little over two years ago as they were leaving Imperial Mercy Hospital in Buenavista. Finnegan had been critically injured in a car accident just weeks prior and had checked himself out of the hospital against doctor's orders. His "daughter," Owens, had picked him up. In the three pictures Mike looked pale and relaxed and maybe a little tired after having half the bones in his body broken, his skull cracked in two places, life-threatening internal damage, and being in a full body cast for almost three weeks.

Hood studied the other pictures, one at a time, still hoping to dredge out some helpful detail he had missed, or achieve some insight that only repetition could spark. One was taken by a German bird-watcher in an ecoresort on the Arenal Volcano in Costa Rica, where Mike was billing himself as Joe Leftwich, an Irish priest. And Arenal, Hood had learned, was where Leftwich had commenced the almost unimaginably cruel destruction of two of Hood's closest friends.

Another picture showed Finnegan/Leftwich at a home Dodgers game in July of the previous year, roughly one month before he arrived in Costa Rica. The subject of the photographer was not Mike at all, but a small boy and his parents, sitting two rows in front of him. Mike was trying to avoid the camera, turning his face away in clear annoyance at being shot. This image was submitted by the boy's mother, a Ventura County assistant DA who recognized the face from one of Hood's insistent e-mails.

Another picture was of Mike and Owens, standing arm in arm at a cocktail party in Beverly Hills. In the picture Owens was a full head taller than he was. Finnegan was smiling resignedly, as if he didn't want to be photographed but knew he should submit to it, but he also appeared happy. The photographer was a professional freelancer who had come across Hood's plea for "Finnegan/Leftwich images" buried in a "Photographs Wanted" search of Google, and recognized Mike.

Hood had not posted the other two pictures, and it wasn't likely he ever would. In some ways, they were his favorites.

One was a group shot that showed Charlie Manson and some hangers-on at Spahn Ranch in the summer of 1969. An L.A. assistant district attorney had come across the picture while digitizing old forensic photos, and seen that one of Manson's groupies looked a lot like the guy that Charlie Hood had been badgering her about. The groupie was obviously a different man, but she sent a digitized copy along as a lark. Hood was flabbergasted to see a dead ringer for Mike Finnegan right in the middle of the hippies, sporting a "Freewheelin'" T-shirt, and his hair grown out in a frizzy halo. He looked to be about forty years old. Hood knew that if Mike had been forty in the Manson picture he would have been around eighty when they met at Imperial Mercy Hospital. Not likely. But even allowing for his own gnawing obsession with Mike Finnegan, Hood could see with his own two eyes that the faces belonged to the same man.

The last image was an even worse conundrum. It was taken in San Jose, California, in 1875, at the hanging of the outlaw Tiburcio Vasquez. It was one of several taken by a newspaper photographer who covered the event. Mike was among the onlookers gazing up at the gallows in a dramatic composition that used the noose itself as a blurred up-front framing device and focused on the well-dressed spectators waiting for the execution. Finnegan. Clearly. Dressed and groomed in the fashion of the day. He looked about fifty years old. Which would have made him 184 years old when, two years ago, lying in his Imperial Mercy ICU bed and tipsy with wine, Mike had recounted for Hood the hanging of his friend, Tiburcio. Mike had quoted the outlaw's last words by memory and this had haunted Hood. So, a few months ago, on a long shot, he had finally ferreted out this collection of photographs. In so doing he had found this image and begun to question the soundness of his eyes and of his reason.

Yet he saw what he saw.

He had had his eyes examined and had spent fifty expensive minutes with a psychiatrist. His uncorrected vision was his usual 20/15. The shrink told him he seemed "sound," given his stressful occupation, ailing father, and troubled relationship with Beth. He said depression was possible, and that Hood should try to experience his emotions rather than direct them. He recommended pleasant outdoor activities but no medication.

In addition to his digital searches, Hood had been handing out Mike Finnegan photo albums wherever he went for about six months now—to law-enforcement people he met through work, to his contacts and informants, to people he met socially through Beth and their growing circle of friends, to waiters and waitresses, clerks and bartenders, once at his own door to Jehovah's Witnesses, trading them for their Watchtowers. Two hundred and forty-eight booklets distributed so far. To manage costs he ordered fifty at a time from the print shop. But the picture books had gotten him nothing, nothing and more nothing.

A familiar chill ran through him as he stared at the Vasquez photograph. He breathed in deeply then slowly out. "Back in ten days," he said. "But you'll keep, Mike, won't you?"

Daisy's tail slapped the tile three times, then stopped. She looked at Hood with a devotion that made him feel undeserving. She sat up and encouraged his self-forgiveness by letting him scratch her throat.

He checked the e-mails and Facebook again and found nothing helpful regarding Mike Finnegan. He got less of everything these days. He wondered if in another year there would be nothing at all. But he knew that Finnegan had not vanished. He knew the man was real and living, perhaps still in L.A. Bathroom fixtures. *It's not nearly as exciting as it sounds.*

In one of the e-mails on his screen now, Hood's contact suggested that he would notify Hood if anything popped, that the weekly reminders were not needed and in fact were a bit of a nuisance. He sent out a fresh blast anyway—982 friendly reminders of who he was looking for, all with the six photographs attached. And another Facebook posting—2,499 people like the last one! More tweets in the thinning search for Mike.

He sighed and found Erin's Web page and looked at the pictures of her performing, and played a video. Not for the first time he was angry at Bradley for putting her in harm's way, and not for the first time he wished that he'd met her first. He felt some shame in this.

Later Hood watched the clear desert stars awhile, then slept poorly, visited by dreams he did not own or understand.

7

AFTER SUNRISE SOMEONE KNOCKED ON her door and Erin rose from a deep sleep and sat up on the bed. She had no idea where she was. She touched the long white nightshirt that she wore but that did not belong to her. When she looked out and saw the palm trees swaying in the orange light and the water glittering between the mangroves she remembered, and her heart tried to climb out from its cage inside her.

A woman's voice. "*Desayuno.*"

"Yes, breakfast, thank you."

The lock whirred and clunked and in walked not a woman but a slender teenage boy with a golden pompadour and a shy smile. He held a folding stand in one hand and with the other he balanced a large waiter's tray over his shoulder. The tray was stacked with stainless-steel warmers that clinked as he crossed the room. At the table he set the tray on the stand and took his time arranging her meal. He changed his mind twice on the placement of side dishes. With a flourish he snapped the napkin and folded it into a loose scallop and set this to the left. Then the flatware.

Erin caught the scent of the meal as it went by and thought it was the best breakfast she'd ever smelled. Her stomach moaned and gurgled. She watched him pour the coffee and the juice. Last he lifted the warmers and stacked them on the tray, then with a matadorial flair swept up the stand and smiled shyly at her again on his way out.

She ate piggishly, slopping the ranchero sauce onto her nightgown and shoveling down fast the tortillas heaped with sweet preserves. She drank the juice and sighed with the pleasure of it: tangerine. She finished it and held her free hand to her belly.

She drew a bath and dried off the derringer and set it on the deck of the beautifully tiled Roman tub. She lifted off the nightshirt and threw it over the shower curtain rod. Her right upper calf still stung from where the taped gun and cash had rubbed and pulled. She disliked guns and the sounds they made. She floated freely in the great deep tub listening to the amplified slurp of the bathwater going in and out of her ears. In these sounds and in their echoes she heard melodies as she had always heard them, the gifts of her nature coming from a universe that, even as a small girl, she had understood was made not only of matter but of music. Straight above her was a raised plaster ceiling painted with the likeness of a young Mayan woman looking down on a warrior who knelt before her. She was long pregnant and she held an urn but Erin could not see into it. This brought tears to her eyes and terror to her heart so she sat up suddenly in the water and slapped herself in the face, hard. You will not come apart. You cannot come apart. She slapped herself hard again.

She dressed in new clothes from the wardrobe, pulling off the tags as she went. They were designer garments, fashionable and well made. She was slender and long-legged and flat-chested but the clothes fit right, even the sandals. The clothes were in colors she liked. She lifted the blouse and stood sideways to the mirror and wondered if they knew.

She pushed aside the breakfast dishes and sat for a long while at the table by the window. She had been to Cancún twice in her life and this place reminded her of it. She and Bradley had stayed at the Camino Real and snorkeled at Isla Mujeres and rented a jeep to drive to Chichen Itza and Tulum. The jungle around Cancún looked like this jungle, only flatter. She remembered the cloud-muted sunlight and the heat. This morning's light was filtered by clouds too and when she touched her hand to the window she could feel the warmth of the day already on the glass.

She reached to open the window but it was not made to be opened. She picked up one of the stainless-steel plate warmers and flung it hard against the glass, to no effect. She lifted a chair and threw it against the glass hard but the glass, if it was glass at all, was very heavy and did not break. She turned and ran to the door and lowered her shoulder and tried to knock it down. She kicked it and hit it with the sides of her fists. She screamed and cursed for anyone to hear and was answered by dead silence. In the bathroom she vomited. She paced the perimeter of her quarters several times, then squeezed into the corner between the wall and the bed and pulled the colorful woven bedspread down over her, curled into a ball on the floor and wept.

Hours later she awakened and threw off the cover and stood. She saw that the breakfast dishes were gone and a light lunch had been left in their place. The chair was back at the table and the plate warmer had been picked up from the floor by the window. She was a heavy sleeper, but she was surprised to have slept through all this. Or maybe not, she thought. You don't get kidnapped every day. You don't see your husband beaten bloody by drug traffickers. She looked outside. From the sun she guessed it was closer to evening than morning. She wondered if the breakfast had been drugged but that made little sense. There was a vase of fresh cut tropical flowers on the table.

She walked the room again and felt the sudden rush of abandonment. She'd never felt abandoned in her life. Not for a day, not for an hour. She had never really even been alone, either. And you have to be alone to be abandoned, she thought, although they were not the same thing. She wanted someone to talk to. And someone to listen to. Maybe if she divided the lunch into two meals and set a place across from her someone would appear and they could lunch. To lunch, she thought. A verb.

She stood for a moment in front of the Hummingbird. It was a beautiful instrument, large and resonant and aesthetically dazzling. It looked fairly old, as did the case. She reached for it, then stopped herself. She felt like Pandora, or maybe like Eve herself, confronted with a thing of temptation that had been forbidden to her. But why forbidden? Who had forbidden it? Herself? Some distant God? She had no memory of the forbidding. In fact, she thought, it hasn't been forbidden; it's been offered.

She picked it up and sat in the handsome leather chair. The strings were new and out of tune. She tuned it and played softly without singing, letting her fingers chase down the music as her ears heard it. The sound led to the feelings and thoughts, and she fetched the paper and pen from the desk and set them on the table in front of her.

Hours became minutes as they always did. There was terror, anger, shame, even hope. She tried to slow the rush of emotion enough to capture the last two days with words, not so much capture as synopsize, sketch, represent. Notes into music. Thoughts into rhyme. Later could come the clarity and the accuracy, the shading and wit.

Later, lost to all this, Erin heard another knock on her door.

"Go away! Marcharse!"

"Mr. Armenta will be here in one half hour." It was the soft high voice of the room-service boy.

"For what? Why?"

Silence.

Think. She put the guitar back in its case and pulled off the three sheets of paper upon which she had written, then put the pad and pen back on the desk. The lyrics she stashed under the bed.

Think. She found a blue dress and bit off the Bloomingdale's tag. It was modest and fit loosely around her middle. Then a pair of new sandals. She turned sideways to the mirror to see her profile and she pulled her stomach in again and when she felt the tears starting up she whacked herself on each cheek and this helped.

From the wardrobe she retrieved the used medical tape and in the bathroom she hiked up the blue dress and used its fading adhesive to fasten the derringer around her unchafed calf. She brushed her hair and pulled it back into a ponytail. She thought for a moment, then changed her mind about the gun and removed it and put it and the tape back where they had been.

Five minutes later she heard the whir and clunk of the door lock and Armenta pushed into the room. He wore a black open-collared dress shirt instead of the Pacifico T-shirt, and a pair of wrinkled linen pants instead of the shorts. His hair was still a mess and his face still unshaven and jowly and his eyes haunted. His sandals were a burnished orange color, similar to that of a sunburst Gibson ES-335 guitar. His matching belt was tooled with crocodiles. Three phones hung from it: one satellite and two cell phones, she guessed.

"I will show you my home."

"Let me go."

He wagged a thick finger at her and shook his head slightly. "You will now see my home."

8

THEY TOOK THE ELEVATOR TO the basement kitchen. It was large and two black women labored over the stoves and another operated a tortilla maker. It was hot and fragrant. Two young men sat in folding chairs by a far wall, weapons across their knees.

"A large kitchen," said Armenta. "Yes, very large."

"Why are the staff all black?"

"I used to live in the Caribbean."

They left the kitchen through steel double doors and entered a warren of windowless vaults that soon defeated her sense of direction. The air was cool and smelled of concrete. Armenta led the way, apparently disinterested and walking fast, revealing the large handgun holstered at the small of his back. But Erin was intrigued by the mystery of this place and she lagged behind to see.

The vaults were large and the ceilings high and all were made of concrete block, unpainted, roughly cemented together. In the first was a bank of four large Honda generators, which groaned along. It was vented to the outside by a network of pipes and grates, and the adjacent vault was filled with fifty-five gallon drums of what Erin figured must be gasoline to run the generators.

In some of the vaults were large quantities of canned food and bottled water, sacks of flour, rice and beans. Others, she saw, were stacked high with crates and pallets of music CDs and movie DVDs.

Thousands of them. She recognized the covers of some—American and Mexican musicians and Hollywood movies and TV shows—and she remembered Bradley telling her that the Mexican drug cartels weren't selling just drugs anymore, but also pirated entertainment and both stolen and counterfeit designer fashion ware. She wondered if any Erin and the Inmates CDs were in the crates. Not likely, she thought, as they were a good band and known but not famous.

One large room was filled with Olmec statuary much like she remembered from the National Museum of Anthropology in Mexico City. She had always been impressed by the great brooding heads with their infinite gazes. Another room had Toltec pieces and another was cluttered with Mayan artifacts, many crumbling with age—stone serpents and jaguars and great blackened blocks that must have come from pyramids or temples or one of the big sporting arenas like she'd seen in Chichen Itza. Armenta stopped and spoke softly into one of the cell phones as he waited for her.

They took the elevator up one floor to the ground-level zoo. It included two tigers, two lions, two leopards, two jaguars, two pumas and two ocelots. Armenta said they were mated pairs. Their separate enclosures spanned outward like the spokes of a half-wheel from the common hub of the Castle's ground floor, then continued out into the jungle behind the structure in widening angles. The runs were separated by metal spike fences that Armenta said were too high even for the leopards to jump. The viewing area took up approximately the rear half of the ground floor of the Castle, and had a cobblestone floor and a low limestone ceiling that, to Erin, gave it the look and feel of a dungeon.

Here in the viewing area the cages converged, each of the enclosures ending at a large rust-eaten barred door that might have come from a prison. Monkeys sat on the cobblestones just out of claw range or walked with tails waving as they contemplated and jeered the captives. A giant sloth slept in a leather chair. A group of coati-

mundis came wobbling in from an opening on one side of the enclosures, crossed in front of Erin and Armenta, and continued out
another. Parrots and macaws in reds and greens sat atop the prison
doors. Peacocks and hens came and went. In the shade near the courtyard stood a large aviary filled with what looked like pigeons.

"I brought the cats in so you could see them."

Erin studied the animals. They looked healthy. Their coats shone
even in the dim light except for the lions, pale and tawny, the color of
the hillsides where she lived. All of the animals were calm except the
leopards. They paced opposite sides of their cage in opposite directions,
six steps from the bars to the raised grates that kept them from their
runs, six steps back, again and again as if counterbalanced. The tigers
seemed curious about her though the lions did not. She recognized the
black jaguar from the third-floor landing and it beheld her again with
its pale green eyes. Eyes like the moon, she thought, eyes like the stone
heads that stare forever. A piece of a song she had been hearing came
to her now and she added to it: *Come to me by moonlight, sugar/Let
the moon be your guide/Be a jaguar in the jungle/Be a cat with Olmec
eyes.* She sensed Armenta looking not at the cats, but at her.

"I give them to friends. I sell them occasionally. They are splendidly
cared for and indulged and yet this changes their natures none. They
are not dogs and can never be as dogs. This is what I respect in them."

Armenta walked to the last barred door and pushed a red button
on the wall. Erin saw the enclosure grates withdraw into their respec-
tive concrete floors and the animals, some running and others walking, travel back into their dark slices of jungle.

Again they took the elevator up, though Armenta pushed one
of the lower buttons. It was a good-sized car, paneled with Honduran

mahogany, which Erin recognized from the precious bookshelves in her father's Austin library. She counted six unnumbered control buttons. She and Armenta looked self-consciously straight ahead as strangers in elevators do. She could smell his cologne and the leather of his belt and sandals.

"How many levels?" she asked.

"Four or five."

"Which?"

"This is level two."

"Why is there no third-floor landing?"

He shrugged and they walked down a marble-floored hallway and came to another armed man, seated outside a door. Erin recognized him from the van. He rose and opened the door for them and Erin stepped into a large, well-lit office. There was a counter with a sink and a coffeemaker and a refrigerator in one corner. The office was carpeted and three of the walls were lined with CD racks. Hundreds and hundreds of recordings, she saw. Some she recognized by their cover art and many she did not. The racks were so high there were wheeled ladders to reach the upper discs.

"From all over the world," said Armenta.

"I thought I had a lot."

Armenta led her past a desk with a sleek new computer on it and little else. He held a door open for her and as she stepped in, Erin recognized the wonderful aural hush of a recording studio.

The control room was large and filled with state-of-the-art equipment—a vintage Trident mixing board, Genelec loudspeakers suspended from the ceiling, a pair of NS-10 near-field speakers and Auratones on the board. She saw the two Studer twenty-four-track tape machines, and the racks with the Neve compressor, a near-holy Pultec EQP equalizer, FX, reverb mainframes dat machines, CD players and tape decks, a dedicated Mac. It was cold as control rooms are.

As she moved slowly through it, looking at the expensive equipment, she felt no warm spots in the room, and she thought of her first recording sessions in an Austin garage when she was so young her brothers insisted on being there with her: the heat and the terrible acoustics and the troubled wannabe record producer who swilled warm beers and smoked joints and finally fell asleep on the floor mumbling sweet nothings to the cover of an Emmylou Harris long-play.

"Forty-eight tracks of analog," said Erin. "And a Mac to store the digital. You have all the good toys," she said.

"I like the warmer sound of the analog."

"I always have too."

He nodded. "However the digital has no hissing, and duplication is very convenient. I do the recording. I am a good engineer. I play accordion, but not well. I sing poorly."

He held open the heavy door and they stepped into the tracking room. The ceilings were high and the rafters exposed and the woodwork and finish were handsome.

"This is more Honduran mahogany," said Armenta.

Here in the tracking room his voice was flat and clear, as if stripped of nonessential vibration. Erin could tell that the baffles and soundproofing were excellent, though hidden within the gorgeous woodwork. The air here was lively in a shimmery way—a tuned tracking room, she thought. Beautiful. There was a big drum booth, a piano booth in which a Yamaha grand piano held court, a vocal booth caked with foam from ceiling to floor. She turned and looked at Armenta.

"Los Jaguars de Veracruz have recorded here. And Mara Graco. Do you know Mara Graco?"

"I love Mara Graco. *La Cumbia de Rosas*."

"And *La Casa du tus Sueños*."

"The House of Your Dreams."

"Her voice is almost that of a man. It is smoking and rich and hides something sharpened. She plays the piano very well but this talent is not featured on her recordings. Until here. Here Mara Graco played the Yamaha. It was . . . extraordinary. I want Flaco Jimenez to come here. So *robusto,* his accordion. I have seen him perform many times."

Erin looked briefly at Armenta. His gray-black hair sprang randomly but his hangdog eyes were intensely focused on her. He seemed flushed by the memory of Mara Graco playing the Yamaha. For a moment his face held a ruddy glow and the hint of a smile. Then these faded and Erin saw the haunted face she had seen before, a man with losses he could not recover and regrets he would not outlive.

"And the Brazilians?" asked Armenta with a small twinkle in his eyes. "Nora Ney? Marisa Monte?"

"*Hipnotico,*" said Erin. "I love the Brazilians. They absorb so much and make it all work. I miss the old sambas."

"I very much love the Irish too," said Armenta. "And when the Chieftains play together with Los Tigres del Norte—"

"The Irish and the Mexicans together," said Erin. "Was 'San Patricio' a wonder or not? With Ry Cooder!"

"Did you know that the accordions were brought here by the German and the Polish miners? Because they could travel with them. And the Mexicans fell in love with this sound. That is why much of our music is polka music—German polkas played faster and with happiness! Oh, yes, then you mix into this the passionate Irish. I reproduced two hundred and ten thousands of CDs of 'San Patricio,' and sold them easily. The Chieftans are excessively popular in Mexico, as are the Celtic Women. I made forty thousands of DVDs of their American PBS special. And the Spanish musicians who are so diverse and unpredictable, I am trying to bring them a bigger audience in Mexico, much bigger. The Arabic musical influence is so distinctive and unusual in Spain. Absolutely! And the Scottish are among my favorites—from ancient highland bagpipes to the guitar of Mark Knopfler! And he mixes them together in 'Piper to the End!' And of course the English, too, they produce greatness. And you Americans. You have Bob Dylan and the Boss and Bonnie Raitt and Taylor Swift. You may wish to know that Erin and the Inmates are beginning to be very popular in this country, especially in the states along the Gulf of Mexico. I sell you very strongly there because many of these states are friends to me. And because Mexicans love women who can sing. So they love you. I sell CDs of American women singers by the many of thousands. Most in Mexico, but many to Central and South America. Not in the United States anymore because of iPods. All of those products you saw in the basement are ready to be shipped. Of course, the downloading of music will ruin my CD business when the iPods become more affordable here. Until then, I will sell to the people what they want."

"You shouldn't rip off the artists you love so much."

He eyed her. The lugubrious expression returned immediately. "Business always must be first."

"Make it second and you'll be happier."

"I will be happy?"

She shrugged and looked out at the gorgeous Yamaha shining in the studio lights. "It's possible that was a stupid thing to say."

"Do you know how many people are trying to kill me?"

"Not exactly."

"Thousands."

"Truly?"

"Very truly. There are soldiers and police and hired assassins and enemies and even mere boys who would kill me without one thought. There are people who would kill me just to have a *corrido* written about it. Yet this is all a part of business. So, as you see, it must come first or I will die. You must comprehend that your world is not my world."

"You're right, Señor Armenta, this is not my world. And you're also right about Flaco Jimenez. He's one robust accordion player."

"Yes. Music. I will tell you about my son someday."

"He frightens me."

"Not Saturnino. Gustavo. I will tell you about Gustavo. He was the beautiful one."

Up on the fourth floor she recognized her hallway and room door. This level spread out logically at right angles, all hallways and guest rooms, like a hotel. Some of the doors were open and Erin saw that the rooms were beautifully furnished and decorated, like hers. Some were closed. They came to seating alcoves with high windows and heavy rancho sofas in leather and cowhide and grand recliners arranged around rustic trunks piled with books and periodicals. Monkeys peered down on them from the curtain rods. Parrots and macaws lined the landing rail and the banister that zigzagged down four floors as Erin looked over. A black man wearing white pants and a white shirt used a step ladder to remove various excretions from the drapery. The bucket on the floor beside him gave up the smell of lavender and Erin saw that a portion of the tile pavers was clean and still wet from the mop.

"In the daylight there are excellent views from these windows. You can see the ruins and the laguna."

"I don't think I'll be free to enjoy views."

He regarded her with a mild shrug. "No. This would not be practical."

The top floor—Erin was fairly sure it was floor five—housed an observatory, a home theater the size of a multiplex, a recital hall, and a game room with billiards, table tennis, Foosball, scores of arcade games from "Cabela's Big Game Hunter" to "Daytona Challenge" to "Kandahar Killers." Father Edgar Ciel sat cramped but splendidly upright in the Daytona car, hands clutching the wheel, blazing his way through the competition while the novitiates watched on.

Back in the elevator Armenta pressed the second button from the top, which let them out on the second story, where they had seen the recording studio.

"The buttons and floors don't match," she said. "They are driving me crazy."

"Driving? As a car?"

"Making me crazy. I mean, how many floors does this place have, anyway?"

Armenta looked at her as if he didn't understand, then let Erin into a gallery. It was spacious and well lit by a network of halogen mini-bulbs. The floor was bird's-eye maple and the walls were white plaster. They were hung with paintings and there were dozens of marble floor pedestals for sculpture from the Americas, some of it pre-Columbian and some of it contemporary. A man with a large black weapon stood in one corner, feet apart, arms cradling the gun.

"These are only a small part."

"Of what?"

"My accomplishments."

Armenta once again turned his back on her to talk into his phone. This time he spoke longer. His voice rose in volume and he cursed happily. In the corner the *sicario* uncradled his gun, lay a finger against the trigger guard and pointed the muzzle to the floor.

Suddenly, Saturnino burst into the gallery. His white Guayabera was drenched in sweat and streaked with blood and his eyes were wild with what looked like glee. There was a gun jammed into the waist of his jeans. He marched right up to Erin but stopped short and orbited her one full rotation, as in a dance, facing her and smiling wild-eyed. "You will be enjoying this!" While looking at her lips he kissed the air and spun off and loped over to his father who stood waiting, the phone still in his hand.

"Felix, papa!"

"Felix, el reportero?" asked Armenta.

"Sí, Padre. Felix! El reportero! El traidor!"

Now the zoo was filled with people. Marimba music came from big speakers hung from the walls and sitting on the cobblestones. Erin was wedged in hard between Armenta on her left and Saturnino on her right. Heriberto stood in front of her. She saw the other gunmen who had kidnapped her and beaten Bradley, and the gentle boy who had served her dinner and poured her wine. There were soldiers and uniformed police and scores of what had to be cartel henchmen, a dozen of the elegant black domestic staff both men and women, and there were Mayans who must have come from the villages nearby. A group of four women and four men stood apart from the others. The women were dressed in white dresses and their heads were covered with the white rebozos, as the women Erin had seen coming from the third floor. The men were dressed in white also, long-sleeved shirts untucked and baggy pants, and their heads were covered not by rebozos but by loose white balaclavas that appeared to be made of a light material. Some of the men and women wore white cloth gloves.

In a row of seats up close to the cages sat the elders, some Indian and some Mexican and others indeterminate. To their left a man screwed a small video recorder to a tripod. Someone turned off the marimba and now a ranchero song blasted from the speakers. The music was festive and loose with up-tempo accordions and guitars strummed on the backbeat and powerful tenors in harmony. She looked through the bars of the cages but saw no cats. The grates were all down and she suspected that the animals were lost to their runs. All this commotion would certainly send them running. No monkeys or sloth or coatimundi. The compound yard was filled with vehicles. The pigeons in the aviary flapped and flitted and cocked their heads toward the ruckus.

Then she saw a beautiful woman making her way through the crowd toward them. She wore a peach-colored dress that was both modest and flattering. Her hair was dark and lustrous. It took Erin a moment to recognize her but when the woman was within ten feet she knew for certain it was Owens Finnegan. It was jarring to see Owens so far from her context of California, but somehow, Erin thought, in some inexplicable way, she fit right in here.

Owens smiled at Benjamin Armenta, then came to him, and when they embraced, Owens looked over his shoulder into Erin's eyes and raised a finger to her own red lips. Her wide sterling silver bracelets slid away and Erin saw the ropy scars that ringed her wrists. They unnerved her as they always had. Then Owens disengaged from Armenta, pecked him on the cheek, glanced at Erin, then settled on the other side of him. Erin watched him put a stout arm around her, lightly and with affection.

Mike Finnegan's "daughter," Erin thought. The Finnegans. Vague, pointless people, in her opinion. They had materialized at one of their Los Angeles gigs one winter, listened to a set, then occasionally shown up to see her perform, club to club, ever since. Friendly enough, maybe too friendly. They always bought the drinks. She could tell their true interest was in Bradley and she distrusted them. Charlie Hood was searching the world for Mike, Erin knew, although she didn't really know why. Or why Charlie was having such trouble finding him. Mike was always turning up, with his laughter-red face and lively blue eyes and his flagrant nosiness about all things.

Saturnino's face leaned near. "Strong men need beautiful women, like her," he said just loud enough that she could hear him over the music. "To keep us strong. And generous. And filled with love."

"You're quite a philosopher, Saturnino."

"You are this beautiful to me. I will be gentle with you." He smiled and raised his hand toward her but stopped short, brushing his fingers in the air as if along the contours of her face. She felt revulsion and she saw the enjoyment of it in his smile. *"Very gentle."*

"Don't try it until after you've shot me."

"I hear this many times. Maybe I will not be gentle."

"I'd still rather die."

"I admire your pride and your courage. I will take them from you."

Saturnino turned to face the cages and Erin saw the black iron grates rise from the cat runs. Like a prison, she thought, everything automatic. Cheers went up from the crowd. Seconds later the cats appeared behind the grates. Erin wondered if they were drawn by the sound of the grates clanging up, or by the crowd. More cheers. Why would wild animals come close to all this noise? But the twelve predators paced in the half-light beyond the grates. A tiger snarled at a lioness and the lioness snapped back, her teeth flashing like yellow knives and ringing off the steel bars of the run.

Two cartel gunmen led a man through the crowd. He wore dirty trousers and a torn shirt and a necktie. His face was swollen and bloody. The reporter, thought Erin: the traitor.

The prison-bar door of the leopard cage rolled open. Erin heard the squeal of it through the beats of the ranchero song. A wave of nausea broke over her and her knees froze as she watched them push the man inside and knock him to the ground. They hovered over him until the door had almost closed then they scrambled, laughing, and squeezed out of the cage. The man struggled upright and faced the leopards waiting on the other side of the grate. The ranchero music blared and the crowd jeered him and the videographer made an adjustment to his little camera.

Erin rammed an elbow into Armenta's arm. "You can't do this!"

He looked at her with a forlorn expression and she tried to ram him again but Armenta caught her elbow in a powerful hand that held her fast. "He is a reporter and a traitor. He writes about me in his newspaper. He tells lies because the Zetas threaten him. The newspaper reporter blames me for the heads in Monterrey but these are done by the Zetas. I forgive him. The reporter blames me for the dead police in Guadalajara but these man are hanged by Zetas. From the bridge. I forgive again. He blames me for Gustavo. My own Gustavo. He blames his death, not on the Americans but on me. Enough. This is the highest disrespect. The newspaper writer is very bad for my reputation and my business. He heats the plaza. I will pay for my own crimes, but not the crimes of others. This writer is now mine and he will write no more words against me or my family."

Armenta dropped her elbow and took a step forward, raising his hand into the air and snapping his fingers. Erin saw Owens looking at her, an unreadable expression on her face.

Then the grate began to retract into the concrete floor and when it was low enough the male leopard launched himself onto the reporter. He screamed and lashed out with his fists but the cat closed its mouth over his face and the scream echoed thickly. The man collapsed onto his back and the leopard raked open his stomach with its hind claws as the female crushed his groin in her jaws and together they carried him out of the cage and past the grate and into the jungle beyond. In their grasp the reporter appeared to weigh little more than the clothes he wore and yet he struggled as he vanished into the darkness.

Erin fainted and was caught by Owens.

9

HOOD SAT IN HIS EXPEDITION in the parking lot of the Jai Alai Palace in Tijuana. The air was hot and smoggy and smelled of exhaust and burning trash. In the asphalt divots stood rainwater from the summer storm.

He looked out at the stately old neoclassical building and remembered coming here with his family for the jai alai games, which his mother in particular had enjoyed. They had made modest bets and cheered loudly and Hood still remembered the resounding smack of the hard, heavy ball rocketing off the walls of the court.

Now the games were gone and the Palace was used for concerts and shows. A sign announced the upcoming events: Lila Downs, a farmer's market, the Exxxpo Erotica.

The prepaid phone rang at three o'clock. Hood flipped it open and said nothing.

"Drive toward Revolucion. Park far in the lot where there are no cars. Stay in your vehicle with your hands on the steering wheel. The hands must be on it."

Hood drove far into the mostly empty parking lot and took a parking place in the open. A moment later two Tijuana police cars swung in from opposite directions and stopped on either side of him. No sirens, no lights. Hood kept his hands on the wheel. Two more prowl cars came in and blocked him front and back. One uniformed officer got out of the passenger seat of each car but the drivers stayed.

Through his side window Hood watched a stocky man approach and wave him from the car. The officer's hand rested on the grip of his sidearm, a large revolver. He wore sunglasses and his forehead was beaded with sweat. His nameplate said "Sgt. I. Rescendez" and his badge and uniform looked authentic.

Hood nodded and opened the door and got out. Rescendez pointed him toward his own vehicle, then reached over and hit the unlock bar of Hood's Expedition. Hood heard the liftgate pop open, then the faint pneumatic hiss of the door risers and the sound of the suitcase bumping on the rear floor. The zipper whined three times. The back seats blocked most of his view but over the headrests Hood saw three men looking down into the rolling case. Two wore the peaked hats of municipal officers and Hood thought that if they were impersonating cops they'd done a good enough job of it. The alternative was even worse.

One of the men said something and the other two laughed. Hood could hear them rummaging through the bundles for dye packs and transmitters. A mumbled comment, and a moment later the zipper sounded three more times and the liftgate thumped down. The men returned to their cars.

"Give me the phone," said Rescendez.

Hood pulled the phone from his pocket and surrendered it. The cop handed him another one, a different make and model, a car charger wrapped tightly around it.

"You are loitering in a public place," Rescendez. "This is a fine of two hundred dollars. You can pay now or appear in court."

"At least I know you're real TJ cops," said Hood.

The man laughed quietly, then pulled a satellite phone off his duty belt. He powered it up and dialed and handed it to Hood. Hood stepped away from Rescendez, listening to the ring.

A man answered and Hood identified himself as Charlie Bravo.

Erin's voice was clear and fearful. "Bradley?"

"Erin, it's me."

"Oh, God, it's so good to hear your voice."

"Are you all right?"

"They haven't hurt me."

"You're going to be okay. I'm bringing the money."

"Please do it soon."

"I'll be there, Erin."

"Soon, please soon. I'm being strong but—"

The phone went silent. Hood tossed it back to Rescendez, who caught it in one hand like a first baseman.

"You are familiar to me, Mr. Bravo."

"I have a common face."

"But where have I seen you?"

"I've never seen you."

"Were you in Mulege?"

"Never."

Rescendez laughed heartily and slapped Hood on the shoulder with a heavy hand. "Maybe your face is very, very common. As you say. Now, please, the two hundred dollars fine is due to be paid."

Hood fixed him with a calm and durable look. "You've fucked with me enough, señor."

"*Sí. Es verdad.* Now you will take the money to Ciudad Juarez."

A city steeped in blood, thought Hood.

"It is thirteen hours with no flat tires," said Rescendez. "That is driving on the U.S. side, of course. You have two days to make the drive. You will stay at the Lucerna. And you will be guarding Benjamin's money very well."

"I understand," said Hood. "Now, you wait here, please." Hood climbed into his vehicle and fetched one of the small Mike Finnegan photo albums from the console. The empty booklet had been complimentary and the cover image was a festive holiday ribbon now out of season. But each page was made of slotted clear plastic and each photograph was well displayed and protected. He brought it to the cop and opened the cover and handed it to him. The plastic pages caught the sunlight and Hood watched I. Rescendez flip through the six photographs, then shrug and hand it back.

"No," he said. "I don't know this man. Who is he and what has he done?"

"He's a bad man."

"The world has many."

"Keep the book. Show the pictures to the men you work with. Your neighbors and friends. Call me if anyone knows of him or sees him. A thousand dollars for any good lead. My numbers are on the back."

"I still think I've seen you before, Mr. Bravo."

Rescendez lifted his cell phone and snapped a picture of Hood.

10

BRADLEY'S CAYENNE ROLLED THROUGH EL Dorado, one of several Baja and Sonora properties maintained by Carlos Herredia of the North Baja Cartel. Fellow LASD Sergeant Jack Cleary sat up front and Deputy Caroline Vega in back. On the freshly bladed dirt road ahead of them were two of Herredia's armored SUVs with ports cut in the roofs for gunmen to stand and fire. Behind them were two more. The gunmen swayed in the dusk. Rainwater stood thinly pooled by the roadside.

Bradley had been here many times and he had never arrived without an armed escort by land or air, and seemingly never taken quite the same dusty labyrinth of roads that led him here now. Herredia forbade GPSs so all that Bradley knew for sure was that he was in Baja California, south of Cataviña, north of Guerrero Negro and east of Mexican Highway 1. Bradley felt the same bristle of excitement he always felt in El Dorado, the same complicity in a world much more violent and profitable than his own and therefore more invigorating. He thought of Erin. And of his mother, and how she had enjoyed danger and would have loved this place. He missed her and knew he always would.

"Sweet airstrip," said Vega.

"And golf course," said Cleary.

"That's a CH-47 military transport helicopter under the camo net," said Vega. "Vietnam. Dad flew one over there. Wow, Herredia's got *two* of them. I wonder how many tons of dope they've moved."

"Nice little course," said Cleary. "Bet he cheats."

"Nobody calls him on it," said Bradley.

"Dad got flak in his ass and a purple heart."

"Better than flak in your heart and a purple ass," said Cleary.

"Captain Obvious strikes again," said Caroline Vega.

"You young people have no sense of humor," said Cleary.

"There has to be some humor in order to sense it."

"Caroline?" said Bradley. "Don't try to impress Herredia with your wit and strength. He's old school and he's got a terrible temper. They don't call him 'the Tiger' for nothing."

"Aye-aye, sir. Should I be strapped when we get out?"

"Leave the guns where they are. Get cool, people. And Caroline? Jack? I owe you for this."

"The fifty grand has me covered for the week," said Cleary.

"I hope we can earn that bonus," said Vega.

"We're going to find her and take her back," said Bradley. Or die trying, he thought, but he did not say this.

Soon they were stopped in the compound proper: the big ranch house, the outbuildings and guest casitas, the swimming pools and sweathouse, the gym and the outdoor pavilion. The parking circle was paved with river rock and a fountain gurgled forth in its center. The gun towers gave the place a prisonlike look. Bradley watched the Federal Judicial Police form a gauntlet around his Porsche and one of them raised a hand to stop him. They were large and humorless, much like the men who had come that night in the rain, but in uniform. Bradley understood that they could be genuine FJP or impersonators, or a combination. In this new Mexico, the old order had been made into no order at all.

That night they dined lavishly in Herredia's ranch house. There were platters of fresh seafood and *bistec* sliced in the thin Mexican style and a dozen salsas from hot to incendiary and guacamole with plenty of cilantro and garlic, fruits and vegetables and afterward, every good tequila Bradley knew and some he did not. All from Baja California, Herredia said, except of course the tequila, which could only come from Jalisco and certain regions of Guanajuato, Michoacan, Nayarit and Tamaulipas.

Herredia was tall and thick and tanned by his many sport fishing hours at sea, his eyes expressive and his hair thick and curly. He told stories of his heroism, spiced by a modesty that was comically false. *And I who cannot shoot well from two hundred meters shot the assassin through the heart with great luck!*

Bradley was glad to see El Tigre taken by Caroline Vega's severe beauty, so much so that he dismissed all four prostitutes in order to focus his attention on her. He moved her to sit on his left, opposite Bradley. Jack Cleary got drunk more quickly than Bradley had hoped but he was a fisherman too. So Cleary appreciated Herredia's tales and smartly made no attempt to match them.

Present were old Felipe and the shortened ten-gauge shotgun that he was never without, and Fidel Candelario, the North Baja cartel lieutenant that Herredia had pledged to Bradley the moment he'd heard of Erin's kidnapping and Armenta's challenge.

Candelario looked to be thirty years old to Bradley and in the prime of life. He was six feet tall, solid, clear-eyed and sharp-nosed, his black hair razor-cut stylishly short. From Bradley's angle he looked

Arabic. He explained in good English that he was from Baja Sur, growing up one generation behind the great El Tigre, whose footsteps he had followed from poverty to power.

He told Bradley that he was in command of a personal guard of twenty men, each one of whom he trusted with his life. They were seasoned men, many with advanced military training in counterterrorism, counternarcotrafficking and hostage liberation. They were professionals, not the beheaders or skinners or other *patologico* monsters who had overrun Mexico. They had of course whatever weapons and communications gear they might need. They had four heavily armored GMC Yukon XL 1500s customized by a Texas company in Laredo. Even the windows repelled small arms fire. If they had to travel long distances, they used one of Herredia's transport helos. My men are the *optimo*, he said, the best of the best.

Bradley looked from Candelario to Herredia, then back to the young lieutenant. "I'm lucky to have you."

"But I am the one who has you," said Fidel.

"Carlos, tell this guy right now who's going to be in charge of those men and this action," said Bradley. "If we're not clear on that, this whole thing is a waste of time and life."

Herredia leaned forward and pointed a thick forefinger at his associate, then at Bradley. "You are partners. You are equal. You are more similar than you know."

"That won't work," said Bradley.

"We will make it work," said Fidel. He said this with a wry smile that Bradley neither liked nor believed. "And when we find Armenta, he will be ours and your wife will again be yours."

"She's the only thing that matters."

"I know this type of emotion."

"You're lucky to know it, Fidel."

Candelario looked at him darkly and Bradley understood. "She and our two children were taken by Armenta's son, Saturnino. He left them hanging in a warehouse and he sent word where to find them. I found them. Just as I will find him."

Later Herredia showed off his newest passion—a horse breeding and training facility. It was tucked back behind the house against the sharp Baja hillsides. He had already built the stables and paddocks and there was an earthen track and an infield of very green grass. The sprinklers came on and Bradley watched their spray criss-crossing in the moonlight.

"I need the stud," Herredia said. "I have the mares but I need a magnificent horse to make my racers."

"I know a breeder in Temecula," said Caroline.

"I want the best!" said Herredia. He gave her his most engaging smile.

"Something tells me you'll find a way to get it," she said.

Bradley saw Fidel look at her with sharp eyes and no expression on his face. You're right, my man, he thought: she's a beauty and a match for you.

They all talked late into the hot Baja night. They sat in an outside pavilion around a rough-hewn table with bottles of tequila sparkling before them. The water of the swimming pool shifted with wedges of light and shadow and above them the stars were adamant at this un-certain latitude. Felipe sat away from the table where the light faded nearly to darkness, his shotgun across his lap, and whenever Bradley looked over at him his posture was unchanged and his withered old face like a gargoyle held half light and half shadow.

Bradley drank slightly and let the tequila-fueled energy rise around him. He had sat here with Herredia so many nights, earning large money, missing Erin, looking into the stars and sending thoughts to her, unable to use a satellite phone for reasons of security, his cell phone useless. Now when he remembered those nights a wave of nostalgia swept him up and he felt weightless and unable to determine his own direction, like a cork bobbing in a hostile sea. His throat tightened and his heart beat hard. He breathed deeply. Keep yourself together, he told himself, for her. He thought a brief prayer to God. And another to El Famoso. One to Malverde and another to anybody or anything that could hear him. *I don't care what you are or what you want from me. Save them. Save them. Just save them.*

He looked at Caroline sitting next to El Tigre and paying close attention to another of his stories. She was two years older than Bradley, dark-haired and brown-eyed, strong and forceful. Her cheekbones were high and scarred by old acne and her tightly gathered ponytail called attention to the scars. Her smile was rare. She was fearless in bad situations and apparently not satisfied with what other people might call normal life. Caroline reminded him greatly of his mother, which was one of the reasons he noticed and later sought her out and brought her close.

But I see that my beautiful dorado is now in the mouth of a great white shark that is the size of Isla Cerralvo and I must land it with my little Shimano reel that is only for the small fish!

Cleary smiled along blearily but when Bradley caught his eye he saw something acute and sober in it. Good, he thought, you'll need all the clarity you can muster, Jack.

Fidel said little at first and appeared to be glaring at the glass of tequila that he had not sipped. He wore a tan T-shirt and a gold cross on a chain, tan camo pants and suede combat boots. Bradley wondered why Mexican outlaws so loved the military. It had to be more than to fool the people they preyed on.

Bradley and Fidel spoke briefly of their families and where they grew up, then of cars, sports, guns, music, Obama and Calderón. Somehow Lorca and Neruda and Urrea came up and they spoke of them too. But all of this had the air of obligation to it and their words came out flat and lifeless because their hearts were in other places.

"Where do you think she is?" asked Bradley.

"Armenta is strong in the south. Veracruz, Oaxaca, Tabasco, Chiapas, Quintana Roo, Campeche."

"But he has safe houses all over Mexico."

"He will take her where he is strongest."

"It's a different world down there."

"Yes, jungle. Rain forest. Not desert. Jungle rots the body and the soul."

"Is Saturnino still his enforcer?"

"Yes. He is a murderer and a rapist."

Bradley felt his heartbeat accelerate. Now this would be added as fuel for his terrible dreams and images. "Maybe we'll both get what we want."

Fidel leaned toward him. His eyes were bright and dark and his nose was hooked. "We have one of Armenta's men. We took him by surprise in the night, much as your wife was taken. He will know where she is. The difficulty is making him want to tell us before he expires."

"Then lighten up on him, Fidel. If you kill him he won't say much."

"We should leave this to our capable men. We all have different natures."

"Let me have a try at him."

Fidel looked at Bradley. "No. You would not have self-control."

"True."

"Only self-control can get you out of Mexico alive."

"I'm getting her out of Mexico alive."

"I will do what can be done. And if it ends as it did for my *mujer* then I will have one more fellow prisoner in this hell that is life. You."

Later when everyone had gone to their rooms Bradley walked past the pool and through the gate and down to the pasture and stood for a while looking at the hillsides to the east, brushed with moonlight. Low in the distance a slick of rainwater caught the light more brightly. Bradley had never seen standing water in this part of Baja. Horses stirred in the paddock.

Again he opened his mind to the raids of memory. What memories were here. For nearly three years, from the time he was just seventeen years old, he had driven to El Dorado once a week and returned home with an average of twelve thousand dollars in cash. The North Baja Cartel took in roughly four hundred thousand dollars a week off the L.A. streets and Bradley drove the collected money south to make his percentage. He had earned nearly a million-six in those first two and a half years, almost pure profit, little overhead and no taxes.

In those early days he had posed as a fisherman, a surfer, a social worker, a church charities representative. He had lugged fishing gear, camping equipment, surfboards, piles of new and used clothing, Bibles and religious literature, cases of canned food and water and sports drinks. He had used several vehicles, some with doctored plates, and several different sets of false documents. Later, his LASD shield became useful at times. Still later, when Herredia brought several U.S. Customs agents under his influence, complementing the Mexican inspectors he already owned, Bradley's job had gotten much easier. The good old days, he thought. Money and more money. He had enjoyed it immensely.

But now as he stood in this desert and looked at the far hills he felt betrayed by what he had once thought of as bravery and confidence. And betrayed by the burden of Murrieta. Wasn't it all just stupidity and foolishness? What had he gotten for it? A small fortune, yes. And for a while, on the legitimate side of his life, good LASD performance reviews and a minor hero's status.

But he had also been shot and stabbed and involved in a shootout that had claimed six lives. This earned him an ongoing LASD Internal Affairs investigation that stopped his Mexico deliveries a year ago and dried up his largest stream of revenue.

One year ago, he thought. One cursed year ago everything changed. IA had begun tailing him at work, then had him reassigned from Narcotics to a desk job in Fraud; they had spied on him during his free time and even tried to spy on him at home; they had interviewed his fellow deputies; and they had no doubt gained access to his phone records and bank transactions. They were a thousand terriers yapping and biting at his ankles. The terriers had only begrudgingly given him these ten days off even though his vacation time would cover it.

A year of bitter suspicion and a drastic pay cut and now, worst of all, Erin kidnapped. And their unborn child. Unimaginable. Fire of my life, Bradley thought, I have delivered you to my enemies.

He closed his eyes and heard her voice: *Come to me by moonlight, sugar/Let the moon be your guide.*

Bradley opened his eyes on the moon and to him it looked not like a guide but an unmoved witness to his own vanity and failure.

11

WHEN HE GOT BACK TO the pavilion Mike Finnegan occupied the chair where Fidel had been. The little man sat up straight, twiddling his thumbs on the table before him, his ankles crossed and the toes of his black dress shoes just touching the ground. He looked up at Bradley. He wore a wheat-colored linen suit with a blue pocket square that matched his eyes and a blue, open-collared shirt.

"I'm deeply sorry for what has happened," Finnegan said. "But I believe we can get her back."

Bradley walked around the table studying Mike. A long moment passed before he spoke. "What the fuck are you doing here?"

"And a good evening to you, Bradley."

"You have no *idea* what happened, you sonofabitch."

"Don't overestimate me, Brad. People know what happened. Many people. It's a statement. Armenta did this exactly so people would know."

"What are you doing here?"

"Offering to help you."

Bradley felt flummoxed and fooled. "You don't know Herredia."

Finnegan's expression was impatient but somehow soulful. "You're so certain of all the things I cannot know! It really is flattering. But Bradley, let's elevate this discourse. Let's get right to the point. What do you see in all that has happened? *Why* has it happened? What are you doing to get her back? It's far too late not to be honest with me, and you know it."

Bradley reached down and took Mike's chin in his hand and lifted up his face so he could more fully view it. He felt the stubble of the red whiskers, the heat of the flesh, the strong bone beneath. In the clear blue eyes he saw concern and intelligence and bottomless optimism.

"What I see is one crazy little shit."

"But I hear the tick of a clock."

Bradley pushed away Mike's face and sat. He pressed his hands to his eyes and ran them through his wavy black hair, then folded them on the table and looked at Finnegan. "I'm down to eight days. I don't know where she is. I don't even know if she's alive."

"But do you have the money?"

"Hood has the money."

"He's your mule? So that you and Fidel can find her first?"

Bradley nodded but said nothing. He had never felt helpless and so furious at the same time. Felt so outsmarted and outgunned. But he felt them all now. He felt that, even with Fidel's band of blue-ribbon bad guys, Armenta had already beaten him.

"Erin is very much alive and well," Mike said. "I have word from someone I can trust."

Bradley sprang from his chair and put both hands on the table and leaned his face into Finnegan's. He watched the hopeful blue eyes and he searched them for the smallest hint of what truly lay behind them. "Tell me what you know. *Tell it!*"

"She has been seen in Quintana Roo."

"Don't toy with me, Mike."

"She has been seen in Quintana Roo."

"How do you know?"

"I have eyes on Armenta, Bradley. But it doesn't matter how I know. It only matters *what* I know."

Bradley shoved off and paced around the big table, his heart beating urgently and his brain firing thoughts he couldn't control. "And she's okay?"

"Perfect."

"Then they haven't . . ."

"No. She's being treated well."

"Did Saturnino ra—"

"*No!*"

"Where is she, Mike! *Where?*"

"She's being held on one of Armenta's properties on the Yucatán Peninsula. Somewhere between Polyuc and the Kohunlich ruins, near the Belize and Guatemala borders. On a map it looks small but in reality it's a lot of jungle. Very dense jungle. We should have a good GPS fix within twenty-four hours."

Bradley stopped opposite Finnegan and again leaned forward into the man's face. *"Should or will?"*

"I do what I can do, Bradley. Every vessel has its shape and capacity." Finnegan took Bradley's right hand in both of his small, strong own. "Let me be your ally and friend."

"What do you want?"

"For you to have everything on this Earth that you deserve."

"She's all I want. I'll do anything to get her back."

"I understand that." Finnegan studied him for a long moment and in his eyes Bradley saw both judgment and sympathy. "Then ask me to be your friend. Phrase it any way you like. Make a joke of it if you have to. The words are what matter to me, not your opinion of them. I need to hear them before I can help you."

Bradley pulled his hand but Mike held it fast and Bradley felt the surprising strength of him.

"Speak to me, son of El Famoso."

"Don't start that shit."

"That's a start."

Bradley pulled hard again, but Finnegan's two fierce little hands were stronger than his one, so he twisted it free with a Hapkido move that left him able to break Mike's elbow. "Okay. Be my friend, Mike. Help me get her back. Or I'll snap your neck, roast you on a spit, and feed you to my dogs. I have twelve of them."

Mike smiled. "What an exceptional proposal of friendship. I accept."

Bradley released his arm and sat back down across from him.

"I'll also need just a few drops of your blood."

"Fuck off."

"I'm serious."

"Blood for what?"

"For everything words can't cover. It's a ritual. I'm not sure why, but it works. It really does. You'll see."

"You're out of your mind."

"Just old-fashioned." From somewhere inside his coat Mike produced a dagger and rested it on his palm for Bradley to see. It was short, mostly handle, and Bradley could tell that the metal was black and old. Before stainless steel alloys, he thought. Before carbon and graphite and tungsten. The flatish handle was wrapped in tooled leather held by rounded silver rivets for weight and grip. "Hand out now and palm up. Just a little prick."

Bradley looked long at the man, remembering that Mike once told him that he had introduced Bradley's parents in order to give him a chance at "magnificence." Mike claimed to be their close friend. And he had told Bradley things about his parents and his ancestors, things that only a very close friend would know. When Bradley had first met Mike three years ago he had sensed a connection but it was a vague sense, and unsteady, a trickle of memory that would flow and evaporate and flow again.

"How long have you known me, Mike?"

"Since your first breath. I've told you this and more."

"And you told me that when I was ready to see I would see."

"First you must look."

"How long have you known Carlos?"

"He was eleven. A critical age. Old Felipe brought him to me. I've always surrounded myself with people of will and talent. Now, hand out and palm up?"

"How long did you know my mother?"

"She was eleven also. It's *the* pivotal age in my view."

"When I was eleven I had a dream that I was on the Oceanside pier one night, and someone dared me to close my eyes and jump off and I was afraid so I didn't. The next day I was ashamed because a friend of mine had done it a bunch of times. I hated being a coward. It ate at me. I badgered Mom to take me to the pier that night but I didn't tell her why. She did. No moon. It was summer but it was cool and every step farther out on that pier I was more and more afraid. Mom carried a big beach towel and my good jacket because I told her I might need them. She wore a red satin blouse and jeans and her hair was full and shiny. I'll never forget how beautiful she was. I just wore my trunks. I looked down at the faraway water. It was heaving and the yellow pier lights gave it a strange glow. I told her about the dream and the friend. And she said, I'll meet you on the beach—and don't be ashamed to take just a tiny peek on the way down, because so long as you know what's in front of you, you'll be fine. I said, 'I love you, Mom.' And she said she loved me and I closed my eyes and jumped."

Finnegan said nothing for a long moment. Then: "Bradley? Knowing Suzanne as I did, and you as I do, that is a truly moving story.

Thank you for it. I wish that she had been better at taking her own advice."

Bradley offered Finnegan his free hand, palm up. "This is for Erin."

Mike gently took Bradley's hand and brought it nearer to him. "You are made by history and history is made by you."

Bradley felt the quick stab of pain. Mike let go and guided the point into his own free palm and he cupped that hand over Bradley's so the two bloods met.

"There," said Finnegan. "I've always wished it would smoke or something. But it does kind of sizzle down deep in the soul, doesn't it?"

"I don't feel anything but rage. Do you know rage, Mike? Or are you just a happy simpleton?"

"Anger. Frustration. Not rage."

"Fury."

"These are destructive. These are indulgences."

"These are what I have now."

Bradley watched the blood from Finnegan's small palm run into his own. He thought of the way his mother had wrapped him in the beach towel and later helped him into his jacket after he'd emerged from the great Pacific, shivering, bone-cold but proud. He thought of Erin on stage the very first time he had laid eyes on her and understood that his life had just changed forever. He tried to picture her exactly right now, held captive by murderers somewhere between Polyuc and the Kohunlich ruins, but this was impossible.

"It's not the blood," said Mike. "It's the giving of the blood."

"Whatever you say." Bradley snatched the blue handkerchief from the little man's coat pocket and stood and clenched it in his bleeding hand. He looked down at Mike's jolly round face, saw the sparkle of mischief in his eyes. "How are we going to find her?"

"The first part is up to you and it is very important: Charlie Hood can't know that we've talked, or that you've seen me, or anything about me. He cannot know about us. Everything that happens from here on will depend on that."

"Done. That's easy. But the Yucatán is still two thousand miles away."

"No. It's just shy of seventeen hundred. So, in anticipation of our new relationship, I took the liberty of consulting with El Tigre. You and your merry outlaws will leave tomorrow in the morning in one of the transport helicopters. Carlos can arrange safe airspace to Veracruz but not farther south."

"What about you?"

"I'll find you there."

Bradley sat again and poured a shot of smoky brown tequila for Mike and one for himself. He glanced up at the moon and thought a message to Erin and when he was finished he felt exhaustion slam down on him. He drank half of his tequila, then dropped the wadded hankie to the table and looked down at his palm. The slice was short and not deep and it had already stopped bleeding. "You cut my lifeline, Mike."

"I love palmistry. It's as entertaining as major league baseball."

"What's between you and Hood?"

"That's even more entertaining."

"Do you know his parents?"

"No. He just came up in the net. But I couldn't throw him back. He's so good. So wholesome. So tempting."

"You just accidentally found him?"

"Through your mother, Suzanne, of course. She was the magnet and Charlie Hood was a small iron shaving."

"He's been looking everywhere for you."

"I know. I receive his requests for information about me every week. Sometimes two or three times."

"What does he want with you?"

"I'm not sure. But I'm concerned for him. He seems to have me confused with an Irish priest who helped build a school in Costa Rica. Imagine."

"You're a meddler, Mike."

"I'm a lot more than just that!"

Later Bradley called Hood on the satellite phone. Hood was on his way to Ciudad Juarez, the murder capital of the New World. The ransom money was safe. Bradley said nothing of Mike Finnegan, the object of Hood's growing obsession. First things first, thought Bradley. Erin first. Nothing else matters.

12

Hood crossed the border into Ciudad Juarez just after dawn Tuesday. He looked up at the mountains above the city and saw the huge sign declaring in Spanish, "The Bible Is the Truth. Read It." The morning was cool and the light was soft. The city looked peaceful enough at this hour but Hood knew its tremendous violence.

He checked into the Lucerna and was told his room was ready. The lobby stood empty except for two men in short-sleeved white shirts and sunglasses who watched him from the far side and were gone by the time Hood was given his room key.

Dazed by the long drive he wheeled his luggage and the small duffel to the elevator bank where the two men intercepted him. One of them reached inside Hood's sport coat and confiscated the Springfield .45 from his hip rig, then started back toward the lobby. The other nodded to Hood to follow.

At their direction Hood loaded his luggage and Bradley's money into the back of a battered black Escalade with smoked windows parked curbside. He sat in the second row of leather seats. The passenger was in his late thirties, he guessed, short in the legs, thick in the neck like a bull, with the diffident air of a gunman. The driver was very big and young and looked intently through the windshield.

They drove the Juarez streets in silence for a few minutes. Hood had never been in the city before. It was said to have the highest murder rate of any city on Earth, including second-place Caracas and third-place New Orleans. The Zetas and the Gulf Cartel had littered the streets with two thousand bodies in the past year alone.

Hood also knew that four hundred others, young women, maquiladora workers mostly, had been raped, mutilated, and murdered in a decade, virtually none of the crimes solved, their bones salting the surrounding desert in shallow graves. Hundreds more of the young women were missing. The murders were the work of at least several men, it was agreed, perhaps working in concert but perhaps not. Violent monsters, certainly. Gangsters and maybe police too. Hundreds of killings and no arrests had been made. And of course the city was dying along with its people. Hood had read Mexican media reports estimating that five hundred thousand citizens—roughly one-third of the population—had left Juarez because of the violence. One hundred sixteen thousand homes had been abandoned. Ten thousand businesses had folded. All blown away by a wind that smelled of human bodies baking in the sun. The living couldn't take it anymore.

Hood looked out the smoked windows at the neighborhood around them—small concrete houses, recently built but now abandoned, covered with graffiti, their windows broken and boarded, no cars on the street, no signs of life, just trash and brown dirt yards.

"Do you know our city?" asked the driver. "This is the Rivera Bravo zone. Once the government said it was a model for the future. Now see it. It is new and almost dead. Anyone who can afford to leave Juarez is doing so. It is having less and less people."

The passenger gave the driver a long look.

"Where are we going?" asked Hood.

"You have nothing to fear," said the driver. He raised his big face to the rearview.

"I have the money. I can show it to you and you can save the cost of gasoline."

"Mr. Bravo, we wanted to talk to you," said the driver. "We wanted you to see our city. There is much history here, much of it bad. But it is not as terrible as everyone in the United States believes. If Calderón can weaken the cartels before he runs out of political support, Juarez will return to normal."

The bull-like man in the passenger seat turned and looked at Hood through his sunglasses. He looked familiar. "Sgt. Rescendez of the Tijuana city police is a man I know," he said. "He told me he recognized you from Mulege."

"I was not in Mulege," said Hood.

"He said you were one of the Americans who rescued the ATF agent, Holdstock."

"No. He is mistaken."

"He has always been an observant man. Let's say he is correct. Then you know that Benjamin Armenta still wants to punish Holdstock and ATF for killing his son."

"I only know of that story from the media," Hood lied again. "Armenta has punished the man enough. Did you see his family on TV? The newspapers said the shooting was accidental. That Holdstock wasn't even aiming at Armenta's son."

The bull nodded. "That may be true. But if Benjamin Armenta believes that you are an ATF agent in Mexico, he will take the money and kill you."

"I'm not an ATF agent. But I think he might kill me anyway. And I don't know where your friend gets his alleged information about me."

"He was one of Luna's men. He helped to rescue the agent Holdstock."

They made two left turns, reversing direction.

"Well, he's working for Armenta now," said Hood.

"There have been thousands of police officers fired across Mexico," said the driver. "Thousands more have quit under suspicion and even more because of fear. There are few livings to be made here by police. So they go where the jobs are. North, or to the *narcotraffican-tes*. Rescendez was once a good man. See? He still offers us informa-tion we can use. For money, however."

Hood considered this. What could be a more dire ailment for a nation than an inability to retain decent law enforcement?

"You are a friend of Bradley Jones?"

"Yes."

"What did he do to Benjamin Armenta to deserve this?"

"I don't know," said Hood. "He's an American cop. He makes a fair salary."

"Yet Armenta sends men to the *Estados Unidos* in order to kidnap his wife? And he wants one million dollars to free her? This makes not enough sense."

"Who are you? How do you know this?"

"This area is called the Campestre," said the driver. "You see the mansions? This was our most expensive district. There were country clubs. Now you see these houses are for sale and for lease. They are falling apart. Nobody wants to live here. Too many murders. Too many beheadings. See the boulders in the driveways? The owners placed them there to slow the vehicles, to make kidnappings and car-jacking and assassinations more difficult. It did not work. So, the prosperous people, they sell. They're in El Paso now, and Dallas and even in California."

A truth began to dawn on Hood, or at least he thought it did. He looked out at the derelict mansions of Campestre. Most of the wrought-iron security gates had been carried off by thieves and the streetlights had been yanked for their copper. The long driveways they once protected were choked with leaves and fallen branches and trash. A pack of dogs rooted through the garbage.

Soon they were outside of the city, traveling into the steep desert mountains to the south, the big "The Bible Is the Truth" sign towering above them. The road turned to dirt, then it cut along flush against the mountain. Soon Hood was looking down on Juarez from hundreds of feet above and he could see the slow brown Rio Grande and El Paso beyond it and he thought: If I'm wrong about this I'm a dead man.

They stopped and the driver shut off the engine. Then he partially turned his bulk to face Hood and show his badge holder. "We are Special Investigations, Juarez Police Department," he said. "We are the most assaulted police force in the world. There is almost nowhere in the city where it is safe to work or even be seen."

The passenger took off his sunglasses and turned to face Hood.

"You are a Luna," said Hood.

"Yes. I am Valente Luna and he is Julio Santo. You are Charlie Hood. Raydel was my brother and he spoke respectfully of you. Like him I have sworn to remove the plague from my country. Raydel died for your friend Holdstock. Now you will take us to Benjamin Armenta, Mr. Hood, and Raydel's death will have meaning."

Hood looked from Luna's badge into his fierce black eyes. He remembered Raydel's similar eyes, the goodness and will and bravery in them. Hood had heard Raydel Luna say one of the most beautiful things he had ever heard said, then he had helplessly watched the man die. Since that moment Luna had earned full citizenship in Hood's dreams and seeing now that some of Raydel was still alive in his brother made Hood's heart glad.

"Right on," he said. "Now maybe you should get me back to the Lucerna before the Gulf people see me talking to you."

The driver started up the SUV.

"Our informants told us where you would be and what you were carrying in the luggage," said Luna. "We assume that they have sold this information to others as well. Information is cheap of course, and can be sold many times. So in Mexico everyone soon knows everything. Armenta has thousands of enemies who would love to find you. We expect the next part of your journey to be fraught with possible danger."

He offered Hood his pistol, handle first.

An hour later Hood answered the knock on his hotel room door. Two men in dark suits and open-collared dress shirts walked past him into the room without invitation or greeting. Hood saw the Mayan blood in them, in the broad cheeks and slightly almond-shaped eyes, the ample ears and compact bodies. Their eyes were quick and hostile. When the hotel door swung shut the heavier man went straight to the suitcase standing upright against the wall. He swung it up and onto the bed and held out a hand to Hood.

Hood tossed him the key and the man caught it and opened the lock, unzipped the main compartment and flipped over the top.

The other man stood in front of the door with his hands crossed contritely in front of him.

Hood watched the first man rummage through the bundles of cash. He pulled some out, then picked up the whole suitcase and dumped the rest of the money onto the bed. He took a packet of fifties, cut through the plastic with a switchblade and extracted a thin stack of bills. These he fanned with a thumb, closely watching the play of the paper in his hands. When he was done he dropped the fifties into the pile and looked at Hood. "Your phone."

Hood popped it from his hip and tossed it. The man dialed and waited a moment, then motioned Hood over to take it.

Hood held it up to his ear and waited. Erin's voice was thin and trembling.

"Charlie?"

"Yes, it's me. Are you okay?"

"I've seen the most terrible things."

"Have they hurt you?"

"They fed a man to leopards and I fainted. I can't lock the door to my room and I can't get out and this man says he'll rape me when he wants to. There's a priest who wears a gun and young acolytes following him around and I don't know where I am or what these people are going to do to me. I'm afraid, Charlie. I'm trying to be strong but I'm just damned afraid I'm going to lose everything, even what's inside me."

"Have they hurt you, Erin?"

"I'm okay, Charlie. Where is Bradley? We only have a few more days. Have you heard from him? Why isn't he here? No! Wait—"

As in Tijuana one of the men claimed Hood's old phone and gave him a new one, another prepaid model, another car charger wrapped around it. The other man handed him a plastic shopping bag containing two Mexico license plates issued apparently by the state of Yucatán. On Armenta's gulf, thought Hood.

"Reynosa in one day. You will be called there. Drive through Texas. It is faster than Mexico and more safe. As soon as you cross into Mexico, change the license plates."

"I have something for you," said Hood. He reached for his duffel and both men drew down on him. Hood raised his hands and they nodded and he moved very slowly, working two of the small photo albums from his duffel. He slipped a one-hundred-dollar bill into each before handing one to each of the *narcos*.

They looked at Hood blankly, then opened the booklets.

"Do you know him? Have you seen him?"

The men flipped patiently through the pictures. One looked up at Hood with an amused smile. The other went through the photos twice.

"No."

"No."

"Keep them. Show them to the men you work with. Show them to whoever you want. I've got a thousand dollars for anyone who can tell me where he is. My numbers are on the last page. Call collect if you want."

"Reynosa in one day."

When the men were gone Hood called Bradley on the satellite phone. "She's okay. I just talked to her. She's scared but she's okay."

"Tell me everything she said."

Hood did. When he was finished he listened to the silence at the other end. "Where are you, my friend?" asked Hood.

"On my way to Veracruz."

"Who aimed you there?"

"Carlos's people. The bad guys always know where the other bad guys are."

"Do you know where they're keeping her?"

"Somewhere on the Yucatán peninsula. Trust me, Hood—when I know where she is, you will too. But I suspect you'll find out long before I do. *If* I do."

"Do you trust Herredia?"

"I have to. I'm lost down here without him."

"I'm guarding this money with my life. I'm doing my job, Bradley."

"Tell me everything she said. Please. One more time."

Dear Beth

*I hope you are okay and that Daisy has been good
company. I'm in Mexico helping some associates who are
in a tight spot. It's a long story and I won't burden you*

with it, although I remember you asking me to share my
burdens. I'm still learning how to do that. I wish I could
blather, warble and yap, as you describe your own talents.
I don't know why I seem to think my burdens are too
special, or maybe not special enough, to share. I miss you
very much, the hope in your eyes and the sweetness of
your breath and the way your hair falls over your
forehead and when I lift it back into place it falls again.
Lots more than that too.

Down here it's another world, Beth. Juarez is
devastated by the murders of the women, and the cartels
have added another two thousand or so bodies of their
own in the last two years. Whole neighborhoods are
deserted now, mostly the more prosperous ones because
the better-off people have left. Anyone who can afford to
leave has gone. The mayor lives in the United States
because he fears for his life. I recount these horrors not to
impress you with my bravery (or foolishness) but as a way
to measure my own puzzlement over why I choose to
work along this border of sorrows. I remember you told
me how you enjoyed the challenge of treating cancer
patients. How you loved the idea that you could win. So I
think you must understand what draws me here. I could
go back to L.A. anytime. I could get back my patrol in
Antelope Valley—you know how I like the desert. But I
stay close to Mexico. Why? I believe that I'm needed here
though I can't prove that my actions and sacrifices, or
those of the brave men and women I work with, some of
which have been far deeper than my own, have
accomplished even one tiny bit of good in this lawless
place so immune to good fortune. I wonder if a man's

soul can grow used to defeat, and if so, can the soul of a place?

There are many beauties in this world but none of them touch the beauty that I see in you.

Your Missing Man,
Charlie

13

"THAT IS NOT VERACRUZ," SAID Bradley, poking his finger against the window glass of the Chinook. The air was spotted with turbulence and the ride was rough. "It's Guadalajara."

"There has been a change," said Fidel. He had piloted the craft for nearly seven hours. They had gotten a late start from El Dorado, which had greatly angered Bradley. "We will stop near Guadalajara."

"But Carlos has a safe strip for us in Veracruz."

"We need to see some people."

"We need to get Erin off the Yucatán. We're eleven hundred miles from the Yucatán, Fidel. You start late. You make changes. You're making me angrier."

"I am so sorry for that. But we have new information. The man I told you about. The one we were questioning."

"We've been in the air all day."

"It came yesterday."

"This is bullshit and I don't like it. Carlos won't, either. He recruited you to help me, not to risk Erin's life."

Fidel gave him a dark look that encompassed Erin within his own history. Bradley saw that his quest to save Erin was only a part of Fidel's quest, a subordinate fragment of the dream that was to avenge his wife and family, and he felt the nearly blind fury stirring inside again. It was always right there, up near the surface, invisible and powerful.

"Would you like to fly us to Veracruz, Bradley?"

"I can't fly this thing."

"No, of course not. Then you be a good soldier and do what I tell you to do."

Someone pushed into the flight deck. Bradley heard the roar of the motor and rotors when the bulkhead door opened and he turned to see Caroline Vega glaring down at him.

"You only missed Veracruz by six hundred miles."

"I was just explaining that to Fidel," said Bradley.

"And I was just explaining to Jones that we have a change of plans," said Fidel.

"Like what kind of change?" asked Vega.

"We need fuel."

"What are all those drums of fuel in the back for? I kicked one of them. It wasn't empty."

"You can never have too much fuel," said Fidel. He turned and smiled up at her. "So now we stop for fuel."

"Who's in charge here, Bradley? Is it you or him?"

"I will let you two decide who is in charge," said Fidel.

With this he clicked off his shoulder restraint, stood and left the cockpit.

"Can you fly this, Brad?"

"No. You?"

"I don't believe so."

Vega worked her way into the pilot seat and surveyed the instruments before her and reached out her hands but wasn't sure where to put them. She looked helplessly at Bradley.

He felt the big machine groaning along but it felt different to him, as if a great weight was climbing onto its back. There was a hesitation and a dreamy yaw that brought his stomach up into his throat.

"Do something, Brad."

He climbed from the copilot seat and clambered out of the flight deck with his hands on the bulkhead for balance and support. He looked back into the huge cargo and passenger bay, where the four black Yukons waited and most of the twenty men napped on litters. Most of the men wore the tan camo fatigues and shirts and desert boots of their leader, but two had changed into navy pants and light blue shirts with white oval patches over the left breast. Fidel was about to open a bottle of Bohemia and sit down with them.

Bradley approached. "You made your point."

The men looked at him with boredom or contempt.

"Good," said Fidel. "In another twenty seconds you would have been too late and we would all soon die."

"And I have a point to make also, Fidel." He swung the barrel of his AirLite flush up against Fidel's forehead, cocking back the hammer midswing. "If you're not on your way to the cockpit in five seconds I'll pull. I'm sure one of these guys can fly this thing. I will not wait six seconds, Fidel. I simply will not wait. And we are not stopping until we get to Veracruz. So now, five, four, three . . ."

Bradley counted fast and on "one," Fidel shrugged away from the pistol and started for the cockpit. Bradley fell in behind him, gun still up and ready, scanning the hostile eyes of the men as he walked. "Remain clear on who's running this show, shitbird. And everything will be cool."

14

SHE AWOKE TO SUNLIGHT DASHING through the open window shutters and a symphony of birdsong in the trees outside. A tangle of melodies, she thought. The sun looked in from the eastern sky like a big red face. The palm fronds lifted and dropped and lifted again.

She lay on her back in the bed with both hands spread over her belly and she silently told her son that everything was good now, everything was good. She thought of Bradley and wondered where he was and what he was doing. She thought of Felix the reporter and banished the memory, and she thought of Saturnino and banished that memory too, and she remembered waking up in this bed, with Armenta and Owens looking down at her as if she were a curiosity or something newly hatched.

The boy with the golden pompadour brought her coffee and breakfast. He said his name was Atlas. As he arranged her meal he asked her in good English if she had played the Gibson Hummingbird yet.

"I haven't touched it," she lied. It seemed mandatory.

"Mr. Armenta would be pleased if you did."

"Well, isn't that just dandy."

He looked at her and smiled shyly. "Dandy?"

"What I meant was, I don't care if I please that monster or not."

With a furrowed look he rearranged the cream and the coffeepot. He snapped the napkin in the air and folded it into a fan and set it to the left of the plate. "He is not a monster. The natives call him *yaguareté*, with respect. It is good to please him. This is his world and he rules over it."

"Will he feed me to the leopards if I don't play his guitar?"

"It is your guitar. When something appears in your room it means that Mr. Armenta has given it to you. My casita is filled with treasures. I have beautiful clothes. I have Rosetta Stone for English. I have a smart phone. But I cannot use it here for reasons of security."

"I don't want the guitar. I have plenty of them at home."

He looked at her and seemed about to speak but did not. He collected his tray and stand and carried them to the door and got his key from his pocket. "Mr. Armenta will be here at twelve o'clock noon, and he will wish you to perform."

"*Perform?*"

"On the Hummingbird."

"Piss on him. Piss on his Hummingbird too."

Atlas's smooth fair face flushed pink and his breath caught. He smiled very slightly and his eyes held both mirth and shame at the mirth, and he backed through the door with tray and stand and was gone.

Armenta stood formally beside the handsome leather armchair. His back was to the window and the shaded sunlight. His hair was a neglected heap and the lines of his face looked like they had been powdered with ashes. He wore a white Guayabera that called attention to the grayness. He was barefoot. He stood a long while in silence and no birds sang.

Erin sat at the head of the table watching him. She felt some fear but mostly anger and helplessness. She wondered what would happen to her and her unborn son if she killed Armenta right now. A quick trip to the bathroom would give her the means. She wasn't sure she could do it but she thought she might. But then what, kill Saturnino too? Then all the Gulf Cartel?

"What is just is not always popular," he finally said. "And what is popular is not always just."

"What does that mean?"

"I'm sorry for what you saw."

"But not for what you did?"

"No. What I did was just."

"I'll never agree with you."

"Justice is nature and I have been just."

"You don't believe that. Your face betrays you."

"Oh?"

"Yes."

"Explain my face to me."

"It looks like something death brought with him in his suitcase."

He studied her. "I loved Warren Zevon. I miss his music. Please. Play one of his songs for me on the Hummingbird. Do you know 'Keep Me in Your Heart'?"

"I know that song."

"When he writes that he is tied to her like the buttons on her blouse. Oh. Perhaps the last song he wrote and he knew this was to be the last. *Valentia*. To create while he is dying."

"Don't we all."

A small twinkle came to Armenta's depleted eyes. "Yes. And what bravery it is."

"The reporter was struggling bravely when the leopards dragged him off."

She looked away from him and out a window to where the palm fronds lifted and rode the steady breeze. A cursed beauty, she thought.

Two pigeons sat upon the railings of her balcony outside looking down on the coop as if awaiting an invitation. She saw two men dressed in white with white balaclavas covering their heads and faces walking slowly up a path toward the castle. The breeze rippled their garments and they looked insubstantial, she thought, like ghosts.

"Who are the people in white?" she asked.

"The lepers."

"Why are they the only ones who go to the third floor?"

"It is theirs."

"Why are they here?"

"Their *colonia* was destroyed by a hurricane so I brought them here. Once, many years ago, I was pursued by killers. I ran until I was exhausted. My friends were all dead. I had a gun but no bullets. I ran to a leper camp. I did not think my enemies would pursue me but they did. The lepers hid me. I buried myself in a leper's bed that stunk with the smells of his disease. Men with guns poked the blankets but not me. I told you I am loyal and do not lack compassion."

She was aware Armenta had not taken his eyes off her. "So you murder reporters but comfort the sick?"

"The lepers are loyal and grateful. The reporter was not."

"You aren't God."

"I do not want to be."

She stood and walked into the bathroom and locked the door. She ran the faucet and found the derringer at the bottom of the flush box and pulled it out and let it drain over the bowl. It was a heavy little thing with a curved rosewood grip and a stainless-steel body and a funny name—the Cowboy Defender or the Texas Slayer or something like that. It fit easily within the span of her hand. The barrels were "over and under," as Bradley had said, and it fired two different and powerful charges but she couldn't remember what they were. He said if she shot at somebody from less than ten feet she'd probably hit her target. More than fifteen feet away just forget it. Head if you can, heart if you can't. Squeeze the trigger, never yank it.

Shoot him, then what? she thought. Easy: dress in new designer fashions. Use his key to leave the room. Outrun Saturnino and all of the Gulf Cartel gunmen, dodge the loyal servants and the gun-toting padre and the lepers and vanish into the jungle. Live on roots and bugs and dew collected in palm fronds. Move by night. Find a village. Use the cash to get a car or boat to the nearest airport. Done. One blast of the Cowboy Exploder and I'm home free with my son safe and sound inside.

She looked down at the thing, its barrels gaping like the nostrils of a pig; then she ran faucet water and quietly set the gun back down in the tank. She thought: I'll kill someone when it will do me some good. Yes. Her hands trembled badly as she splashed water onto her face and dried it and when she went back into the room Armenta was watching her with his lugubrious eyes.

He held the Hummingbird toward her with both hands. "Please now perform."

She took the instrument because her nature was to play it and because playing gave her strength. She heard the faint harmonics of the box and strings brushing through the air as she walked across the room. She sat down on one of the dining room chairs and played the first few phrases of Zevon's "Keep Me in Your Heart."

The guitar had a beautiful tone, rich and detailed and seemingly derived from more than just six strings and a hollow body. The smell of the instrument coming through the hole was a quiet thrill for her, as always. Different smells for different guitars, of course, different woods and glues and finishes. But her hands and voice were afraid and unsteady and she couldn't get them to care. She tried to lose herself in the song anyway but failed, and the failure brought her back to who and where she was. Her voice fell and cracked and she let it lay there.

She carefully set the instrument on the tabletop and glanced at gray Armenta sitting stone-still in the filtered sunlight. He seemed not present. She looked out a window at the rippled silver lagoon and she felt tears coming so she turned away from the man and let them come but made no sound.

"Maybe someday you finish the song for me."

"Don't count on it."

She heard Armenta clear his throat. "Gustavo was eighteen," he said. "He was my seventh child. He was born quiet and he remained quiet all his life. He was gentle but strong. He hated cruelty but he had good courage. When he was very young he was wise and when he grew older he became younger. He loved to read. He loved fútbol. He was a very good horseman. When I watched him jumping it would make great pride in me. When he was ten I could no longer win at chess. When he was eleven I went to the prison for two years and when I escaped and came home he was a man. He was more helping for his mother than the others. The others were good and bad in their own ways but Gustavo was apart. He was not really similar to them. You will see in your life that you do not choose your children and you do not influence them as greatly as you think you will. You are merely the supplier of life. They become who they are in spite of you. So, Gustavo was all this."

Armenta's voice was softer and somehow more pleasant when Erin had her back to him. She picked a napkin off the dining table and wiped her eyes. Toughen up, girl, she thought. You've got to toughen up. She set the napkin on the table by the Hummingbird, then folded her hands over her middle and bowed her head and closed her eyes.

"When Gustavo is fourteen he meets a girl, Dulce Kopf. Her family came to Mexico from Germany in seventeen-fifty-one and they worked in the mines. Dulce is fourteen also and she is very much like him. They become friends. They go places and do the things that they

are allowed to do. And they go and do things that they are not allowed to do. I know this. But I see this love of theirs and I wait for the
love to go away. When he is eighteen he has been with Dulce for five
years nearly. This is more than one-quarter of his life. They are still
the happy children they have always been but now it is time to become adults. They have the best of grades from the private school in
Mexico. They have polo and fencing. They are popular and beautiful.
Did I mention to you that Gustavo was beautiful? They are very good
at languages and technical knowledge and music. They know English
and German. He knows the stringed instruments and she the woodwinds, all of the woodwinds. They have composed music alone and
together. They are both accept at UCLA in California. Very expensive
but I am a wealthy man by then. When they are finished they will be
married. But before the UCLA can begin it is over."

Erin opened her eyes to the heated green jungle and the shimmering laguna. "What happened?"

"Summer. They are living in Buenavista on the border so they can
travel to Los Angeles by car to look for an apartment. And because
they have a love of geography and certain rocks and plants that grow
in the desert. I never understand this love. Gustavo collected many
rocks and raised thousands of strange desert succulents and cactus.
Their home is filled with these things. One night they have dinner in
a restaurant in Buenavista. They sit outside on a patio and it is a quiet
night. I have a picture of them taken by the waiter with Dulce's camera. They are dressed somewhat elaborately for Buenavista because
Gustavo and Dulce loved to wear nice clothes. And of course there is
violence because there is always violence. A gunfight is about to begin
between American ATF agents and two gun smugglers. Gustavo sees
this development and he takes Dulce's hand and they climb the small
adobe wall of the patio and they run off into the darkness toward
home while the gunshots are heard in the restaurant. They are laugh-

ing, Dulce told me. It was so dangerous and almost funny to have a gunfight in a quiet restaurant on a hot desert night, men with guns fighting over more guns. Gustavo and Dulce held hands as they ran. And then Gustavo falls dead. A bullet from the restaurant, fired by the ATF agent Holdstock. One chance in a hundred million that the bullet would find his heart in all of that vast darkness."

Armenta was quiet for a long while.

"Why do you tell me this?" Erin asked.

"Because you played for me. When I hear 'Keep Me In Your Heart,' I think of Gustavo and Dulce. Of course this is why."

"Where is Dulce?"

"Here. She doesn't leave her room very often. It has been two years but he was her whole world and now he is gone. I gave her kilos of American dollars and told her to go into the world, anywhere she wants to go. But no."

Erin stared out the window. The breeze was stiffer now and it hissed through the palms and pocked the lagoon. To the southeast there was an indigo glow in the usually pale blue sky. She wondered why the birds had stopped singing. The pigeons had left her balcony. She thought of Heriberto's hurricane and of Bradley and of the small life brewing inside her. "Is your wife here?"

"She died."

"I'm sorry." For a moment she allowed herself to think of Armenta as a decent man but the moment passed. "Your son Saturnino has threatened to rape me."

"He will not rape you while I am alive."

She turned and looked at him. "But you will let him skin me in eight days if you are not made richer?"

"Yes. That is the agreement."

"You are beyond my comprehension."

"We can comprehend each other through music."

"I will play no more music for killers and torturers."

"Of course you will. It is your weapon. It is how you fight. You will play long and loud and with passion. The Jaguars of Veracruz will perform here the night after tomorrow. It will be a substantial evening. But first, I will give you the stage."

"I will not perform."

"Oh?" Armenta gave his eyes a histrionic roll. He looked away from her and raised his eyebrows. "You should know that your husband's courier is nowhere near here. He has not been communicating with us. I think he maybe has experienced the temptation of the big money."

"What are you saying?"

"Maybe he needs more time to deliver. Maybe the ten days can become eleven days. And with the hurricane coming who knows if the roads will be open? But if you perform on the stage of the Jaguars, I will give you back the day that has been lost. So that the million dollars can arrive here."

"You bastard." Erin whirled and saw the red flush on his pallorous face. She stood and lifted the Hummingbird over her head with both hands and heaved it at him. Armenta scrambled upright with surprising speed and did a little barefoot stutter step, then caught the flying instrument by its neck and body, balancing its weight as he gathered it from the air. "You sonofabitch."

He looked woefully from the guitar to Erin. "Then do not perform for yourself."

"For whom, then? You? For your dead angel of a son? For your living rapist of a son? For Felix the reporter?"

Armenta walked slowly across the tiles and set the guitar back into the case. He closed the lid and fastened the clasps.

He looked at her. "Do it for the child that grows inside you."

15

Hood sat in the Reynosa motel room and looked through *El Universal* newspaper while Valente Luna answered e-mails on his phone. Julio Santo had gone for takeout at a restaurant he knew and highly recommended.

Hood thought that Reynosa should be big in the news right now. Yesterday, the U.S. radio stations had been filled with the story of a shootout between *narcotrafficantes* and Federal troops—four dead in a running shootout that paralyzed Reynosa for hours. But there was no mention of this in *El Universal*. Hood looked over at the television news but there had not been any reference to the shootout on TV, either.

"Nobody in Reynosa talks about Reynosa," he said.

"Journalism is dead," said Luna, looking up from his phone. "The editors and reporters are afraid of the cartels. If they say the wrong thing it heats the plaza, and they're murdered. They have no protection. Thirty reporters killed since Calderón declared his war on the cartels. Some tortured and beheaded. Even the United Nations has been here to see the situation. But they come and they say, yes, this is one of the most dangerous places in the world for journalists. Then they leave and nothing changes. The American media named it *narco-censorship* and I think this is a good word for it."

Hood stood and looked through motel room curtains at the darkened parking lot and the bakery and mini-super and restaurant across the street. There were diners in the restaurant and a little line out front and it was easy for him to pretend that things were good down here, that the law meant something and there were plenty of good people to enforce it.

"Why did you join the police in Juarez?"

Luna looked up from his phone again. "My father was a Juarez police captain. I was born in Juarez. It was a good city. It was peaceful and proud."

"You and Raydel were both police."

"And one more brother, Antonio. Three police. My sister teaches school in Juarez. Sometimes I think of leaving. We only solve one out of every two hundred murders in our city now. That is a terrible truth. Half our department has been fired or has quit. We cannot hire and train new ones fast enough. The government has given us millions of dollars but we still can't find enough men. Where are they? We run the advertisements and they fail to appear. One morning in Guadalajara last month there was a banner hanging from a freeway overpass. It said 'Join the Zetas. High pay. Good benefits. An exciting life.' It was an authentic recruiting attempt. There was a number to call. The banner was removed immediately and the next day it was up again with a body hung on either side of it. Police, of course. Still in their uniforms."

"I admire your courage."

"Then I'll tell you this, my American friend: I called the number on the banner."

Hood looked at Luna and Luna looked gloomily back. "I wanted to know how much the Zetas would pay me for killing my own kind. No one answered my call. Just a recording machine asking me for information. But I have heard that the Zetas pay ten times a policeman's salary. Ten."

Hood looked through the window again and saw Julio waiting in a little group of pedestrians at a traffic light across the busy street, both his hands dangling white plastic bags.

"My dad worked in landscape maintenance but I became a deputy in Los Angeles."

"Why?"

"I did some investigative work in Iraq, with the Navy. I kind of had a knack for it so when I got back I applied. The pay is okay and the benefits are good. I guess I make about what the Zetas pay."

"Then money was not your reason. For an American this is not a lot of money."

"No. It was more going where I was needed. Doing something I believed in."

"The law?"

"Yes. I believe in that."

"If you know people who don't, send them to Juarez. I will give them a personal tour of a city without law."

Hood heard the knock. Through the peephole he saw the distorted and out-of-focus face of Julio. Hood opened the door to a gun blast and the whack of a bullet against his ballistic vest. A spray of blood hit him in the face and Julio collapsed on the landing with the bags of food still in his hands. The shooter was small and tucked close behind Julio and he swept his weapon toward Hood who twisted it away and broke the boy's elbow and nose, then instinctively dropped to the floor, drawing his sidearm on the way down. He heard the three roars of Luna's handgun behind him and the broken-armed shooter fall but two more men rushed from the darkness firing their pistols wildly, as if the number of bullets in the air was the only thing in the world that mattered. Hood rose to his knees and shot the nearest man and Luna cut down the second. Then two more *sicarios* charged from behind the ice machine but by now Luna was through the doorway and he headshot one, then the other, and they fell grotesquely into the planters filled with cactus and succulents and white gravel.

They knelt over Julio and Hood felt his carotid while he watched an SUV far back in the motel parking lot. Men were gathered around it and they looked undecided what to do. They looked young. Hood saw the glint of their weaponry in the weak streetlights.

"If they try again we will move apart," said Luna. "At least one of them might know how to aim a gun and squeeze a trigger." He stood and raised a fist at them, then worked a fresh magazine into the butt of his gun, holding it up for them to see.

Julio lay in a lake of blood and Hood could find no pulse. Across the street people fled from the restaurant and the store, and someone slammed shut the mini-super door from inside. There were families getting churros at the bakery but now the parents were herding away the crying children. Deep in the parking lot the men climbed back inside their vehicle. It was a Durango with a custom purple paint job and a shiny chrome face of Malverde, patron saint of the *narcos*, affixed to one of the side windows. A deep thumping sound came from the vehicle, then guitars and a mournful tenor sang the first line of a *narcocorrido*. Hood watched it jump the parking blocks, roll across the sidewalk and wobble over the curb and onto the busy street, where it disappeared in the traffic.

He rose and went the few steps to his vehicle and threw open the liftgate, then he carried Julio over and shouldered the dead man into the back. Luna ran from the room with the suitcase and hurled it onto a backseat.

"To pursue or escape?" Luna asked.

"Pursue. They won't expect us."

"Kill or arrest?"

"Let them decide."

"I'll drive," he said. "I know the city. They went east for the highway but I know a faster way."

Hood wiped his bloody hands on his pants, then slapped a fresh magazine into his .45. He holstered the weapon and pulled the cut-down ten-gauge from under the front seat. Help us, he thought. Help us.

They pulled onto the Highway 97 on-ramp just ahead of the purple Durango. By the time the driver realized what was happening Luna drove him to a stop against the guardrail then slammed into reverse and blocked his only escape route with Hood's big Expedition.

Luna hit the brights, then he and Hood piled out the driver's side, using their vehicle for cover. Music throbbed from the Durango, then stopped. Its headlights sprayed off toward the highway and into the beams rose dust. The lights of the oncoming traffic advanced brightly and Hood squinted down the brief barrel of the shotgun resting on his car, waiting for gunfire.

"*Policia! Rendir de armas! Policia!*"

The Durango's headlights went off. Hood saw the rear left door swing open but no interior light went on. A slender young man dropped to the asphalt with his hands up, then another behind him. They stood staring to the side of the Expedition's headlights and in the white blast of the high beams they looked to Hood no older than eighteen. Then the driver's door opened and another very young man stepped down, dressed in Sinaloan fashion—a yoked cowboy shirt with mother-of-pearl snaps that caught the highway lights, and black jeans and white cowboy boots. Two more boys came around from the passenger side, hands up, gazing through the brightness in the direction of Hood and Luna.

Then another came through the back door, a heavyset youth dressed all in black with a black bandana tied vaquero style around his neck and a black cowboy hat with a high crown and a silver hat-band. He hustled after his comrades as if he was afraid they'd leave him and when he caught up he removed his hat, then lay facedown to the asphalt and spread his legs and arms.

Luna barked at the others to do the same and Hood watched them obey. When they were down Luna told them to not move and without taking his eyes off them he dug out his cell phone and punched a number and a moment later was giving their location and ordering someone to hurry.

Reynosa police pommander Oscar Ruiz was heavyset and dour and he seemed uninterested in what had happened. The six suspects were locked in a holding cell in the intake area, where a uniformed officer cut away their wrist restraints as they held them out to the bars. The suspects said little and they avoided looking at the local cops but stared sullenly at Hood and Luna.

Hood was directed to the lobby bathroom and here he used a dribble of water and powdered soap to grind the blood off his hands and face. His long run of adrenaline had ended and he felt dazed and displaced. He watched the grainy pink water trickle down the drain and he wondered, as he had in the alleys of Hamdaniya and on the streets of L.A. and in bloody Mexico, how ready men were to die for the things they wanted. To die by the hundreds. By the thousands.

A few minutes later Hood and Luna stood in the compound yard and watched two medics wrestle Julio from the Expedition onto a stretcher, then carry the stretcher into the coroner's building.

"A wife and a daughter," said Luna. "And a very small government payment."

"It could have been me," said Hood. "I volunteered to buy the dinners. But Julio knew a restaurant."

"It could have been you one thousand times in the past. And it might be you a thousand times in the future."

"Your country is beginning to exhaust me."

"It exhausts us all."

Hood made sure the suitcase was still on the rear seats, then swung the liftgate closed and locked the vehicle and set the alarm with his key fob.

The interview lasted half an hour and Ruiz made a few notes, very slowly. He said that Reynosa was being contested by Sinaloan and Gulf Cartel gangsters because it was a lucrative entryway into the *Estados Unidos*. He looked at Hood when he said the gringos were the cause of the drug wars and the deaths of forty thousand Mexicans who had died in those wars, because of the gringo appetite for drugs. Hood said the Mexican appetites for money and violence had plenty to do with it too and this drew a quizzical raising of eyebrows.

Ruiz said that the shooters appeared to be quite young and this could mean they were Gulf Cartel recruits because this cartel had been at war with the Zetas and now the Sinaloans and it had suffered losses. He said that the suspects probably mistook Hood, Luna, and Julio for rival cartel men. There were shoot-outs in Mexican border towns all the time, he said, between such people. These criminals would be interrogated and charged, swiftly. He never mentioned money, or any possible motive for such an attack other than cartel wars, so Hood suspected that he already knew about the luggage and what it contained. *Information is cheap of course and can be sold many times.*

He asked Hood and Luna to fill out their own versions of what happened and he gave each of them a Reynosa Policia Municipal form and a ballpoint pen. Hood finished before Luna and he went back to check on the Expedition. A uniformed officer stood with his back to the driver's door and he stared at Hood. They spoke in Spanish.

—I'm seeing if my vehicle is safe.

—It is very safe. I am guarding it.

—What is your name?

—Reuben.

—It has a very loud alarm, Reuben.

—Yes, I know this model of the Ford.

Hood looked through a back window and saw the suitcase on the seats. They'll be looking for this vehicle now, he thought, and they've got our Mexican plate numbers. He unlocked the Expedition and opened a back door and yanked the luggage out to the ground where it landed on its side.

"Your luggage is very safe."

"Yes. But I may need a change of clothes."

The officer looked questioningly at Hood, but said nothing. Hood rolled the suitcase around to the impound yard and set it down and unsnapped his holster strap and waited. A few minutes later a man in street clothes and a straw cowboy hat walked from the station and got into the purple Durango and drove it out of the yard, through the sally port, then onto the street. Here he parked it and got out and locked it with an electronic key and put the key in his pocket. Hood watched him walk around the corner and out of sight. He waited and watched, then carried the suitcase back inside to the prisoner intake area, where he saw the man in the straw cowboy hat leaning against the bars of the holding tank, talking with the boys inside. One of the boys laughed. The man in the hat glanced over at Hood, then turned back to the inmates.

Luna had come up behind him. "They'll be free the moment we leave," he whispered. "Ruiz is the third police commander in Reynosa in the last two years. The other two were caught running drugs into Texas."

"How did these people know where we were and what we have?"

"In a poor place, one million dollars cannot be a secret for very long."

Hood patted the suitcase. "It's pretty much public knowledge now."

"It's good you have it and a gun to guard it with."

"We need a different vehicle."

"We can do this."

Hood drove away from the Reynosa PD and Luna kept a constant eye out behind them. They were almost back to the motel when Hood's phone buzzed.

"Drive to Merida. Stay at the Hyatt Regency. You have four days."

"Let me talk to her."

There was a shuffle and silence, then Erin's voice.

"Charlie?"

"I'm here, Erin. I'm getting closer with the money."

"Please get here soon."

"Are you all right?"

"I'm all right. But I'm afraid. Armenta knows who I am. He knew all along. He claims he loves my music. He wants me to play for him. Where is Bradley? Why isn't he bringing the money? I'm his wife. I'm not your wife, but you're risking your life for me. I don't know how long I'm going to last around here."

"We thought this would work best. You're going to be okay, Erin."

The connection went dead.

16

"YOU'RE GOING TO LIKE VERACRUZ, Bradley," said Mike Finnegan.
They were walking the *malecón* at dusk. The sky was too
dark for this hour and the wind snapped the Gulf of Mexico waters
into whitecaps. Most of the vendors had packed up ahead of the
storm and the old boardwalk was empty of tourists and lovers.
Finnegan wore red tennis warm-ups and Top-Siders and a USS *Constitution* cap and he toted in each hand a heavy canvas bag.

"Where is she? You said you'd know by now."

Mike stopped and set down a bag and dug a hand into the pocket
of his warm-ups. Bradley noted that the contents of each canvas bag
were covered by a neatly folded plastic lawn bag. Mike handed him a
Villa Rica matchbook. "She is being held in Benjamin Armenta's Castle in Quintana Roo. The coordinates are written inside."

"Castle?"

Finnegan picked up the bag and they continued down the *malecón*.
"There's no really good word for it. It's too rustic to be called a palace
or a mansion. Too large to be called a home. Too homey to be called a
fortress or citadel or bastion. It was always called the Castle. It was built
in the nineteen-twenties by a daft banker who was passionate about
Meso-American native artifacts. A gringo, though his wife was a Chinese woman. Interesting pair. When they died the place was sacked by
vandals and sat in ruin for decades. Armenta bought it five years ago,

through intermediaries, paid more cash than it was really worth so that certain questions could go unasked. It sits squarely in a federally protected archaeological preserve not open to the public. Federal soldiers man the gates and no one can enter the reserve, except for Armenta's chosen few. He pays handsomely for this protection. The reserve itself is managed by a private Catholic league called the Sons of Jesus, heavily endowed by Armenta through Father Edgar Ciel. The Castle is said to be either four or five levels and is of course believed to be haunted."

"Why of course?"

"The Caribbean imagination favors such constructs. A different world down there." Finnegan smiled and tilted back his head and drew a deep breath. "Veracruz smells of centuries, and centuries fire the imagination. But to get to the point, Armenta's Castle is home to a couple of dozen or so of his friends and family. Armed men guard the compound in eight-hour shifts. The off-duty guards live in a garrison back in the jungle. They rotate in and out, always fresh and well rested. Ten armed guards patrol the Castle and its immediate grounds. Then there are three gate guards staggered down the road. Three guards each. And four more men who prowl the perimeter of the property. There is only one road in. The property is not fenced. The jungle is extremely dense and some of it is precipitous. Often, when Armenta is especially fearful for his life, he will increase the number of guards or rearrange them according to his latest intelligence and fears. His eldest son is the head of security. His name is Saturnino."

The name sent a shiver up Bradley's back. Saturnino. He thought of Fidel's wife and two children and of Erin, now in Saturnino's hands. Killer. Rapist. Skinner.

Bradley read the coordinates off the matchbook and committed them to memory. "There are twenty-four of us. We'd be up against at least twenty-three armed men who know the Castle and the jungle around it."

"Don't forget to count Armenta himself, and his personal body-guards, his son and their closest associates. Figure ten more men, conservatively."

"How did you get this information?"

"Contacts."

"Can we get word to her?"

"Possibly."

They continued up the boardwalk. Bradley looked across the harbor to Fort San Juan de Ulúa. Even at this distance and in the failing light it looked unassailable. He imagined Armenta's Castle and it too looked unassailable with its armed patrols and Erin being held God only knew where.

"The Spanish built it to guard against pirates," said Finnegan. "That was in fifteen-eighty-two. Veracruz had already been here over sixty years, if you can believe that. Cortez himself founded it, the first settlement on the American mainland. Sorry if I sound like a seventh-grade history teacher but I love this city—the Maya and the slave trade and the pirates and the drastic attitudes of the Spanish conquerors. What a rich, mad blend. Coming here suggests so much to me."

"Can we get word to Erin or not?"

"What word would it be?"

"Can she get out and come to us, or do we need to blast her out?"

"You can't blast her out. The chances of her being hit by a bullet are far too great. We can't let her or your son or you, Bradley, expire in such a small and pointless way."

"That's why we need a way to communicate. What if she can slip away? I don't know—through a window or a door when the guard takes a break. Or, maybe your *contact* can create a diversion or knock somebody cold for a few minutes so Erin can get out."

"Yes, good. Now, during the nineteenth century, Fort San Juan de Ulúa was a military prison. Some of the dungeons have walls twenty-four-feet thick in places. Imagine the hopelessness! They had nick-names for the hottest and darkest of them—'Purgatory,' and 'Hell' and other rather unimaginative names like that."

"Surprise is what we have, Mike. We can surprise them but we can't overwhelm them."

Finnegan stopped and looked up at Bradley. "It's all you have."

They found the Taberna Roja near the port on a cramped eighteenth-century side street intersecting Zaragoza. The weather-beaten wooden sign hanging out front featured a plump man in san-dals and a poncho running with a grin on his face and a tray of booze bottles held high overhead. Inside it was cool and damp but very crowded and thick with smoke. Bradley saw that several arguments in several languages were taking place throughout the dark, high-ceilinged room. The patrons were almost all men, stevedores and sail-ors and perhaps fishermen. He and Mike took a small high table in the back. A moment later one of the barkeeps arrived with a bottle of rum and a dish filled with lime and lemon wedges and a bucket of ice and two lowball glasses on a tray.

"Welcome, Mr. Fix. How are you?"

"*Perfecto*, Pao. Perfectly perfect now that I'm here!"

Pao spooned the ice into the glasses and opened the bottle and set it beside the fruit dish. *"Salud."*

Mike smiled and Pao nodded curtly, then disappeared back into the noisy throng at the bar.

"Fix?"

"I like it," said Mike. "Uncommon and descriptive. In Spanish I'd be *Reparar*."

Bradley shook his head and smiled. Whenever he thought he'd had enough of the little man, Mike would do something amusing. He wondered if that was how Mike had gotten through his life.

Now Mike lifted one of the heavy book bags to his lap and dug out three volumes and put them on the table. "People tell me all the time that I'm old-fashioned."

"You told me that yourself when you knifed me."

"But try downloading *these* to your reader!"

Bradley looked at the covers of the tattered old books but he couldn't read a single word of the titles.

"Taki-Taki, Papiamento, Quiché," said Mike. "Ancient languages, poorly understood. These are academic attempts. There's a dealer here in Veracruz, one of the Naval Museum curators. He must be two hundred years old. I don't know how he finds this stuff or who buys it except for me."

"Explain something," said Bradley. "Ever since you cut me, the skin won't heal. But it doesn't hurt and it's not inflamed. Did you dip your knife in venom or the plague or something?" He held out his hand and lifted the bandage and Finnegan studied the open gouge.

"This is just a common topical infection, Bradley. Any over-the-counter remedy will defeat it."

"I've been using one."

"Maybe try another."

"How's yours?"

"Oh, I'm a tough old guy." Mike unfurled his hand and looked down into it and Bradley saw the faint pink line of the cut healed over with new flesh. "But here, this is what I wanted to show you."

Mike set the books back into the bag, then pulled out a thin leather folder and handed it to Bradley.

He opened it and looked down at a drawing. It looked like a landscape architect's site plan, an aerial view with buildings represented by rectangles and trees by circles and elevations by shaded cross-hatching.

"Armenta's *Castle,*" said Bradley, his breath catching. "Where did you get this?"

"Some of the source material came from the state of Quintana Roo. I can assure you it wasn't easy to get. American bureaucracy is nothing compared to Mexican bureaucracy. In Mexico, the government is very deep but also very spotty. For instance, things suddenly disappear or are suddenly found or suddenly change. The person of authority on one day is not in authority on another. It can take as many as five people to do something as simple as collecting a completed form, filling out a receipt, and handing the receipt to the applicant. Luckily I was able to find the original construction drawings in a dusty museum collection in San Francisco. And able to cobble this together for you."

"Is it accurate?"

"Of course it's accurate. I wouldn't risk the life of Erin McKenna on a slipshod rendering. The map below it is an area view, putting the castle in a larger context."

Bradley studied both of the maps. "Where is the electronic security, the alarms and sensors?"

"None. Low-tech. Macho. Men with guns."

"Telephone landlines?"

"Armenta removed them." Mike poured the rum over the ice. In the dark tavern light it came from the bottle like gold. "No landlines. He installed cell signal scramblers that cover the whole compound and half of the federal reserve. He relies on satellite phones but he only allows his most trusted men to carry them. Armenta's men confiscate all electronic devices belonging to guests, returning them only when the guests depart. He has no alarms or electronic security, none of the things that you fruitlessly employed against the men who now have Erin."

"How do you know what I employed? You've never even been to my home."

Mike gave him a crafty smile. "I'm trying to teach you something here. The things you thought would protect you—whatever they may be—did not protect you. Oh, good ideas, yes. Terrific technology. But technology is still very fragile and finicky. It's the simple things that really register, really *work*, and always have. The finger on the trigger. The well-timed question. Twenty-fifteen eyesight. Thirty pieces of silver or a million in cash."

"Hand-drawn maps."

"Exactly."

Bradley held up the maps and even in the poor light he could see the smudges left by Finnegan's fingers and the shine of the graphite on the paper. Then he set the papers back in the folder. "Did you make copies?"

"Not prudent. Each is one of a kind. They are yours."

Bradley slowly shuffled them, staring at the close-up, then the establishing shot, one after the other.

"What we need is a way to talk to her, Mike. If we can talk, we can make a plan. Without a plan, it's just bullets and blood."

"I'm working on this. Believe me, I am working on it."

They clinked glasses and drank. Bradley was not a rum man but it was sweet and whole and the lemon finished it cleanly.

"Bradley, have you by any chance mentioned our friendship to Charlie Hood?"

"Why would I do that?"

"That is not what I asked."

"I said I wouldn't. I haven't and I won't." Bradley tucked the leather folder onto his lap and lifted his glass to Finnegan.

An hour later the bottle was half gone and Finnegan had joined a pack of stevedores up by the bar. He was shouting out something about all the gold still left here in Veracruz and why the lazy people on this part of Earth had failed to extract it. Someone laughed and pushed him and Mike laughed and drove a finger into the man's chest and rocked him back. Then he was up at the counter buying drinks and when Bradley looked above the tavern mirror at the same Taberna Roja sign that hung outside, he saw that the jolly man with the booze on his tray looked a bit like Mike. Red cheeks and curly red hair. El Rojo. Bradley shook his head and added a handful of ice to his glass and set the leather folder on the table before him and looked again at the maps of where Erin was being held. This is what connects me to you, he thought: a map drawn by a man I hardly know and barely trust.

Looking down at the maps he thought that the jungle might be an ally rather than an enemy. Yes, Armenta and his people knew the jungle, but if it was as dense and steep as Mike had said, then it could hide things even from those who knew it. Bradley thought that they could get close to the Castle without being seen. Yes, through the unfenced jungle. With a finger he traced the road coming in, then tapped the triangle representing the guardhouse. Using his pocket-knife he estimated the distance from the garrison in the jungle to the Castle proper to be half a mile, based on Mike's scale. If we were quiet, he thought, and Erin could meet us, we could steal her away before anyone knew she was gone. Silence. Cunning. The Caribbean Sea was less than half a mile east. Laguna Guerrero a third of a mile to the west. Trails. There must be at least game trails. Or, water. Come from the water and leave by water. Chetumal was close enough if they could get a decent boat. Chetumal also had an airport. Bacalar was near the lagoon, and very near the highway leading northwest to Merida. Merida: crowds, a consulate, an airport, safety. The same for Cancún. He sipped the rum without taking his eyes from the maps.

Or we can think about using the road, he thought. Be simple and pure and audacious. Surely, if the Castle was locked in the middle of jungle, then it required occasional deliveries of goods and services. Food? Propane? Water? Building materials? Landscape and pool maintenance? Painting? Mosquito abatement? He thought: If I could talk to her she could tell me who comes and goes. If she could get free for just a minute, for just a few seconds, I could get her on her way home before Armenta knew a thing. *If* . . .

He looked at Finnegan, now pushing drinks down the bar toward two men who appeared ready to fight. In his red warm-ups and deck shoes and Navy cap, shouting, his face flushed and his eyes asparkle with whatever high emotions now ran through him, Mike looked ridiculous. But even wearing an expensive-looking suit, as he had worn the other night at El Dorado, Mike still looked ridiculous, thought Bradley, and he wondered if Mike's strenuous efforts to know things and to influence people and to seem important were all attempts to cover this. The little-dog complex. Owens had said that Mike was insane and Bradley had never doubted it. And what did it say about himself that Mike was his greatest ally in this, the most weighted journey of his life?

Through the windows Bradley could see a couple running in the wind and the first drops of rain hit the glass and the bottom of the Taberna Roja sign swaying on its stout iron rod. We will be that couple someday, he thought, Erin and I will run through the rain together again, alive and free and we will never come back to the hell of Mexico again. Never.

Mike was back at the table adding ice to their glasses, then pouring the last of the rum into them.

"No sense leaving now with the rain starting up," he said, smiling.

"None," said Bradley.

Mike held up the empty bottle and Pao left the drink he was making and brought over a fresh one and another bucket of ice. "What are you thinking, young son of Murrieta?"

"Don't call me that. Can we get a satellite phone to her?"

"They say that Armenta is phobic about phones of all kinds," said Mike. "Only he and his trusted few can have one. So, we can smuggle something in to her, but the question then becomes, can she keep it? What sort of wrath would she receive? They'll search. They'll find her things. Oh, Brad. I almost forgot. I've got something else for you here in my bag of tricks."

Finnegan hopped down and lifted one of the bags to the stool and searched through it. From down in a corner he produced a small metal tube and handed it to Bradley.

At first Bradley thought it was a gun cartridge casing but it was far too light and there was an odd clasp affixed to one side. He held the clasp and twisted one end of the tube open. Inside was stuffed some kind of cloth. He worried it out with his pocketknife blade and it dropped to the tabletop. He unrolled the material, fine silk or maybe a sheer linen, and it became a square approximately five by five inches and covered with Erin's tight cursive writing in blue ink.

> *Dear B, I'm okay and so is he. Owens F. is here and she says this will get to Mike then you. She says Arm finds and destroys cell and sat phones but he doesn't suspect pigeons as there are many in the coop and the message containers are easy to hide. She seems to be Arm's but says she is here of free will. Is a very disturbing woman. I am okay but terrified. Please hurry. Get me out of here.*
> *Erin*

Bradley felt the great rush of tears and he couldn't stop them. There she was. Her hand had written this to him. She was alive and well and so was their son. The tears of joy and hope burned his eyes as he stared down at her words. "God, this is great news."

"I'm glad to deliver it to you."

"What's Owens doing with Armenta?"

"They've known each other for years."

"You smuggled her a homing pigeon?"

"Three of them. Actually, I *had* them smuggled to her by an underpaid Quintana Roo propane delivery man. I'll certainly introduce you to him, but to be truthful I was never confident that he'd complete his mission."

"You never told me you kept pigeons."

Mike gave him a boy's grin. "Oh, forever."

A possibility hit him, and Bradley wiped the tears with his hand and flicked them onto the tavern table. "The propane guy also brought three of Armenta's birds out for you. Because we need some that will fly back to the Castle. Right?"

"Yes," said Mike, his eyes sparkling with glee. "I am so proud of me sometimes."

"Then we have a way to contact her."

"Well, three ways. Would you like to see them?"

Bradley slipped the leather map folder between his belt and the small of his back, then pulled on his rain jacket. Mike stashed the newly arrived bottle of rum in one of his book bags then snugged the folded plastic lawn bags against the rain. He looked up at Bradley and gestured at the door like a butler, palm up, scar not visible to Bradley in the poor tavern light.

17

M IKE'S APARTMENT WAS ON AN alley several blocks north and east, off of M. Doblado. It was in the *zona historico*, the oldest part of a very old city. Bradley had trouble keeping up with the little man as he barreled along the narrow streets and by the time they were climbing the stone steps to the front door the rain had slackened and the wind died down.

Inside the apartment smelled of seawater and ancient rock. "Built in eighteen-forty-eight," said Mike. "For Veracruz, practically brand-new. One hundred and one years before Woodrow Wilson's attack. Downstairs was a livery and upstairs the residence. Retrofitted for running water and electricity. Later a hostel."

As the lights fluttered on in the foyer Bradley saw that the main room had a high ceiling and there was a balcony that faced east toward the Gulf of Mexico. The windows had been left open and the wind and rain easily blew in past the grates and swayed what looked like very old drapes.

Finnegan unslung the book bags and pulled the windows closed and motioned Bradley to follow. They passed a small kitchen lit by a very weak bulb. The hallway was long and made of hardwood that creaked under Bradley's boots. They passed a bedroom on the right and another to the left, then they climbed a narrow wooden stairway and Mike was talking as he headed up.

"Yoo-hoo, my fine feathered friends. It's just me again, your favorite creature, bringing someone very special here to meet you."

He turned and drew Bradley by his arm into the room.

"My flock, meet the son of Murrieta!"

Bradley stepped into a half story, smelled the green stink of caged birds, saw the head-high coop that stretched from wall to wall, saw the bursts of feathers and seed as the animals flapped and dodged. Their alarm spread quickly through the enclosure, then just as quickly it was gone and the birds, Bradley guessed maybe twenty in all, settled on their nests and perches and peered out at the men with the curiosity of pigeons everywhere.

Mike was smiling. First at the birds and then at Bradley, then at the birds again.

"I'll bet each one has a name," said Bradley.

"Well, that's Jason in the corner there, and beautiful Ambrosia on her nest."

"It's a hobby?"

"It's one more way to see the world."

Bradley looked around the spacious room. The floor was more brick-red tile and the ceiling paint was peeling. The walls were lined with bookcases to a height of about six feet, and the cases were full. Bradley recognized some of the languages on the spines. Above the shelves the walls were festooned with weapons and devices apparently made for torture, all very old. There was a leather recliner with a colorful serape flung across the back, and a reading lamp beside it. There was a long wooden table in the middle of the room and a wheeled chair. The table was cluttered with books and magazines and sketchbooks and large graph-paper blotters strangled by doodles and notations. A laptop computer sat closed on the blotter. Beside it was a small earthen dish containing a handful of message containers for the pigeons. Some looked well used and others nearly new. There was a short stack of fabric squares similar to the one that Erin had written on.

"You communicate with other fanciers?"

"Do I ever! Of the twenty-four birds in there right now, only six are actually my own. Released from anywhere, within reason, they'll fly right back to me bearing the messages of my friends and associates. The other eighteen belong to friends I've made over time. We exchange a few here and there when we meet, so we always have an adequate flock."

"What do you write to each other about?"

"The Earth and everything upon it."

"For about the same cost as a cell phone, I'd guess. Once you figure in the food and grit and vitamins and vet bills and—"

"Quite a bit cheaper, actually, and of course they breed for free, just like people. But it's not about cost. It's not even really about communication. It's about the medium itself. The medium is the message, as we've been taught, so it follows that a slow method of communication will reveal different meanings than a fast one. You get very different rewards when you compose longhand and deliver your brief notes on the wings of birds! You get shorter, more compact thoughts and ideas. You get ideas that are, well, smaller but larger. And this relative slowness with which they are delivered really does nothing to impede the flow of conversation about Earth's important events because, as you know, important events almost never happen quickly. Earthquakes and spectacular accidents aside."

"You're talking like, geology and history."

"Not *like* them. They *themselves*. I'm quite drunk. Shall we have another? Listen to that rain coming down out there. The lovely Ivana is most assuredly on her way now."

"She's aimed at the Yucatán," said Bradley. "At Erin."

Mike looked into the coop and pointed at a white-and-tan bird studying him from its perch. "He is one of Armenta's birds. I have named him Samson. I will bet that Samson here can fly back home through any hurricane."

"We have to beat the storm."

Mike went to the desk and took a square of fabric from the top of the stack and cleared the books away and set it down on the blotter. From the middle drawer he brought a pen box and opened it and set it beside the fabric.

"It's up to you, Bradley."

"This is going to take a while."

"I would think so. You have only twenty-five square inches on each side, so you must clear your thoughts, condense your language, and solicit specific information that will allow you to form a plan. A plan that cannot fail."

"Would you make me a pot of coffee?"

"The best and strongest in all of Veracruz."

"The rum will keep."

"It always does."

"We're going to get her back, Mike."

"I could see in the tavern that you were giving it some serious thought."

Bradley set the maps on the desk, then sat and took the pen and flattened the fabric so it would take the ink evenly. He pored over the drawings of the Castle and the compound and the surrounding land and lagoon and sea. "The maps help. The maps show us the way. But they can't give us the way."

"No. You must conjure that with words on silk."

"She has to meet me outside the Castle. It's either that or a gun battle. I can't take that chance. I need to know where to find her, that's the main thing. Outside the Castle. I can be there if I only know where *there* is."

"Tell her what you need to know, Bradley. And please, save me a little room at the end. I'll write something brief to Owens. Owens can help."

Bradley stared down at the maps while Mike made coffee. Bradley could hear the buzz of the grinder downstairs. When Finnegan came back a few minutes later Bradley had found what looked like a very promising place where he could meet Erin near the Castle.

"This, here," he said, pointing to a small circle with tiny stylized waves sketched within. "It's a cenote?"

"Yes. Just as I have indicated."

"Five hundred yards from the compound."

"I'm confident of that measurement."

"So the cenote is there. Even if your source material is fifty years old, that cenote will be there."

"Bradley, the cenote is five centuries old. Fresh water, coming up from the aquifer. Fresh water, sustaining thousands of the Maya in that area, for hundreds and hundreds of years."

Mike went downstairs to get the coffee and Bradley slowly and carefully composed the letter. It thrilled him and frightened him that their lives now depended on written words. Every movement of the pen seemed freighted with consequence, every word a potential miracle or catastrophe. He had spent years writing poems, trying to get one like Neruda's but he never even approximated one.

Now he told her, concisely and clearly, where he would be waiting. Using the map, he described the cenote's exact location so that she could find it without difficulty or doubt. He gave her two consecutive days to be there—day ten, which was the ransom day, and the day preceding it. Wednesday. Tuesday. He would be there, all twenty-four hours of each day. He would be there. It was not a promise or an approximation but a fact. Not until he had finished did he write two lines to tell her he loved her more than he loved anyone or anything on Earth. *I will come to you, like you asked me to in your song.* He left room for Mike. Then he turned over the swatch of fabric and faithfully re-created Mike's map of the compound and the surrounding grounds.

When he was finished he checked the map and read the directions over very carefully, then looked up at Mike. "Can we send all three birds? Three messages, three maps, triple our chances?"

"I was about to suggest it."

"They'll take what, four days to get there? If they can make it through the hurricane at all?"

"She's only a category two," said Finnegan.

"Write your part to Owens."

He stood and handed the pen to Mike.

When the letters and maps were finished and rolled and fitted into the containers, Bradley held the birds upside down one at a time while Mike fixed the capsules to their legs. He gave each container a little tug when he was finished. The birds felt warm and capable to Bradley and they allowed themselves to be handled. Bradley said a silent prayer for each one, trying to customize it for the individual bird.

"Bradley," Mike said softly. "You can pray but you will never be answered because God does not listen. He does not control the lives of men. He only influences them through intermediaries. And never because of a prayer."

"What makes you think I was praying?"

"Thoughts can be loud."

"More of your bullshit. I'll pray if I want."

Just before midnight Mike opened the attic window. The air was heavy but the rain had stopped. Bradley held the warm strong Samson in his hands and kissed the top of his head, then he reached through the window and released him into the night.

In the taxi early that morning Bradley called Hood on the satellite phone and told him that he had found Erin. He described the Castle, the compound, and their larger geographical positioning within the geography of Yucatán. He told Hood the GPS coordinates.

"That tracks," said Hood. "Armenta is bringing me to Merida— less than two hundred miles from Erin. How many people do you have?"

"Twenty-four. But Charlie, get this—I don't think I'll even need them."

"Talk."

"I've found a way to communicate with her. I've told her to go into the jungle the day before the ransom is due. There's a path and a cenote. All she has to do is get a few seconds to herself. She's got help. She's made a friend. Anytime she can make it is okay. We'll be there all day. Caroline, Cleary, and I will be waiting."

"She's got a phone?"

"No phones. Pigeons. Long story."

"*Pigeons?*"

Bradley's heart soared though somewhat drunkenly. He had almost forgotten what hope felt like. "It's going to work, Charlie. We're going to pull this off. She's going to be all right. Have you heard from her? What did she say? Please tell me everything she said. Don't leave out one word."

18

FATHER EDGAR CIEL KEYED HIS way into Erin's room that evening and gently pulled the door shut behind him. "You asked to see me."

"Yes, thank you. Please come in and sit."

Ciel was a tall man, though slender, and he crossed the room with an angular grace, watching her closely as he passed her to sit in the old armchair. He wore a priest's short-sleeve black shirt with the white stiff collar and black jacket, pants and shoes. His crucifix was large and silver. There was no gun on his hip that Erin could see and she wondered if in all of her trauma and exhaustion that first day she had only imagined it. He was pale. Behind his wire-rimmed glasses his eyes were blue and luminous.

"I want you to ask the Catholic Church to intervene on my behalf," she said.

"The Vatican is a bureaucracy," he said with a small smile. His voice was soft and clear and unhurried.

"It's supposed to be the greatest church in the world. How complicated is a kidnapped woman? I am a Catholic and proud of it. I have confessed a million times. Do something, Father. I saw them feed a man to the leopards. The devil walks this castle free and proud. Maybe more than one of them. You have sensed this, haven't you?"

"Yes."

"Do something."

Ciel stood and went to the window and looked out. Past him Erin saw the fronds whipping and a dark layer of clouds sitting high in the southeastern sky. "We must deal with practical realities, Mrs. Mc-Kenna. We must deal with your problem directly. I have spoken to Benjamin. He says he will not release you until he has received what he wants. He will not say exactly what he wants. To me, he seems to have less interest in the ransom than he did a few days ago."

"He wants me to sing for him."

"He is expecting you to sing tonight before the Jaguars. But he assuredly wants more than that."

"Why does it feel like you're on his side? Are you? Am I the problem here? A distraction from your fund-raising efforts for the Legion of Christ?"

He turned to her and she saw the dampness in his eyes and the quiver of his chin. "I will do anything in my power to make sure you leave this place alive. My church is thousands of miles from here, and my God thousands more. I am working for your freedom. Until you are free I can offer you comfort in the Holy Spirit."

She remembered Father O'Hora again, from when she was just a girl. He had the same kind eyes as Ciel and the same near hush about him. He had always seemed both faithful and hapless. But he was the man you could trust. He was the man who would do what God would do. God's agent. Legionnaire for Christ.

She looked into Ciel's eyes and remembered O'Hora's eyes at her father's funeral and they were the same in their deep empathy and powerlessness. She remembered despising that powerlessness then, and sensing for the first time that the affairs of God and men were separate. She remembered comparing her father to Father O'Hora, and deciding that her father had been the better man—at once joyful and profane and intensely emotional—not a man caged by faith and controlled by doubt. And she remembered thinking that God himself would strike her dead at age thirteen for such thoughts.

Ciel beckoned her to him with his pale hands. She went to him and he reached his arms around her. She rested her cheek on his chest just above the crucifix. He felt bony and hard. His heart was beating strong and slow and he smelled of soap and vanilla. "'Whither has your beloved gone, O fairest among women? Wither has your beloved turned, that we may seek him with you?'"

"I loved the Song of Solomon when I was a girl."

"'Open to me, my sister, my love, my dove, my perfect one; for my head is wet with dew, my locks with the drops of the night.'"

"Some of it's kind of graphic, though."

"Let me be what you need me to be."

"I haven't had a good cry in an awful long time," she said.

"Cry to me, my child. Cry your tears upon me."

Cry to me, my child, she thought. That's what I want. She let go.

Seconds after Ciel left, Erin heard a tap on the door and Owens Finnegan's voice. "I'm coming in."

"You and everyone else."

Owens stepped into the room and motioned for Erin to come with her. "I got you a hall pass. You're free for a few minutes."

"He'll kill me," said Erin.

"He knows I'm here and he thinks he knows what I'm doing. Pronto, girl. Gift horse and all that."

But Erin didn't move. It came as a dismal truth to realize that she actually felt safer inside the room than outside it.

"Don't be afraid," said Owens.

And Erin followed her out. She had never felt stranger or more displaced than she did walking through the Castle as a free woman, even momentarily. The monkeys watched her from the curtain rods and a large red macaw on the landing rail called *Finnegan! Finnegan!* as Owens strode boldly along in front of her, black hair pulled back in a ponytail, wearing a simple black tank and jeans and sandals. She spoke briefly to the servants in perfect Spanish and they smiled at her and stared at Erin. Erin could see the scars that ringed the woman's wrists beneath her colorful woven bracelets and for the first time she was not disturbed by them. She wondered if she should have brought the Cowboy Defender.

They took the stairs down to the ground level and walked away from the zoo and into the commons where workmen were erecting a big white tent for the party and the early delivery trucks and vans were arriving with food and drinks and barbecues fashioned from fifty-five-gallon drums. The stage was almost complete and the roadies were muscling the monitors into place and a team of boys lugged in armloads of folding chairs and argued about their placement. Men with weapons slung over their shoulders stood in a loose perimeter watching intently. Others with long-handled mirrors inspected the delivery vehicles for bombs. Erin and Owens stood in the shade and watched.

"Benjamin's parties remind me of your wedding," said Owens.

"I was thinking the same thing."

"They're all about the music. You'll be surprised by the people who come tonight."

Erin thought back to her wedding day. Hard to believe it was two years ago, but she could picture it in fine detail—a carnival of live music and dancing and feasting and absinthe and joyously dubious behavior; no children at this event. At Bradley's insistence they'd even rented a bullring and bulls to ride, and they weren't beaten-down animals at all but the real thing and Bradley had nearly killed himself trying to ride one and later someone let them out of their pen to roam the party at will and they'd ended up in the pond to beat the heat. All of her friends and family were there and Bradley was handsome as a man could be and she wore the special dress and looking at herself one last time in the mirror as her maids fussed over her she had conceded that she was, at this one moment, beautiful in the world. She thought of Bradley now and her heart went cold.

"I can see it. But it seems like forever ago."

"Life is slow, then sudden, isn't it?"

"It can turn on a dime."

Erin looked out at the steep green hills that seemed to quarantine the Castle from the rest of the world. The thicket growing on the hillside vibrated in the growing breeze. "Are you here because you want to be or because you have to be?"

Owens looked at her. Her eyes changed with the light, and now in the storm-threatened evening they had the color and shine of a newly minted nickel. "I am free to go and do what I want. That's the first agreement I make with anyone." She held her wrists out for Erin to see. "This made me free. It was supposed to make me not at all, but it made me free instead."

"Why did you do it?"

"I couldn't find anything to live for."

"Not even for the next day or the sunset or to hear a beautiful song one more time? Not one friend you wanted to see again?"

"No, Erin. Not even those. Mike found me. It took him some time, but he made me not want to do it again."

"Then what do you live for now?"

Owens looked out at the compound. "This world is enough."

"I never believed you were his daughter."

"I'm not. It's a thin story but most people don't see through it because they don't want to."

"What's your real name?"

"Owens Finnegan is nice, don't you think?"

"Why not just tell the truth about yourself?"

"Because the truth is harder to understand than a father and a daughter."

"Are you lovers?"

"Oh, no. But I do love him. You can sure be direct when you want to, girl."

"Mom was that way. Partners, then?"

"Sometimes. We help each other."

"Do what?"

"I can act. I have a gift for it, and ambitions. I have had roles. He supports me."

"What's your part of the partnership?"

"I help him in different ways. Some are very small, such as making a phone call to pass information. Some are much bigger, such as influencing someone to do a certain thing. I don't always know why. I persuade men easily. Sometimes I don't know what I'm doing, in terms of consequence."

Erin tried to make clear sense of this, but she couldn't. "What are you to Armenta? How long have you been here?"

Owens looked at her, then away, and Erin thought she saw a slight blush come to her face. "I've been here often enough for the house birds to learn my name."

"Why did you and Mike come after Bradley? You got to know him for your own reasons. I could tell. You befriended me in order to get close to him."

Owens gave her a hard look. "Mike knew Suzanne. And he wants Bradley to do well in life. He's very loyal to the people he befriends, especially to their spouses and children."

A quick shot of alarm went through her and was gone. She wanted to tell the Finnegans to stay away and never come to another one of her shows. But she realized that they now held the only line of communication she had with Bradley and with the world. A small capsule. A piece of cloth. A bird.

She watched the men winching up the big canvas tent. A moment later a large colorful tour bus climbed toward them from the direction of the guard gate. It was painted a shiny yellow and an enormous black jaguar was depicted along its flank, stretching from the nose to the end of the bus. It was not snarling but it looked alert. There were white jungle flowers and toucans and leafing vines and below the cat were the words *Los Jaguars del Veracruz.*

"They're really here," said Erin.

"Erin, I want to ask you to perform tonight. It means more to Benjamin than you can know. And by now you understand that he becomes very angry when he doesn't get what he wants."

"Like that little disagreement with the reporter."

"And others."

"Jesus Christ, Owens. What is wrong here? What is wrong with you people?"

"Can I tell him you will perform?"

Erin held the woman's flat gray gaze. *For the child that grows inside you.* "Fine."

She watched the Jaguars of Veracruz getting off the bus now, walking slowly and stretching and looking up at the looming green hills and the Castle towering high against them. They were two sets of brothers, she knew, uneducated, raised from poverty to international stardom by blending the varied styles of music they grew up with.

Heriberto came hustling from the Castle and hugged a short stout man who walked ahead of the other four. Caesar Llanes, she knew, the front man, singer and accordionist *supremo.* He seemed to sense her watching him and he looked up at her and tiredly raised a hand in greeting. Erin was embarrassed but waved back.

A few minutes later she and Owens stood in front of the big pigeon coop and Erin watched the handsome birds strut and flutter and look back at her with their oddly optimistic expressions. Do you think my letter made it to Bradley?" asked Erin.

"It must have. You'll hear back from him in two days."

"What about the storm?"

"These are strong flyers."

"But in a hurricane?"

"Believe."

"Does Armenta trust you?"

"He doesn't trust anyone. Not even Saturnino."

"But he gave you a key and he knows we're out here."

"He knows you can't go far. If you ran away his men would find you in minutes. The jungle is thick and full of snakes and scorpions and jaguars. And no one can hide their footprints on a sandy beach. But don't run off, Erin. I enjoy your company very much. And Benjamin expects me to keep an eye on you tonight. Don't make me look bad."

Owens winked at her and Erin said nothing. The pigeons cooed and shuffled as if they shared her bewilderment at her circumstance.

"I saw Edgar Ciel leave your room not long ago. I don't know if you find him holy or not, but do be very careful of him. Even with a woman your age he's capable of things that would surprise you. Saturnino will try to take your body but Ciel will use it for more than that."

"I'm at the end of my understanding, Owens."

Owens stared out toward the courtyard and Erin saw the distance register in her gaze. "He's been fathering children all over Mexico for twenty years. Twenty-one mothers, and still counting. The mothers are always beautiful and often poor. He supports them through the Legion. Handsomely. If the mother is too young to raise his child properly, they grow up in the expensive boarding schools he builds for the rich. My school was in Monterrey. I had a terrific Catholic education. I can prove his paternity with one drop of my blood and he knows it. Mike and my lawyers have samples too, and documentation of where they came from. Ciel knows this also. So I have some influence over what he does. He fears and loathes me. I fear and loathe him."

"He carries a gun."

"He used it on my mother. Only the barrel, not the bullets. She was a novitiate like most of the other women he seduces. She was thirteen and angry at him for what he did to her. Her name is Felicita and she lives in L.A. He takes especially good care of her. She lives in a Santa Monica condo and drives fast convertibles. She has psychological and alcohol problems. I see her often when I'm home."

"Ciel seduces those faithful girls who follow him around?"

Owens nodded and looked out toward the stage. "But mostly the boys. Especially the boys. There are rumors of pictures and video."

"I didn't know they made monsters like that."

Owens unfastened her gaze and looked at Erin with a combination of pity and shame. "They're rare."

In spite of the heat Erin felt the chill run from her scalp to her feet. The heat seemed to weigh one thousand pounds upon her but the madness she felt in this place was heavier by far and it seemed to multiply by the hour.

19

A T SUNSET ERIN TOOK THE stage carrying the Hummingbird. She felt awkward and empty and alone. The crowd broke into applause as she walked into the beams of the spotlights and squinted out at them. She introduced herself and began a song off the last Erin and the Inmates CD and was surprised to hear a few Spanish-accented voices singing along.

The night was hot and humid. Her legs had gone weak and her heart beat dizzyingly fast and her eyes kept falling on the gunmen. She closed her eyes while she sang. Let me in, she thought. Please. And halfway through the song the music invited her in and she went. From there she looked out at the crowd and she saw Armenta in his black silk shirt and Owens in a brief floral dress and Saturnino and Ciel and the hundreds of others all looking up at her, and she knew that music was more durable than they were and that long after they were all dead this song would still be played by the living.

When she was done the applause was genuine and for the first time in days she began to feel the comfort and joy of the lives inside her, her own and his. What would she name him? She looked down at the stage floor and at the beautiful boots she had found in the wardrobe in exactly her size, and she waited for the clapping to end. Someone called out a Lila Downs title and by luck it was a *ranchera* she had long loved and translated into English for her own enjoyment and she sang it in that language now and after a few moments of terrible silence the audience understood what she was doing and they shouted out wildly their appreciation. It was an upbeat song so people clapped to the rhythm.

After the song she drank water from a cup sitting on her amp and this brought a rowdy ripple from the audience, who assumed it was something strong. She made a joke in Spanish about sounding better to herself with each drink and someone yelled a reply and this went back and forth for a moment as the man was clearly drunk but good humored. She looked into the lights and wiped her forehead with the back of her hand and suddenly a boy raced onstage with a white hand towel and presented it to her with a short bow, which of course drew more applause.

After her set and while the Jaguars' crew prepared for their show Owens walked Erin through the crowd, introducing her to the dignitaries. Erin felt tired but relieved. She had done all right. Her son was active inside now, as if he was relieved too.

She met two congressmen and their wives, a governor and lieutenant governor, a dozen mayors and at least as many mayoral candidates, all of whom would win their elections next July, Owens said.

"Every one of them? How can you know that?" asked Erin.

"Well, maybe not all of them," said Owens. "Some will be assassinated by Benjamin's enemies. But the ones who survive will win. They have no opponents running against them."

"Because they've been threatened?"

"Or worse. Mayors are important to the cartels, even the mayor of a small town. Because the mayors control the local police. The local police are usually poorly trained and poorly paid. And for a lot of Mexico, there is no other level of law enforcement. The states are stretched thin, and they distrust the locals. The federal troops and

police are under the control of the president and they're deeply suspicious of the state police. And of course everybody hates the federals,
especially other federals. The Navy and Army are famous for their
mutual enmity. So what you have is distrust and noncooperation and
deception and outright competition between dozens of agencies and
departments. Benjamin spends millions of dollars on elections. He
needs mayors who are either sympathetic or at least willing to leave
him alone. The best mayors are the ones who throw the support of
their police to Benjamin. There's a gaggle of mayors and soon-to-be
mayors right over there, at the table by the beer kegs."

Erin looked at them: they were already loud and plenty cheerful,
middle-aged men, most of them with their wives. Most wore Guayabera shirts and slacks. They were laughing and knocking back their
drinks.

"Then over on the other side of the bar, that table is all chiefs of
police. Almost all. There are some captains and commanders also."

These men looked rougher and less festive to Erin's eye. They observed from behind sunglasses even now at night, and were easy to
picture in uniform. Some of them wore business shirts and sports
coats in spite of the heat and humidity. They looked uncomfortable
and impatient for the music to continue.

The congressmen were dapper in the tropical weight suits, and
their wives quite beautiful in pearls and jewelry. The governor's companion was a young *gringa* from Tustin who loved Erin and the Inmates and had seen Erin perform in L.A. The woman seemed
unsurprised that Erin would be here as a guest of one of the most
wanted men in Mexico.

"Where are the Inmates?"

"They stayed home."

"I love Mexico. I feel so much more free down here."

They got margaritas at one of the bars and Erin asked for hers light on the tequila but she saw the bartender pour in two shots any-way. Onstage the roadies were testing out the mikes and monitors and tuning the stringed instruments. Erin saw the gleaming yellow-and-black accordion sitting on its stand.

"Over there are the media people," said Owens. "Some are news-paper or magazine publishers. The fat guy's a famous DJ. The guy in the cream suit is an anchor for a popular news show. The woman with him is one of the show's reporters. Felix, from the other night, he worked for their competition. So you can guess why they're here."

"Because they ignore Benjamin."

"And you won't see a camera between them. It's the new face of journalism, narco style. It's the policy of the whole network now. They leave the Gulf Cartel unnamed. But they will mention the Zetas, who are enemies of Benjamin. However, Felix's network will some-times mention the Gulf Cartel, as we saw. But they never cover the Zetas. The power of the cartels is everywhere. Mike says it's vertical—from the bottom to the top. He says the reason why the Gulf Cartel takes less federal heat than the other cartels is because Benjamin and the president know the same people."

"That's hard to believe."

"Is it?"

Erin sipped more of the drink. It was the first alcohol she'd had in two months and the powerful tequila went quickly to her head. She watched Edgar Ciel and his retinue of young novices making their way along the edge of the canopy. There were four of them now, two boys and two girls. Ciel stopped at a group of the wealthy and it parted for him and the women kissed his hand and the men bowed.

"Why do you put yourself in the middle of all this?"

"Mike asked me to come here."

"To become Armenta's mistress and confidante."

"It's the confidante that Mike wants."

"But why? What does he care what happens down here?"

"He cares what happens everywhere, Erin. You've seen how curious he is about everything. And everyone. In the years I've known him I've yet to find something or someone he *isn't* interested in. He makes friends in minutes and keeps them for life. He gets so wrapped in people and their worlds that he can go a week without sleep, helping out one friend, then going on to help out another, and not show any effects from it. He reads books in a dozen languages. He gives them to universities and libraries when he's done. Hundreds of them every year. He never forgets, even the smallest things stay with him, and he can call up a memory in high, high resolution."

Erin could hear the admiration in Owens's voice. She saw the dilation of her pupils—pride in Mike, she thought. Her boss, father, brother, friend. Her reason to live. And to sleep with a narcotics trafficker and murderer.

"So, that's why I'm here in the middle of all this," said Owens. "I know it can seem cruel and barbaric sometimes. That's what I thought at first. But Mike's world is full of people and music and art and history and incredible energy."

"Mike's world? Not Benjamin's?"

"It's the same, Erin. Mike has known Benjamin since he was born. Did you know that Benjamin was named Mexico's third richest man by *Forbes* magazine? That he donates scores of millions of dollars a year to the Legion of Christ? That his great-grandfather fought with Zapata?"

"I know he threw an innocent man to the leopards. I know he plans to skin me alive if he doesn't get my husband's money in four days. So how can his alleged greatness mean anything to me? I'm supposed to be impressed by him because *Forbes* magazine is?"

"You're an artist so you see things differently. You have to simplify things into songs. So the things you can't simplify you don't see. You make beauty, Erin. What you do is important. But it's not the world.

It's only part of the world. What you see here is another part of it, in all its glory and its pain."

"I'll stick with music."

"You have no choice. You were born to it. Mike said some people are born prone to do certain things and I believe him. He said that you are one of the great surprises of his life. He searched out Suzanne Jones. He found Bradley. And he found you too. He says that truly great men and women are not often found together. That's why we're helping you communicate."

"What if Benjamin knew?"

Owens gave her a gray-eyed stare and ran a fingernail across her throat.

As if on cue Armenta turned to look at them. Erin saw the happy smile come to his face when he looked at Owens, and when he looked at Erin she saw it grow stronger. He raised his hand to his mouth and kissed the air like a chef pleased with a sauce. Saturnino looked at her too, with a smile of a different nature, one that momentarily gutted her courage and made her look away in anger and shame. She wished she had the Cowboy Defender taped to her leg but she did not. It had come to seem increasingly useless.

The Jaguars of Veracruz took the stage at ten o'clock, by which time Erin had seen scores of gallons of alcohol consumed by the crowd of roughly one thousand people. The air hung heavy and sweet with mota smoked mostly from joints but there were pipes and bongs and huge Jamaican-style spliffs being shared too, and beautiful dinner plates piled high with fluffy cocaine being passed around from guest to guest, and they used everything from rolled currency to fingernails to bread knives in order to shovel the stuff home before the plate was passed along or set down and forgotten or spilled and refilled by whomever from a shiny new galvanized thirty-gallon trash can next to the beer kegs.

The Jaguars wore their trademark black satin suits with orange piping and elaborate multicolored embroidery on the shoulders. Their shirts were black. Erin felt swept up in their energy as they took their positions and instruments. She clapped hard but could barely hear her own hands within the riotous tumult of the crowd. When the music started the crowd let out a huge round of applause, then quickly quieted to hear the story.

Story, thought Erin. The Jaguars always tell stories. Tell me a story that will take me away from here. That's what you're doing for everyone else.

She closed her eyes for a moment and listened to the music. The Jaguars were led by Caesar Llanes, who had a frontal, penetrating voice and a strong vibrato that he used to sustain his notes. She had seen the Jaguars perform live but she was struck anew not only by their taut, bright musicianship, but by the emotional level that Caesar brought to each song. He made the words sound so important not by hiking up his voice but by taking it down just a little, making it sound almost factual to better serve the story. The songs were mainly up-tempo, but on the less urgent ones Caesar would roam the stage randomly, delivering the lines as if he were just now making them up. Really, she thought, he does very little. And makes it count for so much. The beautiful black-and-yellow accordion swung in for a fill between the verses and Erin caught herself smiling.

The song was a *narcocorrido* about a couple of young drug runners who die in a hail of bullets fired by American DEA agents in a dusty border town. It was upbeat but haunted by its inevitable catastrophe. She had heard that the narcos commissioned such songs to be written about themselves and their exploits, each cartel boss hoping for a bigger hit song than that of his rivals. Stories again, she thought: sing me a story. She'd also read that the Jaguars sorted through the thousands of letters that came to them or were thrown up onto the stage at each performance, every one a story, most of them true, and they chose the best ones and wrote their songs around them. Erin looked into the crowd and found Armenta and she saw his woebegone face looking up at Caesar as if he was hypnotized.

"He listens to music most hours of the day," said Owens. "He sleeps to music. All that hair of his? He uses it to hide the ear buds. He's always got an iPod hidden on him somewhere. He strolls around the Castle looking so intense and forbidding but he's almost always listening to music. He wears elaborate disguises and attends concerts around the world."

"He looks afraid right now."

"His greatest fear is of being betrayed by his own men."

"He scares me no matter how afraid he is. But he doesn't scare me as much as his son does."

"Stay far away from him."

"He threatened to rape me."

"Benjamin took his key. You're safe in your room."

"How can you be safe in a room where everyone knows where to find you? How hard is it for Saturnino to steal a key?"

"Benjamin rebuked him. Strongly. It's not the key that stands between you and Saturnino. It's his father."

"The head of the Gulf Cartel."

"Let's go sit with him."

"No. Stay here with me. I'm your responsibility, remember? And I can't be that close to his son."

By midnight the wind was slashing through the palm trees and the tent rippled violently to and fro against the tethers and the rain slanted through the open walls. The crowd roared just to be heard and for a moment the Jaguars huddled together back by the drum set, then they nodded and broke the huddle. Erin watched Caesar come back to center stage and peer into the lights until he found her.

—Erin, would you like to join us for some music? And please, we beg Benjamin to come up here and play the accordion for us! Come now, before the world blows away!

Another blast of wind and roar of voices and Erin found herself pushed forward by Owens and Armenta, then Caesar had stepped off the stage to offer her his hand and Armenta handed her up and followed.

Caesar unshackled himself from his splendid accordion and handed it to Armenta, then the Jaguars began their first huge hit, "Ballad of the Red Road." This too was a drug story but it focused on a betrayal by alleged friends. Erin had first heard it twenty years ago and long ago committed it to her singer's memory, a memory that was easily engaged and practically flawless. She laid back and sang harmony and tried to let the music get inside her. Caesar sang and Armenta played much better than Erin had expected, full bodied and melodic. Next they played Linda Ronstadt's "Adios" sped up to the pace of a Mexican bolero, trading verses while Armenta chimed away happily with the accordion. To Erin's ear it had a kind of daft charm but when it was over the crowd rose in ovation, though some of the first to rise with such appreciation were also the first to fall over drunk. Then the Jaguars burst into one of their new songs and Erin was utterly lost in it but she managed a harmony that fit the chorus nicely and the audience was beginning to rise for still another ovation when the wind finally ripped the tent off its stanchions and the pooled rainwater cascaded down through the lights, drenching everyone.

Erin crumpled under the weight of the soaked canvas. She rose to her knees and felt no pain so she swam forward through the clinging material until she reached an edge and lifted it, which allowed it to catch the next blast of wind and suddenly she was standing on the stage with the Jaguars, who were all emerging from the drenched sheet in their black-and-yellow blazers and black shirts with dazed smiles on their faces.

Then Caesar's amplifier began throwing sparks. He dropped his mic to the watery floor and strode off regally as the amplifier exploded into a cloud of white smoke. Manny the guitar player shucked his instrument a second later and so did the bass player, then both of them ran off stage. Overhead the stage lights popped and the glass rained down and a moment later the generators in the basement offered a series of muffled explosions and suddenly the world was dark.

The crowd roared but Erin couldn't tell if it was in disappointment or fear or even the spirit of adventure. She stepped off the stage and in the slight moonlight she could make out the politicians and their wives making for their vehicles and the policemen hustling off for their own and the media people seemingly uncertain what to do without cameras or microphones. Scores more were raiding the bar and the trash can full of cocaine and she saw the gaunt figure of Edgar Ciel gliding through the crowd, his four novitiates fanned out behind him. Armenta jumped onto the stage and started yelling. A group of armed guards detached and ran toward the Castle basement. Owens stood shivering with her arms around herself with the rain pelting down and she was looking up to the sky with a smile on her lovely face.

Erin stole down the walkway alongside the Castle, which in a moment brought her to the pigeon coop where the birds stood dry in the overhang and oddly unruffled by the storm. She walked by them and around a corner to the zoo and she could see that the grates were up and the big cats were visible in their shaded runs, the tigers pacing and the lions lying half awake with their tails twitching and the leopards sleeping big-bellied through all the excitement.

She cut across the clearing to the edge of the jungle and stood still. She saw the headlights of the vehicles crisscrossing in the darkness and she memorized the location, then ducked her way into the wet dark. The branches tugged at her hair and clothes, and the floor was covered with hard roots and some of them were exposed and grabbed at her boots. It was surprisingly cool. She pulled herself through in the direction of the headlights. The lower leaves and fronds dumped their collected rain onto her as she climbed along, lifting her feet high to keep the roots from dragging her down, and she imagined snakes waiting down there to strike and wondered if Jimmy Choo boots were snake-proof but bet not.

At the edge of the parking area she crouched behind a cluster of sea grape. She watched the cars jockey toward the one narrow exit road. Most of them had their windows down and the people sang and yelled and threw beer cans at one another while their stereos blasted away, mostly the Jaguars, but Erin could also hear Fabian Ortega and Los Tucanes de Tijuana and Ry Cooder and Luis Miguel and Julieta Venegas.

She stood on trembling legs, then stepped from the foliage into the parking area. Look calm, she thought. Look assured. Surely, someone will give the gringa singer a ride to town. She approached the SUV and held her hand against the door and saw that it was one of the mayors and his wife and she addressed them in her able Spanish.

—I need to go to town.

—You are a guest of Benjamin.

—I need medicine from the pharmacy in the morning.

—But he can have it brought to you.

—Please, can I get in?

—We cannot interfere. You must talk to the boss.

She grabbed the back-door handle but she heard the click of the locks going down and then the mayor's window rose and closed and the vehicle jumped forward. The front tires dropped into a rain-filled pothole, which threw muddy water against her knees and she could feel the grit of the dirt as the water washed down her calves and into her boots.

She splashed her way to the next vehicle, a late-model Mercedes sedan. The windows were up and the brights went on. With her hands cupped to the glass Erin could see the governor's wife sitting behind the wheel and the governor himself resting an open bottle of tequila on his thigh. The woman refused to look at her and the man waggled a finger in front of his face and shook his head as if Erin were a child and should know better.

She pushed off the car angrily and stood up straight, looked around in the rain for someone who might care. There in a swank metallic cream-colored Escalade she saw the TV network anchor and the reporter and two of the magazine editors that Owens had pointed out. Both of the windows on her side went down and the four journalists stared at her in collective disbelief.

—I need a ride. Do you have room for me?

—Aren't you a guest? said the anchor.

—I am not a guest. I am not here of my free will.

—Oh, Miss McKenna this is very, very bad. However, your music was beautiful tonight.

—He has kidnapped her, said the TV reporter. Her voice was loud, and sharp with alarm.

—Let me in.

—This is impossible, said the anchor. We cannot defy Benjamin. This would only heat the plaza.

—Fuck the plaza, friend, these people are going to kill me.

—Let her in, said the reporter.

Erin pulled on the door but it was locked and the Escalade rolled forward and bumped into the pickup truck in front of it. The cops in the truck started yelling and the anchorman hit his horn.

—Let her in. She's been kidnapped, yelled the reporter over the horn blast.

—Please let me in. I'll tell you everything.

—You will be safe now, said the anchor. See? This is perfect. You now will be safe.

With this the driver's window started up and in the glass Erin saw Saturnino close behind her, his face growing full as the window rose. She felt his hand clamp down on her arm and twist. The excruciating pain that shot into her shoulder collapsed her to her knees in the muddy lot.

—You don't have to hurt her, yelled the reporter.

—Thank you, Dolores, said Saturnino. Many thanks to everyone at 'Veracruz Tonight!'

—Be merciful to her, Saturnino.

—And you be silent, you mouth of a whore.

Saturnino pulled Erin to her feet and marched her struggling out of the parking area and toward the jungle from which she knew she would not return whole if at all.

Deep in the darkness they stopped and he clamped his hands on either side of her face very hard and dragged his tongue against her lips and teeth. She struck him and Saturnino slammed her flush on the jaw with his elbow and she went down. "Sing to *me* now," he said. Through the dizziness she felt one of his hands tight against her throat and the other yanking her dress up over her knees and waist, then tearing and rolling it up to her neck and over her face and she kept flailing at him, but most of her blows missed and none of them had the power to hurt him and she could hardly draw breath. He pulled off her underpants and drove his knees between her legs and forced them open. The jungle floor was cold and sharp against her legs and back but she thrashed and screamed into the fabric piled tight against her face. His hand was rough against her center and he pulled a handful of her hair and said again, "Sing to *me* now."

She heard a loud smack, as if he had hit her, but felt nothing. She wondered if she was passing out. She couldn't feel his hand around her throat as she gasped for a full breath, and she couldn't feel the weight of him between her legs, either. Is this how you survive it? she thought. Do you shut down in shock? Then a more terrifying and practical thought: no, he's let go of my throat and lifted up his body and he's getting himself ready. He's going to do it.

Erin lashed out with fresh terror but her fists found nothing to hit so she dug in her heels and pushed herself backward fast across the slick ground and rolled over to her knees, grabbing two big handfuls of fabric and yanking the dress all the way over her head and covering her near-naked self with it while she panted. She managed to stand and was ready to run.

Air and breath. Air and breath. Two lights. Two men. Benjamin and Father Ciel.

On the ground between them in their flashlight beams Saturnino swayed on hands and knees. He was frowning at her and his mouth hung loose. His head was split open at the hairline, a gash of white skull, a stream of blood running down his face to the jungle floor. He looked insensible but surprised.

Ciel walked around Saturnino without taking his eyes or light off him. Standing before Erin he handed her the flashlight, then took off his black jacket that smelled of vanilla and wrapped it around her while he muttered a prayer.

Numbly she stared past him. Benjamin sat on his haunches a few feet in front of Saturnino, who had collapsed. Benjamin's forearms rested on his knees and the flashlight dangled from one hand, the beam ending at the ground. He looked like a man trying to reason things out. She lifted the torch beam to Armenta's face and saw the agony on it.

20

Late in the black morning Ivana's wind finally pushed the Chevrolet off the highway. The car planed to his right and Hood steered into the drift and touched the brakes and watched the wall of rainwater crest up to his left, then fall. The heavy old Impala righted its course and slid back into its lane. When he sensed that the car wasn't about to slide off again he leaned forward and wiped the fogged-up windshield with a wad of paper napkins, the defroster nonoperational.

"You drive almost as good as a Veracruzano," said Luna.

"It's a bad enough highway without a hurricane," said Hood.

"It's a famously bad highway, even for Mexico. We will stop and stay in Tuxpan."

"A famously bad city for floods," said Hood.

"I hope it is not to be having another."

They had been driving all night, putting all the miles they could between themselves and the Reynosa police, trying to make as much progress toward Merida as they could before Ivana ground them to a halt. One man napped while the other drove but there was no real sleep for Hood, who saw the slaughter of Julio again and again, wondering if he should have said something to Julio as he stood outside the motel room door, something to confirm that he was alone and okay; or if he should have looked through the window to make sure that everything was fine before opening the door. But he had not and the young man was dead along with five baby *narcos* who seemed poorly prepared for the violence they had commenced.

They checked into the Floridita Hotel and got a second-floor room. Hood gave the clerk a photo album of Mike Finnegan pictures with a hundred dollar bill in it, got the usual answer, and made his usual offer. Upstairs in their room Hood handcuffed the suitcase to a bathroom water pipe. He knew the quaint little luggage locks and a mere water pipe were no obstacles to determined men, but might discourage the undecided or the merely curious. They tossed a coin to guard the money or go get food. Hood won and opted to run the errand and took his gun.

An hour past sunrise the sky was a close dark ceiling and the rain continued and the wind buffeted the town. The water was up over the curbs and Hood's shoes were soon soaked but from what he could see it was a pretty little city, built along the Tuxpan River, with Mexican Navy frigates and Pemex tankers berthed against the lush greenery, and nicely kept homes and businesses along the water.

He stopped at a newsstand and bought papers, then found a cafe for coffee and pastries. On the walls were framed photographs of the famous *inundaciones* of 1930 and 1999, and Hood was struck not just by the water standing head-high against the buildings, but by how little those buildings had changed in the sixty-nine years between the photos. He looked through the window at the Tuxpan River and compared it to the river in the 1999 photograph and thought it had a long way to go to get that high. Outside, the rain was steady. A group of children floated plastic boats down the flooded street past a Volkswagen dealership.

A man and woman blasted in from outside in a rush of wind and rain. They wore official clothing—khaki safari shirts with emblems over the pockets and matching drenched baseball caps with emblems also. The man was a large Mexican and the woman a stout gringa who pulled off her cap and shook it outside quickly, then pulled the door shut. She nodded at Hood as the big man went to the counter unleashing a torrent of words to match the rain.

Hood read the logo on the woman's shirt: RC. He picked out a few of the man's urgent words. *Six hundred crocodiles! The rain flooded the ponds and the water rose! All escaped!*

"Crocodiles?" Hood asked.

"River crocodiles," said the woman. Her face was flushed with excitement and she was breathing hard. "They're endangered. We're with the Reserva Cocodrilo in Alamo, up the river. We've raised hundreds of river crocs. The rain in Alamo is much heavier than here but we had no idea the water could rise so fast and we did what we could. We caught some of the hatchlings and juveniles and put them in our pickup truck. But the rest just swam away. You can't rescue a fifteen-foot crocodile who doesn't want to be rescued."

The big man turned with a cup of coffee and handed it to the woman. He looked at Hood and said *buenos dias*, then turned back to the counter woman and continued his tale.

"Where will they go?" asked Hood.

"Where the river takes them. Which will be pretty much right here. Tuxpan. It'll take them a while to get this far, I'd guess."

"Are they dangerous?"

"They're wild animals and they can go twelve feet long in the wild. We have some larger. Quite a few, actually. The big ones weigh over a thousand pounds. Very heavy and wide. They can take off an arm or a leg pretty easy. Then you bleed to death."

"Do they eat people?"

"Not regularly. We feed them chickens and fish."

"Six hundred."

"We're trying to find a way to tell the people here not to kill or capture them. They're *not* a danger unless you provoke them. Or if you don't know what you're doing. I thought of making up some signs, but in this rain and wind . . ."

"What about the radio stations?"

"The Tuxpan radio tower is down. The power lines along Highway One-eighty blew over an hour ago. Long distance is shot. We'll do what we can to let people know. The sad part is the crocs themselves. They'll just wash up downriver and people will kill them."

"I hope you can save a few at least."

"We got twenty or so in the truck outside. Little ones."

"Good luck to you, then."

Hood put the newspapers in the two plastic bags, then shouldered his way back outside. He went to the children with the boats and told them about the crocodiles that might be washing into Tuxpan. They looked at him as if he'd just ruined their day. He led them over and held them up one at a time and they looked into the bed of the reserve pickup at the crocodiles. Some were trying to scamper up the walls of the truck bed, others just lay in the rain motionless and prehistoric, their big tan eyes and vertical pupils wide against the world.

"*Tener cuidado*," he told them, pointing to the river down which the crocs would come.

He began his way back toward the Floridita picturing six hundred fifteen-footers weaving their ways through the streets of Tuxpan. He had seen National Geographic TV crocodiles, and their girth and speed had always impressed him. He looked up and down the flooded streets for the telltale knobby snouts of the crocs but saw nothing.

The bags of food in his hands made him think of Julio Santo. What a pleasant and intelligent young man he had seemed, and proud of his city and of his calling. Proud of Juarez, thought Hood. When human nature seems nothing but bleak you get a guy who's proud of his violence-wracked city and you think well, maybe human nature has a chance.

He strode through the rain past the fountain at city hall still oddly gurgling away during the rainstorm and past the aqua taxi stand, where a family laden with bags of oranges and bananas from across the swelling river was stepping off the boat. Hood paused and shifted both bags to one hand and slid his .45 from its hip holster to the pocket of his water-resistant jacket, by now thoroughly soaked by the storm. He leaned into the wind and kept his eyes moving and every hundred feet or so he looked behind him for gunmen or crocodiles and kept going.

They ate their breakfast and slept and that afternoon the rain continued steadily and the wind was harder. Hood could see from their second-floor window that the street was under a foot of water and there were no children playing and only two trucks still moving, and that people below were boarding up not only the first-story doors and windows but those on the second levels as well.

At three o'clock the power in the Floridita failed or was shut off to prevent catastrophe. Hood slipped a penlight from his pocket and found the candles back on the closet shelf. Luna tried to use his satellite phone but there was no service. Through Ivana's great bluster Hood could hear the sounds of alarm downstairs, voices calling out and the loud thumps of furniture being moved or dropped.

Downstairs in the storm-dark lobby he found the staff and some of the guests using buckets to bail rainwater into wheeled plastic laundry hampers. Young children and old people sat or stood on the check-in desk to be out of the water and some of the children were running up and down the shiny wood counter but others were crying and the old people stubbornly ignored the world around them. One of them held an umbrella over her head. Hood saw that the floor was a foot underwater already and it was pouring in under the door and around the windows and surging up from the basement faster than they could work.

The rain accelerated, louder and faster. Outside the water charged down the sidewalk past the floor-to-ceiling windows, two feet high against the glass and Hood wondered if they would hold up against the debris that was sure to come. A small dog swam with the current looking for dry land but there was none. Palm fronds and coconuts and wads of foliage rushed along toward the Gulf of Mexico. No crocodiles. Hood found a bucket back in the flooded kitchen and joined in.

A minute later he helped four other people trying to push one of the hampers outside to be emptied. They managed to muscle it to the doorway and others held open the lobby doors so they could force it outside and Luna and two other people joined in and they pushed and pulled it into the sidewalk current, but when they tried to tip it over the floodwaters plucked it away from them and down the street it zoomed, wheels up and sinking until it stopped against a car left parked against the curb.

The manager sloshed in from his office with the news that the highway had been washed out both north and south of town, which meant that Tuxpan was now isolated and on its own. "And the airport too is closed, of course," he said. He looked at Hood. "Maybe Señor Bravo, we may let some of the older people and children come to your room for safety?"

Hood thought of the money that was Erin McKenna's life but he did what he had to do. "Yeah. Sure."

Hood and Luna led them up the stairs and unlocked the door and let them in—six elderly, four children and their mothers. The children climbed onto the beds and started jumping up and down while the oldsters tried to shoo them off so they could sit. Luna talked calmly to the children in Spanish while he found a pad of hotel stationery, several postcards and two pens from the desk drawer, a handful of plastic wrist restraints from his travel bag and a dispenser of dental floss from his shave kit, all of which he delivered to the two older kids with orders to share and to play quietly. They looked at the items, then back to Luna hopefully. Then they nodded and quieted down and Hood could see that they were respectful of the thick-necked, muscular bull of a man that was Valente Luna. One of the girls was already wrapping the floss around one of the pens in a decorative flourish.

In the bathroom Hood made sure the suitcase was still locked and he told himself if he just stayed vigilant and alert the money would be fine and the hurricane would pass and he would be in Merida in two days, on time and ready to deal. He could feel the wind shivering the roof and took some comfort that the Floridita had been pictured on the walls of the breakfast cafe, having withstood the flood of 1999, and would surely survive this.

He went back into the crowded room and looked out one of the windows. A drowned cow floated down the middle of the street toward the river. Then a wooden chair painted yellow and a small Airstream travel trailer and a white minivan. There were clots of foliage racing past and a large king palm bobbing upright on the ballast of its root-ball and a larger palm tree snapped off midtrunk. A man rode a truck tire down the rapids, centered on the wheel and holding on to the treads for his life, the tire spinning wildly and flipping over and back and over and back again in utter torture of him. A blue sedan. A Brahma bull. A refrigerator with magnets and stickers somehow still attached to the door.

Hood felt the wind hurling itself against the building again and he thanked God it was built of concrete blocks. He hoped they had used good rebar and lots of it. He knew that so long as the roof held, the danger wasn't the wind but the water undercutting the foundation enough for the heavy concrete to collapse.

He waited for one of the families to come out of the bathroom, then checked on the suitcase and it was all right so he came back and looked out again to where the wind blew the palm trees flat and blew the rain flat too. It looked like they were not being blown at all but rather sucked in by some great beast with its mouth tight to the horizon.

By evening both the children and oldsters were either asleep or wanting food so some of the mothers raided the downstairs kitchen and returned with loaves of bread and a pot of cold tortilla soup from the refrigerator, a bowl of cooked rice, a large tray of flan, bagsful of beers and sodas, flatware and plates.

Hood sat dutifully on the toilet beside the suitcase, dinner plate on his knees, listening to the rain lash the walls and thinking of Beth Petty back in Buenavista.

After an unusually violent flurry of rain and wind, he rose and went into the room and stared through a window to the street. The floodwater was almost to the tops of the ground-level doorways now, its ownership of Tuxpan nearly complete.

An hour before sunset the room shook violently, then pitched toward the flooded street. It felt to Hood as if one corner of the foundation had been pulled away. He lost his balance and fell to one knee. Several of the others fell fully and hard, and the children yelped out, terrified. There was a great grinding roar from below, then the windows burst. Hood knew they were going over and braced himself. A long moment passed. Then, as if saved by invisible brakes, the Floridita came to a shuddering stop and now hung precariously in midair over the street. Hood and everyone else in the crowded room instinctively flattened themselves to the floor but gravity pulled them forward toward the gaping glass-toothed window openings and the raging brown torrent below. He crawled back into the bathroom and found the suitcase slid nearly to the downside wall, outstretched on its handcuff chain. Luna crawled in too and saw the luggage and they gave each other wordless looks and Hood felt the building start to fall again.

He climbed onto the suitcase and reached his arms around it and held on tight. Again he heard the great shear of the foundation parting and again the room hurtled downward. But the Floridita fell faster this time, and it was still accelerating as it whooshed into the floodwaters below, then burst apart like a tower of dominos.

Hood landed hard in the water and held fast to the money. He felt the water pipe break free. He took a deep breath as the current took him down. He had ridden bodyboards in the Pacific and now he tried to use the same balance to control the suitcase but he was rolling over and over in the current and knew his breath would not last long. He grabbed a handle and dropped through the torrent to the street and felt his feet touch bottom then lift off, and when they hit bottom again he sprang skyward and at the apex of his feeble jump managed to suck in one blessed lungful of air.

Nearer the surface the nylon suitcase established buoyancy. Hood held on with one hand and with the other he pulled himself toward an orange tree gliding past and when he grabbed a branch it lifted and pulled him and the suitcase along, floating not sinking. He breathed hard and looked futilely for Luna. Instead he saw one of the children from the Floridita down current, bashing valiantly to stay afloat and crying, and Hood, kicking for all he was worth, was able to steer his barge so the boy could take the nearest handle. The suitcase with its plastic-wrapped million in cash and the orange tree were lifesavers as

Hood and the boy careened down the middle of the flooded street, past the last buildings to where the town ended, then swiftly accelerating straight and deep into the raging Tuxpan River.

They raced. Far ahead through the gray evening and the pelting rain loomed the Navy frigates and the Pemex tankers and the barges and beyond them rose the towers of the oil platforms. From across the suitcase the boy looked at Hood in wordless terror. Hood could see a black dog paddling amidst the logs and brush and suddenly they were among hundreds of rose bushes in blooms of many colors, all in identical black plastic pots, dipping and bobbing wildly, the flowers bowed but stubbornly undestroyed.

Hood felt their slow clockwise pivot as they raced midriver. He tried to kick the crude barge toward the nearest shore but he sensed no influence over their speed or bearing.

—Are we going to die?

—We will live.

—How?

—We're not ready to die.

—Who will save us?

—Whatever you believe in will save you.

—When?

—We'll reach the harbor soon. The water will be slower and we will swim to shore.

—I don't like the dark.

—It's not dark yet, but some of the lights in the harbor are on. See.

—As long as I see lights I can live.

—Good, then. Watch the lights.

—There are sharks in the harbor and sometimes crocodiles but I can live.

—Done deal. I'm Charlie.

—I'm Juan.

21

THE RAIN SLOWED AND THE wind slackened and the evening light turned to pewter. Hood felt suddenly cold and very sleepy. He laid his head over on one shoulder and looked out at the Navy ships and the lights of the oil platforms just beyond the harbor. He could still feel the speed of his makeshift barge but it seemed less now and its rotation was slower too as the Tuxpan River widened into harbor. Hood roused himself and tried to kick them to the port shore, where he could see the smattering of lights and the Navy ships and oil rigs grown taller, looming in the gray sky. The boy was quick to join him, holding the suitcase handle with just one hand and trailing his legs out and kicking steadily.

After tiring minutes of this Hood looked ahead again to judge their progress and saw that they were farther from the port shore than ever and drifting to starboard.

—We can't fight the current.

—Are we going to die?

—Let's go with the river. Let it save us.

—That is the wild side not the safe side. There is only the light-house and swamps and that is all.

—It's where the river wants to take us.

—I'm going to pray again.

They surrendered to the river and it took them toward the starboard shore. Hood floated and watched. Ivana had saturated the world and now the evening cool condensed the moisture into fog. Through this quiet silver blanket drifted the river and its random cargo—not far from him, Hood could see a Ford coupe, a lifeless horse, a tangle of resin chairs apparently lashed together so they couldn't blow away, a wooden picnic table, a freezer with a big Fanta advertisement on it, a cable spool, the roof of a *palapa*, a gate made of palm fronds, hundreds of plastic bottles.

Hood heard Juan's teeth chattering, but the boy said nothing. Hood kicked easily with the current and soon he could see the low round tree line of the jungle. He pointed at the orange tree toward the shore. Voices carried across the river from the port side, a woman crying and men shouting, but here on the wild shore was only silence. He could still see the frigates and the tankers and the barges and Hood thought he saw people gathered on them but wasn't sure. A flare wobbled into the sky and opened into a dome of bright white light.

—Are they looking for us?

—They are signaling us.

—It's not dark yet. They should save the flares. Where are my mother and father?

—I don't know.

—Why are we alone? There were many people in your hotel room.

It dawned on Hood that Ivana might have drowned every last one of them.

—We're safe now. The shore is close. We can walk back to town if there's a trail.

The current eased them nearly to shore and Hood kicked to make landfall. His teeth were chattering too and he felt exhaustion coming over him. The wind kicked up in a furious gust and suddenly the rain was blasting down again. Juan looked at Hood with a woebegone expression, but he said nothing. They drifted for what seemed like hours though Hood's wristwatch proved him wrong. The hurricane weakened and raged, then weakened.

At evening's end and without warning, a branch of the river not visible until now drew them into the jungle. They drifted down the middle of the channel with the mangrove banks on either side. The roots had collected hundreds of plastic bottles that undulated and gleamed dully in the failing light. There were watermelons and pine-apples and mangos bobbing. A fat snake pushed along the edge of the mangroves, head high, then joined the roots and vanished.

They floated into a small sheltered bay. Hood felt the eddy slowly spin them toward a sandy beach. The bay and beach were littered with flotsam and jetsam of every kind, from driftwood to furniture to a Volkswagen van that had floated up against the mangroves. Hood saw that dozens of the battered roses were bobbing just offshore or had washed up on the beach. The beach was strewn with logs appar-ently loosed from an upstream lumber mill. The black dog they had seen was watching them from atop a big shit-stained rock that rose abruptly from the sand.

Then Hood felt the river bottom and he pushed the barge onto the shore. He climbed onto dry land without letting go of the suitcase, then he and the boy dragged the bag onto the sand.

—Do you have your clothes in this?

—Clothes and other things.

—Things that float.

—Thank you for saving my life.

—Thank you for saving mine.

Hood and Juan pulled the suitcase a few yards farther up the beach and lay back on either side of it. For a long while they were silent. Another flare lit the darkening sky to the north. Hood sat up and looked around for a road or trail leading back to Tuxpan, but saw neither. He guessed they were three miles away, maybe four. The dog barked at them once and Hood wondered why it didn't just climb down from the rock and come over. He whistled and the dog stood and wagged its tail and barked again but didn't come down.

Darkness closed and Hood looked at the logs scattered on the beach. They were long, straight and thick, stripped of branches, ready to be milled. Thirty of them, maybe forty. Valuable, thought Hood.

Then one of them opened its very long mouth and Hood saw the pale inside of it and the long teeth, and he heard the wheeze of a yawn and the hollow knock of the jaws closing.

Juan wheeled at the sound and the dog barked.

—Crocodile, he whispered.

—More than one, Hood whispered back.

—They are everywhere.

—The reserve experts told me they don't eat people regularly.

—I heard of a boy who was eaten. I saw one eat a pig. They shake the animal to pieces and then they eat the pieces. These are the very big ones from the reserve. What do we do?

—Let's sit still and think.

Hood watched another of the crocs lurch forward, then stop and apparently fall back asleep. He heard a rippling in the water and when he turned he saw the black shape of the crocodile just now climbing onto the beach. It rose, dripping onto all fours and lumbered curvingly to an unoccupied part of the sand and plopped down. The dog barked until the croc stopped moving.

Hood looked in the direction of Tuxpan. In a straight line between them and the town were a hundred feet of sand beach, eight crocodiles, then miles of jungle.

—Is there a road from here to Tuxpan?

—Yes. It is narrow and dirt but good.

—Do you know where it is?

Juan pointed toward the jungle.

—There.

—Can you find it?

—It is a good road.

—I asked if you could find it.

—I don't want to die.

—I think we can get past the crocodiles and into the jungle. I don't think they will bother us.

—Why wouldn't they eat us?

—Because they are tired like we are and not ready to eat.

—They can tear off your foot and eat it with the shoe still on.

—But after we get into the jungle we can't go to Tuxpan without the road.

Hood watched as another croc stirred, opened its gaping jaws, then slowly closed them. Another jerked forward as if dreaming of a kill. The dog barked and the newly arrived croc snapped at something so fast that Hood never saw the movement, just the afterimage of it. But he clearly heard the meaty whack of the mouth closing.

—They smell us, Charlie.

Another crocodile rose and swung its tail in a big arc that threw sand into the river. It seemed to be looking at them and it took two steps in their direction, then settled back down with a heavy exhale, a log ready for the mill.

—I'll carry the bag. You can go first because you'll be faster.

—I want you to go first.

—Then I'll go first. I'm going to run between that one there, and the two that are on his right.

—But that one is the biggest.

—If we go to his right we will be headed for Tuxpan. And look, there are probably forty others if we choose the other directions.

—Crocodiles like to eat human feet because they know we make boots out of them.

—You can wait and if they come after me you can run where they are not.

—No. I go with you. You have a gun.

—Let's do this quickly, Juan. I'm going to stand, take the suitcase in one hand and my gun in the other, and run like hell.

—I will also run like hell.

—Let's stay close to each other in the jungle.

—I don't know where the road is.

—I know you don't. We can find it. Okay, Juan—let's get it done.

Hood drew his pistol and grabbed the long-side suitcase handle and started up the beach. The bag was waterlogged and profoundly heavy and the drenched sand sucked his feet deep, then closed quickly over them. He was aware of Juan behind him and slightly to his right. He saw the logs coming to life around them, even the ones far up the beach. The big croc on his left suddenly rose and watched them. The two animals to his right both stirred and stood alertly. Fifty feet to the thicket of jungle. His heart beat very fast and his feet were sinking deep and were hard to pull out of the heavy sand and the bag was a cumbersome anchor. Forty feet. The big croc looked at them and Hood knew that their eyesight was excellent. The two animals to his right did likewise.

By the time all three of them had focused and made up their minds to kill them, Hood and Juan were just fifteen feet from the foliage. Under the weight of the suitcase and sunk nearly to his knees in drenched sand, Hood stumbled. Juan appeared on his right. Ten feet to go. Five.

The crocodiles launched with speed supernatural. Hood swept up Juan with his gun hand and held him tight against his shoulder and he charged forward into the black jungle. He churned across the firmer ground, ramming his lowered head and shoulder through the branches and the leaves, ripping the heavy suitcase through behind him. He ducked onto a path through a stand of river cane.

With the harder ground under him he managed a balance between the boy and the luggage and he leaned forward for speed. The dog shot past them, ears back and disappeared around a bend. Through the high walls of Carizzo cane the trail wandered, a faint, meandering miracle. He tried to run faster but had no strength left. He was pretty sure that crocodiles hunted only in water but he didn't look back. He slipped and stumbled but kept a hold on both of his precious bundles. His breath came in short fast bursts and his legs felt heavy and slow. Up ahead he saw a clearing. He told Juan to be ready. Hood plodded all the way through to the end of the clear ground before launching Juan as high into the cane as he could, dropping the suitcase and turning to face the crocs with his gun up and ready, the barrel of it pitching down and up with his desperate breathing like a ship on high seas.

No crocs. Hood tried to hold the weapon steady where the monsters would come in but he couldn't quite. He tried to listen for them but he couldn't stop panting. Suddenly Juan slipped off the thick slick poles of the river cane and landed hard and now he crouched at Hood's side with a short length of green cane in his hand, ready to fight.

—Is there. A way out?

—Yes, see the dog.

—You. Go.

—I fight.

—I won't. Argue.

—You are too fast for them.

Hood stopped and wrestled the suitcase upright, then went down on one knee and rested his pistol on the bag. With the butt held firm he could cover the narrow opening into the clearing. He still had not heard them, no sounds at all coming from the jungle, no monkeys or night birds, no fish hunting in the mangroves or river lapping the shore, nothing but his own deafening breath.

A minute went by. Hood recovered quickly as young men do.

—They don't come.

—I hope you're right, Juan.

—I'll show you the trail. It is made by cows.

The dog vanished again and Juan led. Hood lugged the suitcase from the clearing onto the trail. It was a narrow trail like the other. They marched briskly, taking long strides and the only sound was the sloshing of their shoes in the mud and cow dung and the lighter splashing of the dog up ahead. It was dark but there was enough light for them to follow the trail. Behind him Hood heard a flare pop open and at the edge of his vision he caught an echo of its light.

Half a mile toward Tuxpan the trail broadened to a path and became firmer and Hood was able to pull the suitcase rather than carry it. He pulled it gladly, his left arm aching. He looked at the dog trotting gaily on point and Juan not far behind, and he glanced down at Erin McKenna's rescue bouncing along the muddy trail and he knew that he had gotten away with something huge and impossible to get away with, or maybe possible to get away with only once in a lifetime, and this had been that once.

The trail became a path that became the road and they trudged toward Tuxpan. There were fallen trees and clusters of giant river cane and grass and sea grape heaped upon the road, leaking snakes of every size, and Hood ploddingly dragged the suitcase around them like an exhausted passenger in a late-night terminal.

They walked into Tuxpan just before one in the morning. The electricity had not been restored and the streets were under a foot of water. Most of the buildings were still standing. City Hall was intact and appeared to be open as a shelter of some kind, generators humming, some lights on, people coming and going through the front doors with food and supplies. There was a Red Cross truck parked outside with its red lights flashing. The Palacio Municipal and the downtown shops and offices and hotels looked fine also. People had gathered on the higher floor balconies and they looked down at Hood and the boy as they sloshed along. Some waved. As they walked, Hood saw that a small mercado had fallen in upon itself, and an apartment complex was missing, and some of the humble homes on slightly higher ground above the river were gone also.

The Floridita was now only half a foundation tilted radically toward the street, the other half undercut and washed away by the raging waters. Hood and Juan stood and looked. The quaint old hotel was simply not there—no hand-painted Hotel Floridita sign, no welcoming lobby, no cheerful floral display or ceiling fan visible through the high glass windows, nothing. What was not swept away lay visible before them for a hundred feet or more, the water racing through it like a river around rocks. There were jagged piles of cinder blocks with the rebar jutting out, and the twisted remnants of water pipes and faucets and sinks and bathtubs and toilets—anything heavy enough to sink and resist the flood.

Hood saw that Juan's chin was trembling.

—We'll find them. Let's go to City Hall. Where do you live?

—Veracruz.

—Why did you and your mother come to Tuxpan?

—To see my aunt. My father stayed home to work. What if everybody is dead?

—Let's be hopeful.

—What if God only had time to save us and not them?

At City Hall they found Juan's mother and Luna and most of the other people who had been in the room. Two of the elderly and one child were still not accounted for, and there were volunteers ready to search the riverbanks between Tuxpan and the harbor as soon as there was enough light. There were rumors of government help but no actual help.

Juan fled to his mother's arms and they both cried and hugged each other and Juan's sisters closed in also and Hood felt good in a way that he had not felt good in a long time. Juan's mother looked up at him through her tears and smiled.

Hood and Luna sat on folding chairs in a corner and ate flavorless Mexican pastries and drank good coffee.

"I was worried about you," said Hood.

"I was not worried about you," said Luna. "Not with your bag of pesos to protect."

"It floated me and the boy."

"Eight dead, that they know of."

"I know we were lucky. You should have seen those crocodiles, Valente."

"I have seen them. Very, *very* lucky."

Hood looked at the villagers, many of them indigenous. The Indians were compact and quiet and kept mostly to themselves.

Luna had already checked the Impala, which Hood had had the foresight to park on the second floor of a pay parking lot across from the hotel. Luna had dried the plugs and the distributor and the car was operable even though the highway was closed in both directions. He had also grabbed Hood's travel duffel as well as his own just before the Floridita finally fell into the water. The duffels were drenched but standing side by side in the corner, their zippers open so the contents could begin to dry. Hood briefly pawed through his things, glad to have stored his Mike Finnegan photo albums and the satellite phone in doubled, locking freezer bags. The vacuum-wrapped ransom money was mostly undamaged.

"If we can't use the roads we can't get to Merida," he said. "Armenta doesn't seem like the type to give us a rain check."

"They'll pick us up this evening," said Luna. He nodded to his duffel, where his satellite phone sat atop a wad of plastic grocery bags. "I know a captain with the Veracruz State Fugitive Police. I have done him favors."

"Even police vehicles can have trouble on a flooded-out highway."

"Helicopter."

Hood thought about the difficulty of arranging that, in the middle of such a disaster. "I guess you did him some large favors."

"They were very large, yes."

Juan and his mother and two sisters came over and sat with them for a while. The mother introduced herself as Teresa de Asanto and she never stopped stroking her son's dark hair. She explained to Hood that her husband had stayed home to work and this was good because their home in Veracruz was old and built to take such calamity. He was a manager in the city government. She was a travel agent in a hotel and she wished she would have stayed home too. Juan ate five pastries and was reaching for a sixth when his mother cut him off. Juan had much to say about his night.

—The crocodiles chased us but we got away! Charlie threw me in the river cane!

Hood handed the woman one of his Finnegan photo albums and she looked at the pictures patiently, then gave Hood an odd look before shaking her head no and handing the booklet back to him. He said she could keep it and he told her about the thousand dollars but she refused to touch it when he held it out to her.

—I meant no obligation.

—No. No obligation. But you have my gratitude for saving Juan.

—He's brave and capable.

—He's eight years old and I thank you again.

In the multipurpose room there were cots set up and people slept or read the lobby magazines and newspapers or played cards because there was no way to leave Tuxpan except on foot.

Another rain front crept in and Hood fell asleep to the sound of it tapping the roof. It was a light rain that sounded almost apologetic. He dreamed of crocodiles chasing him through a jungle with his son in his arms and in the dream he was sure they would not catch him. When he came to a clearing he ran into it and spread his nylon wings and flew away.

He opened his eyes early in the evening to find Juan's mother bent over his duffel in the half-light. She set something underneath the bag, then turned away silently and stole back in the direction of her family.

Hood stayed still for a few minutes, then sat up on his cot. He wrote a letter to Beth, about everything that had happened to him in the last days. *Dear Beth, I have seen the most amazing things . . .* He tried hard to explain killing the gunman, and this came easily to him because he had killed in order to preserve his own life, but when he tried to explain how he felt about it he started sounding sentimental and he finally had to settle on the word "bad." Reading over the letter, Hood decided it was a rather dry synopsis of events and he wished he could really write up a story like it was supposed to be written. He liked Conrad and Jack London and Steinbeck and Tom Wolfe and Sebastian Junger. He smelled coffee and heard voices coming from the lobby. Through the window he saw one of Tuxpan's remaining palm trees swaying only slightly in the breeze. *No rain*, thought Hood. *No rain, please.*

He slid his hand under the duffel and brought away what had been placed there by Juan's mother. It was a page from one of the glossy magazines, folded into a triangle. He half expected it to contain money and he hoped it did not. But the page contained nothing but an advertisement for shampoo and some very neat feminine handwriting in the upper left corner.

Taberna Roja
Avenida Zaragoza
Veracruz, Veracruz

Hood memorized the words then refolded the paper and slipped it into the freezer bag with the pictures of Finnegan.

An hour later he sat in the back of a Bell 204 twisting off the roof of the Palacio Municipal and into the spent subtropic sky.

22

BRADLEY LOOKED THROUGH THE WINDSHIELD at the Campeche lowlands. They had ridden out Ivana in the Sierra Madre de Chiapas and he was thankful to be off the precarious mountain roads and making good time on Highway 186.

It was Sunday afternoon on the seventh day after the kidnapping and they were one hundred miles from Erin. Crisp shafts of sunlight came down through the trees. Bradley felt edgy and impatient. A day and a half was plenty of time to travel a hundred miles by truck, he thought, so why was he stuffed with anxiety and dread? Did at least one of the pigeons make it through the hurricane? One, he thought: we only need one. He fidgeted inside the antiballistic vest. The vests were hot and sweat inducing and they pinched the flesh and itched incessantly where it was hard to scratch. His palm was still open from Mike's knife. The wound would neither heal nor fester but rather remained half-closed and half-open, prone to painful accidents. He bummed another cigarette off Cleary and with his thumbnail flicked the wooden Mexican match to life.

They stopped in Las Flores for gas and cold drinks but the *mercado* shelves were practically bare. They found a few cases of bottled fruit punch and discounted packs of old tortillas, along with spicy corn chips and bananas. There were still cases of frijoles so they bought three of these and Caroline got the last ten gallons of bottled water and Cleary bought a carton of Mexican Marlboros. Young Omar tried to buy tequila but Fidel ordered him not to.

Bradley sipped the warm punch and tried to scratch his back against the gas pump while he watched the numbers race and the 1500 suck up almost a hundred liters of Pemex supreme. Fidel joined him, leaning against the SUV. He seemed cool and comfortable and impervious to the vests.

"Two more days, amigo."

"I know what day it is," said Bradley.

"Are you afraid to think about it?"

"I'm more afraid not to."

"You've done what you can. It's now up to her."

Bradley thought of Fidel walking into the warehouse where his wife and family hung dead. He couldn't imagine Erin in such a way and he wanted to say something to Fidel but there were few words he knew that were adequate and not overworn.

"I hope you get your vengeance. I'll help you if I can."

"Your soul is not black enough for that."

"You might be surprised."

Bradley looked at the village. The streets were dirt and the buildings had once been gaily painted but now the blues and yellows and cinnamon colors were long faded. Windows were broken or boarded. In the zocalo there were concrete benches arranged in a circle around a cracked concrete patio. The square was empty except for thin dogs watching them with suspicion and distant hope. The church stood at the far end of the square, its bell tower crumbling. Bradley saw that the *panaderia* was closed and boarded and so were the butcher shop and the shoe store. The newspaper office was doorless and abandoned and there were bullet holes in the windows. There was a mini-super across the street and outside its doorway stood a stout woman in a dark gray dress with two young children. She shooed them inside but stood her ground. Bradley nodded and she did nothing. There was a cantina with three trucks parked outside and an old man sitting out front on a wooden bench. The door was open and Bradley could hear faint music from inside.

"The government fears the Zapatistas in the Sierra Madre," said Fidel. "And they fear the Gulf Cartel. We are in the heart of their plaza. Armenta grew up not far from here. Rebels and drug cartels get along very well because the cartels provide jobs for the poor, growing *mota* and the poppies. Of course this is illegal. But those wealthy cartels that pay their bribes to the police and government, their people can grow all they want. In this way the government and the cartels work together to produce Mexico's most valuable crops. But those without cartel sponsors? Or those who want to work for another set of cartel masters? They suffer. They don't dare pick up a shovel to help themselves. Their fields are burned, or worse. But sometimes even the peasants who have jobs, they get ideas and they make demands of the government or the cartels. That happened here in Las Flores. They demanded that the school be rebuilt and that fresh water be supplied and that their protection payments be made smaller. A cartel enforcer disappeared near here. So the village is being starved. They are mostly Maya—they speak no Spanish and they worship their own gods and they disdain the Mexican government. Military patrols intercept the delivery trucks to this village, and send them back. Gulf Cartel patrols terrorize them with extortion and beatings and the rape of women and girls. So the *mercados* look like the one we were just in. Not enough food. Not enough water. Not enough medicine. In a few weeks the delivery trucks will stop coming here altogether. The people will leave for other villages or cities. For Villahermosa or Campeche or Chetumal. Some of them will disappear into the jungle and live in camps. Sooner or later the government will allow the supplies to come through and things will return to normal."

"Normal."

"Our normal. Mexico is cursed. So far from God and so close to the United States."

Bradley nodded at the aphorism, then took the pump nozzle in his hand to top off the tank. His palm wound barked.

"What I want most out of this is Saturnino," said Fidel. "He belongs to me."

"If everything goes right, there won't be a Saturnino. There will be Erin and we'll get her and get the hell out."

"And what if everything does not go right?"

They passed northeast through Escárcega. The lowlands spread flatly before them, rainforest thick with ceibas and strangler figs and Honduras Mahogany. The highway was straight and narrow and bleached gray by the Yucatecan sun.

Caroline Vega leaned forward from the back bench seat, her shiny black hair flooding onto the center console between the men. Bradley had seen the attraction growing between her and Fidel and it angered him because it detracted from their sense of mission. Caroline rarely engaged anyone, but she was engaging Fidel often.

"How long?"

"One hundred kilometers," said Fidel.

"I like the ruins. Can we stop and look?"

"We're not stopping to play tourist right now," said Bradley.

"I didn't ask you," said Caroline. "And I can't sit still much longer."

"We should keep moving, Caroline," said Fidel.

"Shut up, Caroline," said Bradley.

They passed a clearing on the right of the highway, where a Mayan woman was selling honey in both jars and cans from a horse-drawn cart. She stared at them without expression, her face hard and lined as tree bark.

"I've heard that's the best honey in the world," said Vega. "They sell it in my health food store in Silver Lake but I buy the stuff from Ojai."

"We're not stopping to buy some," said Bradley.

She slugged him smartly on the shoulder and sat back in her seat. "Are we there yet?"

"We can stop and buy honey," said Fidel. "It will improve the flavor of our very old tortillas."

"You gotta be kidding me," said Bradley.

"Fidel knows what he's doing," said Vega.

"Please, Bradley," said Fidel. "I am not challenging your command. A few minutes is all."

"Christ."

Fidel slowed and U-turned onto the opposite shoulder of the highway. Slowly he rocked across the muddy ground and waited for the next vehicle to do the same before pulling back onto the asphalt. When they came to the cart they pulled in and parked but only Cleary and Bradley stayed. The three other Yukons arrived and waited with their engines running but no one got out.

"At least the men have a little bit of good sense," said Bradley.

"This won't take long. It's hilarious watching Vega getting the hots for Fidel."

"It's not hilarious to me."

"Amusing, then."

"I'm not amused, either. I just want to get there and get set up."

"I know. I do too."

"We've stopped for fucking honey, Jack. I can't believe this."

"Remain calm, Deputy Jones."

Nerves make you pissy, Bradley thought. Do something constructive. He reached under the seat and made sure his machine pistol was handy. He slid it out and pulled open the slide just enough to see the sparkle of brass and copper, then he closed it and thumbed down the safety. Sweet. He gave the sound suppressor a snugging turn. It was a small gun, designed and built by a friend of his in Orange County, California, of all places. It was fully automatic, .32 caliber and easily concealable. It could take a fifty-shot magazine, and it had a built-in telescoping butt, similar in design to the retractable handles on luggage. The sound suppressor was removable and worked well. The gunmaker had named his invention the Love 32, due to his fascination with outlaws and lawmen, Murrieta having been shot down and beheaded by a man named Harry Love. Bradley thought that the gun should have been named the Joaquin Thirty-two, or maybe just the Murrieta, but naming it was not his privilege.

He had sold one thousand of them to Carlos Herredia, so his soldiers could match the firepower of the Gulf Cartel. He'd made himself a lot of money too, although Charlie Hood had come very close to busting him on felony gun-trafficking charges. Bradley smiled as he remembered those days, just a couple of years ago. Things had been so easy then. His luck had been so good. Well, things change, he thought. He lay the gun alongside his right thigh, the butt telescoped into the frame for now.

"Don't shoot yourself in the foot, Brad."

"Go to hell, Jack."

Bradley turned around and gave Cleary a look, then he watched Vega and Fidel haggling with the honey seller. Omar looked on. Overhead the sun burned yellow, a searing heat, and the jungle trees still glistened from the storm. Vega pointed and Fidel collected a gallon can from the cart. Vega dug into her pocket for money. Like married people at a Safeway, thought Bradley. Married people in body armor. Wave of the future. They seemed to be moving in slow motion. They

plodded around the muddiest places back toward the SUV and Bradley swore they were taking their time to enjoy the walk together. Fidel
balanced the can on one finger and caught it when it fell. Omar trailed
behind them, head down, dodging the puddles.

After a brief eternity they were back in the SUV and Fidel had
started up the engine while Vega passed around the gallon of Mayan
honey. The label featured the head of a cartoon jaguar being circled
by bees.

"Glad you could make it back before dark," said Bradley.

"We're just over one hour away," said Fidel.

"Then step on it."

Nearer the Reserva de la Biosfera Calakmul the land rose and undulated in gentle hills and atop some of these Bradley could see the
stones of Mayan ruins still staunch against the rain forest. He looked
at his watch, then at the maps that Mike had drawn for him. Sixty
miles, he thought. He studied the minor roads on the macro map, the
ones that would take him deep into the humid coastal jungle and finally to the Castle.

They drove through Conhuas without even slowing down. A few
miles on Bradley saw a sign for the biosphere reserve and he liked the
idea that they were about to enter federally patrolled land. He allowed himself hope. What a pleasure, he thought. What a thing to
have. He looked over his shoulder past Caroline and Cleary and
young Omar, and through the rear window he could see the black
Yukon 1500 behind them and the other one behind it. And another
bringing up the rear.

The column crossed into the biosphere reserve and passed the Be-
can ruins. They were heading almost due east now, and Bradley could
see the rain forest making its slow transition to subtropical jungle—
the trees and plants growing more densely together now, and taller
with the increased rainfall and proximity to the Caribbean Sea.

They dropped into a basin and off to his right Bradley saw a hill-
ock with another nameless, brazenly inaccessible ruin built upon it.
The ruin looked to Bradley like a temple of some kind, square and
squat and overgrown but it was a statement made perhaps six centuries ago that still had a voice if you could only hear it. He wished he
could. And he wished Erin could see it because she could hear that
voice if anyone could. It would mean something to her. Then he wondered if she had in fact seen that very ruin on her way to Armenta's
Castle. Had they hurt her? Did they respect her at all? Did they know
she was pregnant? His heart was an anxious knot of emotions.

The land flattened and dipped and rose again. They had just
topped the next rise when Fidel slowed to navigate around a wooden
cart that had overturned smack in the middle of the highway. A horse
stood a few yards away, looking at them with interest, and two Mayan men were trying to get the cart back upright but were having no
success at it. The cans and jars of honey had rolled unhelpfully down-
hill, some of them already to the shoulder where the jungle crowded
high and close to the highway and the storm water stood in long
pools. Vega and Cleary were craning forward to see and Cleary made
some crack about picking up all the honey they wanted and Bradley
saw that the horse was still tethered to the cart by the rope around its
neck but there was no bit or bridle in sight. The Mayans stopped
pushing on the cart, then let go and backed away a few steps while
looking at them. Bradley saw movement within the jungle, and the
first burst of gunfire slapped against them. Fidel swung the vehicle
around the cart and onto the shoulder, where it quickly spun and slid
sideways toward the jungle, tires digging in, throwing mud rooster
tails into the air.

"*Open the top!*" yelled Bradley.

Fidel hit a dashboard button and by the time the shooters' port
had slid open, bullets were whapping against the Yukon's armor. Vega

and Cleary and Omar sprouted up into the port with military assault
guns and unleashed their storm. Bradley swung himself out the window and held on to the frame with one hand and reached across the
bullet-pocked windshield and shot a man crouched by a strangler fig
and another who was beside him and another who was reloading. In
the periphery of his vision he saw the Mayans running off into the
jungle and the tethered horse bucking wildly at the gunfire and the
second SUV screeching to a stop on the far side of the cart. Its shooters too were up in the port and strafing the greenery fearsomely. The
third Yukon swung to a stop and the storm multiplied.

Bradley pulled himself back into the cab, drove a fresh magazine
into his weapon, clamped another mag crossways between his teeth,
then opened his door and dropped to the mud beside the SUV. He
crawled on his elbows to the right front tire, then lay himself out flat
behind it and waited. The soft mud gathered him down and he had
the Love 32 firm in his hands. As the men in the trees moved and
became visible he shot them one bullet at a time, three men down for
the five shots he fired, and he could see the fear growing on the faces
of the others because they had no idea where the bullets were coming
from and they couldn't hear the report of his silenced weapon. They
were young men and they wore military fatigues but no helmets or
body armor. The "Z" insignias on their shirtsleeves identified them as
Zetas, former Gulf Cartel allies now locked in a murderous rivalry
with their old employers. A rocket-propelled grenade exploded in the
trees and Bradley saw two Zetas twist airborne with the shrapnel,
then collapse to earth with finality.

He watched the fourth of their caravan come to a halt fifty yards
short of the cart. The man they called El Grande, Martin, climbed
into the port opening and launched another grenade. It exploded
deep in the jungle beyond the attackers and when Martin rose again
with the launcher he was thrown back by machine-gun fire. Bradley

heard bullets whistling madly against the armor of the vehicles and he saw that the bullets did not shatter the security windows but left them pocked with snowy divots and small cracks. He shot two more men with his last five shots, then took the full magazine from his mouth and reloaded. A sudden fury of fire from the trees slammed into his Yukon and he heard the lead screaming off the armor and punching through the places between the armor and he wondered if his people were dying just a few feet above him.

The fourth vehicle lurched forward and barreled toward them. But instead of following Fidel's SUV into the mud hole the driver cut fast and hard across the highway, barged through the trees and disappeared into the shooters' side of the rain forest. A moment later Bradley heard the fusillade of gunfire. Some of the ambushers panicked and spilled out onto the highway where they were shot to ribbons. Others must have run deeper into the jungle because the riot of guns and grenades coming from the fourth vehicle seemed to last for minutes. Then the fourth SUV came smashing out of the green and onto the highway, its three gunmen swaying wildly like trees buffeted by a storm but whooping and yelping and killing the ambushers as they tried to scramble away.

When they finally stopped shooting the world went silent. Bradley waited awhile, then climbed suckingly from the mud and stooped behind the hood of the Yukon. He kept his gun pointed to the trees but he looked through the window to see Vega and Cleary standing in the port and Fidel behind his open armored door with a riot ten gauge propped against the frame and Omar slumped, bloody and still on the back bench.

A compact car came up the highway toward them from the west. Sun-blistered paint, Quintana Roo plates. It slowed when it came near the cart, and the family inside it stared wide-eyed at the armored gunmen who raised their hands for the car to stop. The driver was a middle-aged man who looked terrified, raising his hands as if he were under arrest. Three of Fidel's men easily turned the wagon upright and rolled it to the side of the road. When one of them waved the little car on, it accelerated noisily but slowly in a cloud of white smoke while the children in the back seat turned and continued to stare.

Moments later the three other SUVs converged on Fidel's stuck Yukon and pulled it out with their winches. Bradley saw that the armored vehicles were pitted in some places and punctured in others, though less so than the furious sound of the battle had implied. The plastic security windows remained unshattered and the security tires still held air.

He cut the horse loose and it walked slowly off to the side of the road and turned and looked at him. There was no sign of the Mayans.

The men and Vega stood in a loose circle for a moment, blocked from the jungle by their vehicles. An old truck came rumbling down the highway from the other direction and did not slow down. A man whimpered from somewhere off in the rain forest. Eduardo said that El Grande Martin was dead and so were Tito and Raul and Perro Negro and Omar. Fidel said if they'd been wearing their armor as ordered they would be alive, which earned him several hostile looks because three of them, according to Eduardo, had worn their armor. Fidel said they would bury the men properly soon but not now. Caroline Vega had been grazed on the forearm but the wound was not serious. Fidel took a small piece of shrapnel in his cheek.

From the jungle they heard at least two men moaning and Fidel said anyone who wanted to go put them out of their misery was free to do so. The men shrugged disinterestedly and Caroline glanced into the jungle, then at Bradley and shrugged too.

After the men had dispersed for their vehicles Vega pulled the metal from Fidel's cheek and touched the other side of his face gently with her hand. He put his bandana to it and got into the mud-draped vehicle.

Fidel started up the Yukon. Bradley got in and closed his door and looked at the bullet-marked safety glass. Then he looked at his own mud-drenched front side and he thought that losing just five men here on this highway was an authentic miracle. How many Zetas had they taken down? More than a dozen, certainly. Twenty?

"What will people do when they see our vehicles?" Caroline asked.

"They'll stay the fuck away from us like they should," said Bradley.

"And what if we run across soldiers?" said Caroline.

"They don't occupy the Yucatán," said Fidel. "They can fight a battle or occupy a village for a few days. They arrive loudly and without surprise. They arrive with great volume and pageantry and media and politicians. But they never stay. We will make the vehicles appear better. I have spray paint and Bondo for the bullet marks."

"We just killed a whole bunch of men," she said.

"Zetas," said Fidel. "We have helped Armenta even though he's our enemy."

"I feel lucky," said Bradley. "I feel the big luck coming."

It had been a long time since he'd felt the good luck that had so effortlessly accompanied him through the first twenty years of his life. Maybe it's all changing for the good, he thought. Luck. And that means Erin is okay and I'm going to get her out of here alive and the baby will be born.

Some miles down the road their second SUV took the lead because Eduardo knew the area. Fidel followed him onto a narrow asphalt road, past an ecolodge and a mini-super. The asphalt soon gave way to the pale white soil of the Yucatán. Deep in the tall twisted ceibas they stopped and dug five graves, taking turns, the labor utterly punishing in the heat and the mosquitoes and the sudden absence of adrenaline. The earth was sandy and loose and the graves soon filled with groundwater and remained shallow and without dignity. The digging went quickly because of the soft ground and the folding camp shovel carried in each SUV for this exact purpose, Bradley guessed. Carrying the bodies to the graves was exhausting and spirit-killing.

An hour later they were back on the road. Bradley looked out the window for new danger. The Love 32, butt retracted for storage and transport, was under his thigh again. He was suddenly spent, every bit of energy gone. Luck and hope were gone too, two coins lost somewhere back along this road he had taken. He listened to the hum of the engine and the rasp of the tires on the highway. In the cab was only silence and the stink of mud and human fear.

23

ERIN SAT IN THE LEATHER chair facing the window. The poststorm evening was gray and cool and the tattered fronds hissed on the breeze. She wore the white nightgown buttoned to her neck and a pair of heavy white socks that Atlas had smuggled in for her and an embroidered Nahuatl blanket around her shoulders.

Nearly three days had passed since Saturnino's attack and she still could not get warm or comfortable, or more than a few hours of nightmare-curdled sleep. Her rump was bruised and her back was scraped and she was torn and burning with pain where he had pulled out her hair. Since walking back here that night, wobbling and nearly senseless, supported on either side by Father Ciel and Benjamin Armenta, she had kept rolled-up tissue in her ear canals, hoping to stem the aural memories of the awful event. It worked only partially.

For almost three days she slept and roamed the room, the eyes looking back at her from the mirrors dull with fear. The life growing inside her was plainly afraid too—thrashing and kicking violently for minutes, then utterly still and possibly lifeless for hours. She kept waiting for the catastrophic evidence to appear, for that feeling of intimate death to come over her, as it had come before. Then she slept and slept more.

Erin looked at her body in profile several times a day and she could see it clearly now, and she knew they must see it too, and she didn't know why it seemed so important that they not know. Would they not skin a pregnant woman? What would that matter? Maybe Saturnino would delight in it more. Did he have special skinning tools? Did they soak you in brine like a turkey? Would he rape her first? Of course he would. That was what savages did. She pulled the blanket tighter. She adjusted the earplugs. Please don't let go, little man, she thought. I'll take care of you. Her hands trembled and her feet were cold as a statue's and when the tears started up she slapped her face hard to make them stop but they did not.

When she couldn't sleep she picked up the García Marquez book and continued where she had left off. Anything to escape those thoughts. The book was perfect for that, as intoxicating as anything she had ever experienced. She lost herself in the story of Sierva María de Todos los Ángeles, bitten by the dog and waiting for the symptoms of rabies to strike her. But Erin couldn't see how the story could end happily, because rabies was always fatal back in the strange and superstitious Caribbean world of the eighteenth century. She liked the crazy colonial viceroys and Inquisitors and the decaying nobility and pirates, but the canopy of viral doom overhanging the tale wouldn't allow her to truly enjoy it. The priest was going to be disgraced by his love for her and Servia María was going to die. Horribly. In her dreams Erin grew the same hair that Servia María grew after her death—sixty feet of splendid copper-colored waves. Had Armenta left the book here as a message? Then why *this* book, of the hundreds of thousands of them on Earth? And what was the damned message, anyway?

Later Atlas set the serving tray on the table and put out a glass of red wine and a plate of cheeses and fruit. He set a small package beside the food. He looked at her gravely as he worked the plastic wrap off the plate.

"Were you here when I performed?" she asked.

"Was I where?"

"Here. In my room."

"No. I was there when you sang. You were fabulous."

"When I got back I thought someone had been in here."

"Maybe you were mistaken. You must have been extremely . . . *infeliz.*"

"Unhappy? Yes, I was."

"Benjamin will be here in one hour for you," he said in his sweet high voice. "He would like you to be nicely dressed for dinner and have the Hummingbird in its case."

"I'll dress how I want to dress."

"Yes."

"Where are we going?"

"I don't know, Mrs. McKenna."

"I hate this fucking place."

"You will be free in three days. It is planned. The money will arrive and you will be released. I'm not supposed to know this but I do. The servants all know, but some don't believe. They are betting on what will be the outcome. And Benjamin has ordered that the tigers not be fed. It is not difficult to add together what this means."

Erin eyed him over the blanket. "If you know so much, then where is Charlie Bravo? Is he close to us? Did he make it through the hurricane?"

"This I do not know. Charlie Bravo brings the money?"

"He'd better bring the money or Saturnino will skin me alive."

"Saturnino will burn in hell."

"He looked pretty bad off the other night."

Atlas didn't answer for a long moment. "Saturnino does not recognize his father. Or others. He has not spoken one word of Spanish but he now speaks some language no one knows but him. He sleeps greatly. He wakes up for a few minutes and he stares at people without comprehension and he eats. They say he eats gigantic amounts. Then he prays in the language that no one knows. Then he falls back asleep for hours and hours more."

"Something tells me he'll steer out of it. Has he skinned many people?"

Atlas did not look up to face her.

"Oh, God," she said.

"Would you like a Bible to read?"

"What kind of question is that?"

"It is a dependable comfort."

"A friend of mine had a seizure at the Guadalajara airport. She was coming home from a vacation in Zihuatanejo. In the hospital they did a scan and when the doctor came in to tell her the results he said he was not sure how to interpret the scan. He told my friend to have a more advanced test when she got home to the United States. And he gave her a Bible in English, with a page marked and a passage underlined about how you can face death with God and He will be your comfort. And this terrified her worse than anything she had ever read. I do not want a Bible."

"But the Bible also says you can face life with God and He will be your guide. And I thought you might do this because . . ."

"Because what?"

She caught him looking at her reflection in the full-length mirror.

"Because you have two lives that need to be guided."

She looked away from the mirror to the mournful gray sky outside. She wanted to cry and she wanted to kill Saturnino. Maybe Armenta too. It feels like my skin is off already, she thought. They can all get to me but I can't get away. They all know me but I don't know them. They all see the baby growing inside me but I see nothing in them but this hell on Earth.

"I don't want a Bible."

"I brought you one anyway."

"What's in that package you put on the table?"

"A gift from Owens. I deliver it only. I don't know what it is."

Atlas popped the cotton napkin and folded it into his trademark scallop before setting it at her place. From the serving tray he took the Bible and set this beside the napkin. Then he took the tray in one hand and walked over to Erin. He held out his other hand in a fist and she put down the book and held out her open hand.

He dropped something small and light into her palm, then he bowed slightly, smiled shyly and left the room.

She knew what it was without looking. She could feel the encapsulated drama of it, right there in the palm of her hand: the winds of Ivana and her pestilential rains, the softness of the bird's feathers as he labored through the heavens on nothing but his own slight wings, the movement of Bradley's pen across the fabric.

She opened the tiny canister and worked out the patch and read the words. Read it once. Twice. Three, four, five times. Got it, she thought. Yes, I know how to find that place. I think I do.

She placed it between her mattress and the box springs, deep toward the center of the bed, undetectable and difficult to find unless you knew right where to look.

She stood, short of breath. He'll be here the day after tomorrow, she thought. Tuesday! One day before Charlie brings the money. Blessed Tuesday. Fat Tuesday. I'll be at the cenote. We'll get there. The baby and I will get there and we will be waiting for you.

The day after tomorrow!

She went to the table and opened the package. It was a plastic shopping bag with the name and logo of a Chetumal market on it, its handles tied neatly into a bow. Inside she found a freshly laundered white dress and one of the sheer white rebozos the lepers wore.

She walked behind Armenta down the hallway toward the elevator. She wore a long dress and a light shawl over her shoulders and the dress rubbed on her abraded back but at least her legs were free. She had taped the Cowboy Defender to her upper calf and she knew without a doubt that she could use it. Violence has set me free to use violence, she thought, like this country, like the world.

Armenta carried the Hummingbird in its case. She could smell the soap and shampoo on him. He wore a black-and-white paneled bowling shirt and raw silk trousers and the broad mesh of his huaraches shone with polish. The satellite phone and others hung from his belt. His face was cleanly shaven though the lines in it were deep and dark as always. He had attempted to tame his hair, which showed some comb tracks and patches of aromatic product, but was still a thatch. They rode the elevator looking straight ahead in silence.

He opened the door of the recording studio and stepped in ahead of her and turned on the lights. Erin walked in and felt the cool and the heavy hush that lightened her heart a small degree.

Armenta leaned the guitar case against one of the gear racks and waved her to follow. At the far wall he opened a closet door. Erin saw the mikes hanging on their dowels.

"Here," he said. "Look at the selection in the mic locker."

She looked down at the Neumanns and AKGs and Sennheisers. She was a longtime fan of the cheap Shure 58 for stage, but there was no such budget equipment here.

"Which microphone do you like?" he asked.

"I don't need a microphone," she said.

"If you record with me."

"I won't record with you."

"But if you did record with me, which mic would it be?"

"You can't beat the 251."

He took down one of the ELAM 251s and closed the closet door. He went back and took up the Hummingbird case and walked into the tracking room.

Through the window she watched him take the mic to the vocal booth and set the guitar outside an instrument booth. He waved her in. She stepped into the shimmering aural brightness of the tuned room. She could tell that this space had been designed to use the reflections and peaks of sound to best effect. She suspected that even a spoken voice would sound beautiful here and she could not restrain herself.

"I have to hear this room," she said. Her words came out with dimension and specificity. Uncluttered, she thought. Bottom, top, middle. No noise. Then the room closed around them and they were gone.

"You must hear it with music."

"It's as good as the rooms in L.A."

"I have stood in the Boston Symphony Hall."

"My old church in Austin had really good acoustics."

"I designed this room myself. I used mathematics and a computer program that is a room peak calculator. You cannot have a tracking room that peaks or builds up in the frequency. These result in key and pitch and this you do not want. What is incorrect must be tuned out and what is ideal must remain. There are materials and designs that are to reflect. And some that are to diffuse and some to absorb. But the goal is not to create death."

"I think you mean deadness."

"Yes, deadness. You want the correct reflections. And the correct sonics. You must approximate . . . deadness. But not to create deadness total."

She went to the Yamaha and brushed the keyboard lid with her fingers but did not lift it. An elaborate and beautiful accordion sat on the bench, gleaming ivory-and-black enamel with mother-of-pearl and gold inlays, and black straps of intricately tooled leather.

"Play only one note," said Armenta.

She lifted the lid and struck middle C and listened to the note shimmer, then sustain and fade.

"I want you to write a song about me," said Armenta. "I want you to describe the life of poverty that becomes wealth. By using the bravery and the hard work."

"A *narcocorrido*."

"The greatest *narcocorrido* ever written, *Veracruzana style*!"

"No."

"Why?"

"Are you serious? *Why?*"

"Yes. Serious in this."

"I've been kidnapped by you and half raped by your son. My husband has been beaten and you're stealing a lot of our money. I'm pregnant and I'm terrified of you people. All of you. I won't write for you. Terror does not write songs."

He looked at her morosely. He walked to the accordion and laid a hand on it. "We make music to defeat terror."

"We make music to express joy."

"A life without joy needs music also."

"I'm sorry for your life but I won't write a song about it."

"But I am not sorry. I do not regret. I want my life to be told. I want them to know who I was. And what this time was. And this place."

"I won't write for you." She heard her words held fast by the fine acoustics of the tracking room, and she heard the fear and anger in them.

"You have strong convictions and these I understand," he said softly.

"I'm glad you understand."

He eyed her with a cagey expression. "The studio would of course be yours if you wanted it. You can compose in your room or here. You may use the Hummingbird or the piano or both of them. You are to choose. I have pens and paper. Do you like the sheets with the staffs for composing? I have several small digital and tape recorders. If you would like a different guitar, you tell me what it is. I have some very old Martins that have magical properties, and some nice Gretsch hollow-bodies, and some exquisite Kirk Sand guitars from California. I have expensive five-string electrics for the open tunings of Keith, and I have a genuine Monteleone arch-top guitar. They would be very honored to be played. You know how they enjoy it. How only then are they alive. Perhaps you would be more happy here in the studio. It reminds you of other studios and the pleasures of music. It does not remind you of being a prisoner."

"You don't understand. You pretend to, but you refuse to, and this is an insult."

"I understand but I try to persuade."

"You can't persuade me to write about you."

"I will continue to try. For you to write about me you must be . . . *encantada*."

"Enchanted? You do not enchant me. I'm the opposite of enchanted by you."

"Not by me. By my accomplishments. You must have a great *impression* by them."

"I am not impressed by hell."

"Hell?"

"You. Saturnino. This whole place."

He regarded her with a long stare. She saw no guile in it and no anger, but something stonier and less negotiable. Will? Nature? Character? Then he looked down at the accordion and touched it thoughtfully.

"Then this I will do. Enchant and impress. You will now please come with me."

He nodded and motioned her back into the control room with some urgency. She walked out of the tracking room and turned when he had closed the heavy door behind him.

"Where?"

"I want you to see my accomplishments. The third floor."

"That's where the lepers live."

"They appreciate my accomplishments. That is why they live there."

"Accomplishments? I don't understand."

"What I have achieved."

"They must be special if the elevator doesn't even stop there. And if there's no landing on the inside stairway."

His look contained small amounts of joy and conspiracy. "So we take the elevator to the ground floor and we use the outside stairs, yes okay?"

24

THE OUTSIDE AIR WAS WEIGHTED and cool but the breeze felt good against her skin. She hadn't been outside since the attack, nearly three days ago. She saw no remnants of the Thursday night party, nothing of the stage or canopy, not a beer can or a roach or a cigarette butt. Small songbirds splashed in a pool of rainwater and a pig lay on its side in a wallow of hurricane mud. She glanced off toward the clearing where the vehicles had been parked that night and where no policeman or politician or reporter would help her. She saw Saturnino's face on the rising glass of the SUV and felt a cold front shudder down her body.

The stairway to the third story began in a small walled-off patio. The entrance to the patio was through a white plaster archway featuring an elaborate gate made of stainless steel. In the middle of the gate a steel sun either rose or set, the slats of its light fanning up and out to the edges of the frame.

"At first the gate, it was made of black iron. They did not like it. They wanted the hope of light, not the darkness they live in. So I had this made. It reflects sunlight even on a day of clouds. It turns moonlight into sunlight."

"Are they contagious?"

"They are treated by a very good doctor. He is here once a week. They are not contagious. But do not go close to them."

"Why?"

"It is offensive to them. They are proud. They do not want to be near us. It is not true that pieces of their bodies fall off. That is a popular myth. But sometimes there are amputations."

Armenta opened the gate with a conventional key, not a plastic card. He slowly pulled it open, the hinges creaking and the stainless steel sun flashing dully in the low light of evening. He waited.

She entered the patio and stood on the cobalt blue tiles and looked at the clean white plaster of the archway, and at the steps leading up to the third floor. The steps were limestone, thick and wide, the slabs fitting together so tightly that the entire stairway appeared to have been chiseled from one piece of stone. They looked like they had been worn smooth by the centuries and would be worn smoother by many more.

"The stairway once was part of a Mayan ruin near Kohunlich," said Armenta. "It is believed to have been an observatory. The man who built this castle discovered it buried in the jungle. He had the stairway collected and reassembled here. It was built in approximately twelve hundred, A.D."

"Interesting history," she said.

"We are interesting history also. That is why I want you to put us in music. So we will be remembered."

"I will not write music about you."

"Would you write music about hating me?"

"Hate can't write music."

"Fearing me?"

"Fear can't write music, either."

"You are wrong. Music is our protest against hate and fear. You must protest. You must write music about the horrors you have endured here in what you call hell. How else will the world know?"

"Your words only make sense on the outside."

"Will you write music about Felix and the leopards? Who will remember him if you don't?"

"Stop. You're just adding confusion to savagery."

He looked at her evenly, nodding. He shut the gate and the lock clicked into place. He pointed to the west-facing wall and Erin saw the scores of small dark geckos. They looked like commas but they moved every few seconds as they took the mosquitoes.

Erin climbed the steps behind Armenta. They stood at an arched wooden door with wrought-iron straps and a speakeasy with its bars festooned with fanciful copper butterflies. "They will only open the door for the doctors, nurses, one teacher, and for me. No one else."

"Can they go to other floors?"

"They do not use other floors."

"Are they allowed?"

"Have you seen them on other floors?"

Armenta knocked. A long moment later the panel behind the butterflies slid open and Erin could see the twinkle of eyes watching them from the darkness inside.

—Benjamin. Give us a few moments.

—You have all the time you need. We will wait.

The panel slid shut.

"They need to prepare for us. The temperature will be cold for you. Because they wear the long clothes. They do not like having their faces and bodies visible to themselves or other people."

"Why do they wear only white?"

"Black made them look like demons."

A long minute later a latch bolt slid from its strike plate, then a dead bolt, and another. The door opened and Erin was standing face-to-face with a woman wearing a loose white dress, her face hidden beneath a gauzy white rebozo. Recessed in the folds was a healthy looking young face but the hand that held open the door had only a gnarled foreshortened stump of thumb.

Armenta spoke in rapid Spanish.

—Good evening, Nestra. This woman is my guest. I want to show her some of my accomplishments.

—We're always happy to see you, Benjamin. We heard that Erin McKenna would be coming and now, look, it is true.

She smiled and told Erin how much she had enjoyed her songs with Los Jaguars and of course the ones she performed solo also.

Erin thanked her in Spanish and the woman held open the door and stepped back to let them in.

The foyer was cool and penumbral, with the late evening light slanting in from a high casement window. The floor was of ceramic tile, white-blossomed roses on blue backgrounds. The woman shut the door behind them, turned the latch bolt and slid the two dead bolts back into place.

Erin could smell faint bleach and lemons. The acoustics eddied sharply here, suggesting high ceilings and open rooms beyond. They went down a hallway lit by electric sconces. Nestra walked ahead of them, then turned to Armenta and nodded and pushed through a wooden door. Erin could see past her to a short hall that opened to a spacious room with walls made of dull green bricks. The door closed and Nestra was gone.

"Thirteen adults and eight children live here," said Armenta. "A teacher for the children comes. The doctors and nurses. When I was hidden by the lepers they kept me for one week. The only safe way for me to leave was by the ocean. I was placed on a banana boat returning to Salvador with a load of corn and oranges. I slept on deck and was bitten by a bat, but I did not get sick. An eyelash viper hidden in the bananas bit me on the finger, but I did not die. I had pain. The water made me sick. I stayed in Salvador for almost a year. Eleven months, thirteen days.

You never forget such things. Anya. I thought only of her, but I did what I had to do to survive. I had no children then. I made friends there and these friends had hundreds of American guns left over from their civil war. The military was disbanded out of fear they would try to rule the country. Thousands of guns. And these, of course, were badly needed in Mexico. In those days there was no Gulf Cartel. We were young and we had very little money. But I was able to buy the guns on credit from my friends. Because of trust. I repaid them very generously."

"Rags to riches."

"Rags? I don't understand."

"From poverty to riches."

"That should be part of what you write about me."

"Except that I won't."

"No. Sadly." He ran a hand through his tangle of gray-black hair and looked at her with that beaten expression. But she caught the mischief in his eyes and she wanted to strike him.

They stepped into the great room. It had the high ceiling that Erin had sensed from the foyer, and a large open fireplace filled not with flames but with a display of cut tropical flowers. An enormous chandelier with electric candles hung from the center of a domed ceiling ringed with life-sized paintings of the Saints, each peering down from his or her own bower.

Erin felt observed. She saw that two of the walls were made of the same unattractive dull green bricks she'd seen in Nestra's suite and she realized they were not walls at all but bundles of cash stacked against the walls. Ten feet high, she guessed. Twelve?

Next to the fireplace was a very large-screen television playing Mexican fútbol. There were three men watching the game and when they sensed that visitors had entered the room they pulled their white balaclavas over their heads then turned to look at them. They rose crookedly and bowed to Armenta and he to them.

—How are our Red Wolves doing?

—It is tied at two, answered one of them.

—Please relax. I will be showing Mrs. McKenna some of what I have collected.

—Nice to meet you.

—It is my pleasure to meet you, she said.

—I am a fan of your music. I know no English. Can you write some songs in Spanish?

She sensed Armenta's gaze but refused to return it.

—I have written in Spanish, but not recorded.

—Can you record them for us who do not understand English?

—Do not ask the artist to work, said Armenta. She came here on pleasure, not business. But perhaps she will consider to write in Spanish someday soon.

"Pleasure?" With this she gave Armenta the most withering look she owned, borne of the Celtic blood and passion that ran through her, a look that Bradley called "The Firing Squad." It was utterly sincere. She thought, not for the first time in the last few minutes, of the Cowboy Defender taped uncomfortably on her upper left calf. So easily retrieved. So easily operated. Armenta's moment of surprise would be the last moment of his life. Firing squad is right.

—Or perhaps not, said Armenta. Enjoy the game.

They walked along the stacks of cash. She could see that the bills were all American and the denominations ranged from five dollars to one hundred. Each brick was approximately three inches thick, neat, and bound by three rubber bands, left, right and center. Up this close she could smell the money through the bleach and lemons. Bradley liked the smell of cash and had more than once joked of making a cologne of it. A crazy wave of homesickness broke over her, because these bills had been printed and earned and spent in the place she so badly wanted to return to, and because she might not see again her deceitful, money-loving husband who so loved the smell of them.

From the periphery of her vision Erin caught the three lepers looking at them. One arranged his balaclava to more completely hide his face. The fútbol announcer spoke in full-auto bursts and the TV crowd roared and the lepers turned back to the action.

"It is difficult to protect money in Mexico," Armenta said. "For this you need the cooperation of banks and our banks are not trustworthy. In ten years, maybe. Twenty. I have friends in banking and when they become influential, things will change. Grand Cayman, yes, is good now. Switzerland, maybe. It is best to keep the money near you. In the names of others I have purchased land and homes and businesses. Farms and ranches, aircraft and boats. Government employees and many politicians, of course. But mostly, I keep it here. No one here in the Castillo has seen this except for you and the lepers. Everyone else thinks they can get leprosy just by breathing the air of the third floor. Mexicans are very superstitious. I can protect my money in banks, or with guns, or with superstition. So I use the most economical. In this room there are fourteen million American dollars. There are exactly eighty million more dollars throughout this level and buried beneath the tiger and lions in the zoo. And millions of pesos, of course, and Colombian currency and yen and euros and English pounds. I have other properties in Mexico with much more money hidden in them. It is best not to have all the eggs in the one basket."

He studied the stacks of cash for a long moment. "They are not interesting or beautiful to look at."

"But you'll skin me alive for a million more?"

He looked at her with strangely distant eyes and she was suddenly frightened even more than before, more than she ever thought she could be. His tone of voice, which had always been resonant and heartfelt, even when endorsing ugliness and violence, now sounded detached, impersonal, fated. "The million dollars is a gesture of respect from your husband. We are all in this world together and he must know how to cooperate in it. The money is not what I want most. The money represents my power. And yes, I must let Saturnino skin you, as promised to you and your husband, or my power is false and my words are nothing. For the same reason the reporter must be given to the leopards. It is justice as a form of nature."

"And the pain you cause?"

"I would pray that Charlie Bravo is successful."

"You would pray, or I should?"

"You must. My prayers would be only an abomination. But I have made peace with this."

"If you have so much power, fly me home. You don't need the money from me. The rest of what you say is just macho bullshit."

He looked at her and a smile brushed his face. "Do you know this courier? Charlie Bravo?"

"No."

"I suspect that is not his name. I suspect also that he may be an agent of the ATF. I suspect that he might be one of the ATF agents who murdered Gustavo. I have very good sources, all over Mexico."

Openly suspicious, he studied her reaction. Without taking his eyes off her he pulled a cell phone from his belt. He had to look away to push the buttons. He handed it to her, and she saw the poor resolution picture of Charlie Hood getting into a vehicle in what looked like a parking lot. She recognized the Tijuana Jai Alai Palace in the background. She handed it back to him.

"Nope. Sorry. This is the man my life depends upon now?"

"The courier. From your husband. You don't know him?"

"I've never seen him before in my life. Answer me, Señor Armenta: are you going to fly me home?"

"If the money arrives on time I will fly you home. And if it does not, then all is as I promised."

"If I asked for mercy would you give it to me?"

"I will accept the one million dollars and nothing else."

Erin felt the gun taped to her leg. So be it, she thought. "I need to use the bathroom."

"You were in your room only minutes ago."

"Please?"

"Of course, Mrs. McKenna."

Armenta walked her to a guest bath down the hall that Nestra had used. Erin turned on the light and locked the door and ran the tap and hiked her left foot onto the marble countertop. She unwrapped the Cowboy Defender and stood and thought: now you have to stand on your own two feet, girl. The gun was small and heavy and the rounded butt fit easily in her hand. She pushed it halfway into a shallow pocket in her dress, draped the shawl to cover it, and pulled it out and worked it back in again and wiggled it back and forth to make sure it would stay put as she walked. If the hammer was caught snug up under the pocket hem then it seemed okay. But what if it cocked itself and went off? She made sure the shawl covered it. Just barely. Where should she aim? *Head if you can, heart if you can't.*

She took a deep breath and knelt down and vomited into the toilet. Then again. She felt sick all the way to her soul. When the retching stopped she wadded the medical tape in a ball and wrapped it in toilet paper and put it in the trash can. In the mirror she saw her face, pale and glistening, her pupils black pits.

25

A RMENTA WAS WAITING FOR HER when she came out. She forced herself to look at him and noticed that he had tried to comb his hair.

"Come see some of my other accomplishments." He turned to lead the way and she followed with her hands folded in front of her, inches from the gun, but this was an awkward way to walk and she couldn't shoot him in the back anyway. You didn't do that. She had just let her hands swing free to walk naturally when he turned around and looked at her. He had a suspicious expression on his face, but said nothing.

He led her through a spacious kitchen where two white-clad women were preparing a meal. She wondered if, dressed like they were, she could pass as one of them, just long enough to make it from the Castle to the cenote. What if she found one of them on the path? Wouldn't she have to stop, and speak, then be discovered? Here in the kitchen their faces were almost hidden by their gauzy rebozos but their eyes smiled at Armenta as he paused to lift a pot lid and peruse the simmering chicken. Erin thought she might get sick again so she focused her attention on the chains of garlic cloves that hung in the opening of a pass-through. Garlic, she thought, save me.

She followed him down a short cool hallway to another room. Through the shawl she touched the gun but could not draw it. He turned on the lights and Erin stepped in. The lights were fluorescent, jittery and sharp, and the smell of marijuana was clear. The room was large but unfurnished except for several large tables that were piled with larger bricks of several colors. Beneath the tables were more stacks. Against the walls still more. These bundles were roughly the size of shoe boxes and they were wrapped in different colors of plastic.

"Are you sick?" he asked.

"I feel good."

"You are white and perspiring."

"I am pregnant and feeling it."

"My wife was sick every day with Saturnino."

She denied the nausea. "I'm sorry he turned into a monster. No, that's none of my business. I'm sorry. I feel like I'm losing my mind."

"He has visions now. The *curandera* gave him scorpion poison mixed with chocolate and goat's milk. To make the visions stop."

"What do the doctors say?"

"Edema of the brain. He ate one entire box of children's cereal this morning, soaked in tequila."

"I'm sorry, but . . . well, I thank you too. For saving me from him."

He looked at her uncertainly and pointed to a table. "Here, look and see this."

Erin looked down on a pallet-sized mountain of bundles wrapped in blue plastic with lightning bolts on them. There were bundles in yellow plastic with bumblebee designs and the word "BUZZ" on them. Beside these were blue packs with Homer Simpson's face and below his face it said, in Spanish, "I'm Getting Smuggled—What of It, Man?" The next bundles were packed in clear plastic and she could see the swirls of green herb compressed within.

There was another, smaller great room in this part of the flat and Erin saw the hooded children sitting on the floor by the big TV watching a Disney video, and the women just now bringing plates of food to the dining table. This room too had a dramatic chandelier and a high ceiling but the paintings were not of saints but of Mayans and jaguars and birds and snakes. They walked past two men playing chess, and in their white hoods and loose white clothing they looked like ghosts or angels but when one of them looked at her, Erin saw that his nose and lips were gone and only some of his bottom teeth remained, staunch as headstones. She felt herself rising as if levitated and she knew she was fainting. One foot in front of the other. I will be there, Bradley. I will be there. Touch the Cowboy Defender. Saint Cowboy Defender.

A young woman came in from one of the hallways that led into the great room. She moved with an easy grace and she wore the white dress of the lepers but not the rebozo. She looked cautiously at Erin, then walked over and sat with the children in front of the TV.

Armenta motioned Erin toward them and led her over. The woman stood as they approached. She was very pretty and her face was pale and smooth and peaceful. Her hair was honey blond, wavy and fine.

"Erin McKenna," he said. "This is Dulce Kopf."

"Very nice to meet you," said Erin.

"I heard your performance from my room. I had the window open to the rain and wind, so I could hear you. I hope you are enjoying your stay."

"It's been unusual."

"I must get back to the children. There is always so much to be done with children."

"Of course."

"It's what Gustavo would have wanted."

"Oh?"

"We were young then. The Americans killed him without a reason or a word."

She glided back among the youngsters and took her place among them. Armenta signaled her and they walked down another hallway.

"Does she have leprosy?"

"No. She feels good with them. This I cannot explain. She has not been out of the Castle since Gustavo. Two years. I try to do what she wants."

"I feel dizzy and bad."

"We are almost finished."

By then her sense of direction had failed. She had no idea even of north or south, or which part of the floor they had already seen and which part remained new. The next room was filled with bricks of cocaine and the next with heroin and another with methamphetamine. There was another room they could only walk halfway into because the rest of it was filled with bundles of American cash, floor to ceiling, taking over almost the entire space, denying them entry. In each of these rooms guns lay about like house cats, not organized and not stowed in any orderly way, mostly just sprawled on the drugs and cash or propped in corners or laid out on the floor where there was room. Many of them were gold or inset with gold, and some had jewels and mysterious inscriptions, and some had images of Malverde, Patron Saint of Narcos, etched onto the butts or stocks. She was pretty sure she was looking at handguns and combat shotguns and assault rifles, as well as exotic sniper guns and grenade launchers and shoulder-launched rockets. She'd seen them in movies.

Erin stood in the doorway, weak with fear, inhaling a world of cash and drugs and guns. She felt the Cowboy Defender ready in its place but it seemed a hundred miles away.

"And my favorite of all the rooms," said Armenta, walking quickly down another hallway now, turning to wave her on.

He pushed open a door and found a light and Erin stepped in. At first she thought she'd walked into the New World before Columbus.

The room was crowded with jade statues and masks and mosaics, quartz carvings of gigantic frogs and strange gods, a huge stone crocodile and an enormous limestone shark carved in meticulous detail, and hundreds of pots and calendars and tablets covered with Mayan writing. Wooden carvings of birds and monkeys and fish and turtles hung from the ceiling. But there were also tables heaped with modern brooches and watches and rings and earrings and necklaces, and there were wooden bins of loose emeralds and diamonds and rubies, some still uncut, and strings of pearls draped through the shutter slats, and chains of gold and silver that had fallen from the slats and were now heaped upon the floor like something that housecleaning would have to deal with, and crystal vases of loose cultured pearls and freshwater and small black pearls. On the floor stood small golden humanlike figurines and more circular golden calendars, and there were silver suns the size of dinner plates leaning against the walls, and Erin saw a silver jackal standing nearly life-sized, its open jaws draped with thick golden chains, and she saw a silver coiled cobra with its head raised and its hood flared, and a flock of jeweled silver birds sitting on a rod fixed above one of the windows. Most of the things were New World creations but she recognized pieces that came from Asia and Africa and the Middle East and Europe and Polynesia. Plunder from around the world, she thought, the treasure of everywhere.

Armenta smiled and folded his hands behind his back and took a formal step toward her, as if he were going to ask her to dance. "Do you like all of this?"

"So much."

He nodded as if her answer didn't matter. His face was lugubrious and his black eyes threw the sparkle of the jewels at her.

"You are looking to be sick," he said.

"Can I sit down?"

"Here." With one stout arm Armenta swept a bin of rubies off one of the tables. They clattered brightly across the floor and Erin backed herself to the table and hoisted herself up. There she sat and hung her head and through the curtain of red hair stared down past her boots at the twinkling city of gemstones above which they dangled.

"The most scared I've ever been before coming here was when all these tarantulas came crawling across the ground toward me. It was like they had sprouted out of the desert. They weren't there and then they were everywhere. The males come out of holes looking for a mate. I don't know why they all get to feeling that way at once. Like a bunch of guys heading for the honky-tonk after work on a Friday maybe. And every one of those spiders you had to multiply by eight on account of how each leg articulates slowly and separately when they walk, which divides your attention eight ways, which makes you eight times as scared. This was in Arizona. It reminds me of here. Every time I look at something I get scared more."

Armenta said nothing for a long while. He was moving from table to table, looking down at the booty. She could hear him toeing the fallen rubies or whatever other treasures had ended up on the floor. He was humming a Lila Downs song. She knew that this was the time to draw the gun and when he came closer she would shoot him. She edged the shawl away to free the gun and she willed her hand to take it, but her hand did not move.

"Did a tarantula bite you?"

"No."

"When I was young in Veracruz another boy kept a tarantula in a cigar box for an amusement. The boy was older and somewhat cruel. This was a black and red spider, and large. His father worked the docks and he brought Fernando a monkey and several birds and snakes and many exotic insects. Fernando carried it around in the box and he would hold it in his hand if you paid him. He dared me to hold the tarantula so I held my hand out and he carefully picked it up from the box and set it on my hand. It simply stood there. And then Fernando commanded the spider to bite. He said, *morder!* and the tarantula bit me. On the palm. Two marks. It did not hurt but I was very surprised. Fernando looked surprised too. My father said tarantulas cannot hear but I had proven him wrong."

"What did you do?"

"I flung the spider into the air and beat Fernando with much force. I took my money back and all that was his also. After that, we were friends."

"I made friends with a girl who talked trash about me, but I never trusted her."

"In my business loyalty is often tested. And if a man or woman fails the test it is always obvious. In that way it is an honest business."

"I don't like backstabbers. Maybe I can get into your line of work."

"I have one more thing to show you. But first I want you to choose one thing from this room and bring it with you."

"Why?"

"Please just choose one thing you call beautiful. You will find this to be interesting."

Erin looked around and spotted a plate of what looked like solid silver, inlaid with black hummingbirds that might have been obsidian or onyx. It was propped up against the wall near a corner stacked with assault rifles. She wondered fleetingly if the assault rifles were loaded.

"The silver plate."

"Taxco. You may pick it up."

She walked to the corner and knelt down and picked up the plate. When she straightened she again unwrapped the shawl and she felt the cool fresh air on her skin. My skin. The skin he will take. The plate was perfect cover, but she could not make her free hand move to the gun.

"I'll take this," he said, picking up a silver candlestick that had rubies and the patina of history upon it. "Come now."

He led her from the room and down a hallway she didn't recognize, and she saw the lepers' quarters neat and organized. The lepers mostly ignored them but some looked up and acknowledged their benefactor, and Erin saw that some of their faces were untouched and others incomplete and there were missing fingers and missing hands and feet and a stillness about them that suggested preoccupation of the highest order.

She followed him down the outside stairway and into the courtyard and he pushed open the sun gate. He had been right, Erin saw— even in the moonlight the stainless steel shone hopefully. With the candlestick in one hand he led her across the sandy road and onto a jungle trail that wound through the trees.

The trail to the cenote, she thought. Where Bradley would be waiting the day after tomorrow to steal her away from here. Then they could get word to Charlie. And he could do whatever he needed to leave this place alive. Money or not, she thought. The money wouldn't matter. It was like God himself was showing her the way so she couldn't miss it. A rehearsal. The day after tomorrow!

The trail was easy to follow because it was white and the jungle was close and dark. She felt the smooth touch of the sea grape leaves and the tickle of ficus and she heard the shallow crunch of her shoes on the sand and the steps of the man up ahead. The trail branched once to the left then once to the right, as on Bradley's map. They climbed a slight hill and the path went left again and then it ended in a wide flat clearing. In the middle of the clearing was an almost perfectly round body of black water. It shimmered in the heavy air, a ribbon of moonlight across its center.

Just like on the map, she thought. I am here. I will be here in two days and we will escape.

"It is very deep," he said. "Thirty meters. The water comes up from the ground century after century. The Maya used it for drinking and irrigation and for sacrifice. The sacrificed person would be weighted with stone and jewels and gold and silver so the offering was more valuable to the gods. The gringo who built the Castle used breathing devices to remove some of the treasure. He did not want to sell it or give it to the government, so he buried it near the guardhouse. My workers discovered it when they dug a new trench for the sanitation system of the Castle."

"The statues and calendars and plates."

"And the chains of gold."

"The lepers watch over it."

"But I try to add to the treasure, not to take away from it. I like to make it grow. I like to multiply the sacrifice. I have thrown kilos and kilos of the treasure back into this cenote. And not only the original treasure, but gold watches and diamond rings and gold-plated pistols. The WBA welterweight belt belonging to Manny Mendez is down there. And the super-lightweight belt of Julio Serro. There is a gold-top Les Paul guitar once belonging to Carlos Santana that I purchased for a great price. There is a microphone used by Bonnie Raitt that I bought also. There are many Cartier and Rolex and Patek watches that have been paid to me. And one yellow Corvette that belonged to a beautiful American outlaw I admired. All in the water now."

"Why?"

"For balance."

Armenta stepped closer to the ring of black water and he flung the silver candlestick high into the air. Erin saw the faint turn of it in the moonlight then heard the splash. She tried to draw the Defender, but her will was not enough. She watched the rings expand across the water. And she realized that in spite of the fact that he was evil and she was not, he was the stronger here and now. In spite of all the life she had to give, and all the life he had taken, he was the stronger for it.

"Throw in the plate," he said.

She held the plate in both hands, testing its weight and balance, then reached back and unleashed it like a flying disc. It sailed briefly then sliced into the water and was gone.

"Good," he said.

"Yes."

"There is bad news about Charlie Bravo."

She felt her anger spike and her exhaustion return, but she said nothing.

"He was difficult to understand on the telephone. Evidently he became lost in Mexico. He mistook Monterrey for Merida and now the hurricane has closed the highways. So he cannot be here on the agreed day. Of course, he cannot get on an airplane with such money. He begged for your life."

"What did you tell him?"

"Mrs. McKenna, I have never in my life been untruthful to a promise."

"So, on that day you kill me."

He looked at her for a long moment but his back was to the lowering moon and she couldn't see his face. "However I am now willing to negotiate with you."

"So, negotiate."

"I will give Charlie Bravo one additional day to get here if you will write and record the song. It is to be about me and this time and place in which we live."

"I've never written a song in three days."

"The studio would be yours."

"The greatest *narcocorrido* ever written. In three days."

"Yes."

"What if I fail? What if you don't like it?"

"I ask for a work of your heart. Not for the heart itself."

"Or you take my skin."

He nodded as if annoyed. "Maybe you would like to walk from your room to the studio when you desire. Then go back to your room when you desire to go. You would have Owens to be your escort for these small journeys. And perhaps this freedom would help you write."

Erin felt emotions trying to form—hope, joy, gratitude, exultation. But they were only partial, still paralyzed by her fear. One more day to live was one more day to escape. One more day for Bradley to get here, if he was having any trouble at all. Take the day, girl. "You leave me no choice. Yes."

"I am very pleased. We shall now celebrate with a very good dinner. You will tell me about being a girl in Texas. And I will tell you about being a boy in Veracruz. Did you know that Veracruz means true cross? Because Cortez landed there on Good Friday in fifteen-nineteen. Four hundred and ninety-three years ago—the first European city in Mexico. Cortez brought flamenco and *folklorico* and violins and cellos and guitarons! Or, perhaps these came later. We will talk and talk and talk. Then you will begin the writing."

26

THE NEXT MORNING HOOD WALKED through the lobby of the Merida Hyatt Regency, then into the growing heat of the city. Twenty-four hours in Merida and nothing, he thought. Didn't Armenta want his cool million? The thought crossed his mind that Armenta may be playing him like a starting pitcher, letting him go as long as he needed before bringing in the closer—the *sicarios* would just swarm in, take the money and kill him once and for all. He was in the heart of the Gulf Cartel's turf, at Armenta's mercy.

He lost himself in the sidewalk crowd and called up to Luna again. Then he went to the street corner and bought another cup of iced coffee from a vendor and walked back the way he had come, past the lobby, to the next intersection. He stood and watched the cars and trucks go by. He bought a pack of gum off a cart. Merida was a colonial city but the hotel was in the newer financial district. Ivana had trampled the northeast and now the weather was hot and humid. There were still downed trees and power lines and a shortage of fresh water in parts of the city but Merida was back to business so far as Hood could see.

He took his time walking back to the lobby, where he got another newspaper and tried to remain obvious and approachable. He got his boots shined and ate breakfast in the hotel cafe while he tried to read the paper. The satellite phone buzzed on his hip.

"Has he called? Where are you?" asked Bradley.

"Hold." Hood pocketed the phone and went into the men's room, bolting himself in a private stall at the far end of the row. "Merida. Nothing from Armenta. Silence."

"Wednesday's the payday, Charlie. Day after tomorrow. You can't stall out in Merida."

"I can't just show up at the Castle, either. I'm not supposed to know where she is, remember? He'd kill me on principle, and probably her too. Where are you?"

"Close to her. Two-point-four miles of jungle away. I got in yesterday. I'm a gringo fisherman staying at the Hotel Laguna in Bacalar. Cleary is my fishing bud and Caroline Vega is his girlfriend. We've got a rental car and a rental motorboat and tackle for tomorrow. For tarpon fishing off Cayo Lobos, you know? But if Erin can hit her mark, the four of us will be across the Bacalar Lagoon and headed for the airport in Chetumal. We've got Fidel and his men for protection. We'll be in the air about the time Armenta knows she's missing. Now, if something happens to me or she can't get away to find me, that leaves you one day to get the money to him. You're the clean-up hitter, Charlie. If you can't deliver, we'll have to use force."

"Where are Fidel and the men?"

"Camped in the jungle between here and her. We were ambushed in Campeche. Five dead. Nineteen of us left. They've got food, water, guns and ammo. They're ready if all else fails, Charlie."

"Don't storm the Castle."

"I will if I have to. What else can I do? Tell me."

Hood considered. If something went wrong on Tuesday, and Armenta didn't bring Hood to the Castle with payment on Wednesday, as agreed, what other choice was there? "If it comes to that, you've got two more guns."

Bradley was silent for a beat. "You really do love me, don't you?"

"Call me when you have her and I'll try to get back to the United States with your money. If I don't hear from you or Armenta tomorrow, I'll be at the Hotel Laguna before sunrise, day after. And we'll break her out."

"We've got three chances, Charlie. Only one needs to work."

"I'm hoping for door number one."

"So am I. Erin and I could be on a jet for LAX by tomorrow morning."

"If you are, give her my regards."

"Casita four." Bradley hung up.

Hood put the phone in his pocket and walked back to his table. He glanced at the newspaper on the table before him, asked for another cup of coffee. The waiter brought the coffee and the check without Hood having to ask for it, which was unusual in Mexico. A muscular man in running sweats walked casually into the room, carrying a leather messenger's pouch. He came toward him and Hood wondered if his luck had just changed.

The young man glanced at Hood through dark glasses, reached into the bag, drew a cell phone and plopped into a seat with his back to Hood, signaling the waiter with sharp waves of his arm. Suddenly, as if he felt Hood's eyes on him, the man wheeled and pulled off his glasses.

"Can I help you?"

"Sorry. I mistook you for someone else."

"Mexico is no place for mistakes."

Hood paid and browsed the gift shop and the newsstand. He bought Beth Petty a small stone replica of a Mayan temple. She was a collector of rocks and fossils and she would appreciate it. He had the clerk wrap the box in shipping paper and he walked it to the nearest post office and mailed it to her.

He strolled the neighborhood, napped upstairs, read, and watched TV and played peso poker with Luna and waited.

Late that evening as the darkness weighed down on the eastern sky Hood felt it descend on his heart as well and he began to believe that Erin McKenna had only two more days of life on Earth.

27

BRADLEY SAT AT A SMALL desk before the window of the casita, cleaning the two Love 32s he had brought south to Mexico. A desk lamp threw good light on the weapons. It was late evening and he had not heard from Hood. He sipped tequila mixed with bottled water. His untouched room-service dinner sat on a stand by the bed. He could feel the adrenaline buzzing through him, low-level stuff waiting to be turned up.

He worked intently but patiently, the guns breaking down and going back together with an efficient simplicity. Their stainless-steel finishes were resisting the tropical moisture well. Erin moved around in his mind, a changeable resident, sometimes her face and sometimes her voice and sometimes a feeling that she was right there in the room watching him, which made his heart ache most. He could feel her anger at him and he knew full well her sense of betrayal. Would he ever be able to explain the secret life that he had been leading? Was there really any explanation for it, except brute, stupid greed and the pleasures of danger and deception? Would she forgive him?

Through the sheer curtain he could see half of the swimming pool, filled by rainwater clear up to the deck but emptied of tourists by Ivana. There were two tall palms that had survived and one that had not, and Bradley could see the sectioned trunk of the palm lying where it had fallen and been cut for burning. Beyond the pool was the

Bacalar Lagoon, rippled silver now in the fading light. In the little marina in front of the hotel was a handsome Chris-Craft set up for big game—outriggers and a fighting chair and a large bait tank on the stern. There were three *pangas* and a catamaran. South of the pool was a windowless white tower with a cross fixed to the wall. Bradley felt watched by this symbol of the God he had prayed to so often in this last week. These prayers felt earnest but he knew that they were not so much devotion as the covering of bets.

He had already wiped down and stashed the Glock .40 caliber he would carry on his hip when he met her tomorrow, and the eight-shot .22 Smith AirLite revolver for his ankle, and one of the two two-shot forty-caliber derringers that had been passed down through generations of Murrietas from Joaquin to his mother and now himself. She had foolishly given the other to Hood. But Bradley would pocket his gun tomorrow somewhere in his pants or jacket. A talisman, but more than only that. It had a grip of black walnut that was deeply oiled and scarred and a barrel pitted by the years and his mother had told him it had killed men.

He reassembled the Love 32s, their parts warmed by his hands, but there was no excitement or comfort for him in the weapons as there once had been. The grand aphrodisiac of living a secret life had dried up with Erin's kidnapping. The warm gun was now just another tool of folly. Bradley imagined returning home to Valley Center with Erin and burying his arsenal deep and forever, then raising their child and a few more children perhaps, to be productive American citizens, while he worked as a paramedic or a salesman or maybe a cagey independent financial advisor. Erin would write, perform and become rich and famous. Of course he would also have buried the head of El Famoso, and all of his great ancestor's belongings, and likely his mother's revealing journals. How could he not? This daydream lasted a few bucolic seconds, then he abruptly pictured himself slipping off the ranch to rob a fast-food place or a convenience store or perhaps steal a fast car just to drive it for a few days, as his mother used to do. I'm sorry, he thought. I'm sorry I'm who I am.

He took a sip of the tequila and shook his head. There was no escaping himself no matter how hard he tried. He knew that his dream of burying his guns and his past and himself had approximately the same weight as his prayers: both were righteous and good but they were still subordinate to the demands of his unsatisfied young heart.

Before leaving home he had put a picture of Erin in his duffel and now he took it out and propped it up on the desktop and the wall in front of him. It was a candid snapshot he had taken on the front porch of the Valley Center ranch, Erin sitting on a picnic bench with a guitar, looking up at the camera. Her hair was pulled back casually and her eyes were knowing and she had a private, unguarded smile. It was the look he enjoyed most, the look that said: just you and me, baby.

"I'm sorry, Erin," he said softly. He looked at her picture, genuinely amazed that she had married him and was willing to bear his children. Long ago he had conceded that he'd done nothing to deserve her. Nothing, he thought now. When he spoke, his words sounded lost in the little motel room but somehow they sounded right too, and necessary. It seemed like forever since he'd told her what was in his heart. Really, had he ever done that?

"Erin, I'm so damned sorry for what I've done. I wanted to tell you the truth ever since I've known it. A million times. I've wanted to tell you about my quirky ancestors. That Mom came from Murrieta, El Famoso. And so I did too. Of course. I wanted to show you his famous head in the famous jar, right there in your beautiful barn in Valley Center. I could have told you that much without doing any harm, I guess. Some people said Murrieta was a cutthroat and some said he was a hero but really, they killed him in eighteen-fifty-three, so how could what happened to him a hundred and fifty-nine years ago matter to us now?

"Well, I'll tell you how it matters now. History doesn't repeat. It extends. I got his blood and his DNA and somehow his spirit or soul or whatever you want to call it. Not so much into my brothers. But it was heavy in Mom. She didn't know what to tell me about myself and what to let me discover on my own. Should she keep me from knowing my own past? What do you do with something powerful but secret? She died not knowing what to do with it. I've got her journals. She wrote a lot. They sound like her, blunt and brave and half-crazy sometimes. Parts would make you laugh, and parts would make the hair on your arms stand up. Tough Suzanne Jones. Smart and selfish Suzanne Jones. Award-winning eighth grade history teacher Suzanne Jones. She was proud of that—Los Angeles Unified School District Middle School Teacher of the Year. Imagine. But Erin, guess what? She was also an outlaw, an armed robber, a car thief, a shoplifter, an occasional con. She was horny as a mink, vain as a starlet and a terrible, terrible cook. Made some good coin, though, bought Valley Center with it, gave a lot to charity. Though to be honest, Erin, she spent most of it on herself and her lovers and us boys. I've wanted to show you those journals a million times, but . . .

"*But.* If I told you all that, then I'd pretty much have to show you the vault under the barn floor and the money and loot that I have stored up there. I stole every bit of it, just like Mom stole most of what she had. Now, I told you that I earned some money by delivering cash across the border a few times. Well, Erin, I actually did that a lot more than a few times—and I delivered cash and guns and ammunition and hot cars and anything else that would bring a price. I stole a yacht once and paid some guys to sail it down. I stole a trash truck from the city of Escondido and sold it to drug traffickers in Tijuana—they moved tons and tons of dope in that thing, hid all under a layer of garbage. If I showed you the vault under the barn, you'd understand what I'm all about. You'd understand that I have a badge and a gun but I'm not always a cop. Not even when I'm on duty. I don't wear my badge and gun to protect and serve the people. I wear them to protect and serve myself. I am ashamed now and I understand that my shame matters very little if at all.

"So, why couldn't I ever tell you? I always came back to the same reasons. You wouldn't love me. You'd walk. And maybe the worst, and this will make you laugh: You would think *less* of me. Isn't that funny, really? I was afraid that you'd think less of me. Less of your hero, Bradley. In your eyes I would fall. Because you know what, Erin? I exist only in your eyes. I am only what you see. I chose you for this. To dream me. You are my dreamer and I don't want you to wake up. Does that make me less real? Or more? I can't change what you are to me. And if I could, I wouldn't.

"Anyway, it's all in a long letter under your pillow back home. The combination for the vault is in it, and instructions on how you find the vault entrance in the first place. You'll love the way I have it hidden under the Ping Pong table. If I make it home with you, I'll probably snatch up that letter before you see it. But if I don't make it home, then you'll read it and you'll finally see me for everything I was. Don't feel complicit. None of it was your fault. You were deceived. So don't cover yourself up as you march out of Eden. Chin up. Use your new truth and the money and the treasure to make a new life for you and our child. I am so blessed in having known you and in having known this world with you in it. I hope you find someone to love who is worthy of you."

He took another drink and finished reassembling the machine pistols then placed them in the center drawer of the hotel desk, with the restaurant menu and a list of services and some pamphlets on Mayan ruin tours and sport fishing. The snapshot slid down and he set it up against the wall again.

He looked out at the departing evening as a Mexican Army half-track clanked into the parking area and came to a stop. It was olive green and Bradley could see the Army emblems on the side. The engine was running but no one got out. A moment later a second vehicle pulled up beside it, a Humvee, dull and dusty, followed by another.

Bradley turned off the desk lamp and slipped into the bathroom. He climbed onto the rim of the toilet bowl to look out the small window near the ceiling. He guessed his shoulders could fit through. Close. But a Mexican Army jeep was parked there and he could see the exhaust lifting behind it in the humid air and the faint play of light off the guns and faces of the men in the front seats.

He went back to the desk and sat in the near darkness. He felt his heart pounding and the painful lump in his throat and a hot anger break over him. All the way to Bacalar for this? For *this*? He took one of the Love 32s from the drawer and set it on the desk and laid a newspaper over it. He rose quietly and put the second machine pistol on the bed and tossed a bath towel on top.

He sat back against the headboard of the bed and put up his feet and brought the gun and towel close. He switched on the bed stand lamp and called Caroline Vega on the satellite phone. Her room was behind his and up on the third level.

"Army troops are all over us," he said. "You and Jack take the jungle tour. Now. Get to the cenote before sunrise and wait for Erin. Take the boat to Chetumal and take the first flight to the U.S. you can get. I'll see you in L.A."

"How many?"

"Four units at least."

"Are you sure we can't talk to them? Three American sheriff's deputies might mean something to them, Bradley."

"Shit is what we'd mean to them, Caroline. Get to the jungle now. You've got the GPS, so use it. That's an order. This is where you earn your paycheck, my friend."

28

H E HUNG UP, WATCHING THROUGH the window as all three of the Army vehicles turned and drove slowly across the lot toward him. They pulled up side by side facing his casita and their headlights cut through the sheer curtain and filled the room in overlapping girders of light. Outside he saw the shapes of men in the beams, three moving toward his door as the engines idled and the lights shone.

He heard the knob turn, then the door flew open and the three armored men flooded in, helmets strapped tight and machine guns ready. He raised his hands and stood beside the bed and the first man clunked forward and spun him against the wall and ran one hand up and down his body. Bradley could feel the barrel of a handgun against the back of his neck.

—I am a United States law enforcement officer. I am on vacation in Mexico. My badge and identification are in my pocket.

—What is your business in Quintana Roo?

—Tarpon. I have the boat and the tackle rented for tomorrow. From Oscar at the Marina. It wasn't cheap.

The soldier pulled the badge holder and then the wallet from Bradley's pants pockets and tossed them on the bed beside the towel. Then he spun Bradley around to face them.

The captain was short and thick-necked and there was a scar on one eyebrow where the hair no longer grew. He picked up the wallet and compared Bradley's picture to his face, then tossed the wallet to the bed. He examined the badge and dropped it onto the towel that covered the gun. He watched the way the badge holder struck the towel then he pulled away the towel and picked up the machine pistol.

—For the tarpon?

Bradley understood the two possibilities here. One was that these men were legitimate Army soldiers. If so, they were in competition with the Mexican Navy and their actions would be something between aggressive and merciless. He, Caroline and Cleary would be questioned and informally deported and his guns and cash would be confiscated. This was the greater likelihood. The other was that they were controlled and paid by Armenta, to keep himself, his products and his routes protected. If so, then they would take everything the Americans had and disappear all three of them.

He realized that if he tried to pick a truth and was wrong, it would all be over quickly. He looked at the captain's scar and he studied the anger in his eyes and decided.

—Not for the tarpon. For protection from the cartels.

—You cannot bring such a weapon into Mexico.

—Maybe the Army should have them. How many good soldiers have been murdered in Mexico since the war on drugs?

The captain stared morosely at Bradley. Then he turned and barked something at the man behind him, who quickly left the room.

Bradley heard the voices and scuffling outside. In the headlights he saw a group of four men pushing Cleary and Vega along in front of them. Cleary's face streamed blood shiny in the light and Vega's head was down like someone trying to avoid a camera. Another soldier held open the back door of one of the SUVs and they shoved Cleary inside. Vega stepped in after him and the man slammed the door shut, then looked inside as if they might have gotten away already.

The man who had frisked Bradley now came from the bathroom holding Bradley's expense wad of roughly forty-nine thousand dollars and his Glock and the AirLite. All of this he dropped to the bed.

—You killed sixteen Zetas in Campeche yesterday, on the highway.

—We were attacked.

—Where are all of your friends?

—Merida.

—Who are they?

—They are Americans. There are ten of them. We work with Baja state police and Baja Sur and others in the north. Our bosses have talked with Calderón himself.

—I have heard of this weapon you have. It is used by Carlos Herredia and his North Baja Cartel.

—It's a very good weapon. Read what it says on the slide.

The captain picked up the gun.

—There is a telescoping butt, *capitán*. Press on the two small buttons and it will appear.

The captain found the buttons on the rear of the gun, just under the slide, and the end of the butt popped out. He pulled it to its furthest reach and looked at Bradley again.

—May I step into the bathroom, *capitán*? I have some things to show you.

The captain motioned to the first soldier, who then followed Bradley into the bath. He rummaged in the side of his duffel and pulled out the silencer and an extended fifty-shot clip, holding one up in each hand for the man to see. He nodded gravely.

Back near the bed he handed them to the captain, who screwed the silencer onto the barrel threads. He popped out the nine-shot magazine and snapped home the gracefully curving extended clip. Guns and ammo, thought Bradley: the universal language of cops and bad guys.

—It will fire all fifty rounds in five seconds. Or you can leave it set on semi. It's real accurate. Take it. It is a gift from me to you.

—It must be confiscated.

—I understand. Confiscate the one on the desk too. Please.

One of the soldiers strode to the desk and unveiled the machine pistol waiting under the Merida newspaper.

—Of course the cash is for the Mexican Army also. It will buy lots of good equipment and hire some more good men. Please leave me the smaller sidearms, captain. It's not good to be in Mexico without defense. As you know.

The captain looked at the money, then up at Bradley.

—All of this will be kept as evidence.

—Of our friendship?

—Of your crime.

—What crime?

—The murder of sixteen.

—They were Zetas. We did you a favor.

The captain looked at the lead soldier, who pulled a pair of old-fashioned metal handcuffs from his belt and cuffed Bradley's hands behind his back.

—*Capitán?* What's wrong with you? I offer you my friendship and gifts of respect for you and your men. And you do this? I ask you now, man to man, to let me be free in Mexico. I'm not here to fish. I do not like fish or fishing. I'm here to find my wife. She was kidnapped by the Gulf Cartel at gunpoint. From my home in California. Armenta has threatened to skin her the day after tomorrow. I love her as you love your wife. Please, allow me to save her from rape and death. If you can find it in your heart.

The *capitán* listened in intent silence. The hairless patch in his right eyebrow gave him a vulnerable look but his eyes were dark and very alert. The scar continued up his forehead and into his hairline. Bradley could almost see the wheels turning inside the man's brain.

—Where is she?

—Here in Quintana Roo.

—Quintana Roo is very large.

—North of Kohunlich and east of Bacalar.

—This is only jungle. You must have coordinates if you are looking for her. Or a map.

—I have neither. I'm waiting for the information.

—You can continue your story on the way to our base.

—I'm a friend. I'm a cop. We are distant brothers. Let me go take care of my wife. You have my gifts.

—I don't need your gifts. No *gringo* comes to Mexico and murders sixteen men.

—Zetas.

—So you say. But why is a Zeta not a man?

—The Zetas are killers and torturers. And who made you God?

—We go now.

"Fuck!"

The captain nodded at the first soldier. A moment later he came from the bedroom with Bradley's satellite phone clipped to his belt and the bricks of cash in both hands.

Handcuffed or not Bradley held a third-degree black belt in Hapkido, a pain-based Korean attack system designed to break bones, blind, maim, and kill. When the soldier tried to walk past him Bradley kicked him hard on the chin and put him down. The captain swung his AR-15 too slowly and Bradley cracked the outside of his foot against his head and the stout man rocked to his left. Bradley jumped into the air and launched the same foot the other way, the hard top of the arch catching the captain flush on the cheekbone. The man crashed butt first to the floor with a dazed look on his face.

Bradley was outside in a flash. He sprinted around the casita and into the jungle and he could hear the bullets flying past him hitting the trees and branches. But the AR-15s threw so much lead at him that he knew he had to hit the ground or take a bullet so he plunged headfirst to the root-knotted jungle floor and lay there with his heart pounding as the bullets cut through the foliage above him and his hope fled.

Soon they were upon him. He tried to rise and run again but one of the men tackled him and the two others were soon above him, their fists and boots finding their marks. His cheek was smashed into the earth and he felt the grind of mud in his ear then the wallop of a boot to his mouth, then another. But mostly he felt his heart breaking because he knew he had no chance now and Erin would wait at the cenote alone tomorrow. And then what? What would she do? The blows rained down and each one of them felt deserved, a reminder of his spectacular incompetence. Somehow he found his footing and struggled up, but quickly they knocked him back down.

The gringos were taken not to a Mexican Army base but to a decrepit warehouse somewhere near the village of Ramonal. It was a long low building with a colonnade along the street and a veranda that sagged between each column. The window openings were boarded over with plywood and there were no lights outside or in and Bradley could see no entrance as they drove past.

The driver pulled around the south side and parked deep in shadowed darkness. Two of the Army vehicles were already there, Bradley

saw, and the others were behind them and he could see a faint rect-
angle of light from the door that stood open above the loading dock.

—The party house?

Bradley's voice sounded roughly unfamiliar, and with his swollen
tongue he felt the dangling tooth and the sharp edge of its broken
neighbor. His lips burned and felt twice their usual size. His shirt
front had a red swath down the button line.

—Yes. Big parties here, said the captain.

—Why aren't guns and money enough to buy mercy in this
wretched country? What is wrong with you people?

—Get out.

They pushed and pulled him out of the Durango and walked him
up the loading ramp. Inside bare bulbs hung on a cord from the high
ceiling and there were old conveyor belts and rollers scattered, and
packing tables and shipping stations long defunct. Near the middle of
the large open warehouse Bradley saw three ropes hung from pulleys
high in the rafters. Each rope ended in a hook heavy enough to
straighten the rope without a load and fitted with a clip to keep its
cargo fast. The opposite ends were wrapped around the spools of
manual crank winches bolted to the floor.

There were commercial-grade floodlights fixed to the rafters and,
when these blasted on, Bradley saw the blood-stained floorboards
and the bolted rings and shackles and chains and the chain saws and
the red gas cans arranged in a loose row to one side like an audience.
There was a car battery with jumper cables and assorted hand tools
thick with rust, lengths of rope and garden hose, pry bars, gloves and
folding chairs, all frosted and surreal in the white light.

His heart dropped. The sum of all fears in Mexico, right here in
this building. Wrong call. Not the good guys I was hoping for. Armenta's goons. And now we slowly die.

—All this is for your interviews?

—The interviews are long.

—What do you want to know, *capitán?*

—It's very simple what I want to know.

Two of the men wrestled Caroline Vega forward and two more brought an unresisting Jack Cleary into the bright wash of the torture lights. Both were handcuffed and Cleary still bled from the nose. The soldiers shackled each of them to the floor by one ankle, then they clipped a ceiling hook through the chain of Bradley's handcuffs. When one of the men cranked the hand winch, the pulley whinnied far overhead and his arms jerked up behind him and his head dropped forward. Soon there was only an inch of play before the joints of Bradley's shoulders would give way. He stared at the floor. The pain was sharp but bearable though he could feel that it would grow exponentially with even a twitch of the winch.

—*Capitán?* Please tell me what you want.

—Did you bring the guns to sell to Armenta? Or to kill him?

—Are you an honest soldier, *capitán?*

The pulley squealed and Bradley's breath caught and he stood on his tiptoes aghast at the pain and the promise of pain.

—To sell him or to kill him? Why is this difficult to say?

God, my faith is in you, Bradley thought.

—To kill him.

—What did you say?

—Kill him! He kidnapped my wife. I told you. He's holding her.

—I don't believe this. I believe you came to sell the guns.

—I have no guns but the ones I gave to you.

—Then where is your wife?

—I told you. Somewhere above Kohunlich.

—But where? Why are you south if she is north?

—I don't know exactly where.

The man at the winch moved slightly, the pulley shrieked over-head and the pain jumped through Bradley like a charge. He bel-lowed and stood on his tiptoes, his head down almost to his knees, his hamstrings burning.

—If you don't know where she is then how can you save her?

—The Yucatán! Between Kohunlich and the Caribbean.

—This is only jungle. You must have coordinates or a map. Per-haps you are trying to sell weapons to Armenta. Perhaps this is why you slaughtered the Zetas on the highway.

—We were attacked. If Armenta knew I was here I'd be dead. He has my wife. She's a performer in the *Estados Unidos*. Erin and the Inmates, very popular.

The *capitán* looked at Bradley then at one of his men, who shook his head.

—This means nothing to us.

—She means everything to me. Let me go. Let me try to find her. I'm no friend of Armenta. I swear to you on the name of the one God we know and fear.

—You must know where she is. You must have coordinates or a map. We can help you if you tell us where she is.

Bradley pressed up onto his tiptoes. He could feel the impossible angles forced upon his shoulder sockets and the imminent surren-der of the joints. No pain in his life had prepared him for this if any pain can.

—I have the coordinates, he whispered.

The winch man cranked.

—I have them! he screamed.

He felt his feet leave the floor and he dove forward to preserve his shoulders and the next thing he knew the floor had jumped up against his face and the excruciating pain had vanished. In its place was

something duller but better and in the center of it he felt the beating
of his heart.

He felt the rough floorboard against his cheek. The overhead lights
beat into his eye. There was rope piled on his head. He gasped rhyth-
mically, aware but not aware, suspended between the waking and the
other world. The dark shape of a man hovered over him and he understood that this was either the beginning or the end. He called upon
all his inner strength to remember the GPS coordinates accurately. He
summoned them up through the pain and humiliation and they came.
So he shaved the seconds north and west enough to mislead the Mexican Army and he took a deep breath before delivering the most important lie of his life.

—Eighteen degrees, forty minutes, zero seconds north. Eighty-
eight degrees, twenty-two minutes, sixty seconds west. Thirty armed
men, at least.

—You will write this on paper.

—If my arms will work.

One of the men unclipped the hook from Bradley's handcuffs and
rolled him over. Bradley hollered from the pain in his shoulders. He
knew the joints were twisted and stretched but not quite dislocated.
For a moment he squinted against the lights. Then he sat up, his legs
stretched flat out in front of him like an infant. He felt like an infant
also, small and helpless and the object of great attention from larger,
more powerful beings. He nodded at disbelieving Caroline Vega and
the still stunned Jack Cleary, then looked up at the *capitán*.

—Pen and paper, please.

The captain waved one of the soldiers over and the man bent
down and handed Bradley a stub of pencil and a tattered, body-
warmed notepad open to a clean page. Bradley wrote in the coordinates. He wondered if perhaps the federal troops who protected the

Reserva Biosfera de la Kohunlich might prevent these Army troops from entering onto their turf. Sure, he thought: a turf war like the CIA and FBI, or the U.S. Army and Navy might have. Everyone competes. Everyone meddles. Just two days, he thought. Just two days of stalling and posturing, and I can get Erin and be gone.

—If the numbers are different than the ones you told me I'll execute you.

—Check them over, Captain.

The captain took the notebook and read the numbers and looked at Bradley.

—*Perfecto*. You will now come to Quintana Roo Police headquarters. Where you will be safe. The Campeche State Police will travel here to talk to you about the Zetas.

—Tomorrow is all I have, Captain. I've got one day to get her out of Armenta's compound.

—I am afraid that you will be occupied for tomorrow. If we discover your wife we will detain and return her to the United States as our constitution requires.

—I will donate two hundred thousand dollars to the Army if you'll let me go.

—Saturnino offered three hundred thousand and I told him to go to hell. I fear not for myself, but for my family.

—Four hundred thousand. Bring your family to California. I'll get you on with the LASD. Starting pay is around forty thousand a year, plus benefits.

The captain stared down at him while he tore out the sheet with the coordinates on it. Then he smiled bitterly.

—Americanos. You come all the way to the bottom of Mexico to insult me with your bribes?

Bradley awaited the boot.

—Tell me what the cost of my wife is.

—The cost is your business with Benjamin Armenta and the many thousands of men like him.

The captain tossed the notebook back to the soldier and barked an order and marched heavily toward the door. Suddenly Bradley was up and being pushed along behind Cleary and Vega and he knew that sunrise would find him not at the cenote but in a jail in Chetumal, if sunrise found him at all.

29

ERIN LABORED THROUGH THE NIGHT and into morning, fell asleep with the Hummingbird and a notebook beside her on the bed, then awakened after two hours of horrifying dreams.

In one of the dreams Saturnino came into her room while she slept and she understood, in the strange logic of dreams, that if she awakened he would attack her. So she remained still, watching him through her closed eyelids. He had a perfectly V-shaped divot in the center of his hairline where the flashlight had crashed into him. He prowled the room looking for something on the table, then in the desk, his back to her. When he turned and looked at her from across the suite he was a leopard and in his mouth was a baby doll dressed in a blue jumpsuit as an infant boy might be. The leopard looked at her with the doll dangling, then dropped the doll and sprang through the window, silently gliding through the pane without breaking it, and into the dark. The doll ate a box of cereal, then grew roots and turned into a white poinsettia.

She was saved by the knock of Atlas, and she called for him to come in as she wrestled herself up from the nightmare. She was so glad to see him. Her life had come down to this day. Sweet Tuesday, she thought. Please be the day this ends. She cried and hid in the bathroom and checked if the gun was still there and it was. When she came out she asked him for coffee and a light breakfast.

Now she was back in the studio control room, listening to more of the *narcocorridos* in Armenta's vast collection of CDs. She had not changed her clothes or showered. She could smell herself. Her hair was pulled back in a lank ponytail and her temples were dotted with perspiration in spite of the coolness of the studio.

"I'll come back for you if you want," said Owens.

"Thank you. I'm having trouble concentrating."

"Imagine that. Two hours?"

"Good," said Erin. "Maybe we could take a walk later, outside. It would help to get some oxygen to my brain."

Her heart tapped faster and she felt the shortness of breath that always accompanied her fear.

Owens studied her. "When?"

"When everyone rests."

"Siesta. I'll make sure that Benjamin is with me."

"I'm terrified, Owens. What if someone sees me? One of Armenta's men, or a leper, or a servant? I read Bradley's note a hundred times. I know it by heart and I know the map by heart. But what if I get lost? One wrong turn. The jungle is dense. What if Bradley's information is old? What if there's a trail he didn't know about and I make a wrong turn?"

"You'll find the cenote. I know you will."

"What if he's not there? What if they arrested him? Or worse?"

"Believe."

"What if someone is there first? Getting water or taking a bath?"

"Believe, Erin."

"In what? In who?"

"That's your choice. I can't decide for you."

She almost said that she believed in Bradley, but there was such a hollow ring to the idea that she couldn't give it words. A short few days ago, he would have been her answer. Now, no. Ever again?

"Come with me," said Erin.

"You forget, I can leave here anytime I want." Owens brought a card key from the pocket of her jeans and gave it to Erin. Erin looked at it for a long beat, her small plastic rectangular savior. Then she dropped it into her boot.

"Won't Benjamin know where I got it?"

"I stole it from my father."

"Will Armenta feed him to a leopard when he sees I'm gone?"

"Father Ciel is safe from Benjamin Armenta. Protected by the God whose indulgence he sells."

"That's heartbreaking. He's filth."

"He is what he is."

"Owens, why have you helped me?"

Owens gave her a startled look. "Mike says we can only give someone the tools to help themselves."

"Then thank you for the tools, Owens. For everything."

"Do you like what you've written so far?"

"Ask me later."

"Back in L.A.?"

"Deal. In L.A." Erin stepped forward and hugged Owens. Then she took the woman's scarred and welted wrists in her hands and looked steadily into her gray eyes. "Sure you don't want to come with me?"

"I'm where I need to be."

"What if Benjamin blames you?"

"I know how to lie to him."

"An hour before siesta come back here. That will give me time to get to my room and get ready and go. And time for you to get back to Benjamin."

"Before you leave the Castle, Erin, slip the key under the door to my room. Don't forget. If you are caught with it someone will suffer. Maybe me."

Erin sat at the mixing board. Concentrate, she thought. Concentrate. But it was almost impossible to compose now. The more the minutes ticked away the less control she had over her own emotions and words and skills. Her mind was beginning to storm. Bradley. The cenote. How to get from her room to the jungle without being seen. What were the chances? Then, the pathways. The trees. Would the trails be clear? Would Bradley be there?

Concentrate. Focus. She listened to Los Jaguars through the Auratones. The Jaguars were terrific, she thought, but she didn't want to praise violence as they did, and she didn't want to present Benjamin Armenta as a man created by the violence around him. He was not a product. He was self-driven, self-governed, self-made. If there was one thing she had learned from him over last night's long dinner, it was that Benjamin Armenta was utterly aware of himself, without delusion and without excuse.

She had a start on a song but that was all—two verses and a chorus and a tenuous melody to hold them. *What if the trails have grown over?* But she was already two long verses into the song and Armenta was still only a boy. How long was this *corrido* going to be? *What if he isn't there? Where should I go?* One of her favorite gangster songs was Dylan's "Joey," and that went, what, eleven minutes? Thirteen? *What if they follow me, what if Saturnino is feeling strong again?* Worse, she had no bridge in sight and every tempo she tried was wrong. She kept trying to get the odd syncopation that the *corridos* often had, that hurried, sooner-than-expected downbeat that foiled your expectations and made your breath catch and drove the narrative forward musically. Like you're tripping but you never quite fall, she thought. Without it the song was sounding like a *narcocorrido* written by a *gringa*. I have to do better than that. The greatest *narcocorrido* of all time. Jesus please help me. *What if Atlas wants to talk and I've vanished? Will he sound the alarm? What if Ciel tells Armenta his key has been stolen? What if the key doesn't work?*

The notebook was open on the board beside her and she read through what she had written.

City of Gold

VERSE

He was born in Veracruz
Son of a man he never knew
His mama did what she had to do
Lo que tenia que hacer!
Skinny boy long hair bare feet
Hermanos flacos—nothing to eat *(Hey, Flaco!)*
You gotta hustle to get the food
(Your) blood runs hot in Veracruz . . .

CHORUS (x2)

(Benji———)
Ah . . . you do what you have to do
(Benji———)
Lo que tenia que hacer!

VERSE

They beat him bad on his way to school
(La partieron la madre!)
He stole a truck ran down those fools
Took their *dinero* and left them dead
So the blood was turned to bread

CHORUS (X2)

(Benji———)
Did what nobody else would do
(Benji———)
Lo que tenia que hacer!

RAP

Chased through the streets of the City of Gold
Hearts beat strong in the City of Gold
You can feel the Ghost of Cortez in the City of Gold
Lookin' for that pagan treasure in the City of Gold
Better go quick boy you better run
Little Benji hidin' from the things he done
Get a reputation and the money will come
Where the blood runs hot in the jungle sun . . .

The clock on the wood-paneled mixing room wall said 8:25. She took the pen and notebook into the tracking room and moved Armenta's accordion into one of the instrument booths so she could sit down at the Yamaha. Even the sound of her boot on the floor and the piano cover being slid open resonated in this room like a perfect musical chord. She ran through Joni Mitchell's "River" to get her heart and her fingers working together and when she got to the ending quote from "Jingle Bells" it reminded her of Christmas and her home so strongly that tears welled in her eyes and she understood very clearly now how terribly Benjamin Armenta must have missed his home when he'd been exiled in Salvador, so she took up the pen and she listened to the wonderful melody and she tried to keep up with the lines coming into her head:

VERSE

So he hides in a secret place
Eleven months and thirteen days
He grew strong but he had the blues
He longed for a girl in Veracruz

CHORUS

(Benji————)
Sweet Anya in Veracruz
(Benji————)
He did what nobody else would do
(Benji————)
Lo que tenia que hacer!
(Benji————)
He did what nobody else would do

And then she imagined what it would be like to be kept from your home for not just a few days, as she had been, but for months on end, and to never know if you'd be able to go back there. What passion you would feel, to finally return! She tapped the melody on the piano and heard the instruments join in, the accordion and the bajo sexto and the guitars. Yes, it was starting to take on the sound of a *corrido*. Danger. Doing things you never thought you could do:

RAP

Steal back quiet to the City of Gold
Where the blood runs hot on the jungle stones
Get a reputation in the City of Gold
Better than money in the City of Gold
Trade it in for your empty soul

Well, no, thought Erin. Not empty soul. If I write that he'll skin me for sure.

So she scratched through "empty," then the rest of the line, but she couldn't find the right words to replace it. It was a terrible feeling and one that she knew well—the fine and incandescent thing that brought the music to her mind was gone again, vanishing like a far-off filament of lightning.

She took the pen and notebook then walked around the tracking room, past the vocal and instrument booths. She imagined them staffed by professionals who could bring her song to life. *Narcorridos* were almost always sung by men, so who would have the best possible voice for it? Luis Miguel? Jorge Hernandez of Los Tigres? Flaco on accordion, for sure! And Ry Cooder on acoustic and maybe Mike Campbell would play electric, and her all-time rhythm section, Sly and Robbie, would show up with Sam Clayton for percussion and man, what if we could get Linda and Lila for harmonies, yeah, that'll be the day Linda Ronstadt and Lila Downs sing backup on one of my songs. But now she could hear them playing and singing anyway. She stood still for a long moment, hearing fully detailed passages of the song, all of the instruments and vocals working perfectly. She

closed her eyes and walked to the rhythm tapping the pen and notebook against her legs. Eyes still closed, she listened and tried not to
interrupt in any way, scribbling across the pages and turning them as
fast as she could:

Hunger grew in his belly like fire
He used his cenote like a telephone wire
To the Gods that he fed that he hoped to inspire
On the City of Gold they would build his empire

CHORUS (X2)

(Benji———)
Did what nobody else would do
(Benji———)
Lo que tenia que hacer!

LAST VERSE (TO BE SUNG SOFTLY, ACCOMPANIED BY ACOUSTIC
GUITAR . . .)

But the Gods are a fickle crew
And Benji's time had come overdue
A gun in the hand of someone new
Who simply did what he had to do

CHORUS REPEAT FADE OUT

(Benji———)
Ah . . . you do what you have to do
(Benji———)
Lo que tenia que hacer!

This *corrido* is going on forever, she thought. Maybe not the greatest *narcorrido* ever written, just the longest!

Then the music stopped. Erin was left standing in silence before the wall clock.

Ten-forty.

"You are hearing music," said Father Ciel.

He was so close behind her, she felt his breath on her neck and she wheeled and stepped away from him, her heart racing.

"I was trying to. Why are you here?"

"My key to your room is missing. I have not told Benjamin. Did you take it?"

"How could I take it? I can't leave my room. Now it's gone? Who else might be sneaking up on me in my own room?"

He looked down on her. The cold blue light was gone from his eyes and in its place was a moist pity. She smelled his vanilla smell and she thought of what he was doing to the novitiates and she felt revulsion.

"I suspect Saturnino took the key. He is becoming increasingly active. I have come to warn you. You are perspiring and you look alarmed."

"You scare me."

He smiled and nodded as if her confession permitted him something. Then he unbuttoned his coat and let it fall open and reached out with his thin pale hands as if to accept her in an embrace. Erin's eyes were drawn to the revolver in the waistband of his trousers and his bulge. She saw the lights reflected off his glasses and the air-conditioning moved his wisps of thin tan hair.

"Come, my child."

"Do not touch me."

His smile was dry and dreamy. "Who told you that you were naked? The serpent?"

"Don't use those words on me."

"Have you spoken to Owens?"

"She told me everything about you."

"She can so easily beguile. An actor's art. But she did not tell you the truth."

"You should be ashamed."

"You have listened to the serpent. Take my hands and let us pray."

"Never."

"Great men can be brought down by the lies of small people. Owens imagines that her sins are mine. She cannot comprehend that a man may devote himself to the Lord. This is common among the unfaithful. Here—take my hands."

"Go to hell."

"I know that Benjamin has given your husband one more day to deliver the money."

"Why are you here?"

"To give you another day beyond that. And another and another. I can save you if you love me as I love you. In Christ. A holy secret between us. We will celebrate the Lord's love and the flesh that he has given us to celebrate Him. Take my hands."

"I'm not thirteen years old. I'm not overwhelmed by you or what you pretend to stand for. Get out of this room before I scream."

"These rooms are soundproof. Who would hear you?"

"You're worse than the devil. The devil is honest compared to you."

He stared down on her for a long moment. She could not quite see his eyes, only the reflection of the lights off his glasses. A drop of sweat ran from his temple to his chin then hit the floor with a tap.

"Because you have listened to the serpent your child shall be born misshapen and an abomination."

"And you'll burn in the hell you frighten children with."

"I can do no more for you."

"You haven't done one thing for me, ever."

Ciel patiently buttoned his coat while he stared down at her. He was sweating hard now. She saw the waver of his chin and the tremble of his hands on the buttons. When she finally got a look at his eyes he seemed to be focused on something beyond her. Then he turned and walked quietly across the tracking room past the booths and the Yamaha and pushed his way through the door.

She watched him cross the mixing room and vanish into the lobby. She waited a few moments, then sunk to her knees and put her forehead to the carpet and hugged her middle and told the little life inside her to hold on. Hold on, she thought. We're almost free. Please hold on, Baby McKenna.

She knelt there for some time, rocking side to side, listening to the whoosh of blood in her ears and the thump of her heart and the strange infinite silence of the studio, which was not silence at all. It was the sound of nothing. What a beautiful sound, she thought. What could be more pure?

Help us.

Help us.

Help us.

She rose and composed. First at the piano. Then with the Hummingbird in one of the instrument rooms. Finally just sprawled on a couch in the mixing room with the notepad and pen and the air-conditioner breeze drying the sweat on her face and neck.

And after what seemed like hours she finally took a deep breath and copied the song out in its entirety, neatly and clearly, in her best cursive handwriting. She set the time signature and wrote in the chords and the notes of some of the fills and tried to make some helpful suggestions as to tone and phrasing. She knew that *corridos* rarely began with guitar intros but she was a gringa rocker so she wrote out the notes to one anyway, figuring that Armenta's guitarist would likely ignore it. "City of Gold." It was different from the Jaguars' *corridos*, not so much accordion, less of a polka, more stately and restrained. It had a little Carribean in it, too, a little ska. It sounded more like biography than legend, which is what she wanted. There was something almost mournful about it, up-tempo though it was. The melody built slowly and the narrative built slowly too but when she ran through it on the guitar, Erin thought she heard something big and compelling and lushly unpredictable in it. Something aimed at the heart. Something about a man alone. Something about the way things used to be in this world, and still are, and always will be. It took up twelve of the notebook pages, double-spaced, and she estimated it would run about seven minutes if you kept it up-tempo and nixed all solos, the guitar intro and the end fade. Or you could relax it, let the artists strut their stuff, and you'd have nine or ten minutes. She liked that idea. Why did a *corrido* have to sound like a polka on meth? And also: what did it matter? Who was going to hear it? Who was going to play it? In a moment of desperate optimism she wrote out her wish list of musicians to perform the song.

It was two o'clock when she set the notebook square in the middle of the Yamaha keyboard, the pen inserted at the song so Armenta couldn't miss it.

Siesta.

A few minutes later Owens came from the lobby into the mixing room and they looked at each other through the soundproof glass.

30

SHE SHOWERED AND PUT ON a pair of lightweight hiking shorts and athletic shoes and an oversized tee with sequined butterflies on it. Again she had the feeling that someone had been in her room but there was no evidence of this. She pulled the Cowboy Defender from inside the toilet tank and dried it over the sink with a hand towel and she hefted it and wondered exactly why she had been unable to use it. She had clearly seen her reasons and opportunities, but she had not been able to even draw the weapon. She dropped it into one of the flapped front pockets and slid the folded fifty-dollar bills into another. Then on hands and knees she reached her hand far under the mattress and came up with the silk swatch containing the map and her instructions. She looked at them one more time to be sure, then she folded and stuffed it into still another pocket of the shorts.

Next she slipped into the loose white leper's dress that Owens had brought her. In front of the mirror she lifted the white rebozo and settled it over her head and shoulders. She arranged the garments to best hide her hair and face.

At the door she stopped and straightened and took three deep breaths. She remembered her father's wry cool and tried to harness the grogginess of her fear, to turn it into calm and clarity.

Come to me by moonlight, sugar, she thought. No, come to me by sunshine. Come to me any way you can get here. Any way you can.

She pushed the card into the lock and heard the dead bolt disengage. Buzz, hum, clunk. Music to her ears now. She held the door open with her toe while she reached up under the dress and slid the card key into a pocket of the shorts.

The door shut behind her and made its final sounds. She walked down the hallway purposefully but not quickly. She pushed the button for the elevator and waited, praying that no one would be moving about in the heat of afternoon siesta. Four floors, she thought—just a straight shot for four floors and I can get outside, where the lepers come and go without drawing much attention.

The elevator door opened on two of the black housekeepers, who stopped talking to stare at her wide-eyed. Erin saw the worry in their faces and she saw that they wanted to get away from her, but didn't know how, so she bowed her head humbly and stepped aside. The two women bustled past her into the vestibule, then the hallway, hurrying down it, then turning for a quick look back at her before turning the first corner.

Once inside the car she considered the maddeningly unlabeled buttons. Six of them, for either four or five stories—no one would clarify which, not even Owens, who had pushed the wrong ones more than once. Erin was fairly sure that the third highest button was for the first floor, not the second highest button, which would logically service the ground floor, allowing for the basement. Owens's rooms were on the first floor. She went with her memory.

The car was slow as always but it didn't stop at the second floor and the next thing Erin knew the door had slid open to frame the entryway of the Castle, its grand foyer and majestic iron doors. Sunshine fell from the skylights in the ceiling and dappled the floor around the swordlike shadows of the palms. A small monkey sat on the curtain rod above a casement window, eating sunflower seeds and looking down at her with a frankly doubtful expression.

She strode down the hallway, away from the foyer, and when she came to Owens's suite she fished the card key from her shorts, looked up and down the hall, then slid it under the door.

Back in the entryway she walked across the tile and pushed against the massive right-side door. The birds shuffled from on high and a monkey screeched softly. The door was heavier than she had imagined and at first she thought it might be locked. But it finally gave, as if in surrender, and she put her shoulder to it and pushed harder. The door swung and gained momentum, towing Erin into the withering Yucatecan heat.

She stopped in the shade of the loggia, stunned by the brightness that lay beyond. She had never felt so conspicuous in her life, even on a stage with a spotlight blinding her. She pulled the rebozo forward over her head. There was an expanse of gravel between the Castle and the jungle and this gravel was raked several times daily by the groundskeepers and as Erin stepped onto it she saw no footprints coming or going, not even the neat tracks of the crabs or lizards that left their trails everywhere, but were almost never seen.

She came to the jungle and stepped right in. Once inside the shade of the trees she stopped and glanced back at the Castle looming in the midday heat. She saw two lepers, women, coming slowly down the outdoor stairway from the third story. A good thing, she thought. She felt like a character in the Old Testament fleeing some cursed place, surrounded by enemies and observed by a jealous and hot-tempered God. A pillar of salt, she thought. Demoniacs. Bloody altars. Dear Lord, get me out of here. Dear duplicitous Bradley, please be waiting.

She turned and ran. She'd forgotten what a pleasure it could be, heat or not, pregnant or not. But what a wild, dislocated feeling it was to be embarking on the most important journey of her life with nothing but the clothes on her back, a leper's shawl, five-hundred dollars and a gun. Save some energy, she thought. She slowed to a trot, then a fast stride.

The trail was narrow but clear. Tree roots grew the thickness of human arms and they were raised across the path and worn smooth by walkers. The trunks of the ficus trees grew up close to the passage-way and the Carrizo cane grew in high walls and choked out the sunlight and the breeze. Erin could hear her shoes crunching on the sand and the roots but she heard no birds or monkeys or even insects, just the gradually fading sound of the Castle's generators running the siesta air conditioners. She walked fast with long steps, then ran again a short distance, then slowed once more to a walk. For a few strides she held her belly in both hands and talked to her charge: *hang in there, hang in there, little baby. You are one tough little guy.*

She followed the trail she had taken with Armenta. She recognized a very narrow fork that led right and one that led left and she con-gratulated herself for keeping to the true path. The passageway got narrower and the roots were raised and knotted higher but she la-bored over them, holding to the cane stalks for balance and careful not to turn an ankle. Something black and low scurried ahead of her, no more than a blur.

A moment later she stopped and turned and listened. She took a few more steps and stopped again. That feeling of being watched, she thought. She'd had it a million times as a girl, watched or not. She heard a bird twitter and a faint breeze stir the foliage.

She continued. Suddenly she came to a fork that she did not re-member. She stopped again. These paths were not minor offshoots but an almost perfect wishbone—two trails just as wide and well-worn as the one she was on, each leading away at equally obtuse angles.

She stared, disbelieving. As she scrolled through the memory of her walk to the cenote with Armenta, she had that sinking, breath-robbing realization that she couldn't remember this place at all. She could remember the silver plate she had carried, and the hard lump of the Cowboy Defender in the pocket of her dress, and the patches of his hair that Armenta had tried to tame with gel, and the silver jewel-studded candlestick he had carried, but she could not remember this junction, this grand and dramatic fork that they had most assuredly negotiated.

She placed both hands over her womb. She was breathing quickly but not deeply and she was light-headed in the breezeless heat. Panic kills. Dad.

She stared at the two paths. The roots of the left path were worn as smoothly as the roots of the right. The right path had a thin layer of white sand, as did the left. Both were of equal width. Both led through thickets of almost indistinguishable trees and plants. They looked like twins staring back at her. Then she thought she saw something. She knelt down slowly to one knee, balancing herself on her fingertips. This made her dizzier, so she took deeper breaths, and faster. She blinked to clear the sweat from her eyes. In the filtered light she saw the footprint on the right path. It was just a small crescent shape, a partial heel, maybe, with the faint zigzag of a sole pattern within it. In front of it was a larger mark, once an oval, perhaps, marked with the same pattern. Going in her direction, she thought.

She stood and fought off the dizziness with deep fast breaths. She felt a fresh eruption of sweat on her face. Who are you? When were you here? Minutes ago? Days? Were you going to the cenote or somewhere else?

She had heard that there were villages in this direction, east, and a hotel, and a marina. She didn't know the names of them or even what country they might be in. She looked straight up as if the sun could give her some clue but it wasn't visible through the thick copse overhead.

Traveled or less traveled. Frost. All the difference. Some help that is, in the middle of a jungle.

So now what? She had to decide and she knew this, but how? On the basis of what? On the basis of who she was and what she was. What else was there to reckon by? Erin had always believed that human nature and human beings were fundamentally good. Not always but usually. Thus she now told herself that another human being might be some kind of help to her, or at least not a hindrance or a threat. In her life she had seen generosity and selflessness, and sacrifice and goodwill. She had seen their opposites too, but if she had to choose right now, she would choose to believe that people, given a chance, would do the right thing. Mostly.

She stepped over the footprint and followed it down the fork leading to her right. What a strange feeling to have lost the known and then to follow what she only believed. Soon she was halfway there, she thought, based on memory. But how good was it? She looked for more shoe prints and she saw a few but these were yards apart, as if the walker were a giant striding through high grass.

Finally she saw something she recognized, a lightning-blasted fig tree, blown to splinters by the bolt, the splinters black and upraised in the green density around them. She had seen this with Armenta and now it seemed a sign that she was going to find the cenote and Bradley, and in a few short hours they would be in the airport in Chetumal, boarding a plane to home and freedom.

Closer to the cenote the trail widened and she remembered this place too, where Armenta had said that the trees grew taller and more fully because they were drawing on the same groundwater as the cenote. She broke into a trot and allowed hope to spark inside her like the beginning of a fire. Then she had to slow again, short of breath and her legs getting heavy.

Through the trees ahead she saw the first glimmers of the pool.

The water was fired with sunshine this time of day and the surface looked flat as a golden mirror. When she came to the last heavy stand of trees she stopped and stepped inside them and waited for her heart to settle. She could only see a small part of the cenote from here and she knew that Bradley would be hidden, but she was disappointed that he was not the first thing she saw, that he didn't just step from the foliage into a column of sunlight and smile at her. Was this another lie of his? Another betrayal?

When her breath finally slowed she approached the pool, staying along the rim of the trees. Closer the cenote looked perfectly round, as if it had been drilled from solid gray rock. From here, with the sun at her back, she could see the last lip of rock before the water, and it was worn smooth by hundreds of years of people swimming and drinking and filling their vessels with the cold, clean water that was always here. There were crude stone benches set back from the pool, ancient gray-black slabs balanced upon others, and even these were polished smooth by centuries of human touch.

She saw the place where she had stood when she threw the plate into the pool. She imagined the treasures piled up somewhere down in the black water—the Mayan gold and silver, their statues and calendars, the gems and jewelry and valuables plucked from ancient history right up to the Corvette and the musical instruments—and the bones of the sacrificed spiking it all. Nothing ever moves down there, she thought. No flow. No current. No tides. Just stillness forever, amen.

She scanned the far side for signs of her husband but saw nothing. So she stepped out into the open and walked toward the water. When she got up nearly to the edge of it she could see the whole lovely pool. The treetops rimmed the perimeter but directly over the water the sky was clear, and behind her, to the west, the sun angled its rays onto the surface and turned the water to gold. In this gold the reflected trees stood upside down, their trunks rooted to their sponsors at the water-line.

"Bradley?" she asked quietly. Then a little louder, "Brad?"

She watched and waited. A puff of breeze scattered the tree trunks on the water, then they re-formed, inverted again. She looked back down the trail and saw just jungle. She started off along the lip of the cenote, walking counterclockwise around it. She saw a pink rubber sandal with a broken thong sitting on the rock. A small ball of foil. A clear plastic bottle cap.

The cenote was not large and in a few minutes she was standing directly across from where she had started. She squinted across the golden surface at the sun-charged jungle.

"Bradley? *Brad?*"

She walked the rim again. When she was three-quarters of the way around she stopped again and looked around. She felt watched. He wouldn't let her dangle this long, would he? For what possible reason?

Her heart fluttered lightly and she had the terrible notion that he was not here and had never been here and never would be. The idea made her dizzy. Vertigo and nausea. She looked ahead and took a deep breath. Just then a wad of what looked like white printer paper flew from the jungle and landed on the rock, not twenty feet in front of her. She watched it bounce erratically along the rough surface and quickly stop. It almost rolled into the water. She looked into the foliage from where it had come and saw the palm fronds flickering in the breeze.

"Who are you and what do you want?" She waited and heard nothing. She wondered how long it would take to run back around the cenote and down the path and all the way back to the Castle. Because this was clearly not her husband. A child playing a game, maybe. A trickster taunting a leper for the fun of it. "You don't scare me."

With her heart banging against her ribs and her knees wobbling like a stack of empty cans, she lifted the dress and reached into her pocket. She let the dress drop back down, then took her first step toward the round white thing. Halfway there she could see that it was almost certainly a sheet of paper, wadded up tightly. She thought she saw dark markings on the wrinkled facets, letters perhaps or small portions of a larger drawing. But they might be creases. The wad teetered in the breeze.

She stood over it and looked into the jungle, but saw no one. She looked behind her. She looked up into the trees. Then she knelt and with her free hand picked up the paper and stood back up straight. She unfurled it without looking down, alert to the world around her. When it was flat and open she glanced at it and knew what it was.

"Did I do a good drawing of your map?"

She searched for the owner of the voice and it took her a moment to find him. Saturnino stood in the jungle, dressed in camouflage, his face painted like foliage. He stepped into a small clearing and she saw that he had a machete slung over one shoulder and an assault rifle over the other and a proud smile on his face, teeth yellow and lips red against the face paint.

31

ERIN'S WORLD WENT ELECTRIC GREEN—the man she was looking at, the trees behind him, the sky behind the trees. All a green mirage, luminescent and flickering like neon losing its charge. She thought she was going to faint. "I knew you'd been in my room."

"As head of security. Yes, of course."

"Where is he?"

"He is not here. Sadly."

"Did you kill him?"

"He did not arrive. I waited and watched. Hour after hour. I brought food and water and cocaine for alertness and rum to be relaxed. There are rumors of a battle with the Zetas and an arrest by the Army. Gringos are said to be involved. But there are rumors of everything in Mexico. Your husband has failed you again, and this is factual. That's why I am very happy to be seeing you."

Saturnino had powdered his hair green, as well as the bandage at the hairline of his forehead. His blue eyes shone brightly against the makeup. With the weapons and war paint Saturnino looked like some Pacific fighter left behind in World War II, she thought, or an actor in an action movie.

"They said you were damaged," she said. "They said you were behaving strangely and sleeping all the time and speaking some language no one knew but you. They said you didn't recognize anyone."

"But they are superstitious, Mexicans. The flashlight knocked me out. Yes. The *craneo* is somewhat broken. It still hurts. I hear voices when there are not people. I hear music when there is no music. I have seen eight ghosts, one *bruja* and one *chupacabra*. But I still have my very intelligent brain."

"Oh."

Saturnino brushed through the trees and walked around another, then onto the wide rock rim of the cenote where Erin stood. She was bad at judging distance but he did not raise his voice when he spoke and she heard him clearly in the jungle stillness.

"You don't look so much like a leper. They wear sandals, not the athletic shoes. They look at the ground and walk slow. You are very much more beautiful. The map I found easy. The bed is a popular hiding place. I took a picture of the map and put the map under the bed. So you would not alarm. Then I drew the map on the paper."

"You're a clever one."

"This is a joke of me?"

"Nothing in the world about you is funny, Saturnino."

"What is that in your hand?"

"The map."

"No. The shining gun. What is this gun?"

"It's the Cowboy Defender."

"Cowboy Defender! Is very deadly?"

"So they say."

"Do you know how to shoot it?"

"I fired it at a paper target."

"Does it recoil very much?"

"Really jumps."

"The bullets are what design?"

"Beats me. Big slow ones, Brad said."

"Where did you hide it?"

"In the toilet box."

"I did not look there. But the ammunition is now made bad from the water."

"No. The water will not hurt the ammunition."

"But you do not know this."

"I'm taking it on faith."

"Yes? Faith?"

Erin dropped the sheet of paper but kept looking at Saturnino. The gun was heavy. But the sputtering green world of a few moments ago had gone away, and although her knees felt rusted shut her vision was good again and she reminded herself of the cool place inside and tried to find it and go there.

"Are you going to apologize for what you did to me?"

"I wish to complete what I began."

"I thought so."

"You are much of what I have been thinking. And you are in the dreams and the visions I have when I am not sleeping."

"Lucky me."

He looked at her, puzzled.

"Are you going to kill me when you're done? Or just beat me up and rape me and walk away?"

"I would not be likely to kill you."

"Not likely."

"But what happens is difficult to see before."

She considered options. She could not outrun him unless she shot him first. And if she managed this, then what? Try to find the rumored villages and marinas of the east? How far east? Were there trails? Wouldn't the people there just turn her over to Benjamin? She'd be right back at the Castle to continue where she left off, writing a song to earn another day of life? Would Hood deliver the money? Did he even know where she was? Would Armenta honor his deal with either

Hood or herself? Or maybe feed them both to the now-ravenous ti-gers?

"I'm going to the marina," she said. "The only way you can stop me is to shoot me. It was nice seeing you again, Saturnino. Good-bye."

He unslung the rifle. "I will not shoot you. But I shall now explode the Cowboy Defender from your hand!"

He brought the gun to his shoulder and his eye to the rear sight and she saw the barrel roving in a low tight circle. The rifle spat and she heard the bullet whirr past her leg and crack into the jungle be-hind her.

"*Ohhh,*" he groaned. "I have the miss!"

He fired again and this time she felt the tug of it going through her dress and when she looked down there was a small hole in the cotton not one inch from where her right hand dangled, holding the Cowboy Defender.

She raised her gun hand out straight to her side, then lifted it over her head and held it there for just a moment before letting it fall waist high. It was like the routine she did as a high school flag twirler but nobody was shooting at the flags back then. She could see the barrel of Saturnino's rifle tracking her movements and again it barked sharply and she heard the buzz and sensed the shock of the bullet as it screamed past the back of her hand.

"You play with me, Erin McKenna!"

"I do not play with you!"

She guessed his distance at thirty feet and she remembered *more than ten feet away just forget it* but she pointed the derringer at him anyway. And she remembered *squeeze the trigger, never yank it* but she yanked the trigger hard in spite of herself.

The blast screamed through her ears and her hands jumped into the air. Saturnino flinched and lowered his rifle and looked at her. "You?" he gurgled.

"Yes, me, Erin McKenna Jones."

He raised the rifle but as he tried to set the stock to his cheek he somehow missed, and the barrel circled wildly. A bullet whistled far over her head. His torso swayed and she tried to track it with the barrel of the derringer but she couldn't get the timing right and keep the little barrel on target. Suddenly, Saturnino rocked back on his heels and his weapon clattered to the rocks. He righted himself clumsily, overcorrecting, then he reached down to pick up the rifle and toppled into the cenote.

The gun smoke hovered in front of her in the humid air. Her ears rang as they had never rung, not on a stage or in an audience or a studio.

Saturnino floated facedown and he raised one arm as if to freestyle but the arm fell and smacked the water and did not come up again. He tried his other arm but he wasn't able to pull it free to begin a stroke. He was close enough to her that she could see the green dye from his hair mixing with the water, and the blood billowing up around his neck, and the dull twinkle of the machete strapped to his shoulder, blade pointing down at the depths into which it was eager to go.

He stopped moving and she watched him for a minute. Two. The breeze pushed him toward the middle of the pool. The terrible weight of her circumstance came over her at once and she wondered if she could even move. She looked down at the Cowboy Defender, then back at Saturnino. His body bobbed gently and rotated slowly clockwise like a compass needle finding north.

She summoned her strength and concentration then stumbled across the rock rim of the cenote and knelt. She set down her derringer and picked up Saturnino's gun. It was very heavy and slick with something and it felt foul against her skin. She had no idea how it worked. After a long struggle she finally got the breech to stay open.

When she managed this she tilted it over and got a cartridge to fall out. Tears ran down her face. She picked up the Defender and broke it open and the empty shell unseated itself. She pulled it out and tossed it into the jungle. But when she tried to reload the derringer with the shell from Saturnino's gun there was no way the much longer rifle cartridge would fit her trusty companion. The tears poured off her cheeks and chin and hit her hands as she fumbled with the guns and ammunition, and she realized how utterly nonsensical she was being, and she knew that she was only doing this desperate exercise so she wouldn't have to face the choices that she would now have to make. You still have one bullet. The cool place. Go there now.

She dropped the gun and cartridge and walked a few feet to an ancient rock bench and sat. She straightened her back and unwound the rebozo and wiped her face with it, then dropped it to the slab. A bird twittered and another answered. When she saw that Saturnino had vanished she stood with a gasp then caught herself. She climbed onto the bench seat and stood on her tiptoes. With the sun off the water she could see his body out near the middle, suspended in the clear water a few feet down.

She sat and stared and took stock. Bradley was gone, perhaps arrested, perhaps worse. He had ordered her to continue walking east toward the lagoons and the ocean if he was not waiting for her at the cenote. She felt betrayed by him but when she pictured him and the memories flashed across her mind's eye, she missed him terribly too. By now Benjamin Armenta was either aware of her escape, or soon would be. Men would be coming. Hood and the ransom money were God knew where, apparently foiled by the weather. She loved Hood but she felt betrayed by him too. She was hungry and thirsty and her soul was damaged by the killing. She tried to keep these truths from crushing her spirit and her baby. She placed her hands over him and closed her eyes and whispered sweet things to him and she willed her blood to find and fill him with oxygen and nitrogen and hydrogen and all those elements and molecules she could never quite understand in chemistry class. Make him strong, she ordered her blood. Give him energy and power and most of all, durability.

She took the rebozo and walked over to the guns. Ugly things, she thought. But she picked up the Cowboy Defender and closed it tight on its one bullet and slipped it into the pocket of her shorts. Then she rearranged the rebozo to cover her face as much as possible. Sighing, she lifted Saturnino's heavy assault rifle and pointed the barrel to the ground and pushed the live cartridge back into the breech. She pushed a button and the action closed with a metallic clank and she saw the slide switch with the red showing and she was not positive, but she was pretty sure, the weapon would now fire.

She picked up the trail on the far side of the cenote and entered the thick jungle. The late afternoon sunlight had waned and the birds and monkeys had started sounding again. She came to a fork and tried to choose the widest, most popular route. She scraped her toe across the untaken path in order to recognize it on her way back should she need to. A good Girl Scout. But why would there be a way back?

She stepped high over a big root that was a snake and when she put her foot down on the other side of it the serpent coiled and struck. The snake's teeth caught in the loose weave of her dress and when she broke into a run the snagged snake came bouncing along beside her. It was surprisingly heavy. Its body writhed and struggled and slapped against the pathway. Finally Erin stopped and dropped the rifle and grabbed the animal behind the head with both hands and she wrestled the hissing thing free from the fabric and with a scream flung it into the thicket. She picked up the gun and ran on, looking back every few steps to make sure it wasn't coming after her.

The path ended suddenly and absolutely. She stood panting. Before her the trees towered high and choked out the light and the spaces between them were so small she would have to turn sideways and try to squeeze through. Even these openings were owned by vines and branches and flowering tendrils and a leaf-mounted gecko that looked at her unblinkingly.

She heard the voices and the shuffle of bodies from somewhere behind her. Through her frantic gasps she could hear the thump of boots and the jangle of guns and heavy breathing and voices made shrill by the hunt.

She turned around to face them.

I cannot let me die. I cannot let you die.

She flung the rifle into the trees then reached up under the dress and pulled out the derringer and placed it in the crotch of her underpants. It felt genuinely revolting there, a violation. She unwound the rebozo and dropped it to the ground and waited.

32

THE WALK BACK TO THE Castle was brief. Some of the men who recaptured her were the same ones who had kidnapped her from home nine days earlier, which led to some muttered recognitions. Heriberto seemed embarrassed. The day after her performance with Los Jaguars, he had sent to her room a shallow bowl of floating gardenia blossoms, very fragrant, with a note in Spanish praising her singing. Erin knew she had gained esteem in his eyes and that it displeased him to force her back into captivity. He patted her for weapons, lightly and respectfully, not touching her most personal places.

They stopped at the cenote to rest. The men speculated about where Saturnino might be, but they didn't ask her directly and they didn't seem to genuinely care. She glanced out to the middle of the pool several times, but she could not see him. She wondered if she should confess, so as not to spoil the water supply. She decided not to. He would float up soon, right? They'd fish him out and in a few days the water would be clean again. Right? Maybe he was down there hot-wiring the Corvette. Maybe he'd never come up.

A few minutes later the jungle parted and the Castle loomed from the hillside and Erin trudged up the road, across the spacious courtyard to the limestone steps of the great entryway. Heriberto opened one of the iron doors and waited for her. The lepers came and watched her from the third-floor landing, and she saw the black faces of the servants behind the windows, and there were *sicarios* everywhere, even up on the balconies, dark boys with machine guns loitering half-hidden in the riotous potted flowers.

Armenta stood waiting for her in the big foyer. He wore slacks and a floral print shirt that was lumpy around the waist with weapons and phones. He was unshaven and unkempt. The bags under his eyes were dark. "Did Saturnino find you?"

"No, sir."

"Did you see him?"

"I saw no one."

"I think he was pretending to be loco."

"I haven't seen him since that night."

He studied her while he unholstered a phone and listened, grunted and punched off. "Where did you get the key?"

"I have no key. The door is broken. It hasn't been locking on the inside for three days."

"It locked for me two hours ago. And Father Ciel says his key was stolen."

"You should never have given him a key to my room. You know what he is. You know what he does."

He sighed softly and linked his fingers below his waistline, watching her. He nodded and considered. Then he brought a different phone off his belt and worked the numbers without looking at them. A moment later he was cursing fast and soft in Spanish and Erin could see the anger in his face. He told someone to go to hell, then slid the phone closed and put it back in his carrier.

"I do not see things as you wrote them in 'City of Gold,'" he said.

She said nothing for a long moment. Heriberto quickly departed. Beyond Armenta she saw the servants pretending to work, not watching them but listening.

"I can't help that," she said.

"When I look at myself I see only a will to survive in a world that is cursed. To me, this will you write of is a neutral thing, something any animal has in its possession. It is not dignity. It is not to be judged. You wrote as if there was strength and even a small goodness in me."

"I see your world as cursed. But look—you created Gustavo. You made someone beautiful."

"Yes. And in your song, Benji grows strong in a cursed world. He is true to his friends and his family. He speaks violence because that is the language of his time and place. All of this means that I am pleased by the song."

She nodded and looked down at her shoes. The eyelets and seams were still crusted with jungle sand and there were small green burrs stuck to the laces. The Cowboy Defender was irritating her. "I can do better."

"Oh?"

"It was my first *corrido*."

"It is good."

"It's crude and obvious."

He wrinkled his brow and his gaze bore into her.

"Has the money arrived?" she asked. "Am I free? Have you heard from Charlie Bravo?"

He shrugged effulgently, then shook his head. *"Lo siento."*

"You're sorry? Because your son is going to flay me? How do you think I feel?"

"Charlie Bravo has two more days, yes? The agreed day was to-morrow. And I gave him one more day for the song that you wrote. I do not regret it. But we hear nothing from him. He heats the plaza. He has broken the pledge."

"Then I'll write you another song. A better song. If you'll give Charlie Bravo one more day."

And one more day for Bradley, she thought. Two precious days to find her. Two and a half, counting today! *I'll come to you by moon-light. Like in your song.*

His dark eyes roamed her face. They looked intelligent but wild, like the eyes of the jaguar in the Castle.

"How badly do you want your money, Mr. Armenta?"

"Money? Yes, always the money comes first."

"But you want another song."

"I want this song too."

"Do we have a deal, then? Another song for another day?"

"Excuse me." Armenta turned his back to her and yanked one of the phones off his belt and somehow dislodged a pistol that clattered to the floor at his feet. He picked it up and looked at her. Then he straightened and, holding the gun at his side with one hand, brought the cell phone to his ear with the other and launched into a Spanish tirade that Erin could scarcely understand. *Traidor! Pinche* Carlos Herredia! *Exterminar!*

It went on and on. She watched his hair fly and his eyes bulge and the big vein on his neck stand out and she heard the furious rush of words and spittle and his hurried breath.

She turned her back to him and considered the big iron doors and wondered what it would be like to just walk out through them, free and heading home.

She only became aware of the silence when he broke it.

"I am sorry for the activity."

"What's wrong? Why are there gunmen everywhere?"

"This is not of your business."

"Okay, then do we have a deal or don't we? One more song for one more day."

"I agree to this."

"Good. I'm tired and dirty and hungry."

"We will dine early. At six."

"I'd rather eat alone."

"You will dine with me. I have much, much more to tell you that will make your writing very easy. About Veracruz when I was a boy. There was a pig that could do advanced mathematics. And a *curandera* who raised the dead not once but three times. And a two-headed girl who argued with herself. And a moron named Francisco with a very thin head who could crawl through the windows of the prison at Ulúa to find treasure. And my lovely Anya—you should know more about her."

"I won't be good company for dinner. Kind of a big day for me, you know?"

Armenta waved over one of the female servants and handed her a key card and ordered her in Spanish to accompany Erin to her room and prepare a bath and bring whatever she might want. He stood straight and extended one hand toward the elevator.

They sat in Armenta's formal dining room, which faced east and caught a warm breeze off the ocean. Because of the slowness of the elevator and its mystifying arrangement of buttons she had not been able to tell whether they had gotten off on the fourth or fifth floor. She wore a long blue dress that covered the derringer lashed to her calf with a bootlace. The dining table was koa wood, long and wide, and Erin realized she could cross her leg under the table and get the gun loose with one hand and without Armenta knowing.

Through the eastern window she could see part of the loggia and the courtyard below. The sun was setting behind her, but she saw the orange glow on the stone columns and the paver tiles and on the facets of the broad-leafed jungle flora. Shot with gold, she thought. Shot. She saw the surprised look on Saturnino's war-painted face. She saw his pathetic pawing in the cenote as he tried to swim. She saw his blood rising in the clear water and the green dye melting off his hair.

A few hours ago, in her room, she had taken the longest, hottest bath of her life and still she felt filthy and stained and she knew that she had been forced to surrender something she would never get back. He had finally raped her after all. She wondered if she could kill his father also. On the same day, even. Why not? She had proven experience. She had done things here she had never imagined and this made her feel unreal and unpredictable even to herself.

Looking down she could see the *sicarios* loitering in the courtyard and among the columns of the portico. Things were wrong here. She felt the tension and nerves in the still subtropical air, surely as she had felt them when she marched back here a few hours ago. At first she thought it was because of her escape, or Saturnino's disappearance. But it wasn't about either of them, she thought now. Something had happened or might happen. *His greatest fear is of being betrayed by his own men.* She looked down to the driveway where Heriberto, a rifle slung over his shoulder, stood talking to one of the young gunmen. Just minutes ago, on the way here to the dining room, they had passed two more gunmen in the foyer and one standing midway down a long hallway and another who was likely stationed just out of eyeshot outside the dining room entry. Erin wondered if Armenta was protected by them or surrounded by them.

He sat at the head of the table with Erin on his right but they were far enough apart to be strangers sharing space in a cafeteria. Overhead the ceiling fans turned at low speed, their blades bending the candle flames.

Armenta had shaved and his hair had been cut and styled. He wore an expensive-looking black silk suit and a white jacquard shirt with small black hummingbirds flying through the weave. The tailored clothing hid his bulk and the haircut revealed a strong neck and a face of intensity and intelligence. She saw Saturnino's handsome roughness and she pictured his face on the night he attacked her, coming into view on the window of the Cadillac as it shut on her.

A servant opened a French Pouilly-Fuissé and set the cork before Erin, who knew nothing of French wines but smelled it and nodded and tasted the wine. It was cool and light and it offered pleasure, which collided with her fear for Bradley and her worry over Hood and her anger over the killing she had done.

"I'd drink this whole bottle if I wasn't pregnant," she said. "And being held captive by a cartel kingpin. I could use a night of forgetting about all this. Maybe a lifetime."

"I see the unhappiness on your face."

"This was one of the worst days of my life. I've had several of them since I met you."

He nodded tersely. "Why did you run? Where were you trying to go?"

"Away, away and away."

"Mexico can be dangerous."

She actually laughed.

He glanced down distractedly at the courtyard, then turned his attention back to her. "Father Ciel found his key. He had misplaced it. Apparently. Maybe your escape was one of opportunity and not planning."

"Either way is just fine with me."

"Do you hate this place very strongly?"

"I'm going to be a mother soon. I can't describe to you how genuinely awful it is to be a prisoner here. Can't you imagine what Anya would have felt like if she were going to give birth to Gustavo and your enemies were holding her thousands of miles from home? Planning to skin her alive? How can you not understand this? Is your heart that small?"

He looked down and away. The waiter set out bowls of ceviche and guacamole and chips, and refreshed the glasses of wine. "I hope not to remove your skin."

"Saturnino will actually do it. So, no worries for you."

"I never wanted to skin you, of course."

She choked down the mouthful of wine and coughed into her napkin. "From the beginning? A bluff?"

"Oh, no bluff. No, no. I kidnapped you for business and to punish an enemy. And because I wanted to meet you. I was a fan. I love musical talent and skill. I intended to skin you only if necessary. But when I met you my perceptions changed. There is more in you than musical talent and skill. There is something that you have and it is only you. I see it. I understand it. My heart sees it. So I want now very much not to skin you although I have given my word and my word is who I am. I want my money. But I want you to write. And go free. And have your child."

"But you will skin me?"

"I must, if Charlie Bravo fails you."

"You . . . Saturnino has done this to other people?"

Armenta raised his eyebrows and cleared his throat softly and continued to look out the window.

"Jesus H. Christ," she said.

"H?"

"It's a saying."

"Meaning what?"

"Meaning can you just please fly me out of Chetumal tomorrow? Can you let me go home?"

"Impossible."

"Why is it impossible? You're the most powerful man in Quintana Roo. Aren't you?"

He looked at her again, nodded and smiled proudly, then his face fell into a scowl. He unbuttoned his jacket, brought a phone to his ear and listened for a long time.

Erin looked down at the loggia colonnade melting into the darkness. The driveway was a pale swatch through the black of the jungle. The *sicarios* were just dabs in the background now, difficult to see but not quite invisible. Her mind was alive with images of the day and she wondered if it was possible to unsee the seen or forget the unforgettable.

Finally Armenta said *bueno* and reclipped the phone to his belt with an apologetic shrug.

"I think you're lying about Charlie Bravo," she said. "You've misled him. He won't be here with the money tomorrow because you don't *want* him here. Right?"

He shrugged and looked at her, then abandoned his pretense and nodded.

"Or have you killed him?"

"No. He is alive, but not here. He is off course but he has my money."

"How long do you propose to keep me prisoner?"

"I have given this thought. My wish is to own a collection of songs that you have written and recorded for me. Enough to form a body of work, on compact disc. The recordings will of course be basic vocal tracks and you will accompany yourself on guitar and piano. Let us say, twelve songs in all. It will not be sold. This is not commercialism. It is for me only to possess."

"Then you'll fly me home?"

"You have my word."

"But your word isn't true. You've sent Charlie miles from here, haven't you? You've gone *back* on your own deal."

He looked morose at his honor being doubted. "But you are compelled to believe me. Charlie Bravo and his one million dollars are not here. Your weak and fearful husband remains hiding in California, useless to you. These are factual truths. Twelve songs."

Twelve songs, she thought. *Time.* Time for the baby inside me to grow. Time for Bradley and Hood. I could write the songs and lay down the vocals in a week. A week! Earn my own freedom.

"You already have one of my songs."

"But you must record it."

"Then you mean eleven."

"Eleven more written, twelve recorded."

"They could not all be epic *corridos*."

"They will be what you want them to be. I do not have to be the subject. Write whatever you want to write."

She sipped the wine and studied his hopeful face. An idea presented itself to her, and although she had no time to examine it, she felt confident that it was good and workable.

"I know you," she said. "You'll take the million dollars from Charlie Bravo whenever you want to take it. After seeing the treasures in this place, I know this is true. To you, this million dollars is only filthy paper. But it means a lot to me. It belongs to me and my husband and the baby inside me. I earned some of it. So I want it back. I will not write the songs unless you send me home with Charlie Bravo *and* the money."

His frown broke into a smile. It was the first smile she had seen on him and it was wide and robust and genuine. "Would you like to be a part of my organization? I will give you cocaine and *mota* distribution in Los Angeles. The plaza will be yours. The money is very tremendous. And with your contacts, all of the musicians in L.A. will remain high forever and produce wonderful works."

"How about no? No works for me."

"I am kidding you. A joke for you."

"That's very funny, Mr. Armenta."

"I agree, then. And you agree to eleven more songs to be written and twelve recorded. At the end you will be flown home with one million dollars, and this Charlie . . . what is his last name?"

"Bravo."

"Brave. Of course. Very brave when he killed my Gustavo. I had forgotten his bravery. But I now promise I will send him home with you."

"Not to the tigers?"

He shrugged and avoided her eyes.

"You ordered your people not to feed them."

"Agreed. Not to the tigers."

"I will be finished in one week. I believe in you as a man of your word."

Now he seemed to vet her like a taste of product, a pleased look spreading across his face.

"Also," she said. "I need the freedom to leave my room when I want to. With no one to watch me. I need to be free to walk around in your Castle and on your property. Except the third floor, of course. I won't run away again. I give my word on this, and it is every bit as good as yours, and you know it is."

He smiled again but this time there was something amused in it, as if he'd just been told a good joke. "Of course this is impossible!"

"Impossible why?"

"Because I don't trust you. Now the truth is exposed. Neither one of us trusts the other but we are making deals like powerful capitalists in the back room! No. You may have limited freedom but only when Owens is with you. Or you will run away. I can see this happening very clearly."

She took a deep breath and let it out. "Okay."

Looking down through the last rays of daylight she could see that the outside gunmen were gone now, having vanished as they sometimes did to places unseen, and for reasons not apparent.

The waiter brought a tray heavy with plates of seafood and beef, and another piled with tamales and Yucatecan mango-topped enchiladas. He set out dishes of hot sauce and wedges of lime and baskets of tortillas.

Armenta lifted his wineglass to her and she took up her glass but did not acknowledge his gesture. "I am worried about Saturnino. He is never to leave here without telling me."

"He'll probably show up."

"You never saw him on the trail to the cenote?"

"I told you I never saw him at all."

"Then maybe he was not acting loco. Maybe he truly is loco and he has taken off for Merida or Veracruz or . . . who can know?"

She said nothing and watched his face crinkle into a scowl. He set down the wineglass and lifted a phone to his head again.

When he stood and cursed into it Erin heard the gunfire erupt outside, short urgent bursts in the darkness. She saw a ragged flash of orange from the jungle, then came the answering shots from somewhere down in the courtyard. A round whinnied through the night, then another.

Armenta stashed the phone and slid a large holstered pistol around his belt until it hung in front. Then he came around the table toward her and when she stood he put both hands on her shoulders not roughly and he guided her to the floor and under the big table.

"Stay down and the bullets will go over your head."

"Who are they?"

"The same as they will always be."

He went to the armoire that sat along one wall and pulled out an assault rifle and swung the strap over his shoulder and chest. Next came what looked like a shotgun, short-barreled and pregnant with a drum of shells. He looked back at her once then marched from the dining room and Erin could see the silent bodyguard leading the way from the suite. He was an older man like Armenta but they moved lightly and spoke to each other though she couldn't hear the words.

Then the generators went silent and Erin heard gunshots replace their insistent drone and these came from inside the Castle, below her, nasty little rattles that seemed to be arguing with one another. The darkness was sudden and deep. She lay in it with her back to the floor and lifted her knee and worked the Cowboy Defender loose from her calf. When the gun was free she looked to the window and saw below the rim of the tabletop the quarter moon high in the east and the lights of what might have been a commercial jet blipping up and away from what city she couldn't say.

She rolled over and crawled out and peeked over the window frame. The drive below was lined with solar lights set in decorative concrete frogs, turtles, fish and crocodiles, and in their modest light she saw two men sprawled on the drive and two more moving slowly toward the Castle from the trees. Two heavy booms and a fusillade of lighter reports erupted from downstairs. Where in the Castle? she wondered. Had Armenta made it outside? Were all those *sicarios* trying to protect him, or kill him? A flare was launched from the foliage and flew into the courtyard out of her sight. She could see the bright red light of it washing the pavers and the columns of the portico and when the two men ran from the jungle onto the drive they were cut down by fire she could not trace. One of them lay still and the other moaned and rolled back up onto his hands and knees but a furious chatter of fire pocked the sand around him and sent him down absolutely and he did not move again.

The glass above her blasted apart. She slumped down against the wall and felt the shards raining down on her. The main battle seemed to be taking place on the drive right below the dining room but she heard other shots and shouts farther down the driveway and from the nearby jungle where Saturnino had attacked her and from the far side of the building. She crawled back to the table with the glass pricking her hands and knees and the derringer held absurdly in her teeth. She stood and tried to tip over the table but bullets whizzed past her and smacked into the wall and she fell to the tile and rolled flat to the floor under the table. Outside she heard the sound of boots on the crunchy sand of the driveway and men shouting and a scream ended by a volley of fire. The flare light burned into the night from the courtyard and she saw the gun smoke rising into it, then felt the concussive explosion downstairs within the Castle. A grenade, she thought, or a bomb of some kind.

Then she heard vehicles on the drive and more shouting and automatic weapons, and the roar of engines. The bullets twanged against the vehicles and she wondered if they were bouncing off or going in. Then an abrupt silence fell. She lay curled in a ball in the dark hugging herself and talking to the baby inside her about some of the beautiful things he would get to see in his life, beginning in just a few short months. *In fact, you will open your eyes to the sky and the moon and stars and Daddy's and Mommy's faces and the faces of toy bears and lions, and there will be music too, beautiful music, and even though you can't see the music it will make you imagine things that you will see whenever the music plays and sometimes even when it doesn't.* She felt her heart thumping and the cool of the tile against her flank and she could smell the festive smell of gun smoke wafting in through the broken window. She put a stinging finger into her mouth and sucked at the blood.

Men shouted. Then another shot, just one shot, somehow forlorn and final, followed by a silence that to Erin seemed to go on for hours.

She heard muffled sounds downstairs, voices and doors slamming. This took her back nine days to the invasion of her home and she wondered if she had entered some new dimension where violence was the beginning, middle, and end of everything. And she thought if the safe room in Valley Center wasn't enough to keep her safe then this table sure wasn't. She battled against a flood of terrible ideas: that Bradley had been caught and executed just a few miles from here, that Hood was being manipulated and useless, that Armenta was dead and the men who would soon find her here would be a thousand times worse than he was. She told herself and the baby to ignore such thoughts. She heard the voices again downstairs and more from outside on the drive and through the window she could still see the light of the flare thinly red against the dark. She closed her eyes and listened to the strange disturbing melodies emerging from the voices and the sounds and she made up words to be carried by those melodies. The tunes merged and changed and returned but the one constant in them was the dependable beat of her heart.

A few minutes later the generators groaned to life and the lights came on. She took the derringer and crawled out trying to avoid the glass and when she was away from the window she stood. Voices came from within the Castle and from the driveway and she didn't recognize them, though she thought she might have heard Heriberto down by the courtyard.

She stole out of the dining room and across a softly lit living room with old-looking area rugs and paintings on the walls and a fireplace where a gas flame flickered between artificial logs. She stood in a foyer and opened the door and looked up and down the hallway.

She heard the elevator approach and bump to a stop, then the release of voices from around the corner. She backed into the foyer and trotted across the living area and went back to the dining room.

At the window she stood in the broken glass and looked down toward the courtyard. The flare light was gone but the floods were working again. It looked like a forty foot drop from here, plenty enough to break her bones and kill her baby, she judged. Through the French doors was a balcony heavy with vessels and flowers and two monkeys that sat on the wrought-iron railing as if they'd been watching the shootout, cracking seeds and dropping the hulls to the driveway. Down on the sandy drive lay four bodies on four blankets of blood. Two black SUVs waited, doors and liftgates open, engines off and headlights on. Four men she did not recognize emerged from somewhere below her and when they came to one of the dead they took his feet and hands and dragged him to the rear end of the closest SUV. There they swung the body four times, each time higher, and on the fifth heave they let go and she heard the thump of him hitting the cargo space and the waddle of the SUV on its struts.

Erin turned away and her eyes were caught by the bounty of untouched food on the table. Suddenly she was very hungry. She knew this was impossible after seeing everything she had just seen, but what did that matter? No other laws seemed to apply here, so why should any law against appetite?

So she sat back down where she had sat earlier. She put the Cowboy Defender on her lap and the soft cotton napkin over the gun and pulled a warm tortilla from its straw keeper and filled it with shrimp ceviche and thought: if I'm going out I'm going out with a full stomach and a little class. I can do no more in this circumstance. Melodies swarmed her, many with lyrics already attached. She thought of her parents, sticklers for manners, and she straightened her back and raised her forearms so as not to rest on the table. The Pouilly-Fuissé was still chilled in its clay cooler so she poured a little and took a sip.

Outside she saw live men carrying dead men to vehicles and slinging them aboard. Like bags of potting soil. She could not tell the loyalists from the assassins, the good guys from the bad, except for Heriberto, who seemed in charge. Maybe there is no difference, she thought. She could see the lepers peeking from behind the courtyard balustrades. The Castle dogs were newly emboldened and they slunk back into the light to investigate. Occasionally she heard distant pops from the jungle and she avoided conclusions as to what they meant. A few minutes later the men slammed the doors of the vehicles and got in and drove away. Where do you take ten dead men on a hot evening? she wondered. To an air-conditioned funeral home, of course. The Pouilly-Fuissé really was good.

The voices of the men from the elevator got louder until they were right outside in the hallway. Then they went silent. She waited for some murmured discussion or the clank of cocking weapons or for them to crash through the door, but she heard nothing. She loaded up a plate with tamales and small lobsters and dug right in. They could not have tasted better, even if they were hotter. Truly fantastic, she thought. Unbearably delicious. Last supper. Heaven can wait. What do you think, down there, little guy? Good stuff? Too bad your father isn't here but we're only here because he fucked up.

She heard the front door open and close and someone walking across the tile toward her. She made sure her back was straight and her shoulders were not slouched. Armenta came into the room with the shotgun slung over his shoulder. He had a bottle of tequila in one hand and in the other a heavy gunnysack tied off at the top. His face was dotted with blood and so was his shirt so it looked like the hummingbirds were zooming through red rain. His new coif was ruined. His gaze went from her to the shattered window then back to her again.

He slung the gunnysack into the far corner of the living room where it landed with a thud and skidded on the tile. In the kitchen he washed his hands. Then he walked into the dining room and set the gun on the floor beside his chair and plunked the bottle of reposado to the table at his place. He stripped off the bloody shirt and threw it into the kitchen. His undershirt was white and clean.

He looked at her, then sat. For a long moment he stared at his wineglass, then he lifted and swirled it up at the light and sipped. "Can I now tell you about Veracruz?"

"I would especially like to hear about Francisco, the mentally challenged boy with the narrow head."

Armenta smiled. "When we were boys we used to crawl into the fortress at San Juan de Ulúa. This was very early morning, or later in evening, after the tourists had gone away. The soldiers did not care if we offered one bottle of good rum. We would go far and deep into the vaults and storage rooms in search of the pirate treasures that were certainly still there. But we could not get into the torture chambers or the cells because the Ulúa windows were cut into the stone in such a size that no man's head or even a boy's head could fit through them. There were never bars at Ulúa. It was a form of mental torture that no prisoner could fit his head through the open windows and escape, yet there was the window, open and with no bars. So also, we could go no further in search of the gold and jewels that were there. But the head of Francisco? It fit easily, as did his narrow shoulders. He was an imbecile, but still he could pass through. So, one day we pushed him through the window and into one of the dungeons and . . ."

33

RIDDEN BY DREAD HOOD MADE Bacalar in the dark of early morning. The Hotel Laguna was built up a bluff from the lagoon and as he got out of the truck he saw the levels cantilevered up the rise. He heard the palm fronds rattling and the halyards pinging on the masts of the yachts down in the marina.

No one answered his knock on casita four. He glanced at Luna and knocked again. Two days had gone by since Bradley had called or answered his phone, which meant that Erin was almost certainly still a prisoner and Bradley was likely captured or killed. Hood looked at his watch and waited.

In Merida, Armenta's men had finally contacted him, ordering him to Veracruz—hundreds of miles from where Erin was being held. They had given him two days to make the drive. Hood could make no sense of this, so instead of following Armenta's orders, he and Luna had driven southwest out of Merida on Highway 180, feigning a run to Veracruz. Soon they had reversed to the north outside Campeche and picked up 186 for Bacalar.

Now the moths and beetles tapped against the porch light and he knocked once more. Suddenly he heard the shuffle of footsteps in the thicket beyond the casita and both Hood and Luna drew down on a young man who stepped out with his hands up and a contemptuous scowl on his face.

"I am Domingo," he said. "Fidel is waiting. If you have flashlights in the car bring them."

"Is Bradley alive?"

"Alive."

They woke the hotel manager and Luna badged him and paid pesos for a room for one week. Luna ordered the manager to make sure the car was not touched and he handed him more bills. The manager was slender and young and he averted his eyes and quickly filled out the registration slip by hand and in silence. He set a shoe box on the counter and took off the lid and rummaged through it. Finally he handed Luna a room key. Luna asked for a second key and gave it to Hood. The manager said to have a good stay in Bacalar, there is fishing and snorkeling, but he didn't look at any of them when he said it.

Back at the car they brought their weapons from the trunk and Luna locked the doors and checked them all before nodding at Hood and Domingo.

Once into the dark jungle they followed their light beams, trotting down a faint and narrow path. Domingo was stocky and short but he was indefatigable and did not look back.

Hood kept the pace. He had a Remington ten-gauge in his hands and his .45 on his hip and the AirLite .22 strapped to the inside of his left combat boot. His belt was heavy with ammunition and his antiballistic vest was tight and hot. He thought of Hamdaniya and his fear was no less here than it had been there. He synched his breath to his stride and thought about Erin and the bloody hours ahead and he wondered who would survive them and who would not. He thought of Beth at the hospital in Buenavista, and of his mother and father, brothers and sisters. Of Suzanne Jones and her reckless escapades, her appetites and her beauty. Of her son, Bradley, alive still, for now at least, and ready to face a storm of cartel bullets to rescue his wife.

Soon they had run two miles by Hood's guess and still there was no hint of sunlight. He pushed the LED button on his wristwatch and glanced down: 4:24 a.m.

The camp was little more than a crude opening hacked from the trees. The sun's first light had just begun to penetrate the jungle, and the faces that looked back at Hood were suspended in gloom as if painted by old masters. Some were lying down and others sitting and some stood.

Hood looked around in the pale light. A small campfire burned and two enamel coffeepots rested on one of the rocks of a fire ring. He smelled tortillas and grilled meat. There were empty plastic bottles scattered everywhere on the ground. The three vehicles had been parked deep in the forest, scarcely visible, covered in loose fronds, with branches jammed under the tires for traction in the fine loose soil. Two wooden munitions crates sat on the ground away from the fire.

The men were sullen and dirty and looked tired. Domingo said something in Spanish that Hood didn't catch and some of the men laughed and most turned their faces away and others merely stared at him or Luna. *Narcos,* thought Hood. *Sicarios.* Not friendly cops. Bradley had recruited gangsters. Caroline Vega sat cross-legged on a blue tarp and Jack Cleary lay snoring atop a sleeping bag.

"Charlie Bravo!" Bradley called, moving into the clearing from the trees. "You're a long way from Veracruz, my friend!"

He walked to Hood with a smile and a limp. When he came closer Hood saw that one of his front teeth was gone and the one next to the empty space had been broken off at a sharp angle. His face was bruised and his lips were split and swollen and one eye was totally shot with blood. He had not shaven in days, and even his heavy black whiskers could not hide the damage. But the energy came off him, strong and wild.

"Like my new look?"

"It's not bad."

"I have to sleep on my back because my face is smashed up. My mouth hangs open and I snore and keep everyone awake. Meet Fidel."

A muscular man dressed in military fatigues rose from beside the campfire and shook Hood's hand strongly. He was tall, but not as tall as Hood, and he looked to be approximately Hood's age. His hair was closely cut and unlike the others his face was freshly shaven. His eyes were black. There was a medallion of Malverde around his neck and a knife in a scabbard on his belt and another protruding from a pocket sewn onto his boot. He looked to Hood like a Moorish assassin.

"Fidel is Baja State Police, and my right arm," said Bradley. "These are his men, our counterparts in Mexican law enforcement. We're going to rescue Erin, and Fidel is going to arrest the rapist-murderer Saturnino. Or cut out his heart and hand it to him as it beats. Whichever feels right!"

Fidel shot Bradley a look. Bradley smiled and Hood saw the pain of it. Hood introduced Luna to Fidel and he could tell that they somehow knew of each other and that between them flowed understanding and dislike. Cleary rose to one elbow and yawned. Caroline Vega poured two cups of coffee and brought them over. There was a time of silence broken by one nearby bird and a soft occasional pop of the fire. Hood studied the men as they studied him.

Fidel went to one of the wooden crates and threw off the lid. He looked down into it for a moment. Hood tried to read the expression on his face. Fidel lifted a new stainless steel machine pistol from the box and held it up for his men to see. Murmurs. Next he extended the telescoping butt of the pistol and worked it into the crook of his elbow. From the second crate he lifted an extended magazine and pushed it into the handle of the gun. Then a sound suppressor, which he screwed onto the barrel. Hood recognized the Love 32 immediately, one of the thousand such guns he'd let slip through his hands and into the clutches of these men, Mexican *narcos*. Brokered by Bradley Jones. Hood's heart beat with anger.

"Break it down for the men in good clear Spanish," said Bradley. "Make sure they know what they're supposed to do. I'll tolerate no fuckups, Fidel."

—We have these magnificent silent guns, use them intelligently, do not waste bullets, kill every man you see until we get to the *gringa*. Saturnino is mine. We will return here and deliver the Americans to the marina at Bacalar and we will be finished.

Some of the men murmured and some smiled.

—We have all studied the map and the drawings. Do you know your directions? Do you? Answer me.

They answered together, an unintelligible stream of language, then they rose and mustered. They took their guns from one crate and the magazines and sound suppressors from the other, and Hood watched them click the magazines into place and screw the silencers onto the barrels.

In these few moments Hood finally saw answers to questions he had long had: he knew these guns had been made in California two years ago, then sold to Carlos Herredia and the North Baja Cartel. Bradley's friend Ron Pace had designed and manufactured them and Bradley had arranged their sale and transport. How had Bradley found Herredia? That was still a loose end, but Bradley had associated with bad people then, as now. One of them, Hood knew, had been on the North Baja payroll. This could explain why Herredia had the Love 32s and why Bradley had a million dollars in cash ready to pay ransom and why Bradley had Herredia's guns and gunmen helping him now.

Hood watched Bradley as he took up one of the weapons, gingerly extending the butt and fitting the long magazine into it. It infuriated Hood that Bradley and the gun maker had made fools of him and his ATF brethren. Hood saw the excited pride in his face and the familiarity in his movements as Bradley screwed on the Love 32 sound suppressor. The expression reminded Hood of Bradley's wild, lovely mother.

Genes, Hood thought. Genetics. Genesis. Generator. Generations. Genealogy. And Bradley knows this too. Look at him.

Bradley caught Hood's look. "So, these are the guns you think I made, or sold, or whatever it is you think I did?"

"Clever—Harry Love and Murrieta."

"You are once again resoundingly full of shit, Charlie. The only thing I know about these things is that they *work*. Who made them or how they got here? I truly don't know. If you need to blame your career failures on me, go right ahead. But you're nowhere near where the truth lives. Wrong neighborhood. Not even close."

"We'll sort this out back in California, Bradley."

"I look forward to that."

The men stretched into their armor and shouldered their ammo packs. Some had hand grenades on their belts, in case the extraction of Erin turned into a firefight. Hood recognized the grenades as U.S. military issue, which could be purchased by anyone in stateside surplus stores, emptied of explosive and cheap. These practice dummies had been finding their way into Mexico in growing numbers over the last year, where the *narcos* repacked them with gunpowder and plugged the bottoms and used them against one another and the government. If one of those explodes, he thought, there goes the stealth raid. It was hard to imagine forty-five men shooting it out and one unarmed woman living to tell about it.

Hood strapped the shotgun over his shoulder, then took a Love 32 from the crate. It was new and shiny and heavy for its size. He screwed on a sound suppressor. He caught Bradley looking at him, a faint, enigmatic smile just beginning to peek out.

"Oh, cheer up," said Bradley. "It's for Erin."

"California," said Hood.

"*Vamos!*" whispered Fidel.

Forty minutes later Hood and Luna were crouched in a thicket between Bradley and Fidel, looking out at the Castle. It climbed a not-too-distant hillside with its many colors, somehow regal and ramshackle at the same time. Pale smoke issued from a chimney then hovered atop the jungle in the breezeless air. The new sun threw orange light against its face as a dog trotted across a broad driveway.

Fidel whispered into his satellite phone and someone whispered back. He punched off and hung the phone on his belt, then under the cover of the palms he slid hissingly on his butt down a lush embankment. Hood held the Love 32 to his chest and followed.

34

ERIN WOKE UP JUST AFTER sunrise. She was curled up on one side of the bed with the sheet over her, still wearing her clothes from the night before. For a moment she looked out the window, saw the palms unmoving in the orange light, her mind crawling with images of the battle. She felt aged by what she had witnessed, made sadder and more fearful and better able to discern her blessings. The baby kicked and elbowed her. She also felt more determined than ever to preserve his life, to deliver him gasping and screaming into the world.

She looked out at the lightening sky and drew a mental picture of Bradley. She saw him not as a failed man but as a misled boy. Misled by whom? Still, when she pictured him and imagined what had happened to him her heart fell. The failed boy was hers and she had made a deal with him, which entitled him. But to what? He could quite easily have been killed or arrested in the service of trying to help her. *He did not arrive . . . There are rumors of a battle with the Zetas and an arrest by the Army.* She took a deep breath and calmly tried to imagine Bradley gone forever, nothing of him left but a memory and scattered evidence left behind. But she could not make this idea real. It sat out there beyond her understanding and she wondered what she would do if by some miracle they both returned home alive.

She showered and changed and when she came out Atlas had delivered a light breakfast and a large pot of coffee. She drank the coffee at the desk with the Hummingbird on her lap, scratching down the lyrics as they stole into her head.

A few minutes later Owens knocked and Erin let her in. She was dressed for travel in slacks and a smart linen jacket, and she trailed a gold-colored rolling bag behind her. A pair of sunglasses was pushed well up into her hair. "Mike needs me. Benjamin thinks it's his idea that I go. For my safety."

Erin felt more abandoned than she knew she should. "Your safety."

"I'll be back in two days."

"I'll be writing for my life."

"Get the guitar. I'll bring the coffee."

In the tracking room Erin sat at the Yamaha and Owens pulled a stool from the vocal booth. Erin felt her way through a melody one key at a time, a bright Tejano tune, then paused. "I thought I was dead last night."

"I did too."

"But here we are."

"Benjamin told me there were ten men. His men. It broke a part of his heart that his own men would do that. Of course, with what was left of his heart he executed the three who were captured alive."

"Did he put their heads in a bag?"

"Yes, personally."

"Listen to what we talk about here, Owens. We don't say these things in the U.S. There we say *have a great day*. Or *no worries*. Here we say *he fed a reporter to the leopards*. Has an attack like that ever happened here before?"

"There was an attempt on his life a year ago. Here. Two foolish boys. Hired shooters. Nothing like last night."

"And it was so strange, Owens. I watched them load the dead men into the vehicles. Bloody and ugly. Then when I turned away from the window and looked at the food I was hungry. More than hungry—starved. I ate a lot. It tasted so good. I even drank some wine. When Benjamin came into the room I wasn't sure who it was, and I didn't care. I'd given up. I was still eating. I was too terrified to be afraid anymore."

"You'll be home in a week, Erin. Maybe less."

Erin found the minor note she needed and wrote it down. "One week. Eleven more songs to write, and twelve to record."

Owens looked at her analytically. "Write well, Erin. Let the angels whisper in your ears. I'll see you in two days."

Erin studied her face, the black hair and gray eyes, her lovely body and shapely arms, the knife scars ringing her wrists like angry snakes.

Owens stood and took the handle of her rolling bag. "My ride's here. Whenever Benjamin arranges my travel it's always three armored SUVs."

"Will you go anywhere Mike tells you to?"

Owens smiled. "Within reason. Or slightly beyond."

"I worry about you too, you know. I don't like or trust him."

"Mike was hoping that his pigeons might make you reconsider him. He went to more than a little trouble to do that. He wants your friendship and trust. He adores Bradley."

Erin considered. "I don't understand one thing about you but I'm glad you're alive."

Erin listened to the smooth roll of the luggage on the studio floor. She didn't watch Owens leave. She felt that her best and only friend had betrayed her and now the future was even more bleak. One week, she thought. Eleven and twelve. Eleven, twelve and out.

For the next hour the music came clear and fast. Two songs stormed in simultaneously, notes and words falling close together like rain. Erin scribbled the phrases and kept two separate ledgers as each grew. One was the Tejano song that had begun in her room and the other was a lullaby to the baby, a waltz, and it brought a little mist to her eyes as it wafted across the morning and into her ears, addressed specifically to her, sent from that part of the universe unknown and unknowable. The little digital tape recorder was a sound-activated wonder—simple to use and very clear on the playback.

My darling son
    My darling son
On the beach
And the meadow run
    Follow a dream
Follow a dream
    And when you return
A man you will be
But until then darling son
You are my darling son
Goodnight to you
You and the stars tonight
Goodnight

Then suddenly the Tejano song butted in and took over, as if it were jealous of Erin's attention elsewhere. She struck the notes of melody on the grand with her left hand, and scribbled down the words in her notebook with the other. It was a song about a young man racing home to his lover on a dark night and he's driving way too fast, and he gets pulled over by a highway patrolman. The patrolman locks him in the back of his cruiser and gets on the radio. The song is the young man's plea to be let go because his woman is so good and sweet and he hasn't seen her in a very long time. The more the young man brags about her, the more astonishingly beautiful, but less believable, she becomes. But the cop lets him go and in the end the young man makes it home and she is plain and poor but in his mind every bit as lovely as he had said she was.

Time passed. She wrote and rewrote, played phrases one way and then another. She collected them all on the little recorder because sometimes you didn't hear a jewel the first time through. It was hard to free her heart to feel the words and the stories because of the great black hole in her universe that was her captivity, and the lesser one that was her husband.

Later she saw Armenta looking at her through the window of the control room. Heriberto stood behind him with a large black rifle of some kind strapped over his shoulder. Armenta looked weary and absent as he lifted a cup of something to his mouth and gave her a slight nod. She turned back to her notepad and a moment later when she looked back for him both men were gone.

Later Armenta came into the tracking room with his accordion case and set it down next to one of the instrument booths. He was clean shaven and groomed, barefoot, in shorts and a blue wedding shirt. He wore a wide military-style belt outside the shirt, hung with phones and weapons. Barefoot and in shorts and a festive shirt he looked like a tourist arriving at a resort.

"I need to play."

"It's your studio."

"Are the songs coming to you?"

"They are trying."

"I will not be a distraction to you."

"How can a man playing accordion not be a distraction?"

Erin saw Heriberto looking through the glass at them from the control room. He sat at the mixing board on a stool, his weapon peeking over his shoulder from behind him. He said something, but of course she heard none of it. He shrugged and he yelled this time but it made no difference. Looking down at the mixing board he finally found the talk-back button.

"Do you want more coffee, Mrs. Jones?" asked Heriberto.

"No, thank you."

"Do not speak to her," ordered Armenta. "She is creating. She will get her own coffee when she wants it."

Heriberto nodded.

"Why is he here? Are you expecting another attack?" she asked.

"I am always expecting another attack."

"You have less men to protect you now."

"What do you mean by this?"

"I don't mean anything. Only that maybe you need more men."

"More are coming. Why would they not come?"

Erin felt her muses scattering, flushed by Armenta and the suspicion and violence that followed him. Don't go, she asked them, please stay. "Play the accordion. Sometimes chaos is good."

"Yes, it becomes collaboration."

"Not quite, but one thing can lead to another."

He looked at her lugubriously and set down his accordion case and removed his phone-and-weapon-studded belt. He slid one pistol into the back of his waistband. Then he hung the belt over a stool where it clattered and clanked and tried to slide off until he balanced it. Then he brought the gleaming instrument from the case and worked the tooled leather straps over his shoulders and settled the heavy thing against his chest. He stepped into the instrument booth and pulled on the headset and muttered something into the mike to Heriberto.

Erin turned her back to him. She flipped on the recorder and tapped out the melody of the lullaby on the Yamaha keys. It was a waltz and she loved waltzes of any kind. The three-quarter time soothed her darkness and when she considered her circumstances her heart did not fall, even though she expected it to crash right down through the floor. No, she thought. I am okay. I can do this. Bradley was not involved in the Zeta attack. He was not arrested by the Army. He is alive. He is coming. He is close. Very close. Mike would have gotten word to Owens if it was otherwise. Right?

Behind her thoughts she heard Armenta's accordion and it seemed pleasant and thousands of miles away, foreign and of another world. The lullaby grew a bridge and another verse and it felt right. She arranged the chords beneath the melody and for a moment she had that old feeling of transportation, of tagging along on a wonderful ride that required very little of her own energy. And every pinch of energy she put forth came back in ounces of music and this music made her energy grow stronger. Minutes flew, but made no sound that she could hear.

A while later the accordion came piping softly again from what seemed miles away, Armenta finding the fills between the lines of the lullaby. *My darling son/My darling son.* Just as with the Jaguars of Veracruz, he played simply and directly and without great style or ego.

Erin dug in and gave the piano chords some authority, playing the song through once and then again. She looked up and watched Armenta come from the instrument booth, the big accordion wheezing in and out and she had to smile at his shorts and his short thick legs and pale-bottomed feet and the razor-cut hairstyle that barely gave shape to his gray-black thatch. He moved in small steps to the waltz time, left then right then left again, toward her but not directly. He was concentrating on the playing. He stopped and turned his back to her, looking through the glass at Heriberto, and Erin saw the lump of the gun beneath his shirt, and his arms stretching the bellows of the accordion in and out.

He turned and regarded her for a long beat with an expression she'd never seen, nodded, and looked back down to his keyboard. In that moment she saw him differently, not only as Benjamin Armenta the violent drug lord, but as a man who knows that no matter how much money he gives to his Church, or how much treasure he might amass, or how many lepers he might care for, he will never get his sons back and he has not one true friend on Earth. Erin suspected that he would give up his world if he could. To make music, she thought.

She sang to herself, softly at first. But as she read the lyrics off the notepad she believed her baby should feel them too, so she filled her lungs and primed her diaphragm and raised the volume to complement the Yamaha. Armenta was standing across the piano from her now and he stopped his playing and watched her, sleepy he looked, his eyes closed and his face down and just the hint of a smile on his face. When she came to the end of the song she started the first verse again and he glanced at her and she nodded. The accordion notes came aptly and with some joy, and Armenta fitted his chords to those of the piano, and together they formed a firm bed on which to lay her voice.

Not bad, she thought. Not bad at all.

She sang, *On the beach/And the meadow run,* then she looked past him through the glass and saw Heriberto turn toward the door. She glanced back down at the notebook to make sure it was *Follow a dream/Follow a dream* and when she looked up again at Armenta he was smiling. She looked past him over his shoulder and through the glass to Heriberto, but he was gone.

In his place Bradley and Charlie Hood and two other men she did not know were moving fast and low behind the glass, bristling with weaponry and headed for the big wooden door that separated the rooms. She looked back to Armenta and held his gaze to show that nothing was wrong, and she was able to remember the next lines without looking down at the notepad. But her days of terror and anger rose up inside and her eyes filled with tears as she sang: *And when you return/A man you will be.*

And Armenta knew. He dropped his hand from the keyboard and reached behind his back, but the tooled leather straps of the accordion halted his motion. Whirling to face the men he reached for his armament belt hanging over the stool. Erin saw him raise a sleek pistol with each hand and they boomed at Bradley but he did not fall. Instead he rocked back, but his shiny little gun spat away almost silently and the accordion splintered and someone fired from behind the glass and the window shattered and dropped like a curtain. Armenta's pistols roared away through the window and someone fell. He strode across the room to her and she could hear the bullets whacking into the accordion and see jagged pieces coming off him. When he reached her the shooting stopped and Armenta pulled her off the piano bench to the floor. He turned and lunged toward the window opening and climbed onto the sill to fire down on his tormentors but this only gave them a better target and Armenta dropped and staggered back as the ivory keys burst and the ruptured baffles sighed. He reeled against a tracking booth and the little silenced guns chattered at him and Armenta fell to his knees. One of his pistols dropped to the floor. He looked at it as if to gauge his strength against the distance and seemed to forget the gun in his other hand. He looked at Erin for a long moment, then pitched forward to the floor, draping over his instrument.

She stood and walked over to him but there was nothing to be said or done except to watch his blood run. Bradley ran to her and took her in his arms and she could sense the gun held firmly in his hand, but still she looked down at Armenta. She clamped on to Bradley with all of her strength and she felt the flood of hope—alien, forbidden, delicious hope—rushing through her.

Over Bradley's shoulder she saw Hood and a bull-like man she didn't know. The man shot down by Armenta climbed back into view, using the mixing board to pull himself up. He looked Arabic and he steadied himself as he looked at Armenta and felt at the two unbloodied rips in the chest of his shirt. Then the studio door swung open and Cleary and Caroline burst in.

"The Army is here," said Cleary. "We might want to get out like right now."

"I need Saturnino," said the Arab.

"He's at the bottom of a cenote," said Erin. "I put him there."

Bradley pulled her across the studio. In the hallway outside she stepped around Heriberto's bullet-pocked body and followed Bradley toward the stairs. Through a tall window she could see the smoke rising from the distant guardhouse and the tanks and jeeps and trucks rolling into the parking area.

"There are innocent people here," said Erin. "Atlas and Dulce. All the servants and the lepers. The novitiates."

"I didn't come this far to get you killed," said Bradley.

"They're innocent people!"

"We'll get them out," said Hood. "There's time."

"Dulce is on the third floor with the lepers," said Erin. "We have to use the outside stairs."

Erin shoved her way through the massive entryway doors while the monkeys and birds shrieked and scattered. Freedom! But as they ran into the courtyard the troops were already coming up the drive, heavily armed and armored, running past the *sicarios* killed by Bradley and Hood.

Up the road she saw the soldiers coming, some of them carrying olive green military gas containers and she could see that the containers were heavy. The soldiers trotted toward the courtyard. A phalanx broke off and ran in unison around the north side of the Castle while others waited at the foot of the outside stairway as the lepers in white silence ran down the steps and across the drive and scattered into the jungle. Dulce was with them. Erin saw Atlas and half a dozen gray-clad servants hustle into the foliage and disappear. Atlas looked at her. The flames from the burning guardhouse climbed above the tree line, and a small two-winged airplane flew just through the tops of them; Erin saw someone in the open cockpit aiming something down at the scene. More of Armenta's bodyguards lay dead on the drive and they looked frail and very human to her as two jeeps maneuvered around them, soldiers training the big mounted guns on the front Castle door. Erin ducked onto the jungle path behind Bradley, turning once to look back at the flames from the guardhouse climbing the sky.

She held her husband's hand and they soon fell behind the others. Charlie maintained his distance ahead, but Erin never lost sight of him. Before they'd gone far into the forest Erin brought Bradley to a stop and turned his bruised and battered face to hers and looked at him. He smiled largely and she saw the gap of the missing tooth and its sharply broken neighbor.

"It's good to see you, Brad."

"I love you so much. Sorry about my face."

"Don't worry, baby," she said softly. "Don't you worry. You're going to heal up all pretty again."

He touched her pale cheek with one dirty finger and placed his free hand on her stomach. "You are my whole life."

"No, I am not. Your lies almost killed me. And you. And the baby."

"I'll do anything to make it right again."

"It never was right."

A short distance later they climbed a rise and stopped again. Erin turned and saw the Castle sitting in a red meadow of flames, gas-mad fire pouring from the windows and doors, climbing the walls and palms. The four novitiates and Edgar Ciel clambered across the courtyard toward a group of soldiers. Ciel towered above his charges, his arms draped around the two nearest ones as if for their protection. He appeared furious, thrusting his face into that of an officer, then waving his arms high, shouting orders drowned by the roar of the fire.

Erin watched two lions and two leopards break through a wall of flames on the lower level and run into the jungle. Then came the tigers. The black jaguar was last, sauntering up the drive, shoulders rolling and tail swinging as he entered the foliage where Erin had entered it. Sparks arced high into the thunderhead of black smoke that roiled up from the roof of *el Castillo*.

In a small camp pitched deep in the jungle Erin watched Fidel and his men remove cut branches from four filthy, bullet-pocked SUVs. She looked at the men and saw that they were nearly identical to the men who had kidnapped her and beaten Bradley and been left for dead back at the Castle. *Narcos*, pure and simple. Not the Mexican "counterparts" that Bradley had named them. Not his "law-enforcement friends." Or maybe they were. She caught Hood looking at her and she guessed that he was thinking the same thing she was. Hood looked as vacant and betrayed as she felt. She looked away.

Everyone climbed into the SUVs and they drove twenty minutes farther down a dirt road, away from the Castle, toward where she thought the coast was. She heard the engine humming under her and the huffing of the air conditioner and she could not fully believe that she was leaving this place. The jungle scrolled past outside the dirty, chipped windows. She sat back with her hands over her stomach and for the first time in ten days didn't care who saw her pregnant. And for the first time in ten days she let the tears roll down her face without a thought to hiding them or slapping herself silent. A sign, said Bacalar.

In a room at the Laguna Hotel, Bradley opened a big rolling suitcase she recognized from home. She saw the cash wrapped into plastic bricks that nearly filled the space. Exactly like Armenta's. Bradley broke into one of them and pulled out a thick wad of hundreds, which he gave to Hood, and another for her, three for Cleary and Caroline and himself, and one that he held toward Luna, who refused to take it. Erin liked the look and carriage of Luna, though he said not one word to her and little to anyone else. He seemed lifted from another time, a time when honor and integrity and honest work were something more than the handicaps of the ambitious. The opposite of her husband, she thought, and not unlike Hood.

Bradley tossed Luna's money back into the case and zipped it, then turned to Fidel. "Divide five hundred thousand between the living and the families of the dead. Take the rest to your boss. He'll find a way to get it to me. And thank you."

Fidel wordlessly wheeled the suitcase outside to one of the SUVs. He threw it into the back, then beckoned to Caroline and they walked down to the marina together. Erin watched them through a window for a moment, saw an intent conversation, a tender hug and a longing kiss.

Hood appeared beside her and she turned into him and set her head against his chest.

"Thank you. Thank you. Thank you, Charlie."

"Any time."

"How about never!" she whispered, and she was surprised to hear a scrap of laughter come from her. "I have something for you, Charlie. Owens Finnegan was *staying* at the Castle with Armenta. Mike told her to. She helped me send Bradley a letter attached to a pigeon! *Mike's* pigeon! Later she helped me try to escape. Then she left about two hours before you came—luggage and all. I never saw Mike, but he was helping Bradley send instructions back to me. Instructions on how to escape. We wrote on pieces of silk. It sounds unbelievable but it worked. I saw the pigeons and I held his letters in my own hands. They were real. Somehow, Mike was right in the middle of everything."

She could feel Hood's steady breathing and the nearby thump of his heart. She swore it sped up as she talked.

"I'll want every detail, Erin. Later."

"Yes, Charlie. Later."

"I'm really glad you're alive in this world."

She sighed and watched Fidel and his gunmen climb into the vehicles and drive away.

She got a cancellation window seat on the flight out of Cancún to Dallas/Ft. Worth, a flight full of happily sunburned tourists, their eyes bleary with excess and satisfaction. She stank of fear and sweat and didn't care. Bradley came from another aisle and frighteningly cajoled his way into the seat beside her, where he held her hand. He was filthy and unshaven and his wrecked face looked even worse when he smiled and looked into her eyes.

She dozed through the roar of the engines, hearing music in them, dreamed that there was a castle floating alongside her on a nearby cloud. She jerked awake to find her husband gazing at her and a part of her recoiled at the sight of him. He had lied to her and made a fool of her and she had tried very hard in her life to not be a fool. Anything but that. But even worse was the betrayal of trust. Trust had not come easy. She had never had an aptitude for it. But over her life she had learned trust as she might learn a musical instrument. Now this. The signs had been there all along and she knew them and refused to read them. Too much in love. Blind with pleasure and ambition. End of the innocence now, girl. Cover yourself and leave the garden. Leave.

She stared out the window and listened to the jet music. She could feel the baby relaxed inside her, enjoying the peace and the quiet and perhaps even the ride. Just you and me right now, she thought. She watched green Mexico rolling along far below, thought of Hood down there, somewhere.

"I can't believe Charlie didn't come with us," she said. "Just hours from the U.S. and he wouldn't get on this flight."

"Hood's been going a little sideways lately, don't you think? That thing of his with Mike."

"But what's he going to do? Where's he going instead of home?"

"Don't know and don't care. All I care about is in the seat beside me."

"My arm's falling asleep, Brad. Thanks. I'm going to doze awhile."

"I love you."

She closed her eyes and smiled slightly and leaned her head against the cool plastic.

35

Hₒₒᴅ's ᴘʟᴀɴᴇ ʟᴀɴᴅᴇᴅ ɪɴ Vᴇʀᴀᴄʀᴜᴢ that evening just after six. In the heat he walked down the stairs to the tarmac and claimed his bag and found a cab. He stared out the window as they drove into the center of the city.

It was sprawling and built low to the ground, and the damp air smelled of the nearby Gulf of Mexico. Hood knew only that Veracruz had been founded by Cortez in 1519, making it the first city chartered by Europeans in the New World. And that the fortress of San Juan de Ulúa, built to repel pirates, had once housed a prison legendary for torture and death.

Taberna Roja was on the corner of Zaragoza and Baluarte in the historical zone. An old wooden sign outside the tavern showed a portly man in a poncho running with a smile on his face and a tray of drinks held high. Red hair and sandals. Hood thought he looked like Finnegan. Another coincidence? Another false lead? He remembered the strange look that Juan's mother gave him that morning after the crocodiles in Tuxpan. Was she mocking him? Hood still had the folded magazine page that she had slipped under his duffel, safely protected in his wallet.

He went inside and stood at the bar and ordered a beer. The late October daylight came through the windows and gave the room a golden glow. Hood looked outside and watched the pigeons wheeling over the cathedral. He paid with dollars and the bartender looked at him briefly.

He took his bottle and glass to a free table. The room felt cool and ancient. The walls were blocks of gray coral and the floor was limestone worn smooth. There was a table of Navy men in uniform and another of what looked to be stevedores or tradesmen and another of businessmen in pale tropical-weight suits and white Panama hats. The men smoked and argued and a thin gauze of smoke hovered high against the ceiling. The bar itself was heavily lacquered and laced with scars, clearly made in a century long past. Another version of the outside sign hung behind the bar, affixed to the mirrored wall—the happy red-haired fellow with all the good cheer to serve.

Hood took a deep breath and let it out. It was finally over. He felt briefly gratified at having seen Erin alive, at having contributed. She's worth the high price, he thought, if anyone is.

But he also felt ugly from skin to soul. Empty and spiritless and angry. He had killed one of Armenta's surprised men outside the Castle, shot him square in the heart with his Love 32. And another one inside. He had killed the gun boy in Reynosa a few days earlier. This freshly spilled blood he now added to the older vintages he carried: Hamdaniya and L.A. and Mulege. The life list. Ten. Who would balance that equation? When? Did helping save Jimmy Holdstock's life reduce the total by one? And helping save young Juan from the crocodiles reduce it by one more?

Most of the anger was at Bradley, though. For his flagrant selfishness and love of money, his neglect of Erin, his disdain for the law he had sworn to enforce and for the people around him. Carlos Herredia's cop in Los Angeles? thought Hood. Well, that would explain almost everything: Bradley's cash fortune in small bills, the instantly available gunmen and their Love 32s, and Benjamin Armenta's attempt to punish him. A twenty-one-year-old man, Hood thought, graduated from the academy less than two years ago. Descendent of Murrieta. Son of Suzanne. Unbelievable. Unforgivable.

He got up and ordered another beer. As he waited he considered handing out some of his remaining Mike Finnegan photo albums to the bartender and patrons but decided against it. If Mike was a regular here then he might be warned of such an inquisition. Better to wait and watch, Hood thought, though he wasn't sure what he would do if he found Finnegan. He had no extradition papers, no warrant, not even any charges against the man. And the nearest soil where he had jurisdiction was a thousand miles north.

He talked with the bartender as he opened and poured the beer. His name was Rafael. He had the fine-featured face of a Spanish professional, light hair and green eyes. Hood put him at seventy. He spoke no English but told Hood to come back in March when the weather was cooler and *carnaval* was happening. Beautiful women, he said, and happiness for everyone.

An hour and three beers later the tavern was beginning to fill and two more bartenders had arrived. Hood checked into a Holiday Inn hotel across the street, originally a convent built in 1641. It was beautifully tiled and the archways spoke of the shuffling of women now hundreds of years gone. He showered and shaved and slept until nine when the cheerful subtropical sunlight came pouring through a high window. He lay there thinking until a maid delivered the laundry he'd bagged up the night before.

Back in the Taberna Roja that afternoon Hood used the expensive pen and paper that Dr. Beth Petty had given him and wrote her a letter. It went on for page after page, Hood leaning back every few minutes to shake the numbness from his writing hand, hoping to see

Mike Finnegan coming through the door. Then back to the letter. He missed her. He pictured her face and her wavy brown-blond hair and her chocolate eyes. At the end of page ten he signed off with love and put the thick folded packet into an envelope and addressed it, then wandered off to find the post office.

After dark he walked the busy streets. He had dinner along the zocalo and browsed the wares of the vendors, mostly native Indian girls dressed in long black skirts and bright shimmering blouses. Their hair shone lustrously. The National Palace stood behind the zocalo, stately and ornate and washed in lights. There was an orchestra in the square and an exhibition by the Dancers of the Heart Group. The couples danced formally and they were all older people except for one tentative young couple in the corner of the dance floor nearest Hood, their backs straight and their bodies not too close together, staring at their feet as they learned the steps.

He spent most of the next two days across the street from the Taberna Roja, sitting in the shade of the cafe awning, eating seafood cocktails, watching for Mike. No hint of him. The jolly red-haired man on the tavern sign began to annoy Hood. The Finnegan he knew was jolly all right. Daft and fun-loving and quick with a remark. But the Finnegan he knew had also led two of Hood's good friends to death and disease. Terrible death and disease, some of the worst Hood had seen. Sean and Seliah Ozburn had been the golden ones—young and strong and in love. Now Sean was dead and Seliah would never be the same. Mike had orchestrated it just for the fun of doing so, was all Hood could figure: because he *could*. So Hood watched and waited and his heart was cold.

On the first day a pickup truck crawled with the traffic along

Zaragoza towing a wheeled cage in which paced a very large Bengal
tiger. Children ran along beside the cage and the cat looked unper-
turbed. In profile its beard made it look like an important older man,
Hood thought, wise and formerly great. He felt a shiver of awe rattle
through him.

Street vendors approached him every few minutes. At first he po-
litely declined, then he bought three carved wooden bookmarks, a
pair of Ray-Ban knockoffs, a bracelet made from shark cartilage, a
smart white Panama hat and a miniature armadillo made completely
of seashells and sand. Then he girded himself with the shades and hat
and greeted the next sellers with curt shakes of his head.

He broke up the tedium of his vigil by drinking *lecheros* at La Par-
roquia and making calls on the Holiday Inn landline in the lobby.
Beth didn't answer. Hood's mother was worried about what to hand
out to the neighborhood trick-or-treaters next week; Hood's father
was no better and no worse, just the same memory-sanded shell of a
man he'd been for two years. ATF agent Frank Soriana was angry
with the Fast and Furious bullshit and couldn't talk right then. Hood's
departmental captain at LASD said he was tired of sharing Hood
with the feds and they could use him back in L.A., and from what
he'd heard, the federal Blowdown funding was about to dry up anyway. Come home to Papa, he said. Nice to be wanted, thought Hood.

At the end of that third evening in Veracruz he stepped into the
Taberna Roja and took a stool at the bar, ordered a beer, and when
Rafael set it down Hood pushed two photographs of Mike Finnegan
toward him. One was taken in Costa Rica when Mike had been dress-
ing as a priest and calling himself Father Joe Leftwich. The other was
the accidental shot of him at a Dodger game in L.A. Rafael looked at
the photos, then at Hood.

—He is Mike Fix. He comes here sometimes. He drinks rum.

—When was the last time you saw him here?

—Maybe nine or ten days. Before the hurricane.

—And before that?

—He has been a tourist here for as long as I have worked here. That is forty-eight years. He comes for one day or one week or two months. He drinks and talks with excitement and sometimes causes arguments and fights with his words. But he is always happy and never angry. He never misses *carnaval*.

—He looks like the man on your sign.

Hood nodded at the tavern sign behind the bar, but Rafael didn't turn to look.

—Veracruz has many stories and jokes regarding the similarities. One story is that Mr. Fix used to work here when the tavern first opened. And he carried the drinks as on the sign. But that is absurd of course because the tavern is two hundred and twenty-five years old. There is another story in which Mike Fix is a rich gringo who secretly bought the tavern in the nineteen-sixties because he liked the sign. And that he comes to Veracruz to escape the pressures of his business in the United States. Although if that were true he would drink his rum here without charge. But he always pays and tips very generously. When he is drunk he describes the horrors of Ulúa in detail, as if he has seen such things personally. But again, that was hundreds of years ago. Another story is that he is a master spy of the Central Intelligence Agency. Another story is that most of these stories are first told by Mr. Fix himself. This is the one I believe.

Early on his fourth evening Hood was sitting at the cafe, shooing off a vendor when Finnegan came bustling along the far sidewalk toward the tavern.

He was dressed in a wheat-colored suit and a white shirt, with a solid lavender-colored tie and pocket square. His belt and shoes were black and very shiny. His hair was longer now and it stood out in a downy red halo. His sunglasses were current. With him were a tall gaunt priest and two novitiates, a boy and a girl.

Finnegan was half-turned toward the taller man, gesturing intently as he walked. The priest was nodding. The boy and girl walked abreast behind them and they seemed to be more focused on the men in front of them than on the city. Finnegan held open the door of the Taberna Roja for the priest, then followed him inside. The novitiates stood with their backs to the tavern and faced the street, hands folded before them.

Hood ordered another iced coffee and waited. The novitiates spoke occasionally and more patrons went into the tavern. The sidewalks began to fill with people and the streets with cars. Police controlled the traffic. The pigeons, wings raised, skidded through the sky and into the cupolas of the Convento Betelhemitas. The globed boulevard lights came on along the zocalo though the fall evening had still not darkened.

An hour and eight minutes later Finnegan came from the tavern and once again held open the door for the priest. Hood wondered if the priest knew the little man as Mike Finnegan of L.A. or Father Joe Leftwich of Dublin, Ireland, or Mike Fix, mysterious tourist. Or all or none. Maybe this priest was a fake also, he thought. The two men short and tall walked east down Zaragoza and the unacknowledged novitiates fell in behind them. Hood paid and overtipped and eased off his chair and into the foot traffic on the sidewalk.

The entourage headed east along Zaragoza. Hood could see Mike up ahead on the other side of the street, dodging oncoming walkers, sometimes with one foot on the sidewalk and the other off the curb, his short legs working to keep up with the taller man. He kept looking up at the priest. Talking, talking, talking. The young people plodded along behind, scarcely looking around themselves, as if wearing blinders. Just past a small circle they all bore north on Victimas del 25 de Junio. Hood jaywalked through the thick traffic and fell in fifty feet behind them, with a knot of pedestrians, his hat and shades for cover. He felt the sweaty weight and scrape of his holster and .45 at the small of his back, an uncomfortable comfort.

Finnegan went east again on 16 de septiembre then north on M. Doblado. The street was narrow and the buildings were all two stories high, many of them residences, some of them crumbling away. On the upper floors Hood saw window openings with the glass long gone and tropical trees growing through from the inside. The street palms were skinny and their white insecticidal coats were dirty and thin. The streetlights were layered with flyers. Pigeons lined the paneless window frames, fretting and bobbing and fluttering up and back down.

They turned west at the next corner. Hood took his time approaching, saw no street sign. When he stepped into the old cobblestoned alley he saw Finnegan, a hundred feet away already, holding open an ornate wrought-iron gate. A fandango came through an upstairs window opposite the alley. He smelled baking bread. The priest and the novitiates waited. Hood turned away and set his hands on his hips like a puzzled tourist.

A moment later he crossed the alley. There was a *panaderia* with big windows and he stood looking in for a while at the loaves and rolls and the marked-down pastries from the day. He turned casually and glanced across the alley: all four people had gone through. The gate was black wrought iron, round at the top to fit the archway. No number. The small courtyard was overgrown with ficus and hibiscus with small yellow blooms. Through the foliage Hood saw the crooked graying limestone steps leading up to a wooden front door. The door was closed.

He walked the alley back the direction he'd come, past M. Doblado. He came to a small cafe called El Canario. It was painted a pale lime green and there were larger-than-life canaries rendered upon the wall in bright yellow. They sat on branches with their beaks raised as if in song. Hood took a sidewalk seat where he could see the gate. He drank an *horchata* and waited and drank another. The waitress was pretty and smiled at him.

An hour later, just before eight, a black SUV pulled up near the gate. It was new and gleaming and the windows were blacked out and the header growled softly as the engine idled. Hood saw the novitiates step into the alley, followed by the gaunt priest. The girl got in, then the boy, the priest, and Mike. Hood watched the short leg and shiny little shoe pull inside, then the door clunk shut.

Hood ordered a beer and a shrimp cocktail. An hour and a half later he walked back toward his hotel.

For the next two days this pattern repeated: Finnegan and his guests arrived at Taberna Roja in the early evening. They left a little over one hour later and walked back to the alley off of M. Doblado. On the first of these two days Owens Finnegan was with them. She wore loose, unflattering clothes and she stayed close to Mike, holding his arm in a familial way, ignoring the priest and novitiates as if they offended her. On the second day she was gone.

Hood varied his surveillance as best he could and only once did Finnegan appear to look at him at all. This was on Tuesday, the second evening, on Victimas del 25 de Junio. The look was brief and from some distance, and Hood had his hat down low and his sunglasses on. A few minutes later Finnegan and the others went through the gate and Hood sat at El Canario and talked to Josie for one hour, looking past her down the alley with a rudeness he could not avoid. The black SUV arrived at its usual time and Mike and his friends boarded. When it grumbled away down the alley Hood changed from *horchata* to beer and asked for another shrimp cocktail.

—Josie, do you know a good locksmith?

—I know one who is fast and cheap. I used him a year ago.

The next day when Finnegan and priest entered the Taberna Roja, Hood called Roberto Acuna, the locksmith, and explained that he'd somehow lost his keys and was now locked out of his own home. He said that Josie at El Canario had recommended him highly and he wondered if Roberto was available immediately, because he had an event to attend at the Naval Museum. Hood said he was already a little late. He described the alley off of M. Doblado, which Roberto was familiar with.

Twenty minutes later Roberto opened the gate with a universal key. They stepped into the courtyard and walked past the blooming hibiscus and the ficus and palms and climbed the rock steps. The big battered wooden door to the apartment proved more difficult but after a minute of patient exploration and repetition the door swung open.

Hood stepped inside and saw the hat rack in the foyer and he set his Panama on it with the others. The foyer light was on.

—Thank you. How much?

—Two hundred pesos.

—Here. And a few extra for you.

—Thank you. Do you want a receipt?

—No. I don't need one.

—Where did you lose the keys?

—If I knew they wouldn't be lost.

—This is very true! I can cut you new keys in just a few minutes. In case you don't find the old ones. And if you don't, perhaps it would be wise to have new locks.

—I have spare keys here at home. And I'm in quite a hurry. The event at the Naval Museum.

Roberto looked past Hood into the apartment. He picked up his toolbox and Hood shook his hand and shut the door and checked his watch: half an hour.

36

H<small>E STEPPED INTO THE MAIN</small> room. The floor tiles were worn and the area rugs were old and the tall windows stood open. Iron grates protected the windows from entry and the heavy faded drapes shifted slightly in the breeze. The ceiling was high and a fan moved slowly. On the walls were paintings, dark and important looking, of naval battles between sailing ships. There was a painting of the Taberna Roja. They were unsigned. An easel stood before one of the windows, a vertical canvas balanced upright. It was an unfinished view of Veracruz through that same window and its grate, with a broad thin swatch of the Gulf of Mexico in the background, and it made Hood feel imprisoned. Double louvered doors opened on a balcony and through the slats he saw the air-conditioning unit and the rain-stained stanchions of the parapet and the wrought-iron spikes arranged in a sunburst pattern to keep intruders out. The room smelled of standing salt water and rock.

The kitchen was small and neat and sparsely equipped. In the small refrigerator he saw tortillas and fruit juices, eggs and paper-wrapped wares from a *carnicería,* and an open pack of peanut-butter crème cookies. On the counter was a somewhat dated cordless phone, no answering machine.

The hardwood flooring of the hallway creaked. He looked into a bedroom on the left. It was simply furnished with a twin bed and chest of drawers, a wash basin with a mirror. A world map was tacked to one wall but that was the only decoration. The bed was unmade, with two pillows and the sheets thrown back. A tripod stood in the middle of the room, legs fully extended. There was nothing attached to it. He checked his watch.

The bedroom on the right was the master. Hood walked in and caught the scent of aftershave or cologne, faint and musky. The room was spacious and the shutters were closed and when Hood flipped the switch the lights fluttered on, but they were dim and weak against the evening. He saw the neatly made twin bed and the three stacks of books beside it and the nightstand with more books and a reading light. Hood glanced at the titles and recognized only some of the languages. The bath was small and beautifully tiled. The sink was a hollow oval carved from marble and set upon a limestone counter. Beside it stood a hairbrush and a can of shave cream and a swank three-bladed razor and in a tall mug leaned an upright toothbrush. Hood broke off some toilet paper and wiped the razor cartridge and the toothbrush, then folded the paper on itself and pushed it into a pocket. In the wastebasket by the toilet he found a length of dental floss and this he looped into a neat coil and wrapped in toilet paper then put into his pocket also. He looked at his watch: twenty-six minutes to go.

The hallway ended at a stairway leading up. Hood climbed lightly on the stone until he was standing in the open doorway of a large half-story. He smelled the dank stink of birds and heard cooing and across the room saw the tall coop that stretched along one entire wall. The high casement windows over the birds were open for sunshine and ventilation and the waning daylight caught the dust motes. The pigeons studied Hood in their bewildered, one-eye-at-a-time manner. One of them sat atop the coop and Hood saw the canister affixed to its leg.

Three of the walls were lined with bookshelves heavy with volumes. The walls above the shelves were hung with swords and lances, clubs, battle knives, primitive firearms and instruments of torture. There were rusted rings bolted to the wall, laced with chains and shackles.

In one corner was a leather chair and ottoman with a reading lamp on a stand beside them. In the middle of the room stood a banquet-sized rough-hewn table with a laptop computer closed down and material strewn over every other available inch: printed papers, sketches, stacks of yellow legal pads, magazines, compact discs, magnifiers, stacks of maps, cans filled with pencils and pens and scissors. And of course more books in English and Spanish and other languages unrecognized by Hood.

Under the table there were half a dozen wooden orange crates with their trademark colorful labels. Some of the crates housed more weapons and dire instruments, and these looked more Mesoamerican than European—made mostly of stone and wood. Other crates contained yellowed rolls of paper, and others what looked like notebooks and scrapbooks.

He looked down at an old wooden chair on ivory casters and saw that the casters had ground a long shallow trough around the table. It was easy to picture Mike sitting there, rolling about from task to task, now to the computer, now around to the sketch of, well, what exactly was it a sketch of?

He sat down and turned on one of three green-shaded banker's lamps spaced along the table. He looked down at the sketch pad and saw an accurate and accomplished portrait of a pigeon. Turning the pages he found another and another. The book was filled with them.

A different sketch pad offered variety: more pigeons, then several studies of Owens's lovely face, and some sketches of the prison at San Juan de Ulúa. Hood closed it and set it down and tried another, which was filled with drawings of Benjamin Armenta's Castle. How did Mike manage that? From a visit? From a photo? Through Owens? Some pages were filled with tiny crosshatching patterns that weaved and wavered dizzily. A two-page diptych showed the planets of the solar system on their various orbits around the sun but the sun was a heart tilted at an angle, with the veins and arteries severed short and clean so that it appeared almost round. Hood opened the computer and turned it on and tried passwords based on Mike's various names and wide interests. All failed.

His toe touched one of the orange crates under the table and looked down at it. The familiar graphics of the old California citrus industry caught his eye. Hood had always liked the bold colors and romanticized scenes of the crate labels. This label was for Queen of the Valley oranges in Valley Center, California. It showed a regal Indian woman holding a large orange, with a fruit-heavy grove and a perfect blue sky behind her. Valley Center, thought Hood: Bradley and Erin's home. Where he'd first met Suzanne and later her son and his red-haired singer girlfriend.

He rolled closer to the crate, felt the casters following the gentle groove along the floor. The pigeon that was locked out of the coop stood on the mesh roof and looked at him, Hood thought, hopefully. Hood had always been intrigued by the fact that most domesticated birds preferred their cages to freedom. The others fluttered in half-alarm, then settled as he leaned over and pulled the crate closer and lifted another sketchbook from inside.

He opened it at about the halfway point and saw a hasty but identifiable image of Bradley's Valley Center barnyard and the huge oak tree and the west side of the ranch house. The next page was a closer view of the same barn and tree. Distances between the tree and the house and between the tree and the barn were written in the neat hand of an engineer or architect: *"From center oak trunk to deck*

steps of house 68m; from center oak trunk to east barn door 74m."
Hood skipped forward a few pages to an interior drawing of the
barn, depicting the old stalls that Hood had seen with his own eyes
years ago, and the new ATVs and the John Deere and the walls of
tools and false ceiling and hidden room over the bathroom where
Suzanne had once kept the head of Joaquin in a jar of alcohol.

Hood's heart was beating hard now and he turned the pages faster.
There were sketches of the outbuildings on Bradley and Erin's property, and of the hillsides around it and the creek on its southern border. And sketches of the only gate and the eight-foot-high chain-link
fence that stretched up into a rocky escarpment in one direction and
terminated at the densely wooded creek in the other. And of the well
packed decomposed-granite roadway that led to the buildings. And
specific measurements: "*Gate to barnyard .54km; south-southeast
fence .93km to escarpment; south-southwest fence .65km to creek
NOTE: gate secured with silent alarm (phone line run underground
at some expense) but chain-link fence UNSECURED likely due to
natural animal activity including Jones's dogs . . .*" On another page
Hood found a list of dogs by breed and size, twelve in all. Some were
sketched on the facing page. Hood recognized the big husky–St. Ber-
nard mix, Call, the unchallenged leader of Bradley and Erin's pack.
"*Dogs kenneled outside unless cold or rain.*" One of the last pages
was a study of a wheeled measuring device of the type used by fence
builders, leaning against the barn. The artist had taken the time to get
the peeling paint and the shadows and the blades of grass. Hood
could see small Mike rolling it from the oak tree to the house.

He turned back to the beginning pages and found macroscopic
sketches of Southern California, San Diego County, North San Diego
County. A simple map or two would have given greater detail and
Hood realized that Mike had drawn these pictures because he liked
drawing them. They had subtle shadings for mountains and crisply

outlined bodies of water. There was an overview of Valley Center, with S6 running through it and the recommended route to the Jones property highlighted with neat arrows.

Toward the end of the notebook were the details: drawings of each room of the house, rendered in an architect's fine hand, and dimensions of the rooms and connecting hallways, locations of doors, windows, closets, right down to the his-and-her sinks in the master bath. The alarm pad in the foyer took up half a page, drawn to scale by the look of it, and beneath it was the *"deactivation code"* for the homeowner to use upon entering: *"BOACDM11."* There was a sketch of an upstairs closet that hid a *"secret hideout,"* and the location of the switch hidden in the closet. The necessary distances and dimensions had been written in by hand, in metric measures. This is a playbook for what happened to Erin McKenna, Hood reasoned—everything, right down to the code that would let someone barge into her house and turn off the alarm and not bring the cavalry charging.

He checked his watch: eleven minutes left.

Next from the orange crate at Hood's feet came photographs of Erin, mostly on stage and printed on photographic paper, some amateur candids of her backstage with the Inmates. There was a high school annual from an Austin, Texas, high school that had a small picture of her as a junior, and another of her playing a guitar at a gig of some kind. Hood leafed through newspaper and magazine clips and printed Internet blogs taped to the notebook pages—reviews of her CDs and performances, features, interviews. She had been featured just this year in *Guitar Player* and the whole magazine had been slipped into a plastic sheath and sealed neatly with clear tape. Hood read her name on the cover, then set it back in the crate along with the rest.

He pushed the box back under the table with his foot and stood. He felt dizzy in the heat. Nine minutes. His flanks were slick with sweat and the holster dug smartly into the flesh of his back.

He pushed the chair back to where it had been, then turned off the banker's lamps. At the window he let the sweet gulf air waft over him. The hopeful pigeon, a big white and caramel colored bird, eyed him with his head held high. Hood walked over and offered his hand and the bird jumped on. He stroked it and felt its warmth and nervous strength, then he unfastened the small message container from its leg and set the bird back atop the coop. Hood turned and looked down at the alley, then opened the canister and worked out the small, tightly wadded piece of silk. He held it open and to the window where he read the words in the closing light of evening.

Hey Red,

I got six ready and you won't find any stronger fliers on planet Earth. Five hundred each, firm. Let me know soon as I got plenty of other buyers in a hurry.

Jason

Hood read it twice, then put it back in the canister and twisted it shut. The pigeon climbed onto his hand again and Hood pressed the little keg back onto its leg. The other birds scattered histrionically as Hood set the free pigeon back on top of the coop.

Outside the tires must have been screeching before Hood registered the sound of them. Suddenly they were close and when he looked down he saw a loud black SUV skidding into the alley from M. Doblado. Its headlights were on but Hood could see that the driver was a young Mexican man and the passenger was Mike Finnegan. The vehicle screeched to a stop below and Mike bailed out and ran toward his apartment, the tail of his pale suit coat flapping. The SUV tore off.

Hood ran down the steps to the hallway, then past the bedrooms and the kitchen and into the main room. He pulled open the louvered doors to the balcony, but saw that it was ensconced in the decorative wrought iron, at an ankle-snapping height from the alley. He shut the doors and ran to the far and darkest corner of the room and worked himself back into the folds of the heavy drapes. He bowed his head and watched the foyer. Outside another vehicle roared down the alley, then another. The foyer was lit by its single light but the rest of the apartment was nearly dark and he could see the shapes of things but no detail.

A long moment later the foyer light went out and Mike stepped into the main room and stopped. He stood in the gloom, holding what looked like Hood's white Panama hat. "Yoo-hoo. Charlie? This must belong to you."

37

Hood stepped out from the drapes. "Hello, Mike."

Finnegan smiled. "A gun?"

"If you run I'll shoot you with it. That's a promise."

"Run where? This is my home. May I offer you a beverage?"

"No, thanks."

"May I get one for myself? I've just been through a rather harrowing few minutes."

"I'll follow you into the kitchen. If you make a move I'll use this thing."

"Kill an unarmed man in his own home? An LASD deputy and ATF-sanctioned U.S. Marshall? Charlie, don't be bumbling and ridiculous. I am a citizen of Mexico, you know. As well as the United States of America."

Hood stood with the gun at rest in both hands and followed him through the darkened room into the kitchen. Finnegan set the hat on the counter, then retrieved a bottle of an orange-yellow juice from the refrigerator. In the pale light from the appliance Hood found a switch and threw it. The incandescent ceiling fixture offered a thin light. Mike got a plastic tumbler from the cabinet and poured the glass half full then turned to Hood and held it out.

"Mango-tangerine, bit of lemon? Blended just for me."

"No, thank you."

Mike leaned back against the counter and drank. "You look good, Charlie. Healthy and eager."

"What happened out there in the alley?" Hood asked.

"How is the lovely Dr. Petty?"

"What happened just now?"

"Is she tiring of your passion for law enforcement? Then how is dusty, quaint, violent little Buenavista? And your ailing father and long-suffering mother? Converse with me, Charlie. We are acquaintances in a room together."

Hood watched him sip the drink but said nothing. Finnegan had a familiar twinkle in his eye, the look of mischief enjoyed. He drank again and looked at Hood's gun and waited awhile. Finally, he sighed quietly.

"In the alley just now? More *narco* violence, I would guess. We were likely mistaken for cartel gunmen."

"A priest, two novitiates and a short gringo?"

Finnegan shrugged and nodded. "Correct. But the SUV windows are dark. And the level of stupid violence in Mexico has become intolerable. Even in peaceful, merry cities like Veracruz. Or perhaps our driver tipped some bad guys to four easy snatch-and-ransom marks. And the surprise attack was not a surprise to him at all. He did seem rather calm about the whole thing."

"You're going to walk into that room now and sit in the first chair and tell me why you destroyed Sean Ozburn and his wife. And why you orchestrated Erin's kidnapping and Bradley's rescue. Everything. It's full accounting time, Mike."

Mike looked at Hood steadily and not unkindly. "I do love talking about myself. But I'm asking you to leave my home, Charlie. Now. You have not been invited. The maid hasn't been here in days. I can call my contacts here in the Mexican Navy Special Enforcement Unit. They're elite, trained to destroy *narcotraficantes*, but I can tell you they are intolerant of any lawbreaking. Such as trespassing. Did you hire a locksmith? Oh, yes—Roberto Acuna. I've heard of him. And yes, Josie at El Canario is lovely. Perhaps she recommended Roberto? And her *horchata* is so very sweet. You sat there like a spy in a movie. Do you see what you're up against in me? Holster your firearm and leave my home, Charlie Hood. You are neither welcome nor adequate here."

Hood remembered what Mike had told him three years ago, as he lay in a full body-and-skull cast in Buenavista's Imperial Mercy Hospital, drinking organic Zinfandel through a straw: *For example, if I am within eight feet of someone, I can hear what they think and see what they see. Sometimes very clearly. It's like hearing a radio or looking at a video.* Later, Mike had denied such a skill, saying he was only joking, chalking it up to the wine.

"It's gone up to almost thirty feet since then," said Mike. "I'm improving. Evolving, as you are. See?"

Hood waved the pistol toward the big room and Mike set down his drink and picked up the cordless phone.

"Excuse me, then," he said.

"Put it back."

"You are trespassing against me, Charlie." Finnegan looked at him while he pressed the buttons.

Hood took hold of the phone and Finnegan grabbed the gun and they clutched like wrestlers, crouched, pulling and pushing. Hood was surprised by the strength of the little man's grip on the gun. They circled once, then twice, trading control of balance, locked to each other by the objects of their desires. Hood let go the phone, wrenched hard on the pistol with both hands and when Mike stumbled back against the counter the gun flew into the big room, landing with a crack then sliding along the tile.

Finnegan was breathing fast and his pupils were large. "I ask you again to leave my home. Collect your firearm and go."

Hood's anger suddenly blinded him. He had completed his quest and found his man. Now he had no more questions and he wanted no more answers—just swift and severe retribution. He blitzed hard, hitting Mike midbody with his lowered head and shoulder. But instead of taking the man down Hood was solidly repelled, then locked in another wrestler's grip, hand to hand, matched again by Finnegan's lesser weight and greater strength. They circled, hands touching and feinting and pulling.

"I enjoy the ancient sport of wrestling, Charlie. You're heavier but I've got experience on you."

Hood had never wrestled but he'd been trained in hand combat by the Navy and his skills were good. He was rangy and well muscled and fast. He charged into Mike and felt his relative lightness. Then Mike crashed back into him and Hood felt his strength.

"Why did you kill Sean?"

"Sean killed himself. I only challenged his faith."

"Why?"

"To offer him freedom and life. But he chose death."

Hood lunged in, feinting with one elbow and slashing out with the other. He caught Mike flush on the temple and he felt its softness. Finnegan's blue eyes gushed tears.

"Why did you infect Seliah, too?"

Mike charged and drove his head into Hood's middle. The breath puffed out of Hood and he clutched Finnegan's arms and pushed the little man away.

"Seliah was part of the whole project. And Sean and Seliah's parents, yes? And their brothers and sisters, and perhaps even their children and their children not yet born. And you and Blowdown. This is chaos. Chaos is what I create. It spreads like the rings in a pool when a good solid rock like Sean goes in."

They circled and clutched, Hood breathing hard. He couldn't control the smaller man and he began to doubt himself. Finnegan had that light of mischief in his eyes again, and he fought with his head at a cocky angle, talking excitedly and rapidly as if there was no end to his breath.

"But chaos is a *blessing,* Charlie! In it people have a chance to see the beauty and the power and the glory of their own freedom. *Freedom.* It's right there, so obvious in the aloneness that chaos offers. Freedom stares back at them from every mirror, calls out to them in every waking moment and every dream. But not all of you will see it. Some will see it and deny seeing it. Some will curse it. I told you three years ago that I represent a naturally occurring, ordering principle. There is no word for it in your or any other language. And I told you that my highest mission is to demonstrate to men and women that they are free. They are free to choose their acts and to decide what is right and meaningful and beautiful. And what is not. Nothing is *chosen* for them by powers high or low. Nothing is fated or ordained or written. Nothing happens for the better, or for a reason. Angels and devils may scurry about like lobbyists trying to persuade, but men and women are free."

"Got it, Mike. I'm clear on everything now." Hood let himself be drawn in, then he pivoted and drove the heel of his right hand toward the bridge of Mike's nose. It was a devastating blow for a taller man to throw, always debilitating and occasionally fatal. But Finnegan slipped it and crabbed on to him, arms and legs clamping hard, and Hood toppled to the floor.

Finnegan's hold was paralyzing and Hood couldn't figure it. His neck and one shoulder quickly lost their flow of blood and he knew they were close to breaking. He was strong enough to protect them but not strong enough to work them free. Finnegan's stout legs gripped his own just above the knees, which left only his calves and feet to swing free but uselessly. Ears roaring, Hood relaxed one shoulder against Mike's grip, and when Finnegan tightened it, Hood slipped his head and other arm free and locked his elbow just below Mike's jaw. Hood squeezed ferociously and he felt the man shudder with pain.

But he kept talking, his voice reduced to a choking soprano whisper: "Charlie, I *wanted* Sean to choose life. Seliah and the doctors could have . . . saved him. All he needed was to choose . . . with his own . . . free will. Freedom. He broke my heart. Because I loved him. . . . I love mankind . . . You are my . . . music . . . You are what we work for through the . . . ages. The *ages*, Charlie. You are a strong one. Just like Sean."

Hood squeezed even harder and he felt the trembling in Mike's arms. But he couldn't maintain this power. The moment he let up, Finnegan pulled his sweat-slick head loose and turned it away, sucking air. Hood shot one arm under his armpit and around the back of the man's head in a half nelson. Mike grunted as Hood slowly turned him. When the time was right Hood brought his weight and strength to bear. He drove the little man to the floor, hard. Finnegan's shoulder joint separated with a muted wet snap and from deep within Hood's grip came a gasp of pain.

Hood uncoiled and stood. He was dizzy and panting and his eyes burned from sweat. He watched Finnegan climb to his knees and one hand, the dislocated shoulder drooping.

Mike turned and looked up at him. His expression was pained but not anguished. He was pale. He pivoted slowly on his good hand, his little legs churning and his shiny black shoes slipping on the tile. He spun a half circle to face Hood and wobbled upright, then backpedaled until the kitchen counter stopped him.

"Nice moves, Charlie. Sheesh . . . I hate it when this happens." With his good hand he took his dangling elbow and raised it up steady and studied it. He arranged it just so and smiled wanly at

Hood, then buckled his knees and dropped. His elbow slammed loudly into the counter and broke his fall. He pulled himself back upright, shoulder in place again. He straightened and faced Hood, adjusting and smoothing his jacket with both hands, though the seams had burst at the armpits and a button was missing and the whole thing was smeared with sweat.

"Charlie, you have won. Now please go."

"You cased the Valley Center property and passed along the information to Armenta. Why Bradley and Erin? For the same reasons as Sean and Seliah? To destroy what's good? To create chaos and hurt everyone around them and make them all doubt their faiths?"

Finnegan shook his head while he rolled his shoulders one at a time, then together. The color was back in his face and his breathing was even and his eyes were blue and lively. "No, no, of course not. *See,* Charlie. Please *see.* Sean and Seliah were just busywork, to keep me in shape. Very rewarding, though, with strong resonance through strong people. The echo will sound through two generations. Not every job can be an epic. But Bradley is my life work—well, one of them. Bradley is very different than Sean. Sean never believed in himself and I couldn't make him. When he lost his spiritual faith he lost everything. But Bradley believes almost totally in himself now, after his heroic rescue of Erin and defeat of a cartel kingpin. To solidify the remainder of his self-belief is my goal for next year. It will effectively replace the last of his conscience. And what a subject he is. Ambitious. Courageous. Insatiable. His potential is vast. He may even partner with me someday. I tremble with joy at that thought, but it could happen—he has the blood for it."

"Suzanne. Joaquin."

"Oh, them and before them, Charlie. *Before them!* Doesn't your narrow vision infuriate you? And the tight little prophylactic you keep on your imagination? Don't you feel constipated by your *answers?*"

"Erin?"

"A supporting actor, of course. Like you, Charlie. I'd love to help a brave and skillful law enforcer. Or a talented young artist. Any of us would. But we can't get to everyone. You and Erin are too decent and too strong, and not large enough. Your egos lack the monstrous size and weight, the prodigious selfishness it takes to move men and women in numbers."

Hood looked at the little man. "Is that you on the Taberna Roja sign? Or an amusing coincidence?"

"Will you believe my answer?"

"Should I? Once you told me that you rode with Murrieta and saw Vasquez hanged and met a whore in Wyatt Earp's saloon in San Diego. I thought you were simply what Owens said you are: smart and insane. Because those things can't be done, Mike. You cannot be hundreds of years old."

"But I confessed to you that I am a journeyman devil with modest powers. That I have superiors and underlings, competitive associates, good assignments and bad. And partnerships with men and women and a few children. I told you this years ago. I was being as honest and forthcoming with you as I could be. I wanted you to think about these things, Charlie. As a lawman your chance of believing me was very small and I knew this. Most of you are cut from rational cloth. But since then you have witnessed certain acts and discovered certain truths. You have given me considerable thought and energy, as much as any man has ever given me. You have shared your interest in me with the world. So what do you believe I am, Charlie, what do you believe I am, right this minute, right *now*?"

"Does it matter?"

"It will determine the course of your life."

Hood said the words he thought he would never say. It was like listening to someone else. "I believe you're what you said you are."

Finnegan's expression went to cautious wonder. "I am truly moved by your belief, Charlie. I knew you were courageous. But this makes you rare. And dangerous. A man can defeat what he sees. And only through belief can he see."

"I despise you."

"Take your trusty pistol and leave my home."

"You're mine. We're going to the American Consulate now. Then back to the United States."

"Oh, that's funny, Charlie. No warrant, no charges. Forcibly removing a Mexican citizen from his home to another country? You'd be up for kidnapping at the very least."

"I'm federal. I'll find a way to take you back with me."

Hood brought the plastic cuff from his pants pocket and Mike's face went pale again but he crouched and squared off, arms extended for battle and the injured shoulder tucked for protection.

"You don't need any more of this, Mike."

"You give me no choice. And I have asked you to leave. If you don't, then I apologize now for anything that happens."

Hood grabbed the injured wrist, turned it in sharply, then twisted Mike's arm behind him. The little man yelped in pain and spun around. He was facing the counter when he spoke.

"There are clean towels and a bottle of alcohol in the bathroom, Charlie. Your hair will hide most of the scar."

Hood had placed the restraint around Mike's wrist before he understood. He grabbed for the other arm, but Mike turned fast. Hood saw a flash of coat sleeve in his face and he heard a swift grinding sound. He stepped back.

Finnegan's face and coat were flecked with blood. His eyes were concerned and the knife in his hand was dark and short. "I'm sorry. I adore you, Charlie, but you can't take me captive. I'd rather die but that's not an option. Use the alcohol. Tropical infection should not be taken lightly."

By then the blood had sheeted Hood's eyes and his world was a red swamp. He pushed a hand to his scalp and looked out through the hot morass. He could feel the liquid pooling, then overflowing his fingers. Mike was across the room and out the door before Hood had willed the strength back into his legs.

He ran out and through the courtyard past the hibiscus blossoms folded in for the night. He shielded his brow like a man fighting sun, and looked down and up the alley but the blood ran fast and all he could do was blink into the darkness where he saw no Mike, saw nothing with clarity except for the green wall of El Canario and its singing birds. He climbed the steps back into the apartment and in a bathroom cabinet he found clean towels. In the mirror he saw the cut running straight along his hairline, deep and clean pink for a moment before it welled up again and the blood cascaded down.

He pressed the hand towel to the wound and stumbled upstairs and slipped a handful of compact discs into a side pocket of his coat. The pigeons eyed him nervously. He crushed one of the sketchbooks into thirds and jammed it lengthwise into his back pocket, then yanked the plug from the laptop and hefted the machine. In the living room he fetched his pistol from under the couch as his blood splattered onto the floor tiles. He rose and found his way back down to the alley and trudged toward El Canario. When he got close Josie was running toward him as her customers stared.

38

TWO WEEKS LATER BRADLEY LABORED under a fretful November sky, installing underground electrical line for motion sensors on the perimeter fence of his Valley Center property. Last week a crew had added shiny new razor wire to the existing eight feet of chain link. Even on this cloudy day the blades caught the sun in muted flashes that spiraled back and forth along the length of coils according to a watcher's position. Bradley looked at the improving fence. There was nearly a mile of it and it was not cheap but certainly worth the money.

He had rented hand trenchers for the digging. The soil was mostly decomposed granite but there was plenty of just plain granite and the work was slow and punishing. Old friends Stone, the car thief, and Clayton, the counterfeiter, were helping. At Bradley's suggestion Stone was now moonlighting as a GMC salesman up in Escondido. Clayton had a consignment space in the tony SoLo building of Solana Beach where his lovely watercolors were sold.

Bradley had the boom box going and a cooler with ice and beer in it. The dogs were out, some of them crowding the men for a good view of the project, others in the shade of the cottonwoods. The two Jack Russells were digging enormous caverns in search of gophers and ground squirrels. The trencher was gas powered and loud and Bradley wasn't aware of the quad runner buzzing toward the nearby gate until it was practically there.

He hit the kill button and swung the machine pistol around his back. In his peripheral vision he could see Stone reaching for his shotgun and Clayton, never armed, standing with his hands on his hips, smiling at the whining intruder.

Mike skidded to a stop with a flourish, throwing up dust. He wore red-and-white leathers and a matching helmet and goggles and to Bradley he looked, as always, ridiculous.

"Men! How goes the security upgrade?"

"It takes a cold twelve to join the club," said Bradley.

"Fresh out. But you don't mind if I hang around for a just a bit, do you?"

"As long as you don't warble for hours on end."

"Fine then," said Finnegan, pulling off the helmet and setting the goggles up on his forehead.

Bradley saw Stone glance at him as he set the barrel of his scattergun against a nearby sagebrush. Stone thought Mike was a weasel, though Clayton adored him. Bradley pulled the trencher back to life and strong-armed it along the inside of the fence. The powerful machine chewed its way along. His sunglasses were frosted with dust but he was still able to see one of the terriers streaking off from his hole with a gopher locked in its mouth, the other terrier in pursuit.

Mike stood in front of him, backing up a few steps when the trencher got closer. After a while Bradley shut off the engine and dropped the handles and shucked his gloves to the ground. From the cooler he got a beer for himself and tossed one to Mike. They walked along the chain link toward the escarpment to the east, the big husky Call trailing behind them with five other dogs.

"Let's see that happy new smile," said Mike.

Bradley grimaced down at the little man. Only the perfection of the new implants betrayed them. His facial bruises were faint shadows now and the gun-butt cuts up on his forehead were still red but smaller. His palm had finally healed. In an attempt to improve his overall appearance Bradley had gotten a short, smart haircut, something between Wall Street and Camp Pendleton, and was giving himself a close shave each morning.

"What gives, Mike?"

"How is she?"

"Showing more and sleeping less. The ultrasound and tests were all good. The baby's healthy and strong."

"She showed awe-inspiring resolve against Armenta, according to Owens. Has Erin told you what happened to Saturnino?"

"Of course she has."

"Astonishing bravery. I'm happy to have done my small part in getting her back."

"We're happy too."

"Funny that I didn't get one sincere word of thanks from you." Finnegan stopped walking and looked up at Bradley hopefully, waiting. The dogs sat or stood around them.

"Your birds and your research made it all possible, Mike. You and I both know that. I asked you to be my friend and let you stab the hell out of my hand, which took two weeks to heal. So, well, thanks again if thanks are really what you're after."

"Accepted!" Mike raised the beer bottle and drank.

Bradley drank too. "Where is Owens?"

"Laguna Beach. Some well deserved R and R." Mike smiled, looking along the newly installed razor wire.

"I'm surprised you'd pimp her out to Armenta."

"I did no such thing. She helped Erin at no little risk to herself. She was free to decline the job. And free to leave his Castle at any time. *Any* time. She liked him and he was quite good to her. There are costs, Bradley. We all make commitments and sometimes sacrifices in order to achieve success, and reap rewards."

"How long was Owens down there with Armenta?"

"Oh, I forget exactly. Months."

"So it was just a coincidence that Benjamin grabbed Erin when he did?"

"What do you mean?"

Bradley looked down at Finnegan as he upped his bottle and drank. "Hood said you supplied Armenta with everything his men needed to take Erin that night—drawings of the property, measurements and locations, the hideout, even the alarm code for the house. He found sketchbooks in your apartment in Veracruz."

"Why would I do that?"

"So Armenta could take Erin, and you and Owens could help me get her back. So you would gain my trust and we would become partners."

Finnegan laughed quietly. "*Partners*," he said. Bradley heard humor but an odd longing in the word too.

"That's what he said."

"But I already had your trust, or thought I did. Now, after all we've been through, you doubt my loyalty to you because of *Charlie Hood*? Some basic facts, Bradley: how do you know *what* Hood saw in Veracruz? Because I know exactly what he saw and I will prove this to you. Answer me."

"He saw the sketchbooks. He grabbed one before he left but it was full of pigeon drawings."

"I do draw pigeons. I confess. But not sketches of this property, or floor plans of rooms I've never seen. Or your alarm code! Listen to me, Bradley: Charlie Hood broke into my home. I found him there, rifling through my belongings, for reasons I couldn't fathom at the time. It was actually good to see an old friend, but he's changed, and changed drastically. His eyes are wrong, something has become dislodged in him. In my home! The circumstances were an outrage. I asked him to leave, then ordered him to leave, then begged him to leave. He assaulted me, dislocating my shoulder. I am an older, smaller man. I disabled him in order to escape, not to maim or kill. I stand unblemished, Bradley—I had no choice. Let me tell you something. The real tragedy in all of this is that Charlie Hood has lost his sanity. Decent, moral, upright Charlie. We all knew he had become obsessed with finding me. The world is a witness to that. Some might call it stalking. Okay. Fine. I did not judge. Obsessions can often lead to good things. Well, he finally found me. And assaulted and injured and tried to abduct me."

Bradley studied him. "Twenty stitches to close him up. How did you ever get the better of him? He's half a foot taller and outweighs you by fifty pounds."

"Surprise. The same as every street fight."

"Hood thinks you're a devil. Literally. A real one. Not human."

"A devil? Not human? Then I rest my case against the delaminating Charlie Hood. He was muttering that kind of nonsense as we grappled. And therein lies the tragedy of which I have spoken. I don't know why it is, Bradley. Why does a good, strong man like Hood break down? Why is it that people need so badly to believe in gods and devils? They crave the existence of something larger than themselves, or so we are told. But they drive themselves literally insane. Why aren't the travails of humankind enough to keep them busy. *Why?*"

"What do you want?"

"Let's walk. The dogs looked bored."

They climbed the escarpment. The boulders had sheared off ages ago but the face of the wall was still sharp and steep. Sage and dudleya and prickly pear grew between the rocks. Here the fence stopped and Mike examined the end post, kicking away the dirt at its bottom to reveal the impressive cylinder of concrete in which it was set.

"Carlos wants you back," said Mike.

"I can't. I told him that. Look what happened to Erin. Never again. I'm going to be a father soon. Hood suspects what I was doing for Carlos. He won't let go of it because Hood doesn't let go. And IA is still breathing down my neck about last year. I'm done. I'm straight. I'm out."

"But Carlos is heartbroken."

"He's got Vega and Cleary."

"He's insulted too."

"Is this a threat?"

"He's made an offer. He'll let you out of your commitments with no hard feelings. All you have to do is get a horse for him."

"A horse."

"Xtravagan."

"Xtravagan is a million-dollar-a-pop stud. Worth ten times that on the hoof."

"That happens to be pastured less than twenty miles from here."

"Funny."

"But true. For Carlos's fledgling racing program. And don't worry. I know the stable."

"Christ, not again."

"I suggested that your loyalty through the years might have earned you the freedom to raise your family in peace. But he gave me that certain expression. You know the look."

"Where his eyebrows point down instead of up."

"Precisely. They pointed down."

"It's easy to make fun of Carlos until he kills you. I don't take this lightly, Mike."

"I'm urging you not to."

Mike tossed Bradley a flash drive. "Think about it. In the meantime enjoy the show. It's off my security cameras in Veracruz. Motion activated. No way Charlie could have seen those beady little lenses watching him from up in that dark ceiling. And if he gets a little too righteous on you, you've caught him in action—trespassing, theft, assault and battery, attempted wrongful imprisonment. Maybe it's something your Commander Dez should see. Or maybe it would just make an amusing Internet posting. Who knows?"

Bradley finished his beer and looked at Mike for a long moment. For the first time he saw Mike Finnegan as not only cryptic and ridiculous, but genuinely dangerous. Erin and Hood had seen it. How had he not?

Mike spoke with a satisfactory tone: "Well, whatever you do with the video, our poor Charlie now has but a few tenuous holds on the world as we know it. He has his self-interested federal and county employers. His ailing father and aging mother. And of course the lovely, no doubt frustrated Dr. Beth Petty, who helped put me back together all those years ago."

Suddenly Bradley considered Charlie Hood in a sympathetic light. Another first. A day for firsts, he thought. He snapped the beer bottle high into the rocks and listened to the sharp burst and patter of the shards. "I've got work to do."

Mike kicked the end pole with the toe of his red racing boot. "Nobody's going to get through this thing when you're done with it, Bradley. No devils coming for you and your family!"

That evening he and Erin sat on the deck and watched the sunset and ate dinner. Bradley grilled tuna caught by a friend, and vegetables and red potatoes wrapped in foil, and poured a good Sauvignon Blanc. The dogs sprawled and fidgeted on the drive and in the barnyard grass, only Call allowed on the deck proper.

Erin sipped her one glass of wine and watched the hills while
Bradley cleared the dishes and sat down. He firmly believed that she
was to be pampered in every possible way until delivery day, still
some four months out.

"You have that look again tonight, Erin."

"Sorry."

"You okay?"

"Just thinking is all."

"About what?"

"The little one. Us. You know. All the wonderful things to come."

"You're not making them sound wonderful."

"Some songs write themselves."

"I didn't mean it as a criticism."

"I didn't take it as that."

He watched the red ball of sun melt into the western hills. Erin had
become impossible but he could hardly blame her. He knew she was
at the end of all tethers and anything might happen. She could take
no more. He could not clearly imagine a life without her but he could
sense it out there, like a storm still below the horizon, sending up an
eerie light.

It was exhausting to think about so he let his mind wander. It
landed on the men he'd killed in Campeche and later at Armenta's
Castle. These weren't the first in his life but they were the least personal, like enemy soldiers almost, and his memories of them had been
sneaking up on him lately, as soldiers would. One unhappy thought
led to another: Carlos Herredia. El Tigre. Steal a racehorse? Well, he
thought, sleep with a fucking drug lord and what do you expect? As
if surrendering the twelve grand a week he no longer earned from
Herredia wasn't bad enough. It was hard to say good-bye to that a
year ago, but as he saw now, the loss of income was just the beginning
of his troubles. Which led him to think about the terriers of LASD

Internal Affairs, still biting at his ankles about last year's disaster. He wondered if he would have twice as many problems when he was twice as old, at say, forty-two. Or half the problems. Maybe that's how it worked. Who knew?

"Those twenty stitches got me," said Bradley. "Mike doing that to Charlie."

"Me too. I tried not to let him see how awful that cut looked to me. And I believe what he said about Mike helping it all happen—all of it—not just the cut. Everything. I think Mike's evil. I know you disagree."

"I think Charlie's blown Mike out of proportion in order to justify his own madness."

"He put his life on the line for us. Is that what you mean by mad?"

Bradley shrugged and drank. "Charlie needs a quest. Human nature. Why not make it Mike? Mike isn't innocent. He's dangerous. I know that now."

Erin sipped the wine and set one hand over her middle. "Well, when Charlie's hair grows back, the scar won't even show."

"In his mind it will show."

After a long moment Bradley put his hand on hers. It was another of the many acts of tenderness that he had offered since returning home. She had offered him not one. Still just the idea of her affection arced brightly across a dark gap inside him.

"We're all carrying new things now," Erin said.

That night they slept in separate beds again, and in the morning when Bradley came in from his early trenching Erin was gone.

Her note was brief:

Dear Bradley,

I cannot find enough love for you to take us through the coming days. I have searched and waited and searched and waited. When I think back on our joy and passion I see that they were based on lies, but they remain the standards of my heart. I used to have a dream of us, a belief. I will try to find that belief again. Whatever happens to us, your son will always be yours; I will see to that. Nothing can take him away from us.

Erin

39

HOOD WATCHED THE OPERATOR SWING the heavy bucket back over the hole, then lower it in. The excavator shuddered and roared. The rams hissed and the bucket rose, Buenavista rock and sand pouring through its teeth. Dwayne backed and swiveled the Cat, then rolled down the road. He dumped the load on the opposite side of Hood's big lot, where there was already quite a hill forming. Dust rose.

Hood sat in the morning shade on his patio with a sweating pitcher of iced tea on the table. Also there were some notebooks and his laptop and Mike Finnegan's laptop, recently configured by ATF tech wizards to accept the password of Hood's choosing. So far Hood had found many interesting things on the heavy, battered little machine: voluminous files in Mandarin Chinese, Greek, and Spanish. Much of this material seemed travel-oriented—air schedules and fares, hotels and restaurants, tips from pros, blogs by tourists. The scarcer English-language files were mostly natural history articles focusing on a wide range of subjects, from the "earth star," a North American fungus commonly found in damp areas near conifers and sometimes eucalyptus, to incomprehensible astronomical predictions stretching from the present into future centuries.

He looked down at his sleeping dog and touched his fingertip to the scar that ran just above his hairline. It was raised and relatively neat, with the plastic stitches taken from inside. Now, sixteen days after the cutting, it itched incessantly.

The Veracruz doctors had shaved and stitched him and dripped him full of antibiotics and turned him over to a U.S. consulate staffer named Bonnie. Josie had visited him often. Soriana flew down from San Diego, and later came Beth, who had to have an immediate look at the wound—"hmmm," and the Mexican needlework—"excellent." Veracruz Police interviewed him twice. Hood had invented a story about a crazed M. Doblado mugger, believed by neither of the detectives, but he stuck to it and never contradicted himself and that was that. He understood that the Veracruz Municipal Police were eager to be rid of him. Five days after the knifing he was home.

"Charlie, I officially give up," said Beth. "I can't think about it anymore. But I'll do it. I'll try to make the arrangement work."

"I think the arrangement can work, Beth. I don't see a better way."

"All righty then." She looked at Hood doubtfully, then out toward the excavator. "Think Dwayne will get mad if I look in the hole again?"

"I think he'd like it."

Beth moved through the adamant fall sunshine to the excavation site, Daisy trotting at her side. Hood watched her walk. She was wearing cargo shorts and a tank and sandals and a big straw hat against the sun. When she got to the edge of the cavern she turned and squinted back at him, a smile on her face. She squatted on her haunches and looked down. She had already asked Dwayne twice to stop the job, slid down into the growing cavern and retrieved one very nice slab of petrified wood and several rough rocks studded with ancient shellfish. Beth was an enthused collector of rocks, shells, bones, fossils, and bird nests, though she was in Hood's opinion a bit of a pack rat. Dwayne backed up the big Cat 245 and swung the bucket safely away, lit a smoke.

A while later she climbed back out with a heavy bounty stowed in her upturned blouse. She set the treasures on the picnic table one at a time. Hood examined a piece of petrified wood that would clean up nicely with some water and a brush. Beth looked skeptically at the other rocks, nothing truly wonderful, then moved her gaze to Hood.

"It's funny that you're calling this add-on a wine cellar."

Hood nodded. "It says so, right on the drawings."

"An underground wine cellar with three rooms, big enough for ten thousand bottles."

"That's right."

"Plumbing and electric, bath and kitchen."

"By all means."

"And heating and air-conditioning with backup generators, and *six-foot concrete* walls and double reinforcement bar."

"The walls are only three feet thick, Beth."

"But there are two of them smack up against each other and iron plates in between. And the seismic stuff. And the catwalk over it. And the grates, so you can see into every room without having to even leave your house. Do you plan to watch the wine age?"

"It will be secure."

She sighed and smiled slightly, letting him off her hook. "Well, I am surprised and happy that you bought a home in Buenavista. I wish the reasons were somewhat simpler. But we've been over it and that's the last I'll say."

"It's best."

She took his chin and turned his head slightly so she could look at the cut. "Well, you might be half crazy but you're healing up good and clean."

"I don't believe I'm half crazy."

"I really don't, either. But I think you could become that way."

He nodded. They sat and watched Dwayne carve away the earth. Hood felt the sun on his legs and it was good.

He had almost nodded off when Beth put both her hands on his face. He opened his eyes to see her up close, studying him. Her fingers were cool.

"I worry about you, Charlie. Don't let Mike take you over. He isn't your superior. My training won't let me believe he's what you think he is, but I've been wrong before. Maybe what we call him doesn't matter. Don't let what he did to you and your friends determine your whole life, just part of it. Charlie Hood is the biggest and most important part of you. So take care of you. I'll help within reason. But I have my limits, and I've got me to consider too. I listen to my heart, not the other way around."

"I know. That's good and true and as it should be. I love and treasure you, Beth."

Her fingers trailed off his face as Hood looked out to the east where the dirt road climbed from the flat desert into the hills. A vehicle came forward dragging a cloud of dust behind it and there was no leisure as it barreled toward them.

A moment later Erin climbed from the SUV and Hood and Beth walked into the shade of the carport to greet her.

ACKNOWLEDGMENTS

A million true thanks to Tom Bagley, Joseph Gauthier, and Kevin Kimmel, who told me how things work in that magical place known as a recording studio. They use words like "slapback," "aural nodes," "tuned rooms," and "critical listening." Music is at the heart of this book and without these guys, there would be none in it. All musical miscues are purely my own.

The lyrics to "City of Gold" were written by Tom Bagley and Nelson Soler, based upon a few lines of my own and a character of my invention. Peter Dobson and Sue Cross helped Tom with the musical grid. I thank you all for a beautiful song—you brought it to life.

On a different note, many thanks again to John Torres, Special Agent in Charge of ATF, Los Angeles, for his continuing support, high energy, and good humor.

Also sincere gratitude to Dave Bridgman for his advice on guns and ammo and how they work, and for pointing out a host of other things in early drafts of this novel. If I've made still another firearm blunder in this book, all the blame is mine and none is his.

Again I thank D. P. Lyle, MD, who was kind enough to explain modern medical suturing, complete with a video showing how it's done.

Thanks once again to Mike Dee, this time for the crocodiles.

Thanks once more to the *Los Angeles Times* "Mexico Under Siege"

Acknowledgments

team for their excellent reporting of the many travails south of the border, and what they mean to that fine country and to us in the United States.

And once again I'd like to thank Robert Gottlieb and all of Trident Media Group for their expertise, good judgment, and unflagging enthusiasm. You are my allies, and I value you.

Last and certainly not least, thanks to Brian Tart, Ben Sevier, Sandy Harding, Christine Ball, Jamie McDonald, Caitlin Mulrooney-Lyski, and all of the other fine people at Dutton and NAL for making these stories real. You're a splendid team.

Photo by Rebecca Lawson

T. Jefferson Parker is the bestselling and award-winning author of eighteen previous novels and a three-time winner of the Edgar Award. Formerly a journalist, Parker lives with his family in Southern California.

Read on for an excerpt
from T. Jefferson Parker's

The Famous and the Dead

Available in hardcover from Dutton

2

CHARLIE HOOD'S FIRST BIG UNDERCOVER assignment began with a nineteen-year-old girl living in a small town in Russell County, Missouri. Her name was Mary Kate Boyle and she had first told her disturbing story over the phone to a girlfriend recently moved to Los Angeles, who happened to have just read a piece in the *L.A. Times Magazine* about a cool G-man.

The G-man was the Special Agent in Charge of the Bureau of Alcohol, Tobacco, Firearms and Explosives in Los Angeles, and Mary Kate took a very long Trailways journey to come find him. In conversation Mary Kate got the *A*, *T*, and *F* correct but kept getting the order wrong, calling the bureau FAT. It was her first time away from her little piece of Missouri.

The SAC heard her out before handing her down the line to an ATF-led task force working guns along the Mexico border. She told of four men—three of them Russell County deputies—who were stealing confiscated evidence and selling it. Mostly guns and drugs. Of course any cash they just put in their pockets. This had been going on for more than a year. Three of them were headed to California to do some business, hoping to find some drug cartel "beaners" with money to spend. The city of El Central was the place to be, they had told her. They wanted to find straw buyers. Cash, cash and more cash, all that profit from the drugs the cartels sold. Plus one of the deputies had a friend in El Central with a restaurant that had the best burritos in the world. So they could eat there for cheap. You know how cops are. Oops.

All of this she had overheard, in pieces, during the last months of her senior year of high school. Last week she had been assaulted by one of those men, beaten sharply, and thrown out of his double-wide. His name was Lyle Scully, Skull for short, the leader. Now here in the ATF field office in Buenavista she sat, skinny, fair and freckled. Mary Kate had an eye swollen up the color of a plum and a deep continuous split in both lips, but she still talked more than a little.

"And I don't think too high of that kind of treatment. Skull says I was born trash and will stay trash and it may be true. That sure didn't stop him making me pregnant, now, did it? God knows it took him long enough and I thought maybe a ring would come attached. It didn't. His divorce is long finalized. So I got the procedure. And now I'm here in California and that's behind me and I'm not going back. Never. Except maybe to get some things. I always wanted to rent one of them You-Haul trucks and just drive away from Russell County. I like the ones with the palm trees and water skiers on the side. I'm going to be an actor, model, or nurse, whichever happens first. I told all this to your boss up in L.A. and he told me you're the people who can get things done down here."

Hood kept notes but mostly he just listened. He was a Los Angeles County sheriff deputy assigned to the ATF Operation Blowdown task force. The people in this room were part of his Achilles team, Mary Kate notwithstanding. Fourth year now for Hood. He thought of ATF not so much as Alcohol, Tobacco and Firearms, but as GDT— Guns, Dust and Treachery. ATF was chronically understaffed and the caseload was heavy, but scandal had further lowered the bureau in the public eye and sent its supporters in high places running. Certain ATF supervisors had implemented some bad ideas in an operation dubbed Fast and Furious, and gotten bad results. Even before this calamity, ATF had been an easy political target but now it seemed nearly friendless. Hood had always thought that, just for starters, ATF had it rough because most Americans *liked* alcohol, tobacco and firearms, and disliked regulation. Hence the agency was spooked and defensive. He chuckled when Mary Kate called it FAT. But Hood enjoyed the work because there was action, and he felt it was necessary work. Hood wanted to be necessary. He was a Bakersfield boy and he had served in Iraq, Anbar Province. He was thirty-four, tall and loose, with an open face and strong eyes.

"El Centro?" asked Janet Bly. Janet had been the senior agent of this Achilles team and still seemed to think of herself as such. Last month ATF had brought in a more senior agent, Dale Yorth, who now sat at the head of the table with an eager look on his face. He'd come in from Miami and the team jury on him was still out.

"Yep. Skull said El Central, pretty sure." Mary Kate dabbed her lips with a tissue.

Hood saw the still unhealed split and felt bad but he also thought that a beating and an abortion might in the long run be a fair trade for escaping a life tied to Lyle Scully. The womenfolk in her part of the world tended to bear the brunt of things, or so he'd read and seen in movies. But Mary Kate would have to stay escaped, of course. Would have to *want* to stay escaped. People had surprising needs and default settings.

"What happened to the fourth guy?" asked Bly.

"Went missing three months back? Not a trace. Disappearo."

"Do you know what contraband they have to sell?" Yorth asked.

"Not exactly. But there's plenty of crank since a lot of it's cooked up right there in Russell. It's high-grade stuff so far as that kinda thing goes. I tried it once and didn't like it. Then there's always plenty of bud to be smoked. Heroin's still pretty popular but the pharmaceuticals are taking it over. Two guys broke into like four Jefferson pharmacies in one weekend, helped themselves, but the state police sent the videos around and guess what? The crooks were from our own neck of the woods. So Russell busted their butts. Skull and his team grabbed most of the evidence when no one was looking and him and his crew sold almost all of it. Right out of Skull's truck, he said, like a roach coach for drugs. Also I know they got lots of guns. Most of them were stored in the property room, some for years. I know this from Skull. And a course they're supposed to destroy the guns once the trial's over but Skull worked it so the paperwork got sent for destroyal but he took the guns himself. Don't ask me what kind or how many. Except once we all went out to the woods so they could try out this new gun they got, and it was a big honkin' thing that had legs on one end and a big round doughnutlike thing on the top. Loud. And heavy, even for Skull who is approximately two hundred pounds of solid muscle. He laid on the ground and fired. Then he got up and braced it on his hip and had to put some back into it. Shot up a bunch of watermelons. I don't like guns any more than I like crank, though I don't see any harm in putting food on a table, which of course ain't what a gun like that gets used for."

"Legs on the end?" asked Hood. "A bipod?"

"Yeah, the far end, like two legs. For when he laid down and shot."

"And a black doughnut? Do you mean a drum attached on top, flat to the frame of the gun?"

"That's what I mean, valentine." She smiled, then winced and brought the tissue back to her mouth. "Ouch. That's what I get for funnin'. Story of my life."

He smiled back and shook his head. And thought, *An old Lewis Gun?* Not exactly state-of-the-art weaponry, though it was a bruiser. It was the only machine gun with an ammo pan on top that he could think of. Belgian. It was a popular machine gun in World War I, and into World War II, but they hadn't made one in seventy-something years. Of course, if Pace Arms could make a thousand Love 32s in Orange County, anything could happen. He'd seen pictures of the Lewis Mark I, and a total of one in the flesh, in his entire life.

"Where do you think they'll go when they get here?" asked Velasquez. He was the youngest of this team and the only one with a master's degree, which was in economics.

"To a motel I guess," said Mary Kate Boyle.

"And to get the best burritos in the world," said Hood.

Yorth leaned back and set his hands behind his head. He was a big man with short yellow hair that was dark at the roots. "You know the name of the restaurant?"

"I'da told you if I did. How many burrito restaurants can there be in El Central?"

"Probably twenty Mexican restaurants," said Hood. "That's just a guess."

"Call Skull and ask him which restaurant, Mary Kate," said Yorth.

Hood saw the tick of worry cross Mary Kate Boyle's face.

Janet Bly rolled her eyes and groaned.

Velasquez tapped his fingers on the tabletop.

"Why not?" asked Yorth. "Call him on your cell and tell him things are just fine in here in Russell County but you miss him. You just want to talk. Hoping you're okay, Skull. Just reach out. Get him talking to you. That's all."

"I ain't doing that."

"If you want Lyle locked away safe in prison, you better consider it. Because if you don't cooperate with us, our chances of putting these boys away go way, way down."

"I still ain't calling him."

Yorth stared at her. "What about testifying in court? You told the SAC in L.A. you'd do that."

"Testifying is one thing, but sneaking up on a man you're done with is something else."

"You started sneaking when you bought that Trailways ticket, Mary Kate."

Mary Kate colored and looked down for a moment and took a deep breath. When she looked up again, she had sharp anger in her eyes. "That isn't sneaking. I never asked Skull to steal. I told him not to. I didn't ask him to go bragging on and on about it. And I didn't ask to go out to the woods to shoot that big old machine gun. And I didn't ask . . ."

"For the cool stuff he bought you with money you knew he'd stolen," said Yorth.

"Knock it off, Dale," said Bly.

Mary Kate stood and slung her bag over her shoulder. Hood and Velasquez stood, too.

"There wasn't that much cool stuff involved," Mary Kate said. "I took a bus here to help and you call me a whore. You're as big an asshole as Skull ever was."

"Sit down," said Yorth. "I was out of line."

"I'm outta here and you can't stop me." She looked at each of the other three agents in the room. "You, you and you got my number." Then she aimed her battered face down on Yorth. "You don't."

"Way to handle a cooperative informant," said Bly.

Yorth shrugged. "You've got her number."

"Christ, Dale, put her back with *him*? She should stay as far away from that guy as possible. Look what he did to her."

"Then we have a difference of opinion. I cleared the idea with L.A. Now, here's what these heroes look like." Yorth handed out photo prints and bios of the cops, and mug shots and a criminal record of the third man. "I've sent these to your phones."

Hood squared his sheets and looked through them. Two pictures of each bad guy per page, along with brief descriptions. The great leader, Lyle Scully, two hundred pounds of solid woman-beating muscle, had a shaven head and a goatee, and was a thirty-year-old sergeant-detective. Sgt. Brock Peltz was fifty-one and heavy. Clint Wampler looked chimplike, with big ears and small eyes and an early Beatles pageboy. Hood thought of his own pronounced ears. Clint was twenty-seven and unemployed, with convictions for drunken driving, aggravated assault, and burglary. He'd done a year. Hood also saw that nineteen-year-old Clint Wampler had been questioned in the torching of a Russell County post office on April 19 of 2005. The FBI had charged two known associates but not Wampler. "That was the ten-year anniversary of Oklahoma City," said Hood. "When Wampler's buddies torched the post office in Russell County."

"I see he's got like-minded friends all over the country," said Bly. "Militiamen in Montana, the Minutemen here on the border, and the good old Aryan Nation boys out in Idaho. Even the Covert Group—the old guys who wanted to poison a small town with ricin gas. Apparently he's been in touch with them, too."

Yorth groaned. "But not with Islamic extremists? They should throw in together and share expenses. Islamamerica, how's that sound?"

"That's ridiculous," said Bly, then she muttered, "Least I hope it is."

This got a brief laugh. In the ensuing near silence the agents pored over the images. Hood heard the central heat come on. Two or three times a year Buenavista was the hottest place in the nation, but in February the little border town could get cold.

"So then," said Yorth. "Where do we find Skull and his merry band?"

"Maybe from an informant we *haven't* run off," said Bly.

"I hear you, Janet," said Yorth. "I hear you, I hear you."

"The Palomino Club in El Centro," said Velasquez. "It's popular with narcos and straw buyers. So are the El Pueblo Restaurant and the Fuzzy Dice bar."

"There's the Monterey Restaurant on Main Avenue," said Hood. "They have a sign out front that says something about their burritos. 'Best in the west,' or 'world's best' or something like that."

Yorth smiled. "Has ATF ever gotten anything that easy?"

"L.A. should have the phone tap warrant by this afternoon," said Bly. "I'll badger them, as I'm so good at doing. Then there's the gun stores. These guys might just watch the customers come and go, pick out a likely buyer, and make an approach. They'll want to get in and out and back home to their families and illustrious careers."

"Charlie Diamonds should be that buyer," said Hood. "He's been in all those clubs and restaurants and stores, and others. He's made some small legal buys. So now he needs a machine gun. And more. He's a familiar face and a fat wallet."

Bly nodded. "I like that idea."

"I do, too," said Velasquez.

Yorth locked his hands together behind his head again. "Ready to fly, Charlie?"

Hood smiled and the diamonds of his left canine caught the light.